POOLS OF DECEPTION

(A CURVE OF HUMANITY STORY)

BY

MAQUEL A. JACOB

Cover Design by Roslyn McFarland
https://www.farlandspublishing.com

Published by
MAJart Works LLC
2001 NE Aloclek Dr #211
Hillsboro, Oregon

https://www.majartworks.com

ISBN: 978-1-950438-24-2

CHAPTER ONE

Breaking the Surface

Bubbles gurgling on the clear blue water's surface, caused ripples in the water. A shadowy figure emerged from below, the black swim cap more visible the closer it came. The roar underwater echoed in the young man's ears, getting fainter until he burst out, gasping for air.

Thunderous cheers erupted. He removed his goggles to squeeze excess water from his eyes and focused on the three quarters full arena of spectators.

He swam smiling big to the edge where a small ladder allowed him to haul his slender, fourteen-year-old frame onto the cold hard tile. The cheers continued as the AI announced his judges' scores ranging from 9.7 to perfect tens. His dive's difficulty level at 3.5 made the score even better.

After the final round of diving for the Olympics, he had secured the gold medal. His teammates rushed him, slapping his wet skin and shaking him.

"And Francis Donovan, the youngest competitor this year, has won gold, taking the title of best diver in the world!"

A reporter came running towards him, microphone in hand, holding it out for him.

"Francis Donovan! How does it feel to be the youngest gold medal winner in diving?" Her words came out rapid fire, giving her no time to catch her breath. "What are your plans now?"

Francis laughed, scratching his head, messing up his matted hair.

"The next Olympics, I guess." He frowned. "I'm glad all my hard work led me to this win. I couldn't have done it without the support of my coach and teammates."

"There you have it," the reporter beamed into the camera. "A new Olympian on the rise. We look forward to seeing you in Tokyo, Japan."

When she left, her cameraman trailing behind her, Francis looked over at his coach. The man's grin showed so much pride, he almost felt self-conscious.

How embarrassing!

"Come on gold medalist. Let's get you some grub then ready for the ceremony." He glanced at everyone on the team. "We did it, kids. A gold for Francis and silver for the team. Time to get serious."

The cheers from the audience intensified. His coach patted him on the back as he headed for the sprayer to rinse off. Shivers went through him the moment he reached open air and whipped off his cap. Lukewarm water sprayed out, easing his discomfort.

From the window seat of the coach bus, Francis admired Japan's landscape. The Olympics were over, and he had the most exciting time of his life. Diving was his passion. Since the time he could swim, the feeling of weightlessness as he soared into the air towards the deep waters captivated him. The water made him calm; it enveloped him in soothing tranquility. People would say he moved like an eel, slithering along the surface, sometimes below.

He placed a hand on the window, spreading his fingers. Leaving seemed bittersweet. But now they all needed to train for the next one. Four years may sound long. To them it was a blip in time. They had to qualify for regional and world championships. Only the best were allowed to advance and compete in the Olympics.

Time to get serious?

That was an understatement. As the youngest gold medalist, he would have to prove himself because in the next one, he won't be. He will be an eighteen-year-old adult. No more notoriety. With a heavy sigh, he turned away from the window and caught his coach's knowing stare.

He realized it too.

MAQUEL A. JACOB
U.S. Aquatics Complex Colorado State

The best divers and swimmers in the United States filled the Olympic sized pool area. Reporters, sponsors, family, and committee leaders sat in the bleachers observing the elite athletes training to keep their place on the Olympic team. Whistles blared, mingling with the shouting of coaches at their wards. The slapping and splashing of water created a strange rhythm.

Fifteen years after the catastrophic alien crash landing of 1974, the world discovered their survivors living on Earth breeding with humans. The introduction of Bi-Genetics, the scientific term for hybrid humans, sent the sports world into uncharted territory.

Many of the hybrids could shift their sexual orientation at will. Schools around the world created new departments separating academics and Athletics. Those children who didn't land in one of those categories the administration placed in General Studies.

The aliens' enemy showed up a decade later, declaring war. They gave humans fifty years to advance their technology for a fighting chance. World leaders tapped their country's athletic departments to find the best athletes to represent them. The Olympics became a contest of who had the biggest sack and the most talented specimens.

Instead of every four years, the Olympic Committee voted to hold them every two, alternating the summer and winter games.

Every major city around the world built facilities in preparation for hosting the games. There would be a lottery instead of each country bidding against the others. No one got the option to bow out.

Hybrids rotated on both teams at intervals. The committee implemented one rule to level the playing field. If an athlete was on the men's team, they could not also be on the women's at the same time. They would have to wait until the next season.

The Aquatics division was no exception. For the past ten years, the United States dominated the field, boosting their status among the other countries. Still looked upon as selfish, hypocritical, bullies, its leaders hoped those young athletes could change the image.

That was the US Olympic committee's task.

A married couple representing the committee sat in the bleachers observing each swimmer and diver with eagle-like eyes. Catching every mannerism and body stance. As former Olympians themselves, they took stock of the young athletes' form and times. One or more of them would be groomed for success to become the face of the nation.

After an hour and a half of brutal heats, the head coach called an intermission. A few athletes exited the pool to rest. Others continued playing in the water.

Francis laughed as he and four others splashed water on each other. His diving teammate got a mouthful from one of the two swimmers.

"Ack!" He sputtered, letting the water spill from his mouth. "That was dirty!" He went to splash the guy back, but Francis got ahead of him and missed, getting the other one instead. "Oh, ho!" He clamped his hand over his mouth.

"The hell, Francis!" The swimmer yelled.

Francis waded past him. "You mad? Come catch me."

He took off swimming, the other three in tow. In the split second they caught the swim coach's eye, he took out his stopwatch. They were near the starting point for 400m. He wanted to see if his boys' time would improve in a relaxed state.

Halfway, he realized they were not closing the gap on Francis, and they were going hard to reach him. Francis' coach and the two committee members noticed as well.

As Francis tagged the other side of the pool, the other three coming behind doing the same, laughing merrily, the coaches went silent. The swim coach stared at his stopwatch. Francis Donovan swam a 400 meter heat a few seconds shy of the world's record with no effort. He turned to the diving coach. An ominous vibe crept into the aquatic center.

The Olympic committee members leaned towards each other, whispering. The dive coach felt a stone drop in the pit of his stomach. Nothing good would come from this.

"You're being selfish, Ken!" The swim coach, Craig Bergenheim, yelled at the diving coach. "He would guarantee a gold medal for the swim team."

"That's not what he wants! He's a diver!" Ken Scholes replied in aggravation.

"Who can swim like a goddamn fish. You know better than anyone how we look to the rest of the world right now. This would solidify our status. Regain trust. He'll get over it."

"Is that what you'd say to your boys?" Ken snapped. He knew Craig would never use his own athletes for something so sinister. "Just because you have no respect for your team doesn't mean I don't."

"The hell did you just say?" Craig's fist rose to his side.

"That's enough." Sharice Montgomery of the committee came into the room.

Her tall frame immaculately dressed in a skirt suit; Sharice gave an angry stare. As the heir to her family's billion-dollar empire, her seat on the committee had been bought by her father, Phillip. Her husband, Gerald Ivers, a former three-time Biathlon gold medalist, stood beside her.

"There's no call for such language." She got closer to them and let out a sigh.

Gerald went to Ken's side. "No one is telling you to kick him off the dive team," he said in a reassuring tone.

"The hell I'm not!" Craig retorted.

"That helps no one," Gerald snapped. He addressed Ken again. "There is no rule that says it can't be done."

"I propose something different," his wife said. They turned to her. "He can stay on the dive team as a permanent alternate. That way he keeps his spot."

"He won't take that! You're basically cutting him off at the knees. What kind of plan is that?" Ken snapped.

"He'll take it." Her eyes seemed to gleam with malice. "What athlete would turn down guaranteed gold medals?"

"There is no guarantee!" Ken spat.

"With me coaching him," Craig smirked, "it is."

He walked off, feeling victorious, with Sharice following.

"Be smart." Gerald said to Ken. "Tell him gently, and let him know the stakes. Contrary to what you may believe,

I don't like what my wife suggested, either." He squeezed Ken's shoulder. "We can't lose him. For any team."

Gerald left Ken alone in the locker room, fuming. After a few minutes, he calmed down. Telling Francis he needed to switch to the swim team would devastate him. He already knew he would feel the same.

"What? No!" Francis' face turned bright pink with fury. "I'm a diver. I like diving! Why? Why'd you let them do this?"

"Francis!" Ken grabbed hold of his shoulders. "I did not let them do anything!" He cupped Francis' face in his hands. "I know this is not what you want." He leaned forward so their foreheads touched. "You need to comply for now. Stay low, do as you're told, and don't make any waves. We'll figure it out. I promise."

He leaned back and stared into Francis' teary face. The rage he held inside emitted from his soul. Something wicked surfaced and Ken let him go, stepping away.

"Fine." Francis' voice quivered. He wiped away snot and tears with one hand, flicking the residue on the tiled floor. A sign of disrespect for the pool area. "Whatever." He turned away from him. "I know you mean what you say. Problem is, you can't fix it." He glanced back over his shoulder. "They got us both by the balls. We won't ever win."

In that moment, Ken saw Francis age intellectually from fifteen to thirty. A new understanding of the situation. He hung his head, watching Francis leave the area.

The kid's right.

That didn't mean he would give up on trying to get him back on the diving team, where he belonged.

Eighteen Months Later

The whistle blared. Every swimmer in the pool stopped.

"What the hell was that?" Coach Craig yelled. "More! Get the lead out of your asses and swim! And you!" He pointed to Francis. "You think half assing it is going to make this all go away? You have one job. Win a gold medal. Now act like it." He blew the whistle again. "That goes for all of you!"

They went back to the starting end, their morale sinking. Francis stared at the coach with deadpan eyes. He sank down into the water and let it take hold of him. His frame of mind needed recalibrating. The rippling motion echoed in his ears, lulling him to relax. It muffled the coach's screaming above. He counted to ten, slowing his heart rate, then emerged from the water.

"You ready to take this seriously now, princess?" The coach chastised him. Francis grabbed the edge and propped his feet flat against the pool wall. "I want to see some improvements." He blew the whistle.

The team pushed off for a 200 meter backstroke heat. A skill that became Francis' specialty.

An intermission called two hours later saw the team exhausted and miserable. The World competition was coming up in less than four months and the coach had lost his mind scheduling more training sessions than necessary. All for Francis' debut as a member of the swim team.

The two swimmers he had raced for fun a year and a half ago sat next to him on the bleachers. Ravi Abenashid had a towel around his neck while Blane Hardy had his draped across his lap with his head tilted back. Francis ran his own towel over his wet hair and left it there.

"He's a goddamn menace," Blane said with his eyes closed.

"I get it, he wants us to be some kind of powerhouse," Ravi said.

"That doesn't mean he has to be a dick."

Francis leaned back, exhaling slowly.

Ravi stared at him. Blane peeked over, opening one eye. Francis used to find it creepy how they scrutinized his physique. Now, he found it funny. Almost everyone experienced growth spurts. At fourteen, his height was five feet ten inches. Now he stood at six feet two inches with a body of all lean muscle and still time to grow a little more.

"I don't see the reason to push us so hard when the whole thing hinges on you." Blane sat up and leaned forward, letting his arms dangle between his thighs. "We'll get gold regardless."

"He'll get gold," Ravi corrected him. "We get gold if his

time pushes us over the edge. None of us are as fast as him."

"Stop," Francis held up a hand. "I'm still just a kid."

"With an Olympic gold medal and a team silver." Blane snorted. "Yeah, you're so not intimidating."

"Maybe if you taught us your technique," Ravi shrugged. "We could get close to your level."

"Hey!" Blane nodded. "That's a great idea. We could have like private lessons from the master."

Francis rolled his eyes. It wouldn't solve anything but indulging them wouldn't hurt. Why not?

World Competition New Mexico

The black skull cap pushed securely on Francis' head hid a surprise underneath. He laughed at himself for coming up with a genius way to debut his swimming career. The coach would have nothing to say. That was step one. The next step loomed just ahead at the registration table at the end of the corridor down the hall. Floor to ceiling windows lined the entire way, giving access to the view of the mountains.

Hushed conversations popped up every so often in the quiet corridor. Wearing his USA Team uniform, a red, white and blue tracksuit, he hummed happily as he walked. On a whim, he removed the cap to let his now dark blond hair with a few highlights, cut in a layered shag that touched his shoulders, flow down.

A man came out of the side door ahead of him on the right. Tall. Only an inch or two taller than him. His demeanor held a swagger of confidence. The dark tailored suit hugging his body nearly blended with the dark brown hair that fell across his shoulders in deep waves.

Their eyes met. Francis froze, as did the man.

Though he had never experienced the feeling before, he knew it immediately. That undeniable connection of two hearts and minds intertwining with ease as if they had become one being. Soulmate. Shifters had a psychic bond to theirs when they found each other. The man placed his hands in his pants pockets and approached him.

"Francis," the man said.

"It's Frankie," he replied a little too harshly. He looked away, embarrassed.

"Frankie. Sorry. I'll remember that. I finally get to meet you." He glanced at Frankie's hair, amused, but didn't say a word.

"Oh?" Frankie raised an eyebrow.

"I'm Gerald Ivers, one of the US Olympic committee members." He didn't extend his hand, knowing Frankie wouldn't take it.

"So, you and your wife are the ones who railroaded me into the swim team?"

Gerald seemed to rear back as if struck.

"I didn't want that."

"Then why didn't you fight harder to stop it?"

Gerald stared at him. Frankie knew he had asked a stupid question. His research found the wife held the most seniority and clout as the daughter of a billionaire sponsor with pull among the Olympic conglomerate. His words would mean nothing.

"I hope to see you win. That's the only way this will be worth it."

Too close.

Every step the man took towards him, Frankie would move back. He now stood against the wall with the Gerald mere inches from him. He planted both hands on the wall on each side of Frankie's face.

"That's some move," Frankie snorted playfully, hiding his nervousness. "If you're not careful, I'll report you as a dirty old man."

"I'm only thirty-one."

"And I'm a minor, so." The man slid his hands away and stepped back. "Don't you have a wife and kids to think about?"

"I do." The sadness in his voice made Frankie wince. Rumors about there being no love in that marriage were crude and borderline hateful. "I wouldn't make a scene."

"Good job. If you'll excuse me." Frankie pointed to the registration table. "I have to get my stuff so everyone will know I'm an Olympic hopeful."

Gerald gave him a disappointed look. Frankie knew what it meant. He had changed a lot since the switch. And not for the better. Gerald walked the opposite way. When he had gone a good twenty yards, Frankie whispered, "Would you even wait for me?"

To his surprise, Gerald answered without stopping.

"I would for as long as it takes."

By the time he got back to the hotel, the rest of the team were in the main hall getting lectured by the coach before heading to the aquatic center. Frankie snuck past them and reached the elevators before anyone noticed.

He got to his room, a small space with four beds, two on each side facing each other. He quickly threw his stuff onto his duffel bag lying on the one by the window on the right. Sliding the lanyard over his head, he left.

This time, the coach caught sight of him as he tried to blend in with the rest of the team. The man stopped yelling mid-sentence and his stare bore into him like a laser beam. His teammates turned towards him. All eyes would be on him from now on.

The massive aquatic center loomed ahead as the buses turned onto the main road leading to the entrance. Security checked each vehicle before raising the gate arms to allow passage. Security led sniffing dogs around to detect illegal drugs or bombs. A sign planted in the grass on the other side mapped the layout of the premises. Two Olympic sized pools awaited the diving and swim teams representing countries from around the world.

Once escorted to the locker rooms, the team stripped down to their swimwear. Everyone had their design preference. Frankie went with leggings that barely set at his hips, showing the cut muscle right above his pelvis. Ravi wore the tight thigh length shorts while Blane went full Speedo, the sides of his ass cheeks exposed.

The diving team geared towards those two outfits so the judges could better see their form. A sense of envy gripped Frankie. He wanted to compete in the diving competitions.

A former teammate came up behind him and slapped the middle of his back.

"Don't worry about us. When we need you, we'll let you know. Go out there and show those assholes what you're made of." He walked past him. "Cool hair." The smile on his face let Frankie see sarcasm.

Frankie watched the diving team head for the opposite side where their pool waited. The swim team lined up and entered their competition site. The pool didn't seem too impressive and the water, too blue. Fresh chlorine. Which meant it had not been cleaned beforehand, and the standard ozone treatment wasn't being used. Thank God for goggles.

Off to the side, the coaches and committee members were having a shouting match with the facilities manager about the water. There was no reason in the current era for any aquatic venue to not use ozone for sanitization. A few places were stuck in the old ways and the backlash increased. Frankie had a feeling the venue would switch by next year.

While the team settled into their area, the coach came up to Frankie.

"You pace it and win for the next heat. Nothing else. Don't you blow that world record until the Olympic games, understood?"

"You want me to go slow on purpose?" Frankie's eyes bulged with outrge..

"Is there a problem? You have one job. Win gold. Get into the Olympics." The Coach leaned closer with gritted teeth, "Win. Gold. And set a new world record."

Frankie felt a boulder hit the pit of his stomach. The games had become a gauge to show the alien races on Earth that humans were capable of fighting for themselves. That we had skills to contribute to the cause when the enemy came knocking. Each country vied for leadership, citing their popularity at these events. The United States had lost favor over time due to arrogance and now they wanted to show the world they were still relevant. Still a superpower.

I get it! And he didn't like it.

"That's…"

Frankie struggled to find the words for such a farce.

"What the committee has agreed on," Coach Craig finished for him. "We don't show all the cards in our hands. This is just a taste of what America can do."

"I don't…"

"You will do as you're told, Francis Donovan," Coach Craig seethed.

He walked off, leaving Frankie in a state of despair. This isn't how he wanted to debut.

"It's Frankie," he whispered to himself.

He looked around at the other swimmers, getting ready to prove themselves for their own validation and the country they came to elevate. What the coach suggested spat in the face of their training. Their efforts would be for nothing because his actions determined the pace and who went into which heat.

Breakfast resurfaced, climbing up his esophagus. He ran to the restrooms, bursting into a stall and leaning over the bowl, vomited everything in his stomach. He spit out the last of it and slammed a fist against the stall. Tears dripped onto the seat. He knelt by the toilet while it flushed.

"Hey! Frankie! You in here?" Blane's voice startled him. He saw purple and green wet shoes from under the stall. "You okay?" He swung the unlocked door open. "Oh, man, are you sick?"

"I'm fine. Just didn't feel so good. Breakfast is gone."

"Well, that shit sucked anyway. You'd think they would give us better food. Being Olympic athletes and all." He held out a hand. "Come on. Before the coach realizes you're missing."

Frankie took his hand and let himself be pulled up. He went to the nearest sink and rinsed his mouth out. Outside the main door, Ravi stood waiting. He ran his fingers through the side of Frankie's hair.

"You sure you're okay?"

"Yep." Frankie took a few deep breaths. "Let's get this over with."

The Olympics Tokyo Japan

Frankie cursed himself for being late again. His room-mates, Ravi and Blane, did not wake him up when they left for registration earlier. Now he had to run to the main complex and get all his credentials before opening ceremonies. At the table he rested both hands on the top and gave the woman checking in athletes a wink.

"Hey beautiful, I'm here to get my documents," he spurted out of breath.

The older woman looked up from her tablet and frowned. She moved a mound of free swag to the side. "What's the name?" The man sitting two feet from her gave Frankie a side glare.

"Well, you see." Frankie pulled a folded document from his uniform jacket's breast pocket. "I have a name change for competition purposes." He handed it to her.

"Francis Donovan." She pulled up his information on the tablet, then hit the edit button." She typed in the details from the document. "Your competition name is now Frankie Mel Donova." Her face scrunched in distaste.

"Exotic, right? The ladies will swoon."

The woman finished his registration, printing a new badge and paperwork. She handed him his lanyard along with a large packet she stuffed the papers in.

"Yeah, good luck with that."

Frankie put the skull cap back on, tucking away any stray hairs inside. He collected his things and headed back to the dormitory. The coach and his team were in the common area waiting for him.

Shit!

"Donovan! What the hell do you think you're doing?" The coach's face reddened with each word.

"It's Frankie…"

"Why are you late? You think you got some sort of special privilege?"

"Mel Donova."

"What did you say?" The coach demanded.

Frankie raised his lanyard so he could see.

The team got a good look, too.

"Huh? When did you change that?"

"I petitioned for it months ago. My parents signed off since I wasn't eighteen yet."

"Are you serious?" One teammate asked incredulously.

"Well, Frankie," the coach said his name with disdain. "You'll have to get up to speed from your fellow team. I'm not going to repeat myself." He folded his arms. "And take that damn hat off! It's eighty degrees outside."

Frankie lowered his lanyard and took off his cap. His now fully blond hair spilled out, each layer falling in place and settling on his shoulders. Some of his mates gasped and snickered. Coach Craig did not look amused.

"What's the meaning of this shit?"

"New name, new look?" Frankie shrugged.

Exasperated, Coach Craig turned away.

"The buses are here. Everybody load up." As Frankie got on, the coach leaned over and whispered, "Don't you dare make a scene, Frankie." Again, he spat out his name like venom.

"Don't worry, coach. I got this." Frankie patted him on the shoulder, then went to his seat.

Inside the stadium, the jubilant atmosphere nearly choked him. So much nervous energy and excitement combined with the masses felt stifling. Like he was being squeezed into a bottle. The Parade of Nations was underway. In the main corridor below the dome, each country's athletes lined up ready to display their pride to the world.

Frankie stood at the front of his procession, bearing his country's flag. When the committee selected him, the other teams balked, forcing the committee to step in to justify it. Swimming proved to be a shoe in for America with gold medals. As the guaranteed hopeful, Frankie fit their narrative. He already practiced a routine to perform as they marched through the crowd.

Two legendary athletes would walk beside him a little way back to avoid getting hit by the flag. He told them his plan ahead of time.

They mocked him for his young mind and over joyous antics.Inching forward, they waited for the previous country to clear the opening. A group of volunteers on each side held them at bay until they received the cue to let them go. When the one on the left gave Frankie a hand signal to move, he grinned, gripping the flagpole.

Showtime!

Past the barricades, Frankie started his high step march while crouching down. He hiked the flag up and down with the beat of the music. A fourth of the way around the route, he began spinning the flag like a baton, whipping it around his waist. He brought it back, always making sure the flag continued to wave fully in the air. He did his routine every hundred yards, waving and blowing kisses, raising one finger to let everyone know he was number one.

The crowd cheered his display of arrogance. He represented his country well.

Frankie followed the succession towards the section reserved for the United States of America close to the center of the main stage.

The setting sun triggered the overhead lights to flicker on. The sound decibel pounded in his ears, penetrating the plugs he had inserted earlier for that very reason. A slight drop in temperature brought a warm summer breeze through the stadium, ruffling his hair. It carried with it the powerful scent of sweat, perfume, and heat. He gagged.

"Right?" Blane exclaimed. He had to yell for anyone to hear him. "Like, it's summer. That shit lingers."

"Some of us got to impress potential hook ups," a teammate said.

"You're sitting with the team and marching with us. The only people you'll be near is us," Ravi replied.

"And we ain't impressed." Blane side eyed him.

Frankie snorted. He really couldn't say anything after having his hair dyed to impress the world. They made their way to their seats and waited for the lighting of the torch, signaling the start of the games. The opening ceremony delivered its own over the top spectacles with performances from major stars and well renown troupes.

POOLS OF DECEPTION

The harsh beams obliterated the dark of night and its stars until the fireworks began blending in. Frankie wore sunglasses to block the brightness. He knew what he looked like when the cameras panned over. The All-American boy, now eighteen and dominating the world.

The first heats of the game didn't bring much fanfare. People usually waited after the qualifying rounds to finish before placing their bets on the finals. The aquatic complex was different. Spectators jampacked the stands. Reporters, with their cameramen, and sponsors jockeyed for the best angle views.

The one person they came to see stood wearing hip hugging spandex leggings while standing on the cool tile stretching his long arms.

Frankie Mel Donova. The crowd had already gotten a taste of the new and improved Francis. Now an adult, he was blond, ambitious, and cocky. It irked many, but the media drank it up with fervor. Even though they knew he would qualify, swimming for gold and no doubt winning, watching him compete mesmerized them.

He still plunged deep underwater and stayed down, observing the flow of the ripples. A technique that acclimated him to its characteristics so he could navigate it better. That moment of personal tranquility on display for the world to see made him appear humble.

Coach Craig came to Frankie's side.

"You remember what we talked about? Same as before. This time, you pull out the stops in the final heats. Got that?"

"Yeah."

His deadpan response didn't sit well with Coach Craig. He got closer.

"Listen to me. This ain't about you. This is for your country. You get to ride the coattails of notoriety. There isn't a sponsor on the planet who's not trying to get you to endorse their shit. Get your act together and do your job."

Frankie turned to him; his eyes filled with rage. "I heard you." Coach Craig stepped back.

The coach left to sit with the team members waiting to

compete in the heat. Camera shutters clicked and flashes created a field of overlaying spots in the area.

The AI announcer's feminine voice boomed through the PA system.

"Competitors, please proceed to your lanes."

The heat would start in a few minutes. Frankie secured his swim cap and rinsed off one more time before walking to his lane. He slid down into the water, taking a slow deep breath before going under. The water caressed him, gliding over his arms and torso, its rushing sound thumped in his ears. Through his goggles, he watched the way it moved, not quite still, having a life of its own despite being encased in walls of white tile and concrete. He let out a bit of air and watched the way the bubbles floated to the top.

A loud klaxon marked his time was up and he resurfaced. The other swimmers were already getting into position for the backstroke. Frankie lazily grabbed the ledge and brought up his feet until his knees were right under his chin.

Slow and easy.

He exhaled. That meant going at three-quarter speed. Enough to qualify yet keep the audience guessing if he's still got the juice or working up to it. So disgusting.

"Swimmers, on your mark." Some adjusted their feet. "Get set." They all leaned back ten degrees.

The horn blared, starting the heat. Frankie pushed off halfheartedly and took long, broad strokes. From the stands, he appeared to be leisurely going about his business. No rush. Except he had already surpassed four other swimmers.

He only needed to get in the top four to qualify. On the last turn, he decided to go for third. No reason to leave any-thing to chance. The second he touched the wall, completing his heat, he heard the murmurs of surprise and excitement.

"Frankie Mel Donova squeaking by to place third in the first qualifying heat for the 200-meter backstroke. Let's hope he gets his rhythm for the next rounds."

Frankie smirked as he took his cap off, dipping it in the water and dousing his head with its contents.

Trust me, I already have it.

Crushed Dreams

The hallways on the third floor of the dormitory sat empty. Everyone had gone out to celebrate the first days of qualification. Already a week passed and some athletes' journey for the games was over. They went out to drink their tears away. Others locked themselves in their rooms to mourn failure alone.

Frankie could hear the soft padding of his gym shoes on the thinly carpeted floor. Every corner light remained dim. He remembered this was the quiet floor. No parties or loud conversation allowed. Exploring the place seemed like a good idea, since he had nothing better to do. Japan's drinking age was eighteen, but he didn't find it fun after the first night which saw him puking his guts out.

A door shut behind him and he turned around. Gerald came out of the stairs exit and walked towards Frankie. He wore a high-end dark suit tailored to perfection. His dark hair in the same style as before, layered to accent his waves just below the shoulders. He finally looked up and saw him.

"Frankie." His voice made Frankie shudder. "What are you doing roaming around?"

"Could say the same to you."

"I had official business and didn't want to run into any paparazzi. So, I took the stairs."

Frankie's mouth down-turned at that. He forgot those vultures lurked around the first two floors hoping to get a glimpse of athletes behaving badly. Gerald got within a foot of him. They were now the same height, so their eyes met.

"The committee didn't agree with your opening ceremony march, by the way."

"Hmph! I livened things up. They should be thanking me."

Frankie leaned against the wall to get some distance between yet Gerald got closer.

"That's not the kind of attention they want." He sighed in defeat. "Please keep a low profile when not competing."

"Hey. You know, you're getting a little too close to me. Someone would call you a dirty old man again." Frankie gave a nervous grin, hoping to deter him from moving in.

"Why would anyone call me that, Frankie?"

"You're kind of hitting on me, right."

"You're not a minor. Frankie."

"Last I checked, you're still married with like kids." Frankie regretted bringing up that sham of a marriage. If Gerald could get out of it without causing too much disgrace, he would end it in a heartbeat. "I'm sorry. I didn't…"

"Frankie…" Gerald sighed. He hung his head, as he got closer.

When he raised his head, his lips found Frankie's. The softness of them made Frankie feel like he was melting. He gave in, opening his mouth a little. Gerald took advantage, slipping his tongue through.

Hot!

Frankie's body heated up fast. His hands balled into fists at his side as he struggled not to push him away. Gerald pressed his body against his. *Please!* He wondered what he pleaded for. To stop or not? Then it did stop.

Gerald pulled away slowly, the touch of his lips lingering.

"Don't tempt me, Frankie. I don't have the kind of restraint you think." Frankie slumped, angry for letting himself get carried away when he wanted more. "Focus on winning." Gerald pushed off the wall and stepped back.

"You won't even want me a few years from now, anyway." Frankie said nonchalantly.

"I'll always want you, Frankie."

Gerald continued down the hall to the other staircase that only went up. The next elevators that gave access to the suites were on the fifth floor. Frankie watched him go through the doors. He flinched when it slammed shut. His lips felt moist, so he licked them, tasting Gerald.

Why?

He heard of stories where soulmates skipped generations, causing age gaps. Some suffered, deciding to continue their fate with the person they wound up with instead of going with their true mate. It always ended badly with suicides unless they saw reason.

Frankie knew Gerald would end his marriage if the opportunity arose.

But I have to wait.

One of the room doors opened and a Ukrainian athlete came out, their roommate following close behind. They stared at him for a moment.

"This not your floor, American." The first said, confused.

"Paparazzi. Both floors below." Frankie pointed down. The two athletes tsked in disgust. "We're all taking the stairs."

"They will find way in stairwells too," the second one said.

Frankie shook his head.

"That would mean someone gave them access with their keycard. I hope no one's that stupid."

He came off the wall and headed for the same stairs Gerald took to his room on the sixth floor. Going up three flights would give him a little exercise. The Ukrainians went the opposite way to go down. Those stairs ended near the kitchen for staff only, circumventing any reporters lurking near the dining hall.

Inside his room, it surprised him to see Ravi and Blane playing cards lounging on Ravi's bed. A medical textbook lay open, face down on the pillow behind Ravi.

"What you bring that for?" Blane asked, nodding at the book with disgust..

"I need to keep up on my studies so I can apply for a work study."

"At some shitty clandestine clinic?"

"I am striving to be an innovator of medical science. We are on the cusp of perfecting procedures that benefit…"

"Rich assholes." Blane interrupted. "And I'm pretty sure

that shit ain't sanctioned by the medical board."

"Yeah? What are you striving for with your degree in physical education?" Ravi slapped down a card.

"We were required to attend college." Blane snapped. "So why'd you go the doctor route?"

"Because that's how my family rolls. It's become part of our culture. You're either a doctor, a lawyer, or an engineer."

"So you're a walking stereotype?"

"Pretty much."

"How about doing what you want?"

Ravi's eyes gleamed. "I am." He glanced at his cards again.

Something about the way he answered sent chills through Frankie. They finally looked over at Frankie as he plopped down sideways on his own bed and spread his arms out. The blinds were still open, giving a view of the nightscape. Off in the distance, the Olympic torch blazed. He stared at the scenery for a while then rolled over on his side.

"I figured you guys would go partying with everyone else."

Blane frowned at the thought and his crap hand of cards.

"Nah. They were getting all sloppy."

"We could do that in the room." Ravi leaned down and pulled a bottle of liquor from under the bed. "Got juice and sodas in the fridge."

"The coach would murder us if he found out." Frankie laughed, imagining the look on Coach Craig's face.

"Why are you back here?" Ravi asked.

"Was checking out the place and heard about the vultures casing the first two floors."

"Why they always gotta' ambush somebody when they trying to be left alone?" Blane tossed two cards down on the bed. Ravi looked at them and let out a heavy sigh, tossing his own on the pile. "My win."

"Want some?" Ravi held the bottle's neck and rocked it back and forth.

"I have a meet tomorrow." Blane and Ravi looked at him, puzzled. "Diving." Frankie smiled wide. "I'm a permanent alternate, remember?"

"That's right. That one kid popped his piss test and you had to qualify." Ravi slid the bottle back under.

"You look happier than a pig in shit," Blane said tersely.

"Yeah." Frankie rolled over on his back again. "Can't wait."

Coach Ken paced the floor of the locker room as he waited patiently for Frankie to show up. True to their word, the committee allowed the swap. The moment the doors opened, he saw the shit-eating grin on Frankie's face and relaxed. This was his wheelhouse. Nothing to worry about. Frankie would forever be a diver.

"How's it going, coach?" Frankie came up to him, adjusting the duffel bag strap on his left shoulder. "Heard you need the calvary."

That part Coach Ken didn't like. Bitterness and anger changed Frankie into what stood before him now.

"Stop being an ass. You're not the almighty. Get changed. You're up in thirty." He turned away and went through the doors leading to the pool. "You better not be rusty."

"Huh?" That offended Frankie. "I qualified for this meet."

"With an eight point seven," Coach Ken tsked while glancing back.

"I was restraining myself." Frankie snapped. Then he smiled. "I'm going all out today." Frankie's arms spread wide. "Put your faith in me."

Coach Ken rolled his eyes and resumed walking. Frankie stripped out of his uniform. The two dives he would perform had difficulties of eight or higher. One being what he earned a gold medal for at his first Olympics with near perfect scores.

He saw Frankie come out and head for the rinse station. His body had evolved into a swimmer's. Tall, long, and lean. Coach Ken hated to admit how much it suited him. Frankie let the water wash over him. His hands slicked back stark blond hair that went dark when wet. He turned off the water and went to the wait station for his cue to climb up.

The current competitor made his way to the edge of the diving board and got into his stance. A mid-range dive with an average technical difficulty. He dove off and Coach Ken immediately saw his form give way. His body went into the water with a splash. Lackluster claps followed mingled with disappointing, 'Aww's.

At the bottom, Frankie shook his head in amusement, relishing in the young man's failure. He could hear the clicks of cameras catching the moment. Once the athlete cleared the pool and they announced his scores, the administrator gave Frankie the cue to head up.

Those long legs took two rungs at a time effortlessly. The whole time, he smiled, waving to the audience. Many indulged him, standing to clap as he ascended. At the top, he kissed two fingers and gestured them towards his fans.

"Representing the United States of America, Frankie Mel Donova." The crowd cheered.

"Frankie Mel Donova will be performing the reverse four and a half somersault in pike position. Technical difficulty three point five." The commentator informed the masses. "The last time he did this dive was in Rio at the age of 14. Let's see if he still has the form."

Frankie heard that and smirked. He shook out his arms and raised one to signal his readiness. He walked to the start position. With pure abandonment, he charged forward. The balls of his feet hit the edge of the board and he leaped off, soaring into the air. His body folded in half with his fingertips touching his toes to clear the board. He appeared to be suspended in time, his rotations flowing with ease before lying back out to come down. Coach Ken stood mesmerized, not sure what he was seeing.

Frankie entered the water with surgical precision. A few ripples formed on the surface. No splash occurred. A nanosecond of silent awe erupted into a roaring cheer. Even the commentators let out yells.

"My goodness! Did you see that?"

"What a performance! A perfect dive."

Coach Ken could already see the seven judges conversing, frowning. They despised Frankie. But they knew giving him a bad score would cause more damage to the games and their reputation. The commentators noticed it as well.

"They need to be real careful how they score this. You may not like his style, but he brings the receipts."

Frankie came up and swam to the edge, where Coach Ken waited with a towel. He rose out and stood next to him, waiting for the score. The AI announcer read the scores as they came on the giant display.

"Nine point seven, nine point five, nine point seven."

A few boos crept in with the cheers.

"Nine point seven, nine point six, nine point seven, nine point nine."

The last score being a slap in the face when everyone knew it should have been a ten.

"Those sons of bitches," Coach Ken spat. Frankie's eyes narrowed. "Come on. No point in arguing about it. You got to prep for your next dive."

The rest of the dive team slapped him on the shoulder and back as he walked past them to the rinse station. They too, had sour expressions on their faces. That dive should have been a perfect ten across the board. Coach Ken saw the way Frankie closed his eyes as he wiped water upward from his face and over his head.

He won't be denied.

Coach Craig scanned the spectators waiting for the final heat of the 400 meter freestyle to start. Cameras were everywhere in the hands of regular people, mounted on scaffolds, resting on the shoulders of news station personnel. Coaches gave last minute pep talks to boost their confidence. The sounds of talking and movement along the tiled floor filled the complex.

Frankie came out of the rinse station donning his cap, tucking in that atrocious blond hair. Coach Craig motioned for him to come closer.

"Don't overdo it. If you get two seconds off it, great. More than that and we get too much attention. The last thing we want is to be accused of genetic modification."

"It's not true." Frankie snorted.

"It doesn't have to be for there to be an investigation and putting doubt in their heads."

"Fine. I'll time it."

"Good. From here on out, you better win every race. Not silver, not bronze. Gold."

"Roger that, master," Frankie laughed, walking away.

Coach Craig caught him by the forearm.

"I'm not being funny."

Frankie looked down at his hand on his arm and met his gaze. Coach Craig flinched, releasing his grip. He had never seen such malice in someone so young. *Is this my fault?* Not long after the committee, and himself, berated and beat him into submission, Frankie changed. His smiles were no longer genuine, his usually subdued responses became snarky.

He watched Frankie go to his lane. For the first time, he got a good look at him. Six foot three, all lean muscle, slightly tanned skin, and an aura of superiority that demanded he be seen. That they only needed to acknowledge him as king. The other competitors seemed to feel it, glancing over at him, trying their best not to be intimidated.

And would get worse when he breaks all the world records during these games. Coach Craig felt queasy.

"All competitors, please go to your assigned lanes." The announcer boomed.

Frankie stretched his long arms to the sky and clasped his hands together, twisting side to side. He swung his arms out like a windmill and shook them out.

"On your mark." The swimmers bent over, their fingertips resting before their toes. "Set." They hunched down, their buttocks high in the air. The horn went off and they launched into the water.

Frankie led the pack, his long, graceful strokes pulling him further away from the rest. He touched the other side and catapulted off, gliding across the lane with ease, not showing any sign of struggle or fatigue. Like he wasn't trying.

The crowd broke into an uproar as the numbers on the timer showed his speed. Cameras flashed as coaches and teammates yelled at their people to pick up the pace. Coach Craig shook his head. He had no reason to do any of that.

It was a done deal.

"Oh my goodness!" An announcer cried out over the feed. "This is unprecedented! Frankie Mel Donova is about to break the Olympic world record by one...no, two seconds!"

POOLS OF DECEPTION

At the end of the last lap, Frankie tagged the wall and breached the surface. The thunderous cheers assaulted his waterlogged ears. He bobbed a few times before grabbing the pool ledge to steady himself. Whipping his cap off, he looked over at the timer and let out a victory yell. He slapped the cap on the water and hauled himself out.

Like a modern-day Adonis, he climbed onto the diving board and blew kisses to the crowd, raising his arms in a V. The smile on his face said it all. Worship me.

The scene repeated throughout the games.

"Frankie Mel Donova has set yet another world record in the 200 meter backstroke!" Frankie took his cap off while still in the water and did a fist bump in the air. A devious grin on his face signaled there was more to come.

"And another Gold medal for Frankie Mel Donova in the 100 meter! He's on a roll and there's no stopping him." The commentator said. "He is here to let everyone know that was no fluke when he won golds in diving at age fourteen."

"He has truly grown up," the commentator's female counterpart added.

"Another Gold for Frankei Mel Donova! That makes four in swimming and one in diving. What a show he has put on in these games."

Frankie walked up to the podium for the fifth time to claim his Gold medal. His competitions were done and he could rest or enjoy the games with others who had completed their heats.

Like before, he stood proudly atop the first-place step in the center. His blond hair stood out against his tanned skin and white track suit jacket. The administrator came over with the medal. He bent down and let him slide it over his head. When he stood, Frankie did his usual V then waved and blew kisses.

The national anthem came on as the American flag rose above him. He placed his hand on the left of his chest and mouthed the words with fake adoration. He couldn't wait for it to be over. His 'job' was complete. In the distance, his teammates frowned.

Envy was a dangerous thing.

And they all looked a little green.

~

Too many parties.

After hitting three of the ten going on in establishments around the complex, Frankie and his roommates tapped out and went back to their room. They flopped on their beds, exhausted from being in closed spaces with so many people. The digital clock on the wall showed 1:00 am. Still early for a weekend.

"Since we didn't really drink at those places," Ravi reached under his bed and pulled out the bottle of liquor he kept hidden.

Blane jumped off his bed and went to the mini fridge, pulling three kinds of juices. Frankie sat up with one knee bent in front of him and his other leg hanging over the edge. Ravi got up and grabbed three plastic cups from the stack next to the coffeemaker. He stood blocking Frankie's view as he made a mixed drink for him, Blane standing close by watching.

Ravi turned around and handed the cup to Frankie then made one for Blane and himself. The two sat on the bed across from Frankie and raised their cups.

"To being Olympic medalists," Ravi said.

"Speak for yourself." Blane gave them both a nasty look.

"Hey," Ravi nudged him in the ribs with an elbow. "You were so close. Hell, I fought hard for that bronze."

"Yeah, Everyone should feel sorry that you placed fourth in the World." Frankie gave him a side stare.

Blane leaned back.

"Hmph." He raised his cup. "Congratulations to us, then."

Frankie took a swig of the drink and winced. His head fell back and he shook it from side to side, his eyes squeezed shut. He raised his head and stared into the cup.

"Holy shit, that's strong!" Frankie's mouth opened in an O as his eyes widened.

Ravi took a sip, winced a little then shrugged.

"Really? Tastes about right to me."

Blane did the same and nodded in approval.

"Yep. Just right. Hits the spot."

"You guys really trying to get me drunk." Frankie laughed as he took another harsh sip.

Ravi and Blane glanced at each other. They watched Frankie take a few more swigs before starting small talk about the games. Within half an hour, Frankie fell asleep still sitting upright on his bed, the cup empty.

Sunlight poured into the dormitory room, causing a white out in Frankie's retinas. He squeezed his eyes tighter, feeling the sting of the light invade all the way to the back of his head. The bed sheets tucked around him made him struggle to get his arm loose, clamping a hand over his face.

"Ugh!" A sour taste lingered in his mouth. Residue of vomit. He knew it well. The slight hint of the drink mingled with it. "My head."

Under the covers, he wore a tank top and drawstring lounge pants. He didn't feel icky yet his whole body hurt. He sat up and slowly opened his eyes. The pain intensified before subsiding. He sniffed himself and didn't smell soap. Yet, he was sort of clean.

Ravi came out of the bathroom. He looked over at Blane sleeping like the dead, his body half off the bed, both arms spread out. Frankie got his attention with a wave of his hand.

"What happened? Did you wipe me down? Pretty sure I rolphed. Can still taste it."

"Huh. We rinsed your mouth out best we could. You weren't that cooperative."

"Damn." Frankie scratched his head, mussing up his hair. "No more of whatever that concoction you mixed was."

"You're just a lightweight." Ravi ran his fingers through the side of Frankie's hair. "As my father would say, strong liquor puts hair on your chest."

Frankie moved away from him and flopped back down.

"No thanks. I have an image to uphold. No hairy chest involved."

Ravi went to Blane's bed and pushed hard up and down on it with both hands. Blane kicked out, missing his head by less than an inch.

"Get up!" Ravi demanded. "We're going to miss breakfast. It ends in like an hour."

"Ew," Frankie gasped slowly. "Food. I can't."

"You especially need to eat something," Ravi glanced back at him. He whacked Blane in the back of the head. "Get moving."

Blane scrambled up into a kneeling position and pushed Ravi hard into the empty bed across from him.

"Fucker! Don't hit me. I heard you. I'll get up on my own."

Frankie rolled out of bed and stumbled, doubling over. He clutched at his stomach.

"Ahh, man. My insides hurt so bad." He managed to stand and headed to the bathroom. "I'm not drinking with you guys ever again."

⌇

"Flight 1127 to Los Angeles has been delayed by two hours. Please check with the airline for any necessary accommodations regarding connecting flights."

The U.S. aquatic teams let out collective cries of outrage. Coaches converged off to the side of the gate to talk about solutions. Combined aromas from the food court created a sickly, greasy scent. Along with the dirty carpet from heavy foot traffic and body odor, Frankie wondered how no one gagged. He felt the stirrings of sickness in the pit of his stomach.

He surveyed the teams crammed in one area and had flashbacks of when his physical education teacher saw potential in him during swim class. Schools separated students based on skills not long after Bi-genetics made up nearly twenty percent of the population.

For sports, the divide went deeper to weed out the best Olympic hopefuls. Aquatics included diving, swimming, water polo, and synchronized dance. The teacher had Frankie immediately transferred to the sports department, no longer allowed to take remedial classes.

Now here he sat in an airport stuck with entitled athletes who would have endorsements waiting for them in their hometowns.

New protocols cited that after a competition, all athletes had to fly back to the U.S. Aquatic Complex for a debrief then released to fly home. He hated that rule. His new bed in his newly purchased condo called to him.

Frankie held his phone to his ear while slumped in the wide seat, his head resting on the back of it. He stared at the ceiling while he listened to his sister's voice on the other end.

"We really are so proud of you, Francis," his sister, Dana, gushed.

"It's Frankie," he tried to correct her.

"A true Olympian. Wow. We have to celebrate when you get back. What do you want to do, Francis?"

Frankie let out a sigh. "That would require those people to be in the country."

Silence fell. Frankie waited for her to counter.

"Mom and dad are just on a short trip. They'll come back if you set a date for them."

"Did they tell you they were proud of me?"

"Francis…"

"Did they?"

"How can you say that? Of course they're proud. Francis, please don't be like this."

"It's…" Frankie gave up. "I'll be home in a couple of days. If you want to stop by, we can have lunch or something."

"Good. I'll let them know. Oh! You have to meet my fiancé. He's dying to finally meet you."

Frankie made a face, rolling his eyes towards the windows. More family drama. Their parents hated her betrothed. He didn't have any feelings towards the man one way or the other. It was her life, not his. He realized he had gone silent.

"Sure, bring him. Can't wait."

"Are you being sarcastic again, Francis?" Dana's tone skeptical.

"No, no. I mean it. Sorry, it's a bit distracting. Our flight got delayed and everyone is freaking out."

"Nothing serious, right?" He could hear the paranoia in her tone about being stranded in another country. "Let me know if I need to contact the embassy or something."

"It's fine. Talk to you later."

"Okay. Have a safe trip. And congratulations, Francis, on being a world record holder!"

With that, she hung up. Frankie closed the phone and tossed it in his open duffel back at his feet. His parents hardly know about his meets, let alone watch them.

Proud? More like relieved he didn't cause a scandal or became a breeding candidate for some affluent old rich man.

I proved them wrong.

Training for the next games would be underway in two months. He just had to get through the world competitions. As the current record holder and gold medalist, Frankie knew the masses would scrutinize his every move to see if he could sustain his status.

Bring it! I'll prove you all wrong, too.

Making Waves

Here he comes.

Frankie could hear Coach Craig stomping down the hall, his alligator boots striking the tiled floor. His attire bordered on business casual coming from a committee meeting. The slicked back salt and pepper hair made him look more like a hitman than a coach. The scowl on his face clued Frankie in on his mood.

"Mel Donova!" Coach Craig yelled as he got closer to the café inside the hotel. "We need to have a discussion. Right now!"

He grabbed Frankie by the arm and hauled him into the nearest restroom. A man came behind to enter and the coach slammed the door shut in his face, leaning on it so no one else would interfere. The man banged on the door, cursing and yelling for him to open the door. Coach Craig paid it no mind.

"What's got you all mad?" Frankie rested his butt on the edge of the sink, crossing his arms.

"First you pull that stunt at the university pool then spew that bullshit about our country's toxic culture during the interview."

"I was only being honest." Frankie smiled.

Coach Craig was on him in a split second, his hands tangled in the front of Frankie's shirt. His eyes nearly bulged out their sockets as his face turned pink.

"Don't you fucking give me that bullshit! I tolerate a lot from you, Mel Donova," he said the name like a curse. "When you put all our careers in jeopardy, I draw the line."

"Let go of me," Frankie said calmly.

Their eyes met. Coach Craig finally released him and stepped back in time to push the door back shut as the man on the other side along with another tried to come in.

"If they had certain things they wanted me to say, they should have given me a script."

"You're not a goddamn child anymore. You turn twenty one in a few months. What excuse will you spout then?"

"I'm doing my job. Anything else is extra." Frankie walked past him and opened the door. Coach stepped forward, angry, ready to burst. "Move." Frankie gave him a stare that frightened him into obeying. The other man stepped to the side.

Not feeling the need for a snack as he originally wanted, Frankie headed for the elevators. He felt used, violated. The company endorsing him scheduled a video shoot later in the day for a commercial. They were footing the hotel bill and travel. Which saved the organization money since the world competition took place in the same city and the team stayed in the same hotel.

The reason Coach Craig had arrived two days early was because the committee needed him to keep Frankie in line. I don't need a babysitter! He got to his room, inserted the keycard, and went in, pulling the deadbolt over.

A room all to himself. He wouldn't have to change it when the rest of the team arrived. Ravi and Blane would be disappointed even though their relationship had soured. They assumed he wasn't teaching them everything to improve their time. Frankie repeatedly told them his technique would not work for everyone. That they should take what he showed them and make their own plans.

He stood at the window overlooking the city. Here, he would stake his claim for the Olympic team once again. His college life put on hold until after the next Olympics. It sucked because he only had one year left with a solid three-point eight GPA, which he didn't have to try to maintain.

The perks of being smart.

Sitting on the plush sofa in front of the wide screen television, he turned on a cartoon show to pass the time until the company representative came to collect him.

At a park in the heart of the city, barricades erected at the shoot cordoned off the cameras area. Under the trees away from the primary shot path, sat a white canopy for the catering inside. A chair with Mel Donova on the back awaited him. The assistant director handed him the script as he sat down. Skimming it, he chuckled.

"Wow. What narcissist would say this crazy stuff? Who wrote this?" He grinned mischievously.

"Is it not what you wanted?" The assistant director asked. "I was under the impression you had a hand in crafting this." Frankie stared at him for a moment until the man caught on. "Oh. Right." He left.

The make-up artist came to give him a touch up, using her fingers to adjust his hair after dusting on another layer of foundation that he didn't need. My skin is flawless.

"Okay, we're ready for you, Mr. Mel Donova," the set coordinator called out.

Mr. Mel Donova?

Frankie snorted, hauling himself out of the seat. He went to his mark, handing the script to another assistant. The audience on the other side of the barricades grew and law enforcement moved in for crowd control.

"And, action." The director said, waving two fingers.

Frankie walked down the trail, a sinister grin on his face.

"As an undefeated world record holder and seven-time Olympic gold medalist, I have to make sure I have a clear mind, good rest, and a perfect body. Genex natural herb blends offer an array of products that help do just that. I trust them to keep me in top shape so I can enjoy life, and places of nature like this," he looked up towards the trees while raising his arms out, "and continue to bring pride to our country by winning gold at the next Olympics. Genex naturals. It's what the best athletes, like me, use for optimal performance."

He walked a little farther, the smile glued on his face.

"And, cut!" Crewmembers scrambled to reset the area.

The director got up from his chair.

"That was perfect. Let's do it one more time like that and we can wrap it up."

"Sure thing."

Frankie gave him his fakest winning smile.

At least I'm getting paid.

⁓

The Aquatics World Championship flashed in bold red, white, and blue letters on the digital billboard. Hundreds of athletes and their coaches flooded into the complex to get ready for the competition. Inside, the crowd split in two as the women's teams went to the right and the men to the left. Light conversation flowed while an announcer gave information over the PA system.

Sponsors talked business with committee members about endorsements. Cameramen set up their equipment for pregame interviews in the lobby. Only previous medal winners and potential hopefuls would get the spotlight.

Sharice caught sight of Frankie Mel Donova walking down the hall towards the arena. She excused herself from the dull conversation of sports memorabilia and heeled him until he stopped at a swag table to check out their wares.

"If it isn't our famous troublemaker," she said coyly.

Frankie, his head bent down to get closer to a trinket, looked over at her. His blue eyes were like a storm. The blond hair sticking out from under a backwards baseball cap with Team USA stitched on it made him look like a Greek Adonis. This is the person whose career my husband is obsessed with. She too had come to scrutinize him more as his antics and wins dominated the news sphere.

"I haven't done anything that would constitute trouble." Frankie stood. "I'm just living life."

"On your own terms at our country's expense."

She gestured for him to walk with her. He swung his duffel back behind him using the strap and turned to stand beside her. They walked down the hall, avoiding others as they passed.

"You're young. Impressionable. I'm sure you'll realize your mistake and correct accordingly."

"Like I said, I haven't done anything wrong."

"We've invested a lot into your career. You don't get to play games anyway you wish."

Frankie stopped. "What is your deal? Why are you riding me all the time?"

"Your arrogance makes our country look bad. You need to rein it in."

"No." Frankie turned those stormy eyes on her. At six feet tall, and a former volleyball player, she intimidated most men. She wore four-inch heels that put her an inch above him. His expression burned into her. He was not afraid of her. "This is what you people wanted. You forced me into it. This is what you get."

She stepped back in surprise at the animosity in his tone. He always came across as a brat of smaller stature in her view. That was a mistake. She knew that now. Frankie was not someone to toy with. Which made her angry.

Why do we have to baby him? Kowtow to his whims?

She wanted to find a way to bring him down a peg. Show the committee, and her star-struck husband, that they could replace him if necessary. He was nothing special anymore.

"Oh, really? You could have said no and ended your Olympic career right then and there."

The way Frankie's eyes widened with fury, she felt fear for the first time in his presence.

"Is that a threat?" He asked it so calmly; she wondered if she was hearing things.

"Just do what you're told."

"Everybody needs to stop saying that to me or I will do something you really won't like."

The rest of his team were up ahead, and Coach Craig looked back to see them standing together. Her expression must have given him a hint of the argument because he frowned and headed towards them. Sharice pursed her lips and shook her head as he approached.

"What the hell are you doing, Frankie? If anyone sees you talking to a committee member, all kinds of rumors will spread. Stay with the team," he snapped loudly.

Frankie said nothing. He went to join his team, leaving Sharice standing in awe at his audacity. Coach Craig folded his arms.

"Look, I got this. No need to involve yourself personally."

He turned and walked back to escort his athletes.

A familiar presence came up behind her.

"That was dangerous," her husband said in her ear. "It looks bad."

"As opposed to you chatting with him at every turn whenever the two of you are in the same vicinity?" She turned to him. "Your obsession is the problem."

"I only give him advice and make sure he's doing okay. This situation is not easy for him."

"He looks like he's doing fine to me."

"Well, he's not."

Gerald walked back to the lobby, leaving her in the thickening foot traffic. She frowned at his words, not believing them. Then her mind went back to when Frankie stared at her moments ago. She could see the faint covering of foundation under his eyes. His tanned skin seemed paler than normal. Those stormy eyes were lackluster, reminding her of malnutrition.

Was he eating properly?

That won't do. He was their prized athlete. Coach Craig saying he had it under control now smacked of a lie. There's no way he didn't know of Frankie's health.

At the same time, she wanted to see him falter just once. Proof that he was nothing more than a hybrid human with flaws like all the rest.

⌒⌒

The pool appeared clean, which made Frankie breathe with relief. He brought one arm across his chest and held it with the other in an elbow grip. He pulled, feeling the muscles stretch, then switched to the other arm. His only mission for the championship involved feigning a struggle to keep his world record. An easy competition that required no exertion on his part.

He watched the other competitors go all out in the current heat and commended them on pushing through it. When his teammates competed, he cheered them all with extra condescension.

Two team members from another country stood near the bleachers, observing his show.

"What an asshole," the first one said, tsking.

"He's not just an asshole. He's a whole ass," the other said.

One of the American team members turned to them.

"You hit the nail right on the head. We can't stand him either."

Frankie glanced over at them while clapping for a teammate making his last lap. He heard them. Sometimes he used his extra sensory hearing to spy on people. It was no great talent like being able to hear a mile away. He just adjusted it to boost the sound. A whole ass, huh?

It amused him because none of them had come close to beating him in the past four years. The cheers grew louder as the first swimmer reached out to touch the wall. The rest followed seconds after each other. His heat was up next, so he headed to the rinse station. On the way, he slapped the back of his teammate coming out of the water.

"Good job!"

"Fuck you, Frankie."

His teammate gave him a nasty look.

"Love you too!"

Frankie stood in front of the world championship backdrop while cameras flashed in his eyes. He held his medals chest high with both hands, smiling wide. The white track suit seemed to glow under the bright lights of the press section.

"How are you feelings about going into the next Olympics still holding the world record?" A female reporter asked, shoving her microphone closer to his face. The stanchions connected by thick velvet ropes stopped her. "Do you think you'll be able to hold on to it?"

"What?" Frankie smirked, tilting his head back. "Heck no." The reporters went silent, dumbfounded by his remark. "Why would I want to hang on to it? I'm gonna' break it."

The room went into an uproar.

"Are you saying you can swim faster than the current record?"

"What's your strategy for that?"

"How does your team fit into this?"

All valid questions. Frankie forced himself not to sigh by taking a deep breath and looking straight into the nearest camera.

"I live to swim. It's only natural that I would get faster over time. As for my team, I have their full support and look forward to competing with them again in Paris."

Coach Craig came into their line of sight with his arms spread open to block the flashes.

"Alright, that's it for today. Our golden boy needs his rest. Thank you all for coming."

The press shouted more questions while he escorted Frankie out of the bubble and towards the elevators. A few paparazzi followed them, only to be shut out as the doors closed. Coach Craig exhaled slowly, closing his eyes for a moment before opening them to stare at Frankie.

"Have you lost your ever-loving mind?" His calm voice had a vicious tone.

"Huh?"

"You're going to break it?"

"MmHmm." Frankie rearranged the gold medals around his neck. "That's what I said."

"We need to have a discussion." Coach Craig pointed a finger between the two of them. "That's not something you just announce without any receipts."

"Have I not delivered when I said I'd do something?"

Coach Craig mouth gaped, shaking his head in disbelief.

"That's not the issue. You're already the fastest swimmer on the planet."

"Recorded. Pretty sure there's some alien laying around in his pajamas talking shit about how slow I am."

"Don't be cute!" Coach Craig pinched the bridge of his nose. "The committee is going to have a field day. You just can't open your mouth and not have bullshit come falling out, can you?"

Frankie curbed his anger. They created this monster and now they don't like the way it speaks! He shoved his hands in his pants pockets.

POOLS OF DECEPTION

The urge to punch his coach dead in the face overwhelmed him. He knew that would be a bad idea.

Rolling Tides

The after party in the suite on the top floor made Caligula look tame. Business executives, sponsors, athletes, press agents, and random partygoers invited in passing, crammed inside eager to engage in debauchery. Frankie hurried out of there before he got trapped. Two women tried to grab hold of him as he made his way to the door.

Outside in the hallway, he breathed a sigh of relief, bending over to rest his hands on his knees. He could faintly hear the thump of techno music coming from the room. A couple walking by stared at him and moved to the other side of the wall. Frankie stood waving at them.

He went to the elevator and pushed his floor button. Four levels down, it stopped. The doors opened and Gerald stood on the other side. He stared at Frankie before getting in. He glanced over at him.

"Rough night?"

"It was like hell on Earth. I barely made it out alive."

Gerald laughed, cupping a hand over his mouth.

"Really, Frankie?"

"I'm being serious." Frankie looked at the panel. "You didn't push your floor."

"Oh. I have time. I can walk you to your room."

"Let me guess," Frankie tilted his head away from him. "Paparazzi."

"I can't just want to walk with you even for five minutes?"

The elevator dinged and the doors opened on Frankie's floor. The two walked side by side towards Frankie's room. At his door, Frankie leaned against the side of it.

"You really shouldn't be here with me. Sinners like us get

caught easily."

"That's not…"

"I mean, there's no reason for you to wait for me."

"Frankie."

Gerald moved in and kissed him deeply. Frankie felt his body sag as euphoria washed over him. He tried to grab hold of the wall to keep from falling.

"No, Frankie. I can't wait any longer."

He found the room key in Frankie's jacket and inserted it in the door. It barely had time to click before they stumbled into the dark room. The door slammed shut. Frankie couldn't hold him back. He never disengaged his lips while he stripped his and Frankie's clothes off. In full heat, Frankie shifted to his female form. They fell onto the bed.

Gerald leaned over Frankie, finally ending the kiss. His eyes smoldered with lust. There was no warning as he entered her with one hard thrust. Frankie gasped, her back arching from the shock. Gerald took hold of her calf and pulled her down closer to him, forcing his cock deeper.

"I warned you, Frankie, not to tease me." His voice deep and lush.

His fast pace and long thrusts were forceful. Frankie felt her eyes roll back as her walls contracted.

"Ahh, Frankie. Don't."

Her juices flowed freely, making his strokes glide easily into her. *It's hot!* Her body burned from the inside. She slammed her hands on his chest, bracing herself to endure his wrath. Like a starved, hungry animal, he took everything he wanted. He grabbed her wrists and pushed both her arms over her head, clasping his fingers with hers.

"Look at me, Frankie," he breathed.

Frankie forced her eyes open and took a sharp intake of air. She wasn't prepared for such a sight. His sweating face and dark hair hanging in his eyes made her heart race even more. She met his stare and her soul ignited.

"I'll never give you up, Frankie. Not ever."

He leaned down and covered her mouth with his. His tongue invaded her, finding hers. She had never been kissed like that before and wanted more.

He drove his cock deeper, forcing her to open her mouth more as she tried to moan in ecstasy.

I can't! It's too much! Frankie cried inwardly.

The tears streamed down her face. He let go of one arm and she used it to grab the back of his head, her fingers tangling in his hair. The moment his lips left hers, she felt herself come with him. His head arched back as he let out a pained growl.

Frankie cried out as if she had been murdered. She might have been, for all she knew. Her body went limp, all the life energy drained, and her eyes fluttered, wanting to shut forever. She had almost drowned once when she was ten and this felt like that only tenfold.

Gerald sat atop her, catching his breath. Their sweat drenched bodies began to cool. His head fell forward, and he looked down on her.

"Don't ever let anyone touch this way but me, Frankie."

He caressed her cheek. The last thing she remembered before the little death took hold, bringing sleep.

Gerald woke up groggy, his crusty eyes refusing to stay open for a moment. Exhaustion consumed him. He glanced at Frankie, fast asleep next to him. The clock on the nightstand showed ten to six. He could see the sun's rays peeking through the curtains move across the ceiling. Leaning over, he kissed Frankie softly on the lips.

"Sweet dreams, Frankie."

He got up and found each piece of his clothing strewn on the floor from the door to the bed. Signs of the desperation he felt when he realized Frankie would let him do what he wanted. His room keycard had fallen out of his pocket and lay at the edge of the bed. Being as quiet as possible, he left the room, gently shutting the door, and went to the elevators.

The inside of his room sat empty.

No sign of Sharice returning. He checked his watch. Six twenty. Once again, he stripped naked and went into the bathroom to take a shower. He let the hot water ease the tension in his muscles. Being in the same room he shared with his wife erased the relaxation he felt before. He hated the fact that he had to wash off Frankie's scent.

The way it lingered on him made him relive the brutal, passionate sex they had just hours ago. He always knew when Frankie came in his vicinity because of his unique smell. A faint sweet cream with a hint of cinnamon. It could find him from across a room. He leaned his head against the wall, letting the water beat down the back of his neck.

Dressed in a black suit with a white shirt, the top two buttons undone, Gerald picked up his phone and opened the picture a sponsor he chatted with earlier sent. The man stood in the forefront while various forms of promiscuity and sexual activity went on behind him.

The caption said, 'You're missing a great party! It just went full porno about an hour ago.'

The same party Frankie had come out of. The activity at the party he couldn't care less about. What concerned him lay far in the background. No one else would probably make it out, but he noticed almost immediately.

On her knees in front of a big plushy chair, his wife's head lay embedded between the thighs of a man sitting in it. The way his pants seem to sag at the sides let him know they were undone at the crotch. He could point her out because of the dress she wore when she left.

He tossed the phone on the bed and went to the floor to ceiling panoramic windows to check out the view of the sunrise over the city.

The door clicked open. Sharice came in, carefully closing the door so it didn't slam. She turned around and stopped. Messy hair crowned her head, and her dress appeared hastily put on. Her shoes dangled from her left hand.

"You're up." She came further in, dropping her shoes by the dresser.

"We have a meeting at eight. Nothing fancy. I can go solo if you want to get some sleep."

"No, no. I'll be fine."

"That must have been some party."

"It didn't start to die down until like an hour ago. Some

went for breakfast. Granted, they were young, too."

He watched her waddle towards the bathroom.

"Is something wrong with your leg? You're kinda limping."

"Oh," she tilted her head back at him. "It's from sitting for so long on that horrible couch. A few sponsors basically talked my head off. A hot shower will knock the kinks out."

The way she lied so easily boggled his mind. They had been married for twelve years. He knew what she looked like after a night of rough sex. And that she could barely walk if it went too intense.

Nausea came over him. He wanted out of their marriage more than anything. The prenuptial agreement stated there had to be just cause. He had no real proof of her infidelity. For all anyone could see, she may have been merely leaning over to talk to the man in the picture while relaxing on the floor at a party.

It wouldn't be the first time she had been unfaithful. She was quite good at hiding it from their friends and family. Not long after she gave birth to their second son, she started using her charms to woo potential clients. That's what angered him the most. She only slept with other men for the advancement of her career. To line her family's pockets.

She didn't have the thoughtfulness, decency, or cared enough for his feelings to fall in love with someone. He would have accepted that scenario given his current issue. This was the first time he had ever cheated on her. There were so many opportunities to follow in her deceit.

At least he had found his soulmate. Not a random piece of ass to seal a deal.

Hearing the shower turn on, Gerald picked up his phone and headed out of the room.

He needed air.

CHAPTER TWO

Swimming Debut

A group of reporters huddled in the press area at France's International Airport waited for the American teams to show. Especially the Aquatics team with Frankie Mel Donova who would once again grace the world with his presence. The Olympic committee once more changed the summer and winter games to be held every two years. They felt no reason to spread them out any longer since the athletes didn't get a break, competing in World Championships each year in between.

Frankie's schedule became jampacked with interviews, sponsor spots, and extra training.

"Did you hear the rumors?" A popular sports podcaster asked in a hushed voice while he looked around at the other media outfits.

"Yeah, that can't be right," his cameraman replied.

"I mean, drugs? Really?" Their female reporter and interviewer scoffed.

"No way he's putting that shit in his body," their writer added.

"From what my sources say, it's not just rumors. People have seen him doing it." The podcaster said.

"If that's the case, he should be disqualified."

"Right? How could he pass a piss test? No way the organization would allow him to compete." The reporter frowned.

"Apparently he flushes his system out beforehand," the cameraman offered.

"Well, he's not stupid," the writer shrugged.

Commotion at the baggage claim made them perk up. Coming down the escalators were the Americans.

Cameramen closer to them scrambled for the best shots. The small group bided their time. No need to bumrush the athletes. They were jet lagged and tired. Questions and congratulations rose to high decibels, making some athletes wince at the noise.

Ten minutes later, the swim team came down. Madness ensued as reporters and cameramen went up the opposite escalators, trying to get at them to the chagrin of the patrons riding it. Frankie Mel Donova wore dark shades that covered most of his upper face. His blond hair lay under a backward baseball cap, the rest falling past his shoulders.

A lollipop stick hung from the corner of his mouth.

He looked put out by the chaos, a sneer creeping. The blue track suit with red and white stripes along the sleeves and down the sides of the pants fit a little tighter than the rest of his team. The matching duffel bag's strap was slung across his chest. As he stepped off into the baggage claim area, he pushed past the paparazzi without saying a word and followed his team to collect their bags.

"Oh, he's being rude and crude today," the reporter in the small group said.

"Should we chance it?"

The cameraman checked his handheld one last time.

"Screw it! All he can do is either ignore or answer us," the podcaster snapped.

Two other groups arrived in the press area amid the chaos.

Frankie came within a few yards of them, the microphones already whipped out, stretched towards his face. The reason for the press area was to limit disruption in the airport and keep some distance from the athletes. No handshakes, or possibilities of getting sneezed on.

"Are you excited to be here at your third Olympic games?"

"Are you still looking to break your own world record?"

"Are the rumors true that you're a drug user?"

All three questions came at once. The last one made him turn to the person who asked it, his face contorted into a nasty stare. The woman journalist leaned back in shock at the response. A silence fell on the crowd. Coach Craig pushed his way through to reach him.

The podcast reporter leaned forward.

"I hear you are looking forward to trying the country's top cuisines. Have you made a list yet?" She gave him a bright smile and patiently waited for a reply.

Frankie's scowl faded, and he lifted his shades to see her better. He returned the smile.

"Not yet. But if you have any suggestions, let me know." He winked at her before lowering his shades.

"Alright. That's enough." Coach Craig maneuvered Frankie back into the fold with the rest of the team. He glanced at the journalist who asked the drug question. "You oughtta' be ashamed for asking that."

The aquatics team exited the airport and loaded into one of the coach buses on the other side of the pickup lanes.

"Nice going," a female reporter in another group next to the podcasters said heatedly. "You ruined our shot." The group at the end gave her incredulous stares.

She looked around. "What?"

"No, he wasn't going to answer any of you guys' questions after asshat here," the podcsaster pointed to the journalist, "threw that bomb out there. You're lucky he even said anything at all. You should be thanking her." He gestured towards the female in his group.

The older female tsked and went to the other end to attack one of the well-known track medalists with a barrage of questions.

"He didn't look so good," the podcast reporter said softly.

"Yeah." The cameraman checked his recorder to make sure he got what little there was. "He seems tired. Not healthy, either."

"He's also diving this time again too." The writer said. "They just aren't giving him a break."

"Drugs help," the nasty journalist added as she came back, denied a shot at her other prey. "Maybe he gets caught and he can rest up for as long as he likes cuz his career will be over."

"Wow. Tell us how you really feel." The podcaster snapped.

"It'll be his own fault." The journalist walked off to find a more cooperative athlete to harass.

The moment Frankie stepped into the dorm room and saw Ravi and Blane, he mentally cut off his disdain so it wouldn't show on his face. Their stares followed him to the bed, where he dropped his duffel bag on top and shoved his suitcase underneath.

"No hard feelings, right Frankie?" Blane asked, leaning back on his bed. "We just want to be teammates and friends like before."

Ravi sat with his legs crossed atop his bed.

"We were frustrated. You know how that feels."

Not really. Frankie thought about how effortless swimming was for him. Life, on the other hand.

"Sure. Let's wash it under the bridge." Frankie flopped on the bed and stared at the ceiling.

"We got that welcome party tonight. Coach says it's mandatory." Blane snorted.

"Fuck." Frankie closed his eyes.

The last thing he wanted to do was schmooze with a bunch of bureaucrats and other USA teams drinking and talking about how great they were. He turned his head towards the digital clock on the nightstand.

"How much time we got?"

Ravi pulled out an itinerary from his bag.

"It's three o'clock now. It starts at eight, so five hours. I say we take a two-hour nap, get showered and dressed, then get down downstairs to the bus on time."

Frankie didn't reply. Ravi looked over at Blane and found him passed out as well. Dropping the paper back in his bag, he laid back and drifted off. At the last minute, he reached over and set the alarm clock.

At five fifteen, the alarm went off. Blane jumped out of bed like a scared dog and rushed first into the shower. Ravi sat up with a start, wiping his face with his hands.

Frankie bolted out of bed, headed towards the window as if he'd been shot, looking around confused, like he didn't know where he was. He calmed down and slumped on the window seat.

"Jesus! Warn us if you set that thing. You know they don't

know to put normal sounding ones in here."

"Yeah, sorry. I forgot. Scared the shit outta me too. Blane probably damn near pissed himself. That's why he got in first."

"Hey!" Blane popped his head out the bathroom door. "We ain't got time to be wasting water. Get in here."

"It's not that kind of shower," Ravi protested. "We won't all fit."

"Wrong. This thing is huge. Hurry up! I got the water going."

They could see steam fog up the mirrors inside. Ravi glanced at Frankie and shrugged.

"Fine. Let's do this." Frankie took off his jacket and pulled his shirt over his head, tossing it on the bed. The rest of his clothes went right as Ravi walked naked past him into the bathroom.

With their outfits lying on their beds, the three sat for a moment to get their bearings. Four other teammates from across the hall had come over filling all four beds. The others had not gotten dressed yet either. Everyone made small talk, laughing at stupid jokes.

Frankie let out a laugh as he took a small tray out of his bag and set it before him on the bed. His damp hair hung in stringy noodles while he wore nothing but his boxers. Then he pulled out a small baggie of white powder and shook some onto the tray.

"What are you doing?" Blane asked, cautiously. Ravi's eyes went wide.

"I kind of need something to make me last through the night," Frankie said as he used his room keycard to chop up the powder. He divided it into two rows. "The right way is to make sure the lines are not too thick or too thin."

His teammates stared at him in awe. "You want to be able to get it all in one go. Can't have them too long either." He bent down while holding one nostril and snorted up the first line. "And definitely don't do just one side." He snorted the second/ They watched his pupils dilate when he raised his head. "It won't feel right." Frankie sniffed hard. "Whoo!"

"What the actual fuck, Frankie!" A teammate yelled.

"Everybody calm down," Ravi said.

"Are you kidding me?" Another teammate cried out.

"What? It's not like I'm going to pop my test before the meet. Chill." Frankie gave them a winning smile. "Trust me." His voice seemed to slur.

"I'm out."

The teammate closest to the door stood and left.

"See you at the party," Blane said, giving a two-finger salute.

"Same here." The other three followed, the door slamming shut behind them.

Ravi glanced over at Frankie. Blane shook his head.

Frankie started laughing. So hard, he fell back on the bed, holding his abs. Tears formed at the corners of his eyes.

"Get dressed, Frankie. We don't wanna' be late." Blane scooted off his bed and picked up the one suit he had brought with him. "Damn, Frankie."

"I aim to please." Frankie reached over and slid his suit towards him. "Time to party."

⌒

Red, silver, and blue balloons floated along the banquet hall's ceiling with matching streamers cascading in a criss cross pattern. White linen covered round tables, large enough to seat ten people. Simple flower arrangements of the same color scheme in clear vases were the centerpiece.

At the far end near the stage sat the biggest, gaudiest American Pride cake Frankie had ever seen. It took up an entire table and had to be at least four or five layers.

A disc jockey set up in the stage's corner spun some old school hip hop and Frankie watched some of the older party goers move rhythmless to it.

Oh God. He didn't want to see that.

Off to his right, he caught sight of the committee. Sharice and Gerald weren't standing together as usual. Why do they stay in such a loveless marriage? Sharice's father came into the group and started talking. That's why.

Frankie tried to move away before Gerald spotted him. He failed. Their eyes met for a second, yet he could see, and feel, the longing. He resumed his conversation.

Sharice caught their exchange and stared at Frankie with indifference. In her eyes, he was nothing to fear.

Think again. Frankie gave her a crooked smile, grabbing a champagne glass off the tray speeding past him, and raised it in a toast to her. She grimaced and turned away to finish her conversation.

"What was that about?" One of the dive team members asked as he came behind him, throwing an arm around his shoulder. "She doesn't like you at all."

"Something like that."

"I don't get it. Why the hate?" He took a few sips from the champagne glass dangling in his hand. "She's the one who advocated to take you off the dive team. We barely win these days except when you come in and do some crazy, amazing feat."

"Stop." Frankie glanced angrily back at him. "Don't say that. You guys are damn good. No one should expect perfection in any of these competitions."

"True. Come on. I'll try to keep your coach and those two asshats away from you as long as I can."

"That would be much obliged." Frankie sipped the champagne and nearly choked, stopping short of spitting it out. "Aww, shit!"

"Yeah, It's nasty." He pointed at a slew of people on the other side of the room waiting in line. "To the bar?"

"Absolutely." Frankie wiped his mouth.

He placed the champagne glass atop another tray passing through, his teammate doing the same.

"You usually don't drink alcohol."

"I'm starting to think I should more often." He saw Coach Craig scanning the room. "My freedom looks short-lived."

"Not so fast."

His teammate pointed to Coach Ken coming around Coach Craig, blocking his view of Frankie. Coach Craig looked flustered, attempting to go past him. Coach Ken calmly talked him down, grabbing a cocktail off the tray a server presented.

The two men engaged in a terse conversation.

"Now's our chance."

They hurried towards the crowded bar. To their surprise, they were allowed to cut the line.

Hangovers made one regret mass quantities of libations the night before. Frankie always laughed at the athletes stumbling around during breakfast in obvious pain. He didn't feel like laughing today as one of those people. His head thumped, making him squeeze his eyes shut in agony. He had thrown up twice in the early hours of the morning, still tasting the liquor that came with the smell of rotting fruit and overly warm meat.

Shouldn't have ate from that charcuterie platter.

The thing had been sitting on the table all night. By midnight, the cheese had curled with hard, oily edges, and the meat a shade darker. He needed something to combat the alcohol swishing around in his stomach.

He sat upright on the bench in the garden area. People strolled the paved walkways, admiring the bright flora and tall trees. A fountain sat five hundred yards behind him, the gushing water soothing to his ears. A small tree and some bushes blocked the sun on his right, so he didn't need to raise his hands to provide shade for his poor eyes. The light still stung, though.

Frankie reached into his sweatpants pocket and pulled out a baggie of green herbs with rolling papers inside.

Maybe this will help.

Two British athletes walking along the path that curved close to the benches laughed about the American party last night, amazed at how over the top it was. As they got closer, they caught sight of Frankie leaning over, doing something with his hands in his lap.

The first guy slapped the other in the chest, stopping him as he halted. His eyes bulged.

"Is that Mel Donova rolling a fag? Doesn't he need like good lung capacity? Should he even smoke?"

"That's not a fag." The other guy replied, shaking his head.

The two turned to stare at each other.

"Holy shit," the first guy whispered. Then he got angry. "That the hell?"

"Right? What kind of detox is he doing to pass piss tests?"

"Can't be anything on the market. Probably some experimental shit from their government."

"No way the Committee would allow him to compete if they knew."

"Wanna' bet on that? They'd do anything to keep their golden cow."

The first guy raised his arms towards Frankie. "He's not even trying to hide it! He's rubbing it in our faces!"

"Let's just go." The other guy steered them in the opposite direction. "Fucking disgrace."

Gerald found Frankie at the bench and stood over him as he rolled the greenery in the papers.

"Frankie. What is that?" He breathed.

Frankie looked up at him with tired eyes. Fatigue lined his deep expression. He finished rolling and lit it with a small lighter. He leaned back and blew out the smoke.

"Just some herbs to stop me from being nauseous."

"Don't let people see you smoking that. They'll get the wrong idea."

"Holy hell, that stinks," a passerby exclaimed. They waved a hand to their face. The person next to them looked over and gaped at Frankie. "What is that?"

Their partner elbowed him and nodded towards the bench. Both their mouths went wide as they hurried down the path.

"Too late for that. That's kind of the point, though. No one ever asked me."

Gerald sighed and bent down until he was level with Frankie's chest. He reached up and placed a hand on his left cheek.

"You need to take better care of yourself. I'm worried about you, Frankie."

"I'll rest after my last heat."

Gerald dropped his hands, letting them hang between his thighs before standing up. Frankie didn't look well and the amount of drinking he did at the party did him no favors. It surprised him to see Frankie consuming alcohol as if he were a veteran drunk.

"Promise me."

Frankie took a few more tokes, blowing more of the foul smoke into the air. He locked eyes with him. Neither wavered for a long time until Frankie lowered his gaze first.

"Fine. I promise." He suddenly sat up and pitched forward, projectile vomiting on the pavement. "I don't feel good."

Some people nearby stopped, gasping in horror.

"Eww!" Another athlete across the grass yelled. "Jesus, Frankie! Can't hold your liquor?"

Gerald glanced back at the man with burning hatred. The guy's face changed to shock at the stare and walked off.

"I'm taking you to the medical center."

Gerald helped Frankie off the bench, grabbing the baggie and shoving it in his jacket pocket. The half-smoked roll he put out in the grass and tossed into the thicket of bushes.

"I don't need to…" Frankie retched. Nothing came out.

"Don't argue with me. Come on."

Inside, Gerald found a maintenance tech and explained the situation. They didn't seem too happy about cleaning up puke from a drunk athlete.

"What the hell have you been doing?" Sharice yelled at Coach Craig. "You're supposed to be watching him!"

The small, overcrowded hospital room held Coach Craig, Gerald, Sharice, and two other committee officials. Frankie lay asleep, heavily sedated, on the bed. The instruments hooked up to him beeped softly. An IV drip attached to his arm administered the sedative and recovery concoction.

"He's not a child! I didn't know he was drinking his damn weight at the party!" Coach Craig's face contorted in anger, flushed pink. His ears were almost red.

"That's the least of our worries," one member snapped. "We got reports of him smoking weed in the goddamn courtyard."

"His actions show a total disrespect for the games. How is he passing his drug tests?"

Coach Craig stared at them, flabbergasted. Gerald could't make out if he had no idea about the rumors, which he found unlikely, or had no answer.

"What the?" He wiped a hand down his face. "Frankie's not stupid either. No way he lit one up for all to see in broad daylight."

"Want us to pull up the footage?" Sharice snapped. "He's out of control. You need to fix this, or I will."

"Really?" Coach Craig snorted, folding his arms. "You gonna sanction him? Bench him for the games when he's the most decorated gold medalist with the world record?"

That rendered the other committee members speechless, halting their upcoming tirades.

"Don't tempt me, Craig," Sharice seethed.

"And don't threaten him with no inclination to do so" Gerald retorted. She glared at him. "No one would let Frankie off the hook if the rumors were true."

"Did you not witness him smoking a joint with your own eyes?" The other member cried. He turned to Sharice. "If this goes on any longer, we will lose face with the rest of the world."

Thoroughly disgusted, everyone exited the room, leaving Frankie to rest. Gerald watched Coach Craig pacing the hall, scratching his head. Things were going to get hard for Frankie going forward. His freedom to roam would be cut off.

Coach Craig stood over Frankie in his dorm room. He had kicked Ravi and Blane out, putting the deadbolt on the door so they couldn't get back in.

"You think I'll let you tank this whole team with your antics?" He drummed his fingers on the backs of his biceps. "Doing drugs in front of everyone..."

"Didn't ..."

"Making a mockery of their training. Is that how you get off?" Coach Craig barely contained his rage. "I swear to God if we didn't need you, I would have cut you from this team years ago. Don't you fuck this up, you fucking junkie!"

Frankie reared back at the onslaught of profanity.

He didn't deserve that. Too weak to fight, he laid sideways on the bed and closed his eyes. Coach Craig sputtered, realizing he had just unleashed a barrage of frustration on a sick person. Exasperated, he gripped his arms.

"Get some rest, Frankie. You gotta be in top shape for your meet tomorrow afternoon." He hesitated to pat him on the head, then decided against it, too angry to feel that level of sympathy. "I'll have the doctor check you in the morning before your drug test."

He undid the deadbolt and opened the door. Ravi and Blane were standing on either side while a few team members hung out their room doors, listening.

"Stop being nosy and get back inside! I don't want to hear about anyone not getting enough sleep."

The room doors slammed shut. Ravi and Blane went in and glanced at Frankie before going to bed. Coach Craig waited for the door to close.

"I need a drink."

Tragedy in the Water

Angry posts about Frankie Mel Donova flooded the Olympic's online forums. Demands for his expulsion from the games and to be removed from Team USA bordered on vulgar. Sharice didn't have to scroll through them. With each new entry, the screen moved to show more.

Other athletes called out the unfairness, having trained hard only to be outclassed by a druggie.

Most of the posts were anonymous. The ones who didn't care who saw how they felt, their icons displayed top left of their rants. The screen's light flickered from scrolling, creating a strobe effect in her dark office. She enjoyed being in the dark when going through the feeds. The images reflected in her eyes as she absorbed them.

Another anonymous post pinged.

'Why do we have to endure this shit? Can't the committee do something?'

Sharice leaned forward. She typed a reply under her personal user handle not associated with the committee.

'Their hands are probably tied. Nothing they can do unless he fails his drug test.'

A different poster chimed in.

'That's BS. I could take care of this if I was in charge.'

Sharice became intrigued. *Oh, really?*

'Yeah,' the first poster sent. 'Easy remedy. Then someone else can win some medals.'

A feeling of trepidation mixed with excitement rushed through Sharice. Maybe? She private messaged the two and entered a separate chat that showed her committee credentials.

'What do you mean, easy? He's the American golden

goose. Plus, he's never been caught…ever.'

The second poster started with a rolling eyes emoji.

'We just need to take him out of the equation.'

'How?' Sharice sent a shrugging emoji.

The first poster was typing.

'All we need is a drug that will take him down for good.'

'Something powerful,' the second one sent.

'There would be no disputing it when it shows up in his system. You want him gone just as bad.'

Sharice thought for a moment. A drug. Taking Frankie out of the loop. He'd be hit with sanctions, not allowed to compete for two years, and required to go into drug rehab.

'If you guys are serious, I could help with that. You can't tell anyone what we're doing and that I'm involved.'

'Who would we tell?' The first one typed. She could tell his tone screamed with indignation.

'You get us what we need, and we'll take care of the rest. No more Frankie headaches.'

'Deal.'

She closed the chat room and exited the site. More posts had come through, getting nastier by the minute. Frankie had a lot of enemies.

By the next day, the three had formed a plan on how to get the drug in the two posters' hands. They established a code name for delivery to the dorms. Sharice worked on finding the best drug every chance she got between meetings and interviews. Frankie Mel Donova won two more medals. She seethed, watching him smile and wave to loud cheers that had diminished over the week. The rumors were spreading.

A week later, the drug she had found through her connections arrived in a puffy manila mailer. The man she purchased it from warned her that too much would cause severe sickness and heart palpitations. It would amplify any drug in Frankie's system tenfold. She made sure to write detailed instructions on how much to use and insert them behind the shipping pouch.

There would be no way for him to pass a drug test with that. Sharice smiled deviously. It turned upside down thinking about her husband. He would defend Frankie to the ends of the Earth. She snorted. Not this time. Her father won't let him back himself into a corner, ruining the family's status.

She went to the door of her office and looked around.

"Richards!" She called out to her father's assistant.

"Yes, Mrs. Sharice?"

"I'm going out for a bit. Check on the athletes at the dorms. Will you let Gerald know?"

"Of course. Will you be back for dinner?"

"I'm not sure. I'll call if not."

Edward bowed his head and went through the suite to the other side where her father kept his office.

Sharice turned around, grabbed the package and a windbreaker from the hook behind the door and headed out. She hailed a taxi, not wanting her driver to know her business.

Getting out at the dorm, she hurried into the common area and went straight for the mailroom. The attendant wasn't there, so she found an empty slot where she placed a sticker with the fake name and slid the package in.

Right as she rounded the corner leading back to the common area, the attendant walked past her. She smiled, proud of herself for the perfect timing. Taking out her phone, she texted her two co-conspirators.

It's here.

⌒

Sharice sat in the box seats of the arena with her husband for the 200 Meter backstroke finals. Frankie Mel Donova's best competition that he held the world record in. A frown graced her face. She had hoped the two posters would have spiked his food or drink beforehand. Then she thought about it. Frankie not competing meant disaster.

Good call.

Her husband seemed disinterested in the meet, but she knew that wasn't true. He probably felt as anxious as the other committee members in attendance to witness Frankie deliver another upset and break his own record.

She peeked over at the rinse station and saw Frankie chatting with his teammates while he stretched. Not a care in the world. It made her blood boil. The cameramen and commentators had taken their positions along the sidelines. She settled into her seat, folding her hands in her lap, a scowl on her face.

Frankie smacked his lips, running his tongue along the inside of his mouth. He had eaten a piece of Blane's energy bar. Only a tiny half inch square, but he could still taste it. His mouth felt super dry, as if dehydrated.

"Hey!" He called out to Blane and Ravi. "Toss me one of those bottled waters." He usually didn't drink before a heat, but this was an exception. Ravi reached into his duffel bag and threw a mini bottle at him. Frankie caught it with one hand. "Thanks."

He cracked open the top and took three sips. It tasted off. Probably from mingling with that nasty piece of bar he had. Not quite satiated, he took a few more small sips.

The Announcer's voice echoed in the area.

"Contestants, please proceed to your designated lane."

Frankie closed the bottle and tossed it back to Ravi. He donned his swim cap and walked out to cheers as he headed for the dive board at his lane. Coach Craig stood akimbo near the edge of the pool with the other coaches. The glare he gave him made Frankie chuckle.

He stepped down into the water and submerged. His vision went a little funny and he adjusted his goggles. The water looked especially wavy today. He came back up and turned around to get into position. His fingers tingled.

Am I nervous? This was a big deal, after all.

"Assume starting positions." The announcer instructed. "On your mark."

The buzzer sounded and the swimmers pushed off. Frankie glided towards the other side to finish his first lap. The cheers from the crowd became more muffled than usual. On the third lap, the butterflies in his stomach intensified. He felt his chest tighten as he struggled to catch his breath.

Something's wrong!

Then everything stopped as his body went still, his eyes staring up at the sky, seeing nothing.

Screaming erupted as the crowd watched Frankie stop moving and sink to the bottom of the pool. Officials ran to the edge as three lifeguards dove in to retrieve him. Sharice's eyes went wide in horror. Her husband shot up from his seat, ready to go down. She grabbed hold of his arm to stop him.

"Don't! Let the medics handle this." She, too felt worried.

Coach Craig slid to the lane where the guards hauled Frankie up. A medical team had arrived on the scene and immediately took possession of him. The first technician pulled out a scanning wand and felt his neck for a pulse.

"He's not breathing. No life signs," he called out. Another medic came around the other side to give chest compressions. One push sent blood and water spewing from Frankie's mouth. The tech pushed him back. "No!" He looked at the scan image on his tablet. "His heart is shredded. Looks like it imploded inside his chest."

"What the hell?" A third medic stared at the image in shock. "How does that even happen?"

"Get the defibrillator rods. We have to try and get it started somehow." He turned to the medic.

The other medic pulled a rolling container next to Frankie and brought out two metal rods attached to a mini electrode machine. Using a scalpel to make two incisions in Frankie's chest above his heart, he inserted the rods.

"Give me five," the tech instructed. The medic turned the dial on the machine and a soft thump sounded. The scan image showing his vitals stayed flat. "Four more." The medic turned the dial further to the right. This time, the scanner came to life after the thump. A faint wavy line scrolled across the bottom of the tablet screen.

"Contact the main house and tell them we need the tissue growth gel now. We gotta keep his heart going before transport or we lose him again." The medic sent a text at lightning speed on his phone.

A barricade was erected around the medical team. Volunteers pulled one of the drink station tents over to block the overhead cameras and spectators' view. Coach Craig made his hands into fists, clearly distraught. He didn't know what to do. The head technician glanced over at him.

"You need to contact next of kin. He might not make it."

Coach Craig jumped up and ran out of the pool area. Security ushered the rest of the swim teams out of the way along with their coaches as four more medical technicians came running. The first of them entered the makeshift tent and produced a giant syringe filled with thick yellow gel. He knelt by Frankie and plunged it into his chest right as the second medic removed the rods.

They all watched the scanner with bated breath. The heart muscle struggled for a bit, then they saw some of the ruptures tighten, closing the damage. The second tech motioned to the others. They came forward and unfolded a portable gurney.

"Alright. Lift him up gently." The first tech said. "You got a cover for him?" He asked a tech unfolding the gurney.

"Yep. No one sees his face when we take him out of here."

Four of the techs surrounded Frankie while another slid a stabilizing board underneath him.

"On three," the first medic said. He counted and on three, the four medics lifted Frankie off the tile and onto the gurney. "Let's go."

The medics threw a dark sheet over Frankie as they hauled him out, exiting the tent faster than the cameras trying to catch them.

Gerald wrenched his arm from his wife and pushed past her to follow the medics. The look on his face frightened her. More than worry, or anger, his soul seemed to have been ripped out of him.

This isn't what I wanted!

She covered her mouth with one hand. A short squeak followed by a shuddering intake of air escaped. Her father came behind her and his hand came down on her shoulder. She fought back tears.

"I don't know what just happened, but it will be a tragedy regardless."

The Olympic committee officially postponed the 200 Meter Backstroke race.

Chaos engulfed the medical center.

The committee contacted a team of specialists. Frankie must live. And to achieve that miracle they had to stabilize him. Sharice's Father went to the nearest doctor handling the case.

"Hello. I'm Philip Montgomery, the head of the American Olympics committee. We are going to need a full blood work analysis and stay abreast of his condition."

"That's protocol with any incident of this magnitude. I'm sure our coordinator will be in touch."

"Of course. Good to know."

He turned away and walked over to Gerald. The man looked hollow. A mere shell standing in the visitor wing. Sharice seemed nervous as she tried to coax him out of it. That's the most affection I've ever seen her give that man.

On the visitor waiting room's wide screen, the news broke about Frankie Mel Donova. Within minutes, his phone vibrated incessantly. He pulled it from his breast pocket and saw massive posts on the Olympic feed. Sharice also looked at her phone. The vitriol was astonishing. The first poster said something about a drug overdose and the rest took it from there.

The way Sharice went pale, he felt the same. Shameful behavior from fellow athletes, whether anonymous or not. Frankie may have been a pain in the ass but he didn't deserve this. Even if the rumors were true, resulting in this.

Dr. Alois Novak rushed down the medical center hall, weaving through medics doing their jobs. More advanced than the hospitals in the country, they catered specifically to Olympians and their family members. He tried to stay calm, failing with every thought about the blood test results. His lab coat whipped behind as he walked faster than normal towards Frankie's room.

He opened the door and found Gerald standing at the edge of the hospital bed. A barrier surrounded Frankie to create a germfree environment. Tubes ran from his chest and arms. The container the catheter emptied into was a quarter full with blood and urine swishing together.

Frankie lay intubated. Powerful drugs fed intravenously put him in an induced coma.

Round the clock surgery lasted for two days, ending with a barely functioning heart and a body too weak to fight.

"You're with the committee?" The Doctor asked with disgust.

Gerald turned to him. His eyes, devoid of life, made the doctor flinch.

"What is it?" Gerald's brow furrowed.

"About the blood test."

"Tell me." Gerald's eyes suddenly blazed with fury.

He knows something is off.

"Frankie Mel Donova had five different narcotics in his system. One of which is an experimental drug no one can get unless they are in the trials for it."

"Is that so?"

"His name is not on that list." Dr. Novak stepped closer. "His drug test before the meet was clean!" The doctor balled his hands up. "Someone tried to … "

Gerald grabbed hold of the doctor's shirt and pushed him into the hallway. He brought his face really close to him so no one else could hear them.

"You need to keep this to yourself. No one wants to hear that. Especially the committee."

Dr. Novak slapped his hand from the front of his shirt, forcing him to release his grip.

"They need to know that someone on that team or even one your people tried to murder a top athlete. Why would they sweep that under the rug?"

"If you want to keep your position as a top Olympic doctor, you need to keep your mouth shut."

"What is the committee going to do then?"

"I'll take care of Frankie. You do your job and tell no one about this."

"I have to give a report on the results," Dr. Novak snapped.

"Then do that. And nothing else."

The doctor could see the malice etched on Gerald's face. It dawned on him. He may be a committee member, but he didn't condone every decision they made. They were both in the same shitty boat with their careers on the line.

He walked away from Gerald and headed to an intensive care room being used for the meeting with the committee representative to go over the blood results.

Montgomery stood waiting in the dimly lit room. His tailored navy blue suit accented by a yellow tie with tiny red polka dot design made him look important.

"Dr. Novak. Good to see you. What do you have for me?"

Angered by his calm demeanor, the doctor frowned and took a step forward.

"My job as a doctor is to make sure my patients get the best care. I don't know what kind of scheme is going on, but I won't any part of it." His raised voice made Montgomery raise his brow. "I compared Mel Donova's drug tests from before the meet and after. He tested clean hours before that meet. You need to find out who tried to kill him!"

The silence that ensued made him realize he may have spoken against his better judgment. Gerald had been correct in his assessment. The committee was about to fuck him.

"I think," Montgomery began as he pushed his hands in his pants pocket, "your talents could be better used at a different facility." Dr. Novak's expression went slack. "Maybe take some time off to destress before transferring."

"Are you threatening me?"

"I am merely giving you an opportunity to broaden your skills in a new environment."

"I won't be bullied or silence…"

"You will if you want to keep your position." Montgomery's expression turned cold. "We'll make sure Frankie is well taken care of." He turned to exit, stopping at the door to glance back. "Telling anyone else about this will only hurt Frankie."

The doctor stood in the room alone, full of rage that deflated to sadness. He had treated Frankie for fatigue, overworked muscles, and sleep deprivation over the years. The only thing he ever consumed were vitamins and herbs. He treated his body bad physically yet like a temple to keep it going.

"You deserve better, Frankie."

News stations all over the world slandered Frankie, making him the most hated athlete on the planet. Other competitors grabbed their fifteen minutes of fame to say cruel, nasty things, most of it untrue. The small monitor on the wall across from Frankie's hospital bed played the highlights.

Gerald frowned at Frankie's sister standing in front of it, arms folded with one hand zipping the single jewel on her necklace back and forth.

She finally saw him and dropped her arms. Tall like Frankie, only two inches shorter, her hair was a light brown with a hint of red, taking after her mother. Her face was plain unlike Frankie who had a natural beauty regardless which sex he was.

"How did he become such a disgrace to our family, and our country?" She exhaled loudly. "This is going to affect my reputation at work. Our parents are just livid"

"Is that what you're worried about?" Gerald asked heatedly. "Go home. I'll take care of your brother since none of you won't!"

"And who are you supposed to be? His savior? Did you know about his drug use? Why didn't you stop it before it came to this?"

"You need to leave," he said in a vicious tone.

"I have to sign the request for transfer to the United States." She pointed to herself. "I am his next of kin, not you."

"Are you going to take over his care?"

She stared at him blankly. "I don't have the money or resources to do that." She replied haughtily.

"That's what I thought."

Back to the Surface

Gerald returned from the medical center feeling worn out. He hadn't been that tired since his days competing. The rental home appeared empty of sound until he heard his wife's voice in the office on the other side. A man responded and he recognized her father's gruff tone. After a while, the man came walking down the short corridor, nodding to him before going into his own section.

Tossing the keycard that opened the main entrance on the living room table, he went to their room overlooking the riviera. They had been there six weeks so far since the incident. The games were long done, all the athletes back at home, and France resumed its normal life.

The core committee members for the United States had to remain until Frankie was life flighted out. So much paperwork and emergency meetings consumed their daily lives. Gerald hung his head, sitting on the sofa, his hands dangling between his legs. He raised them to cover his face, calming himself down with a breathing technique. For close to four minutes he stayed like that, not wanting to do anything.

With a sigh, he dropped his hands and went over to the desk where stacks of invoices and bills lay haphazardly atop it. He shuffled them around to glance at the sender names. No use in delaying the inevitable. Bills had to be paid and letters answered.

He leaned to the side to get the letter opener sitting on the windowsill. Not sure why it was there. Some sticky residue with pieces of manila paper stuck to it. *Must have opened one of those express packages.* He wiped it off on his pants and went through the stack.

One correspondence addressed to Sharice caught his eye. Something about the person's name made him curious. He pulled out his phone and did a search. The name popped up as a researcher at the clinical trials institute where the drug in Frankie's system came from.

No. That can't be right.

His insides seemed to flip and he got woozy. He steadied himself by placing a hand on the edge of the desk. There had to be an explanation for it. Because the other option was vile. Unconscionable. Lightheaded yet determined, he made his way to Sharice who stood in her office talking to her monitor.

"Answer you fuckwads," Sharice demanded at the screen.

She had been trying to get in contact with the two posters since the incident. They were AWOL until now. Her question glared on the screen.

'What the hell were you thinking?'

The two posters icons blinked with the words 'typing'. The first one finally replied.

'What are you mad about?'

'Right?' The other replied. 'We said we were going to get rid of him.

She stared at the screen incredulous at their response.

"The hell?" She furiously typed her response.

'Why would you even think of something like that?'

'We solved both our problems. You sound ungrateful,' the second one sent.

"Ungrateful!" Sharice yelled while typing her reply. "You almost killed him! I didn't sign up for that!"

A cold, menacing presence hit her right as she finished speaking. She stood straight and turned to see Gerald in the doorway. His eyes burned with a hatred she had never seen before. Her mouth opened but she couldn't say anything.

Her reply ran across the screen beneath theirs.

'What would you have done if he died?'

She glanced at her monitor, not sure what to do. Shutting it down wouldn't solve the issue at hand. Gerald slowly walked towards her, his eyes catching the chat on the screen.

"This was your doing?" His even tone simmered with restrained fury. "You planned to do that to Frankie?"

He had his hands around her neck in an instant, pushing forward to ram her into the opposite wall. His face contorted as he got close enough to kiss her.

"When I saw that letter from the research coordinator, I thought to myself, no, she isn't that evil. To commit such an act on an elite athlete. For what?"

"Please, Gerald!" She gasped, "You're hurting me. Please, listen to me." She managed to take another breath. "I never wanted to kill him! I only wanted to…"

"What the hell is going on!" Her father came into the room. "You better get your hands off her, right now."

Gerald shoved her into the wall, backing away from her.

"I won't be married to that monster one moment longer." He pointed to Sharice. She slumped to the floor, holding her neck. "I want out of this marriage without penalty!"

"What are you talking about?" Her father approached him.

"Go on!" Gerald seethed. "Tell him what you've done!" Gerald backed out of the room. "I'll be gone by the end of the day. Stay away from Frankie! I will handle the rest of the logistics for the committee on his behalf."

He went back to their room and slammed the door shut. Rage consumed him as he paced between the bed and the desk. He stopped and looked over at the letter sitting where he had left it. Not leaving anything to chance, he pulled out his phone and took a picture of it and the envelope. Then he went to the closet and pulled all his belongings out.

The pain in his heart weighed on him, and he stopped midway. With total abandon, he fell onto the bed and cried, curling into a fetal position with his fists on the sides of his head. He wailed loudly, not caring who heard him. After what seemed like an eternity, he fell into a deep sleep.

Silence permeated the office. The monitor sat askew and the rest of the surrounding items previously on the desk littered the floor. Sharice did not get up while her father read the posts on the screen. He didn't say a word afterwards. She finally got the courage to get on her feet.

"Dad," she called to him.

He raised a hand to stop her. The blank expression covering his face signaled his anger as he contemplated the situation.

"What have you done?" His calm tone frightened her. "This travesty will ruin us all. Our family connections. The Olympic committee." He turned his gaze on her. "Everyone."

"I swear to you, my intentions…"

"Your intentions were ground in deceit from the start. Colluding with these," he waved a flat hand at the screen, "lowlifes who have the nerve to call themselves Olympic athletes."

"I never wanted to hurt Frankie. Just teach him a lesson." Sharice felt her tears stream down her face. She tried to wipe them away despite the fact that they kept coming. "I don't know how to fix it, Daddy."

"Fix it?" He shook his head. "There's no fixing this. The only thing we can do now is go with public opinion."

"But!" She clasped the front of her blouse. "None of it is true!"

"Which is why we only tell them what they want to hear and support Frankie behind the scenes. We will make sure he recovers. Whether he can come back to compete again is another story."

"Gerald. He…"

"Your marriage is indeed over. I won't make him suffer such a fate even if I don't like him. He will stay on the committee. I won't let him get out of that after this is over. You two will act like nothing is wrong. For now."

Sharice stared at him with shock. Her father left her alone in the room. The monitor mocked her, the chat still up. She swiped it to the floor with a backhand motion and heard it crack as it fell. Throwing her head back, she yelled at the ceiling, slamming her fists on the desk.

The committee's private jet took off from the country's airstrip to its destination in the United States. On board in a secured cabin, Frankie lay sedated with four medical technicians on hand. Gerald leaned back in his seat in the main cabin, a half glass of bourbon in his hand that flopped over the armrest. No one else had accompanied him on the flight.

He preferred being alone at the moment. The thought of seeing another member, let alone his father-in-law or wife, made him angry all over again. No. They could all go to hell. All he wanted was for Frankie to wake up. He took a few slow breaths and raised his glass, taking a big swig. The liquor burned his throat. He gladly let it, indulging in the short-lived pain.

His wristband beeped. He glanced down at it and reached over to tap the screen in front of him. The American Olympic committee was holding a press conference. Off to the side stood the games committee members. Sharice kept close to her father as he stepped up to the podium and placed both hands on its edges.

"Today, Frankie Mel Donova returns home. Not as a celebrated hero." Montgomery made a dramatic pause. "But as a disgraced Olympian bringing shame to his family and our country."

The camera shutters clicked, and flashes bombarded the stage. News crews and affiliates filled the ballroom. Everyone would watch, even those in other countries.

"It is with a sad heart that I am announcing the medals awarded to Frankie Mel Donova in the Paris France games will be revoked." Gasped erupted along with some claps. "His place on the USA Aquatics Team is hereby terminated."

Questions flooded the room, overlapping with each other. Father raised a hand, motioning for everyone to calm down.

"We will not be taking any questions today. Please defer them to the Olympic Organization Members. He gestured to the people waiting in the wings. "We wish Frankie a speedy recovery and that he reflects on his actions. Good day."

Once the Americans left the stage, the stern-faced head of the Olympic games committee stepped forward. Reporters resumed their slew of questions.

Gerald turned the screen off. Watching that farce made him want to puke. None of those things were happening.

The American committee quietly moved funds to cover Frankie's hospital bills and aftercare. They assigned a trained nurses to his house, following his release from the hospital. From what the doctors told him, Frankie needed two more months of down time before they brought him out of his coma.

Disgusted with the whole situation, he drained his glass and set it on the side tray. He fell asleep. It would be a long flight and he needed the rest to combat what was to come at the airport.

Protest signs rose up and down in the air while the mob chanted vile insults towards Frankie who would never hear them. Gerald stood on the third level of the airport watching the scene. Close to fifty people had gathered on the outskirts of the road, knowing the plane had landed. One sign said, you should have died in the water, junkie! Another said, Frankie the Junkie.

An attendant tapped Gerald on the shoulder.

"Excuse me, sir. All your luggage has been transported into the cargo van. Your driver is waiting."

"The unmarked ambulance?" Gerald turned away from the mob scene.

"Already enroute to the Olympic high security Medical Center. A decoy will be behind you."

"Thank you."

Gerald went to walk past her and saw a frown form.

She clenched her fists, then released them, staring him in the face.

"I don't believe it, you know." Gerald tilted his head. She took a deep breath. "I mean, none of it adds up. I think someone did something to him."

Gerald stared at her, surprised by the outburst. He heard whispers of conspiracy theorists finding evidence to debunk the rumors. Bless their hearts, as his grandmother would have said.

"You might be right," Gerald whispered.

The woman's eyes widened. "Then they shouldn't be condemning him without an investigation!"

"They would have to want to first." Gerald realized this was a dangerous conversation. "Thanks again. You should refrain from spreading your feelings about Frankie."

He walked off and took the elevator to the ground floor where his cargo van awaited. The empty ambulance sat behind it ready to go. Both vehicles drove down the road once he secured himself in the van. The mob came into view and, to his and the drivers' amazement, people threw things at the ambulance.

Some even leaned forward into the road to spit at it.

"What is wrong with these people?" The man in the front passenger seat yelled. "Last I checked, Frankie didn't kill nobody."

"That's a whole lot of unnecessary for a kid fighting for his life after a little mistake," the driver added.

"I mean, damn. It was drugs. Big deal."

Gerald couldn't agree more. He had a clue how it went so far, so fast. Whoever was jimmying up the rumor mills went at it hard and heavy. And the committee decided to let it happen to continue their own narrative.

A strangled, high-pitched gasp broke Gerald out of his slumber in the chair next to Frankie's hospital bed. He jumped up and caught Frankie's hand as she clawed at the air. Her back arched off the bed, the tubes going taut as her garbled breathing turned to a succession of screams. The sound itself tore into Gerald's soul, almost making him let go. He tightened his grip and used his free hand to hit the alarm.

Nurses and doctors rushed in within seconds, getting on both sides of Frankie to hold her down. One nurse leaned over to stick a syringe in the IV spout and pushed the plunger.

"It's okay, Frankie," Doctor Novak said calmly. "You're alright." Frankie's screams turned to wailing. "I know. It hurts. We gave you something for the pain. Just relax."

The nurse removed the syringe and Frankie's body went slack. Her grip on Gerald's hand remained firm as she turned her head and their eyes met.

"I won't leave you, Frankie. Not ever. I told you that."

Gerald caressed her forehead.

"Welcome back to the living, Frankie," Doctor Novak said, patting her on the leg.

The sedative finally kicked in and Frankie fell asleep. The beep of the heart monitor evened out, the graph showing the up and down dots forming wave patterns.

Doctor Novak motioned for Gerald to step away. He reluctantly let go of Frankie's hand when it went limp. They stepped out into the hall while the other doctor and the two nurses did routine checks on Frankie.

"I know that was probably hard for you. But we needed to make sure her pain receptors worked. There's a lot of damage to her entire biological system, let alone her heart."

"Is it repaired, regrown? What did you do to it?" Gerald crossed his arms defensively.

"A bit of both. We repaired the tears by regrowing the outer tissue. It's not perfect, and the organ is weaker than before. She'll recover. Whether she can compete is a whole other story."

"I don't care about that right now. How long?"

"If she sticks to a strict plan and doesn't overexert herself? I say in six months she'll be able to walk around on her own. She's actually recovering faster than we expected."

"She's an Olympian. Her body is stronger than most."

Doctor Novak gave him a dubious stare. Gerald could tell where his doubt lay. He had seen many pro athletes during his practice and equated Frankie with that level. That was his mistake. Olympians, especially hybrids like Frankie, were in a different league.

"Well, it also has to do with the condition of her body at the time of the incident." Doctor Novak frowned. "Which is strange since I've only seen that kind of devastation occur if the body was healthy. There's no indication of drug abuse in any of the fluid workups."

Gerald leaned closer to the doctor.

"You should keep that observation to yourself. If you insist on voicing that, the committee will find another doctor for him."

Doctor Novak glared at him, a silent rage building.

"You people will never get away with this. At some point, the math is going to add up. You all essentially vilified Frankie, tanking her career over a lie."

"No one's caught on yet," Gerald sneered.

"Frankie won't forgive you."

"Frankie knows the ugly side of the organization better than anyone."

Gerald turned away and went back into the room right as the other doctor and two nurses finished up their duties. They left in a hurry, hearing the call for another code. He sat back in the chair and held Frankie's hand, stroking the back of her hand with a finger.

"One day. Maybe not now or even ten years from now. But, one day," Gerald bent down and kissed her hand. "They will pay for this."

Churning Waters

Sharice paced the floor of her bedroom. The morning sun peeked through the sheer curtains, casting a pale-yellow light along the walls. Her silk nightgown grazed the carpet along with the matching robe worn open. The fabric billowed around her ankles. She let the carpet's plush fibers squeeze between the toes of her bare feet.

With Gerald's belongings gone, the room felt hollow. She half expected an echo whenever she talked on the phone, its vastness making her seem small. Her right thumb rested on her lips as she chewed the nail. Anxiety made her doubt her decision to not find out who the two chat posters were.

Her father had chastised her early on about making sure she knew all the players when doing backdoor dealings. She didn't do her due diligence, forgot her teachings. They had to be American swim team members. No one else would have direct access to Frankie.

The team's reaction to his near death brought to light how many despised him. And for no good reason other than envy. Jealousy. It made her realize her own feelings towards Frankie stemmed from his good nature in the eye of any storm.

And we ruined it.

Frankie became exactly what they wanted him to be, the direct opposite of his true self, and she hated him for it. He could have said no. Or not act like an ass out of retaliation against the committee. His ambition. That's what angered her. No matter what anyone threw at him, Frankie managed to prevail.

She reflected on her own shattered Olympic dreams after pushing herself too hard just to get a medal. Any medal.

All those extra hours of training to beat the top five in her event led to multiple injuries during the World championships. None of the techniques she stole from them worked.

Finding herself getting lost in reverie, she shook her head to clear it of past regrets and went to her closet. She had a meeting with her father, then another with the committee. An emergency session had been called.

Only two things would cause that. Blackmail. Hordes of conspiracy groups demanded investigation into the incident. Or it had something specifically to do with Frankie.

Her chest tightened thinking about him. None of it should have happened. She couldn't get her mind to stop replaying that image of Frankie floating lifeless atop the water, his eyes open, before sinking. The way Gerald jumped up at the exact same moment, clutching his heart. She now understood his obsession with Frankie.

Soul mates. It happened often. She knew her and Gerald weren't a match. His parents had an inkling that he may have one lurking about who would be a hybrid. Their loathing of Bi-Genetics wouldn't allow them to let their son be mated to one.

Of all the people in the world, it ended up being Frankie.

Which made her role in his demise worse. Their two sons, upon hearing him spew hateful words at her during the divorce, treated Gerald like an enemy. Her father advised to let it be unless she was willing to confess her sins to them.

Sharice perused the rows of suits and landed on one she could tolerate. A beige pants suit with wide straight legs. The jacket stopped right at the hips. She picked out a dusty pink blouse and matching heels. Nice, subdued colors that gave her a wholesome appeal.

Time to put on a show.

⌒

The president of the Olympic organization sat at the head of the table in the center of the large conference room. They had rented out a suite at a hotel in the city overlooking the skyline. A grand view for the shit show to be discussed. Members of both committees, dressed in business casual, feigned a relaxed atmosphere. The group hadn't been seated for less than a few minutes when he cleared his throat.

"This travesty has gone on long enough."

Sharice grimaced. That word got overused as time went on. Of course, they had no other way to put it.

"Yes," Madam chairwoman said. "We never thought punishing him would be an invitation for the world to spew such hatred."

"Most of it is all conjecture. Did they just throw the truth out the window?"

"Which truth is that?" Gerald sat on the opposite side of the table, away from Sharice. The room went silent. "The one we fabricated for the media or the real one?"

"Your anger over this is quite excessive." Madam chairwoman said. "I know you invested a lot of time giving him guidance as a former Olympian."

Gerald leaned forward, ready to say something he might regret. Sharice could see it in his eyes. Before he could speak, Madam Chair did.

"If this doesn't make any of you just as angry, I fear for our athletes."

"This was a one off," another committee member chimed in. "There's no way we would have known someone would try to assassinate another team member. It's inconceivable!"

"And we still don't know who the culprits are," Montgomery added. "Our investigators went through every trash bin in the area. My guess is they took whatever it was with them."

"What about the footage?" A committee member asked.

"It seems to have been erased," the head chair replied. "Which means this was a coordinated effort."

Sharice felt Gerald's stare. She braved a glance and flinched at his horrified expression. Only those under the committee's umbrella would have access. She didn't know the details, but her father had certainly seen to its destruction after watching it.

My father knows who they are. And he's not telling me.

"I say we start sending out small press pieces, interview clips, and such to curb the animosity. Frankie doesn't need this during his recovery." Madam Chair laced her fingers on the table. "He's our most decorated athlete. We need him for promotions."

"How about this." The president leaned back in his seat. "Since we have not actually expunged all his accomplishments, let's give him a chance to redeem himself."

"What?" Gerald cried out. "How?"

"When he is back on his feet and swimming a little, we will invite him to record his time. If he can still hit his world record, we reinstate his status."

"You," Gerald had not sat down and now braced himself on the edge of the table, "are all nothing but monsters. You expect him to swim at his previous speed after all this?"

Sharice had to agree. It was beyond cruel.

"No cardiologist worth his salt would sign off on something like that!" The first committee member retorted. "IF they do, they should have their license revoked."

"I'm done." Gerald pushed off the table to stand straight.

"Sit down." Montgomery commanded, not looking up. "You will finish this meeting like the rest of us."

Gerald hesitated, looking around the room. None of them wanted to be there. The president's gaze bore into him. He too silently demanded he take his place at the table and endure it. Relenting to the pressure, Gerald slowly took his seat.

"If he does manage to keep his time," the president resumed, "we can put him back as dive team alternate."

"Or maybe this is the time to double our status and switch Frankie over to the women's swim team. More bang for our buck." A member piped up cheerfully. "It would be within the guidelines for swapping him out. Frankie could stay in female stage for a round."

Gerald placed both hands on his face and brought them down enough so he could rub his eyes with the tips of his fingers. He looked distressed and ready to have a breakdown. His body shook.

"You would need to run it by him, of course. These are merely options. Frankie can always say no." The member raised both arms in an exaggerated shrug.

Gerald bolted out of his seat and left the room, his hands balled up in fists gone red from blocking circulation. Sharice fought the urge to go after him. She was the last person he wanted consoling from. Her father placed a hand flat on the table and tapped it a few times.

"Leave him be. He has one priority. Taking care of Frankie's needs." He looked at the president. "Your option is disgusting. And I'm being generous with my assessment."

"You Americans," the president laughed. "Always so cocky, thinking you are above the rest of us. How does it feel to be brought down a peg, hmm?"

Sharice winced. Her father would not take that from anyone. Something bad brewed in the president's future. As if noticing the tension in the room, the other committee members averted their eyes.

"What? You are offended? Think you can come for me and not have consequences? Try me!" The president scoffed, waving a hand dismissively.

"I will gladly oblige." Sharice's father's eyes narrowed.

The meeting ended with an agreement on how much funds to allocate for Frankie and a list of news outlets to tap to fix the damage to his reputation. Sharice followed her father to the car waiting in front of the hotel for them. The driver held the door open as they got in and shut it behind them.

"Father." Sharice settled in the seat beside him and clicked her seatbelt. "Was the footage really erased? If I could see it, maybe…"

"There is no footage." He reached over and opened the mini fridge embedded in the back of the driver's seat. "If you had done this right, we wouldn't have to worry about those jackasses showing up in the next year or so to blackmail you." He took out a mini bottle of gin and cracked it open. "I'm not a fan of Gerald but you fucked this all up."

Her father drained the little bottle.

Drinking it straight signaled his rage. The problem was she didn't know if his anger directed at her, the head chair, or both.

The ground level condo sat nestled on the corner with trees surrounding the right side and left front. A paved walkway curved to the entrance where one short step led to the decorative white door. Midday sunlight broke between the leaves casting their shadows on the tiny porch. Birds chirped happily in the distance.

Gerald ran his fingers through his already too long hair. It had grown another two inches, touching close to the middle of his back. Week old stubble graced his face and itched from lack of moisture. Release forms for Frankie arriving from the doctors interrupted his daily routine.

The ambulance brought her home yesterday in female stage. Her body couldn't handle shifting back. They advised him maybe in another month or two.

Checking his charcoal black suit with the top three buttons of his white shirt undone, he produced a keycard and held it against the security panel on door 's the right side. He heard the whir of the locking mechanisms click, popping the door open an inch.

Gerald went inside and scrutinized the place. Immediately to the left sat a full kitchen enclosed at the entrance by a waist-high counter. A six burner gas oven sat against the wall under a panoramic window overlooking the front yard. On its right was a dual door smart refrigerator. Cabinets above the counter were on the right facing in. The island sported a double basin sink with a detachable sprayer.

More storage space underneath.

Directly across from the kitchen lay the dining room slash living room. A small square table with four chairs sat on the threshold of the beams separating the space. Beyond that sat a sectional couch positioned in front of a retractable screen for the projector installed on the beam above.

He glanced to his left where a waist-high wall separated it from the entrance. A king-sized bed with the headboard lay against the outer wall. The bay window on the side had a view of the bushes, blocking most prying eyes. A short, narrow walkway across from the bed led to the bathroom.

Gerald walked around the separator and went over to the chair he had set near the window. Frankie still slept; her face scrunched up as if she were having a bad dream. A weighted, light blue comforter covered her so she wouldn't toss and turn, aggravating her condition. Four pillows bunched behind her kept her head stable. He stroked her hair. Frankie's eyes fluttered open.

"Shhh." Gerald leaned forward and kissed her forehead. "You don't have to wake up."

"Why?" Frankie's voice croaked, barely a whisper. "I never hurt anyone," she cried. Tears ran down the sides of her face. "I don't understand. Why would anyone do this to me?"

Gerald couldn't answer that. He watched helplessly as Frankie cried her eyes out. Being an asshole didn't mean you deserved to be killed. He slid onto the bed and lay next to her, wrapping his arms around her shoulders. After five minutes of crying and another fifteen of silence, Frankie wiped her eyes and pushed the top of the comforter off.

"Are you okay to eat something?" Gerald asked.

"Did they find who did it?" Frankie countered. "Are they in jail?"

"No. Let's not talk about that now. You need to put something solid in your system."

Frankie would not be denied. She struggled to sit up, shoving Gerald off the bed. Her anger felt like heat coming off her.

"Why not? How can they not have been caught?"

Gerald sighed as he stood.

"Because that would cause too big of a scandal for the Olympic committee and the organization itself."

They met each other's eyes and in an instant, Frankie understood.

"You agreed to it."

"I wasn't given a choice. But I made sure none of them were in charge of your care."

"What about your wife?"

Fury consumed him.

He stopped for a moment, staring into nothing. He finally glanced down at Frankie. The way her face transfixed in terror watched him made Gerald realize how he probably looked.

"We're divorced. I refused to stay married to her one more day after that."

"Then, you're free," Frankie whispered.

Gerald bent down and kissed Frankie hard, re-wetting her dry mouth. When he disengaged, Gerald walked to the kitchen.

"I'll make you some broth and toast. A travel nurse who specializes in nutrition will be here starting next week. I have a few meetings."

"So not free." Frankie frowned. "The committee won't let you go. Not with something like this hanging in the wind."

Gerald felt the pit of his stomach tighten again. Frankie knew the score better than most. He had become jaded.

I don't want that for you.

"They're paying for all this, aren't they?"

"Yes." Gerald poured a bowl of pre-made soup from its carton and stuck it in the microwave for two minutes. "You don't have to worry about anything." He turned around and saw Frankie clutching her chest. Her lips pulled back, baring teeth, while her eyes narrowed. "Frankie?"

He went over to her. Frankie took a sharp intake of air.

"I need you to calm down. Don't stress over this. You just have to bide your time."

Frankie glared at him for a second then let him lay her back, rearranging the pillows so she could sit upright comfortably. The microwave beeped and Gerald left her side to get the soup. He decided against the toast for now. Frankie only ate half the bowl before dozing off to sleep again.

Gerald cleaned up the dishes and sat in the chair beside Frankie. He got a good look at her. Frankie looked like shit. Gaunt, pale, and weak. The blond hair had long grown out and Gerald had it cut off, leaving four inches of dull brown. Her blue eyes had gone dark, almost navy. A tell-tale sign of her body's betrayal.

Frankie knows who did this.

And he had a feeling so did his father-in-law. But not Sharice. The culprits would have a hold over them. That didn't matter. Gerald vowed to make them pay once he found out who they were.

Frankie's sister, Dana, stood on the porch, hitting the doorbell until it opened. An older woman a few inches shorter than her stared up at her with disdain. She didn't say a word, just stepped to the side and gestured for her to come in. She headed into the kitchen area.

Dana stared at the small condo's interior. Not much had changed since the last time she had been there six months before the last Olympic games. She figured the place would have gone up for sale, since no one stepped up to handle its upkeep. He must have used every dime of his savings to hold on to it.

She nodded to herself. This place is probably the only thing of significance her brother owned. Movement on her right made her look over to see Frankie stir in his bed. He looks terrible. Shockingly so. She felt bad for her younger brother, but he had brought this on himself.

"You're awake." She moved closer to the foot of his bed. "Figured I'd at least check on you."

"You don't have to," Frankie said softly. He sounds super tired. "I'm sure you have better things to do."

"Look. I'm disappointed in you, that's a given. But, you're still my brother."

"When has that ever been a factor?"

His tone came out tense.

"If you hadn't done drugs in the first place…"

"I didn't."

"None of this would have happened. We expected better from you."

"That's enough." A man's voice yelled at her. "If all you came to do was berate him instead of being his sister, you should leave."

She didn't notice the door open, and Gerald walked in. He too looked a bit haggard, his long hair going wild on his head. The suit appeared slept in despite the obvious quality. He slung the plastic shopping bag in his hand over the wall onto the kitchen's corner counter.

"That's not what I'm doing," she snapped.

Frankie had fallen back to sleep. Her demeanor changed. She didn't like seeing him this way.

His fall from grace was ugly to witness.

"I only…"

"The one thing he wanted his own family couldn't give him. He needed you to be there for him. Instead, you walked away and let other people handle him."

"Like you? A committee dog with his own agenda?"

"My only priority is Frankie. You can leave and not come back. I know I've told you this before. He doesn't need your brand of love or pity."

Dana left after talking with the nurse about Frankie's condition. She got the feeling the woman didn't want to take care of someone like her brother. *Isn't that your job?* Sure, if they assigned the woman to take care of a criminal or whatever, she could see that. Frankie just made a mistake with drugs.

The whole nastiness that came out of the community towards Frankie came swift and over the top. His family had a right to be angry. These people didn't even know him. Not really. She got in her hybrid vehicle and hit the start button. The near silent engine booted up the system.

"God, Frankie. What have you done?"

She leaned over the steering wheel and rested her forehead on its top. Their parents hadn't contacted her since the transfer from Paris's medical center. They wanted nothing to do with it or Frankie.

They just need time, she thought hopefully.

Her phone vibrated. She saw her husband calling. Not now. Her current state wouldn't allow her to talk without breaking down into tears. She did love her brother. Gerald stating otherwise angered her to no end.

How dare he say that to her?

A large pit in her stomach warned she missed something important in all this. But it made no sense for the committee who condemned him to then turn around and cover all his medical costs. And possibly the condo.

Thinking about it logically, Frankie would have had to authorize someone to pay for the utilities and housekeeping. He was in a coma at the time.

So, who foot the bills?

Gerald had money, but not that kind. She shifted the car into drive.

Frankie being taken care of meaant she had no financial obligations. Her husband would be relieved.

⌇

Children screamed in delight as they ran around the restaurant's outdoor dining area with an open layout showcasing the landscape. At the end of the main footpath, a large play area with a mega slide looming above the trees awaited them. Servers wearing all black, including the apron, weaved through the chaos to deliver their table orders. The soles of their dress shoes clacked against the patterned stone.

Multiple conversations mingled into a wall of sound.

Gerald and his two sons waited at a small table with benches near the back entrance of the establishment. He opted for one without the giant umbrella since the sun had moved on to the other side. With his legs crossed, he rested his back against the stone wall with foliage spilling over its ledge. A branch brushed across his suit jacket. He wore a white shirt unbuttoned at his chest and dark slacks. His hair hung loose, the waves framing his face.

The lunch rush tapered off around one thirty. He watched the surrounding tables empty out. Bavarian cuisine had taken off in the area. No matter what day, the restaurant seemed packed. Especially in the summer with school out.

Across the bench, his sons glared at him. The oldest, Payton, named after Sharice's great grandfather, had dark brown hair touching his shoulders. He sat with his back erect, picking at his coleslaw with a plastic spoon. The younger, Garbiel, Gabe for short, sporting short curly hair, sipped his drink through a straw, his blue eyes focused like daggers at him. Their silent rage more deafening than the people talking. Payton plopped his fork down.

"Granddad says we have to keep quiet about you being with Frankie. So, we're supposed to just accept you ditching mom for some druggie who's a national disgrace?"

Gerald marveled at his sons' intelligence.

They attended the top prep school in the country, which

the old man demanded. At ten and twelve, their knowledge surpassed others the same age.

Gabe stopped sipping and raised his head.

"You were probably cheating on her the whole time. That's nasty." His eyes narrowed. "You could have given her some STD or something."

"I don't care what you think about this situation, since you are quite wrong." Gerald leaned back, resting one hand on the table. "But, I will not tolerate your disrespect."

"Or what?" Payton spat. "Gonna' punish us? You're not home anymore."

"You can't do anything." Gabe laughed. "We only listen to mom."

"We're leaving." Gerald uncrossed his legs and sat up.

They both stared, stunned, at him. This was their favorite place. A doggie bag never appeared at their table, the two eating everything on the plate.

"We haven't finished eating," Payton protested.

"You must be if you have no intention of spending time with me, as your mother asked. I won't sit here while you spout hate at me for no reason."

"We never said that!" Gabe cried.

"You did." Gerald didn't want to bring up the scene when they first discussed it and Payton screamed out he hated him. "Let's go."

"We didn't ..." Payton struggled to finish his thought.

"We'll stop, okay," Gabe looked teary-eyed. Gerald let out a sigh. "This is the only time we get to see you."

"Fine." Gerald settled against the wall. "Eat your food."

They consumed their meal in normal fashion, taking their time to chew. Gerald could see the heartache in their demeanor. He preferred remedying a little disrespect over them finding out their mother's secret.

◠

Phillip Montgomery sat across from the university dean in the man's office. Both men stared at each other, gauging their resolve. Dean Stevonovich leaned back, swiveling in his plush leather chair, one hand raised, rubbing his fingers together.

"So let me get this straight." His gaze didn't waver. "You want me to let Frankie Mel Donova back on campus to finish his degree? And you don't think that's a dangerous idea?"

"Isn't that what security is for?" Montgomery tilted his head down. "You would deny a young man on the brinks of recovery an education to start his life over?"

"His scholarship was pulled."

"Money is not a problem. The remainder of his tuition will be paid in full."

The dean leaned forward, causing his chair to buck. He placed his hand on his desk.

"What the hell is going on? You people fucked him, didn't you?" Stevonovich's eyes burned with indignation. "He wasn't a druggie. You let those murderers off the hook for some more potential medals."

"You should tread carefully," Montgomery warned.

"Fuck you. The committee wants to pay. Fine. I'll keep your little secret. But Frankie will be the only one I talk to about his college needs. Your people stay out of the loop. Just keep the checks coming."

Montgomery tilted his head to the side.

"You like to live dangerously, I see. Very well. We need Frankie back on his feet." He stood. "We will be in touch."

"No," Stevonovich retorted. "You just need to send the money. I don't want to see or talk with any of you ever. Poor fucking Frankie. He didn't have a chance in hell." Stevonovich waved his hand at Montgomery. "Get out of my office."

Sitting back in his chair, he let it tilt back halfway as he ran a finger along his bottom lip. A good chunk of the conspiracy theories he heard made sense. He didn't give them much thought until that committee guy demanded a meeting and came up with that proposal.

All the pieces fell into place, and he felt sick.

Frankie acted like the big man on campus for a reason. He could back it up. Olympic Gold Medalist, brand endorser, and held a three-point nine GPA after his last semester. The only reason for it not being above a four-point O was because of his training schedule. He majored in Aquatics Science with a minor in archeology. The kid had an amazing brain.

Knowing the committee would make good on their promise, he booted up his computer and began the process to reinstate Frankie. Only two classes would be on campus. He didn't want any more trouble than necessary.

CHAPTER THREE

Land Life

The sound of water rushing enticed Gerald to ease into Frankie's bathroom. Inside, behind the frosted doors, stood Frankie leaning against the wall with his eyes closed while water pelted his head. Dark hair now past his shoulders lay slicked back. The faint scars from his heart surgery turned red from the heat.

Gerald stood mesmerized by his beauty. Seeing him not moving, he opened the door and shut off the water. Frankie opened his eyes and glanced over at him. Gerald pulled the towel from the rack and wrapped it around him.

"Come on. You need to rest."

"I'm tired of laying around. I want to do more."

Frankie stepped out of the tub into Gerald's arms.

"I know. But you need to gain more strength. You're not eating enough either."

Gerald dried him off and helped him back to bed.

"I'm not helpless," Frankie said angrily.

"You really think you're strong enough to do anything?"

Gerald leaned forward, forcing Frankie back until he flopped onto the covers. His lips found Frankie's and he kissed him deeply. Not stopping even as felt Frankie's body shift. He ran a hand across breasts that fit perfectly in his palm. Frankie gasped, letting Gerald sink his tongue further, blocking air. He stripped naked, only disengaging when he thought Frankie had had enough.

His lips pulled away, coated with his saliva mingled with Frankie's.

"You know I love you, Frankie."

He entered her without warning.

Her back arched, allowing him to run his arm behind to bring her closer to him. His other hand grabbed the back of her thigh and spread her legs more as he thrust hard.

"Uhn!" Frankie tried not to cry out. Pain etched her face.

"I'm sorry, stay with me."

Gerald tried to go slower. Euphoria overtook him and he continued with abandonment even when he saw Frankie clutch her left breast. She reached out and slammed her fist into his chest, her face contorted in agony.

"Please, almost. Stay with me, Frankie."

The second after his release he almost regretted it. Frankie's eyes rolled back in her head and her body went limp. In a panic, Gerald felt for a heartbeat as he laid her down flat. Feeling the hard thump against the palm of his hand, he breathed in relief. He slid off her and took the heart rate monitor out of the nightstand drawer.

The gadget made successive beeps. Too high. There was medication to bring it down. He walked naked to the closet, where he stored an emergency kit. He found the right one inside and went back to the bed.

"Frankie. Open your eyes. I need you to take this." For what seemed like an eternity, Frankie finally did. Tears filled her eyes. "I'm sorry. I couldn't stop. Here." He placed the pill between her lips and brought one of the mini water bottles to them. Frankie guzzled half of it to swallow the medication and closed her eyes again. "That's my girl."

He kissed her softly.

Gerald moved Frankie under the covers and took the wet towel back into the bathroom. He crawled in bed beside her and held her close to him. They both fell asleep like that.

~

Lena, the younger of the two nurses assigned to Frankie, entered the condo hauling two grocery bags, one in each arm. She swung them onto the kitchen counter and proceeded to put everything she wouldn't be using right then away. Out of the corner of her vision, she could see her charge fast asleep on the other side.

She swiped a lock of her chestnut hair from her face and placed both hands on her hips. The media had painted him out to be some kind of monster. What lay before her was a broken child. At nearly forty, anyone in their twenties she called that.

At the same time, she wasn't sure if she should have any sympathy for him.

Her counterpart, Nurse Audrey, who took care of him on the odd days told her that if their employer really wanted Frankie back on his feet, then we shouldn't pamper him so much. A few times, she had forced him to make his way to the bathroom on his own. When he took too long, she went in and found him slumped against the wall near the toilet. He had gotten dizzy and fell.

Mr. Ivers had shown up the next day and inquired Nurse Audrey about the bruise on the side of Frankie's forehead. Luckily for Lena, she took the blame, ending up in a shouting match with Gerald.

Today, she would prep his meals for the week and administer his shot. An easy payday. It was rare for him to be alone in the condo. Mr. Ivers must have stepped out for a short while. While she cut vegetables and pureed fruit for smoothies, the man himself arrived. She took a deep breath to calm her nerves. Gerald, though quite sexy, intimidated her.

He wore a dark blue suit with a sky-blue shirt and a matching tie of a tiny paisley design. His freshly coifed hair fell just below his ears against a clean-shaven face. He looked like a powerful business executive.

"Hello Mr. Ivers." She greeted him without looking up.

"Nurse Lena."

He gave her a nod and went to check on Frankie.

"I'll be done in a second. I got his shot ready in the fridge."

"Thank you."

She washed her hands, donned a pair of surgical gloves, and took the shot out of the refrigerator. When she got near the bed, Frankie seemed in pain, her eyes glazed as if she was out of it. On second glance, she noticed bare skin under the covers and the curve of breasts.

"What have you…how could you?" She stopped and stood

straight. "You can't do that. Unless you want to kill him."

Gerald glared at her.

"I would never hurt Frankie. This wasn't…"

Nurse Lena went to the side of the bed and pulled out Frankie's arm. She used an alcohol wipe on the spot she wanted and tapping a vein, plunged the needle.

"You think because he can move a bit on his own that he has the strength to do whatever." She placed a small gauze bandage from her apron pocket on the entry point. "Well, he can't. Maybe you should learn to restrain yourself."s

"You're not here to lecture me," Gerald said heatedly.

"No. I'm here to make sure Frankie recovers. You're not helping."

She went back into the kitchen and disposed of the needle in the sharp container on the side counter. Her view of Mr. Ivers went down a few pegs.

What a selfish man.

⌒

Farmer's markets always made Nurse Lena feel better. The bright colors of the harvest, the people chatting with others from their community. It made her more relaxed. She went to a local florist's booth and browsed through the array of pre-made bouquets, bending down to smell them.

A familiar voice floated in her ears. She turned around, scanning the crowd, and found her counterpart, wearing tight jeans, a white tank top and a leather jacket, laughing with a group of women in similar attire. Well-worn boon-dockers adorned her feet. Her slicked back gray hair showed off her light-colored eyes.

"Mrs. Audrey?" Lena one called out.

The woman stopped mid-sentence and glanced over at her. She held up a finger to her friends and approached. The two met halfway.

"What's going on?" Lena asked.

"Oh, I'm headed to a show. My favorite band is in town. Hitting it with a few girlfriends."

"Wow. That's great." Lena squinted. "I thought this was your day to care for the Donovan kid."

"Yeah, he'll be just fine. Not like he can go anywhere. He doesn't have classes today."

"But, he's not supposed to be alone. Do you want me to go in your place? I won't tell if you don't.

Audrey waved away the idea. "That's not necessary. He'll sleep most of the day and you'll be there in the morning. No harm, no foul."

"Are you sure?"

"Don't you have something to do too?"

"I, well. I do have a show myself to go to. A musical I've been wanting to see."

"Then go. Have fun. I know I will." Audrey winked and walked back to her group.

Lena felt uneasy at first, then decided her counterpart was right. Nothing to worry about.

⌒

Frankie woke up alone in his condo. He searched the dark room and saw the curtains drawn shut. Bright sun rays made their way between slivers of openings. The clock said four in the afternoon.

Oh damn.

He had a meeting at six with the dean of the university to discuss his schedule. Finishing his degree would give him more options when he got better.

Sliding out of bed, his legs gave out the moment he put weight on them. His body felt weak, and he collapsed onto the bed, turning sideways to stop himself from going to the floor. He took a few deep breaths and tried again. This time, he half crawled to the bathroom. Grabbing a washcloth, he leaned over the sink to wet it and pumped the soap dispenser twice. He sat on the toilet and slowly wiped himself down with the warm, soapy cloth.

He came out of the bathroom naked and went to the closet. Pulling open the first drawer, he took out a gray t-shirt. From the second one, he got a pair of black sweatpants. Socks were too much of a hassle. His hands shook slightly. The feeling of weakness combined with the light-headedness, forced him to move slow.

In the kitchen, he opened the refrigerator and found a sealed packet of soup. He leaned over the counter at the sink and tried to tear it open for the bowl nearby. After the third try, the edge ripped apart, spilling it across the sink.

"There goes that." He nonchalantly pushed the dripping packet to the side and grabbed a banana out of the fruit bowl. "I gotta' go."

Frankie found his phone and texted the ride service. He nibbled on the banana while waiting for it to show up. A small sling pouch with his ID and credit cards rested across his chest. Once his ride arrived, he walked out to the curb and got into the black sedan.

Stevonovich observed Frankie from his chair, trying to determine if he should tread lightly. The boy looked unhealthy. He saw the slight shake of his hands. *How did he even get here on his own?* His outfit seemed to swim on him, he had lost so much weight.

"How are you doing, really, Frankie?" He asked cautiously.

"Better. I'm still alive." The way he said it let the dean know he understood what happened. "I do want to finish what I started, though. Education wise."

"You don't look so good. When did you eat last?"

Frankie frowned. "Yesterday, I think."

Stevonovich restrained himself from cursing. That won't solve the issue.

"Well, I'll be honest. I'm not giving you a full load. You only have a few credits left, but you need to take it slow."

Frankie's demeanor deflated, then shifted. He wanted to get it over with, yet also knew he couldn't handle it. The dean got angry at the committee for him. With the advancements in medical technology, there was no reason for Frankie to still suffer like that.

"I get it." Frankie lowered his head. "It just sucks that I don't have the energy to go hard like I want."

"You'll also have access to the aquatic center if you ever feel up to that. I heard it's low impact strength training." Stevonovich grimaced at the thought of exercise.

Frankie's stare went far away, as if his soul had left his

body. Then it came back, and he focused on the dean. A hint of sadness and rage flickered.

"I'll think about it."

They talked for a little longer and Frankie left with his packet of information and a new student badge. Stevonovich swiveled in his chair as he watched him lumber down the hall. He could already see the wheels turning in the young man's head. Frankie would get back in the water.

Hard stares followed Frankie as he made his way through the campus to the pool area and sat down in the bleachers. The dimmed lights made the water look dark, with black ripples rolling across the surface. Memories of being submerged in its embrace flooded his mind. He hadn't thought much about swimming since he woke up screaming.

His life, thus far, only involved pain and weakness. He could hardly stay conscious for more than a few hours at a time. Even screwing could kill him. As much as it hurt, he didn't want Gerald to stop.

How stupid!

That's not the way he wanted to go out, no matter how romantic it sounded.

I have to get better.

He rested his elbows on his knees, placing his hands on the sides of his face.

The water seemed angry at him. Like he had betrayed it somehow. His body reacted with remorse, shivering at the thought of actually going in despite its longing. He had been robbed of his passion. The culprits had no such remorse. They went on with their lives, competing to try for medals they didn't deserve.

A group of six people wearing swimsuits came into the pool area. Two of the women tucked dry hair under their caps. He sat up, silently admonishing them. The two men looked over and sneered.

"Looks like we got a loser watching us," the first said.

"Maybe he's feeling nostalgic," one of the women said. "Since he's no longer an Olympian."

Her nasty expression puzzled Frankie.

He had no idea who any of those people were yet they assumed to know how he felt.

"Yeah, his days are over." The second guy scoffed. "How's your heart?" He laughed.

An awkward silence filled the room. The others averted their eyes from him. He became nervous, his brow furrowed at their reactions.

Frankie tilted his head, not satisfying them with an answer.

"Let's just get some laps in," one of the women said.

One of them held a timer in his hand and set it down. They all picked a lane and the guy hit the start button. They swam with all their might. Frankie stared at the timer as two of them touched the wall after four laps.

How slow.

When the driver picked Frankie up, he walked around to the passenger back side and opened the car door for him. Frankie got in and immediately fell asleep. During the ride, his charge slid to the side laying across the back seat. Knowing something was wrong, he hurried back, driving faster than the speed limit.

He parked the car at the curb in front of Frankie's condo and got out, lifting one of Frankie's arms over his shoulder to carry him to the door.

He got the keycard from the pouch and tapped the sensor. As he placed Frankie on the bed, he woke up, clearly out of it.

"I'm sorry. I didn't mean to trouble you," Frankie barely spoke, almost whispering.

"Not a problem. Are you sure you'll be alright?"

"Yeah."

"Okay. Call me if you can't get a hold of anyone else." He set the keycard on the nightstand and left the condo. Getting in the car, he shook his head. "Why would they leave him alone?" He drove off, keeping his phone handy next to him.

Frankie lay in the dark, falling in and out of sleep during the night. He had to pee and struggled to get up. At some point, he couldn't hold it much longer. Again, he crawled to the toilet, barely getting his pants around his ankles, and peed sitting down. He reached back to flush, then pulled his pants back on while he tried to slide gracefully to the floor.

For a few minutes, he lay there before making his way back to the bedroom area. He slumped against the wall near the side of the bed and fell unconscious.

Gerald came into the condo, witnessing the harrowing scene. He rushed over to Frankie and grabbed his head in both hands. At already ten in the morning, he didn't find neither nurse.

"Frankie! Can you hear me? Talk to me."

Nurse Lena stepped into the wide-open door and gasped.

"Oh my god." She ran into the kitchen and pulled his shot out of the fridge.

Gerald pulled Frankie off the floor and onto the edge of the bed. She came and administered the shot.

"What happened?" Gerald demanded.

"Guess I got a little weak," Frankie laughed softly. "Didn't get to eat. I had an appointment with the dean."

Gerald saw Nurse Lena stiffen.

"What do you mean, you didn't get to eat?"

"I tried to," Frankie nodded towards the kitchen sink, "but couldn't get it right."

Gerald stared at the mess, then at the nurse.

His eyes narrowed.

"When was the last time you had something?" Gerald asked, horrified.

"Two days ago. I ate a banana yesterday."

Gerald stood and glared at the nurse.

"Explain this. Why was he here alone?"

"I…Nurse Audrey must have been sick," she stammered.

"And didn't call you to cover? Where were you then?"

"I had a show to go to. I didn't know he would be by himself," she lied.

"That's not true," he called her out. "If you have such disdain for your patient and can't bother to care for him as you're being paid to do, then leave. I will find another service to replace you."

She walked angrily away, disposing of the needle, then

went to clean up the mess. He had offended her. *So what?* Her and the other nurse's neglect could have cost Frankie his life. No excuse would suffice.

"I'm good at my job," she finally said, slapping the washcloth into the sink. It smacked against the metal sides. Her eyes got red and teary. "I didn't think she would endanger him."

"No, you didn't think at all. If you had, the moment you realized she wasn't coming to care for him, you should have. That is part of your contract."

He got Frankie out of the t-shirt and sweats and into a microfiber tank and thin pajama pants. With Gerald's help, he got under the covers right as he fell asleep.

"I'll need to wake him up in a couple hours so he can eat," Nurse Lena said.

"Why are you still here?" Gerald walked out into the small hallway.

"Doing my job," she snapped. She turned around and glared at him.

Gerald sighed loudly, not wanting to deal with her anymore. He went into the living room and settled on the couch, turning on the television. To both their horror, the world championship games were being broadcast. Even worse, the 200 meter backstroke was in progress.

A young Italian swimmer far ahead of the others raced against the timer that ran off to the side. The crowd went wild, erupting into cheers as he touched the wall point zero three nanoseconds behind the world record previously held by Frankie. He raised a fist in the air and let out a victory yell.

The commentator sounded just as joyous.

"And Italian swimmer, Paulo Boresccio, has broken the world record! Frankie Mel Donova no longer holds that title. We have a new reigning champion. What a great freshman showing at these world games!"

Gerald tsked in disgust. Nurse Lena looked down at the floor, her expression one of sadness.

Frankie's eyes opened, smoldering as he stared at the wall beneath the window.

Back in the Water

The American committee's phone number displayed on Frankie's phone glared at him. He hadn't tapped the dial icon yet. Gerald seemed to be keeping something from him after the world championship results. Trust had to be a two-way street. The last thing he wanted to do was contact the committee. He sat on the left side of his bed so he could lean on the entryway separator. Staring at his phone a little longer he tapped the icon.

After three rings, the automated system connected.

"Thank you for contacting The United States of America's Olympic Committee. For general information, please press one. To get a copy of our public resources and bylaws, press two. If you are a current or former athlete, please press three. All other inquiries stay on the line."

He pressed three and a real person answered.

"Good afternoon. Thank you for contacting the American Olympic Committee. Can I have your name, please?"

"Francis Carmel Donovan."

He could hear typing on the other side of the line. A pause followed.

"Francis Donovan?" She asked, unsure. "Could you hold for a moment?"

"Sure."

The call time passed the seven-minute mark when the line clicked over and the person came back.

"Umm, Mr. Donovan. I've been informed to send you a meeting invitation for the day after tomorrow. Please look over it and accept if the time is doable."

"Okay," Frankie replied, confused.

"Is there, uh, anything else I can help you with?"

"No. Thank you."

"Of course," her nervous tone made him uneasy. "Have a wonderful day."

She disconnected before he could answer.

His phone chimed with a notification right after. He opened the invitation and saw the meeting landed on a day he would be on campus between classes. They knew his schedule. It didn't surprise him as much as irked him. Nothing seemed sacred when it came to his life.

He wouldn't tell Gerald.

Depending on the secret determined how angry he'd be. Frankie let his head fall back as he sighed, holding the phone away from him as if it were contaminated.

No turning back now.

⌒

College campuses received upgrades across the board to accommodate the extra curriculums after the hybrid crisis. The courtyard and grounds had immaculate landscaping to ensure the students would experience a relaxed environment.

Nature went undisturbed. The weeping willows brought plenty of shade for the benches nearby. A few students lounged beneath them having casual talk, studying, or taking a nap. The afternoon sun had moved so its intensity had waned.

"Over here." He heard Phillip Montgomery's voice.

That stopped him in his tracks. For the man to show up in person meant the meeting involved something serious. He sat at a small patio table with two wrought-iron chairs painted white. The branches of the trees hung down, brushing the tip of his left shoulder whenever a breeze caught it.

Wearing a dark brown suit and a mustard shirt accented by a black tie of argyle design, he stood out like an eyesore. Thankfully, no one wanted to approach him. Frankie made his way to sit in the other chair, his cautious demeanor not lost on Montgomery.

"You're moving much better. That's good."

"My workout regimen got switched out for more weight training."

Montgomery raised his brow. "I hope that means in the water. Lifting actual weights is not ideal."

"They're small weights. I do my own water exercises."

A silent moment stretched between them.

"You long to get back in the water. You miss it." Montgomery said bluntly. Frankie looked down at the table. "Having some random half talented swimmer break your world record made you wake up."

This time Frankie met his gaze. The fury in his eyes burned within. He never wanted to admit how he truly felt about it. This man hit it right on the head.

"I could've beaten it faster than that if I'd..." He stopped, clenching his fists on the table.

"Did Gerald not tell you about the Olympic Organization's proposal?" Frankie perked up, his eyes wide. "Of course not. He doesn't want you to get hurt by heightening your expectations."

"What did they say?"

"If you can swim at your world record time, we will reinstate it on the official books. That would still mean that Italian brat holds the record, regardless how puny his advantage is."

Frankie's heart thumped hard, and he placed a hand on his chest, resisting the urge to grab hold. To do that, he would need to train. He didn't know how much his new heart could take, but in small increments he was certain he could get back to that level.

"And you would be back as a permanent alternate on the diving team." Montgomery added.

Frankie's head shot up.

Why? Why would Gerald keep this from me? Not letting me get hurt? What a flimsy excuse.

There had to be more to it.

"Is that for real?" Frankie's eyes narrowed. "Or is this some other trick to screw me over?"

"No tricks, Frankie." Montgomery casually picked at a lifted piece of white paint, flicking it off his fingertips with an air of importance. "They put the deal in place before you were sent home." He glanced up at Frankie. "We are waiting on you."

Frankie laid his hands flat and leaned back in the chair.

"Is there a timeline?" Frankie asked.

"Yes. Yours." Montgomery folded his hands on his crossed knee. "What do you want to do, Frankie?"

The wheels turned in his head as he called up the games' timeline from memory. To have his record back on the books before the next Olympic games, he would have to get it in before the world championships set for next year.

As if reading his mind, Montgomery addressed him.

"You have eight months before the world championship trials. If you do that, there would be nothing stopping you from breaking even that. Frankie Mel…"

"Frankie Mel Donova is dead." Hearing himself say it, a huge boulder lifted from his soul.

"That's understandable. Okay, Francis. It's your turn. Prove us all wrong."

Frankie rubbed his face with both hands. A bit of anxiety crept in. *Could I? Restore my accomplishments with just one small thing?* First, he had to confront Gerald.

An angry lover awaited Gerald when he walked into the condo. At first, he thought maybe Frankie felt frustrated again for being bedridden the past few days. Then he happened to see his father in law's card lying next to him while he sat with his back towards him on the bed.

Shit!

He tossed the bag of takeout on the counter. No doubt, old man Montgomery had told him about the Olympic organization's proposal. From the way Frankie avoided looking at him, he was considering it, which put him in the crosshairs of too many enemies.

"You're mad at me. I get it."

"Why didn't you tell me." Frankie didn't turn around.

"Because I wanted you to be free of all this."

"You had no right to keep it from me. It's my decision to make, not yours," Frankie snapped.

Gerald walked around and sat before him, face to face.

"I know. I'm sorry." He rested his forehead on Frankie's. "Please, hear me out."

Frankie leaned away. "You always do that. Try to protect me from everything. I'm not a child."

Gerald reared back. "I have never treated you like one. How could you say that to me?"

"It's how I felt." Frankie tilted forward, connecting with him again. "I'll be careful. Can't you trust me this time?"

Gerald wrapped his arms around him and pulled tight.

"It's not you I don't trust, Frankie." After a moment, he raised his head. "Only if your doctor gives you clearance. There's no point in starting this if your heart isn't strong enough."

"You'll set up an appointment for me?"

Gerald slid one hand behind Frankie's head and kissed him. Softly at first then deeper, slipping his tongue between his lips. When he disengaged, Frankie opened his eyes and stared at him.

"Mmhmm. Tomorrow."

"Take this seriously," Frankie chided him.

"I am. More than you know." Gerald kissed him again, pushing him down flat onto the bed. "Tomorrow."

$\backsim$

The elevator dinged when it reached the tenth floor of the medical center's office complex. Frankie stepped through the opening doors and walked towards the glass double doors at the end of the hall. A receptionist at the desk set low at eye level greeted him as he came up.

"Good morning, Mr. Donovan." They came from behind the desk and escorted him to an examination room towards the back. "Dr. Holgate will be in shortly for your checkup."

They left Frankie alone in the cold, white room with a sink, exam table and an adjustable swivel stool. The glaring lights hurt his eyes. He could feel the lack of sound close in on him. Twenty minutes went by. Dr. Holgate entered the room with a wide swing of his hand against the door.

He spun the stool until it came waist high, then sat down, leaning sideways on the wall where a rolling station with a monitor screen sat in front of him. His bored, exasperated look let Frankie know he had no interest in his wellbeing.

He never did.

"What brings you here?" Dr. Holgate asked in a huff.

"I need medical clearance to start a new aquatic exercise regimen."

"And? What's your point?"

"You're my doctor. The committee needs an exam with a full report."

"I'm not wasting my time on examining someone as careless as you so that committee or whoever can pat themselves on the back for you being alive. I couldn't care less what some junkie does with his life."

Dr. Holgate sat straight and started typing into the system. He hit the print button and the printer in the corner whirred. The four sheets that came out he handed to Frankie.

"Here. You're cleared. Go drown in a pool."

With that, the doctor waited for Frankie to leave the room.

Frankie figured as much. His cardiologist was one of his haters. Not privy to the truth, he had developed his own prejudice against him and didn't bother to do the routine test for a person with heart issues.

That's fine! I'll get better on my own.

⌒

The desk inside the grey metal cubicle with cloth walls sat bare except for the computer setup, a penholder, and a sticky note pad. Directly from its opening lay the walkway to the elevators. Two cubes on each side faced the opposite way so their occupants couldn't be seen at that angle. The fluorescent strip lights cast an equally gray blanket over the entire office floor.

Frankie sat in an ergonomic chair, adjusted specifically for him by the admin. He wore plain, gray shirt and black slacks, making him blend with the décor. His fingers typed rapidly on the keyboard, filling a registration form on the screen. A pair of earbuds attached to an MP3 player hung from his ears. The muffled music seeped from them.

After graduating with honors from the Berkeley University of California, he took a mediocre data entry job at the Aquatics center. The pay left little to be desired, and the hours sucked. He ended up getting to the campus pool two hours before closing during the week. On his off days, he was allowed to use the pool at the Aquatics Center as long as he left before the American teams showed up for practice.

A lock of his dark auburn hair, grown past his shoulders and hitting the middle of his back, swung forward, obstructing the view of his left eye. He moved his head to toss it back, his fingers never stopping. The boss liked how efficiently he finished each task.

The timer he had set on the screen beeped right as he completed the form and sent it on its way to the administrator's email. He logged off, removing the earbuds, and cut off the player.

As he stood, his six foot four frame towered over the top of the cubicle. Tucking the player in his messenger bag, he lifted it over his shoulder and headed to the elevators.

Outside at the front of the building, his driver sat in the sedan reading a magazine. Frankie heard the door unlock as he approached. He slid into the back seat, tossing his bag next to him.

"Everything okay?" The driver asked, setting the magazine on the passenger seat and driving off.

"Same old, same old," Frankie replied. "How's traffic?"

"We'll get there the usual time."

Frankie rested his head against the back seat and closed his eyes. He could go to work, go swimming, but not drive himself. There was nothing wrong with his heart anymore, save the minor damage. His doctor refused to sign off on the paperwork for the DMV.

The sedan pulled up to the side entrance of the college's aquatics department and Frankie got out.

"See you in a couple of hours," he said, closing the door.

He knew the driver would go park further down the street so he could turn around easily later. The man did not like being too far away from him in case of any emergency. Everyone acted too cautious in Frankie's opinion.

The pool sat empty and dark. Overheads in the center were dim while the outer ones lit the tiled walking areas around it. Frankie sat down on the edge and slid off into the water, careful not to make a splash. The ripples resembled tiny eels racing out towards the middle. Its warmth wrapped around Frankie's waist as he eased down further until he was underwater.

He swam a few laps without timing himself. Getting his rhythm down the only goal for the day. A few other swimmers had showed up, occupying the other lanes on either side of him. One guy swam ferociously three lanes away on his left. On the right, two lanes over a young woman waded. She swam towards him while he treaded water near the wall.

"Come here often?" She spewed water from her mouth and smiled.

Neither of them had a swim cap on, a no-no according to regulations. Who would tell an hour before closing?

"Is that supposed to be a pick up line?" Frankie ran his hands back across his head.

"Maybe. You're a pretty good swimmer." She came within inches of him. The buoy line bobbed between them as she ducked under.

"I'm trying my best." Frankie gave her a grin.

"We should swim together sometime."

She swam to get around him, but he turned with her. They circled each other a few times.

"Aren't we doing that now?" The left corner of her mouth twitched up mischievously. Frankie gave her a serious expression. "You don't want to be associated with me."

"What?" She laughed. "And why is that?"

"You don't know who I am. People won't like it."

"I think I know how to make my own judgement."

The sound of multiple sneakers squeaking on the wet tile echoed in the pool area. Frankie wiped his face with one hand and got a clearer view of the group of guys standing in their white college Aquatics team uniforms with red and blue design.

We'll find out right now.

Frankie already knew how it would end.

"What are you doing talking to that loser?" The bigger man in the group's front yelled at the woman.

"Get away from that fucking junkie."

"What the hell are you talking about? Don't talk to me like that!" She retorted.

"Don't you know who that is?" The guy behind the leader asked. "That's our illustrious disgraced Olympian, Frankie Mel Donova."

"Real shameless of you to come up in here and swim in our pool like nothing's wrong," the leader said.

The woman's face scrunched as she swam backwards away from Frankie.

"Eww! What the fuck?" She caught Frankie's gaze and flinched. Her expression fell in an instant. Not wanting to lose face in front of the guys, she mustered up the courage to spit out a nasty insult. "You shitty has been. They should have let you die to save us all from embarrassment."

"Ooh!" The guys erupted, a few of them placing their fists against their mouths while bending over with laughter.

"Sick burn, Tina!" The second guy said.

"Shut up," she yelled, pulling herself out of the water.

The leader grinned at Frankie. "See? You can't even convince chicks to be down with you."

Frankie didn't engage. He simply watched Tina dash past them, a hurt look on her face.

Yeah. What you said was evil.

The guys left the pool area. A few minutes later, the closing announcement for the Aquatics center came on.

Time to get out.

When Frankie got home, he found Nurse Lena finishing up in the kitchen. Gerald had long dismissed her, but she refused to leave. Her reason being it would take too long to replace her, and he needed constant care. He couldn't argue with that at the time. Now he could fend for himself.

Or so he liked to believe.

There were still bad days where he felt weak and went down hard. It happened only three times in the months since he started training. Gerald, angry at his decision, came by less. The last time being a month ago. They talked on the phone twice a week.

"What are you doing here so late?" Frankie asked, going over to his bed and flopping down. "Your shift was over hours ago."

"I made you a light dinner since I know you just left work and went straight to the pool again without eating."

"True. I'll eat it in a minute." He felt her iron stare on the back of his head. He turned around and sure enough, she had a steely gaze. "I promise. I really am hungry this time."

She relented and went back to wiping down the sink counter. Drying her hands on the dish towel, Nurse Lena grabbed her purse from the corner and walked around to the door.

"Call me if you need anything else."

"Have a good night."

"Thanks. You too, Frankie."

The door shut after her and Frankie exhaled slowly. He was hungry and also tired. Since he promised, he struggled to get up and went to the kitchen.

A small grilled chicken salad with cherry tomatoes cut in half, sliced cucumbers, and hard mozzarella sprinkled on top sat on the counter accompanied by a ramakin of vinaigrette.

Frankie got a bottle of mineral water from the fridge, grabbed his dinner, and went to the dining table. He didn't turn on the projector. Watching anything made him anxious.

Last month, he shot a commercial for a clothig brand company. His name wouldn't be used. As if that's going to stop people from noticing me! He smirked in disgust. The contract hadn't been fulfilled because of the incident and the organization didn't want to lose their money.

He ate in silence, thinking about the looming deadline. In two days, he would be off work and headed to the Aquatic training center to use the Olympic sized pool for better timing.

⌒

The American Olympic Committee meeting turned ugly after ten minutes of heated debate regarding their up-and-coming athletes versus the veterans. The conversation in question involved the swim team. As the new head of the committee, Montgomery oversaw the proceedings.

The dark wood furniture in the conference room, meant to induce calm, didn't seem to work. The dim light of the three table lamps placed down the center of the table made it somber.

There went that plan. He sat in the middle seat on the right side of the table, remaining quiet while the others yelled and cursed as usual, not getting anywhere. The arguments would eventually lead to Frankie Mel Donova. He waited for it to come up.

"We're losing our edge!" The first man yelled. "Not one of our athletes has won a gold medal."

"Ravi K won another bronze in the 200 Meter breast stroke. Hardy is holding on to his fifth in the world status and Fitzsimmons won silver in the 800 Meter freestyle." The woman on Montgomery's right said. "We do have a few in the top ten, including the relay team."

"That doesn't cut it," another man snapped. "We even lost the world record." He turned to another member. "How much faster was that Italian kid?"

"Less than two nanoseconds," the man replied.

"It's a tiny margin," Montgomery added. "Not important enough to mention." He sat back in his chair. "We didn't know how much we needed Frankie until we didn't' have him."

"You'd think Coach Craig would have trained another prodigy by now," Sharice said.

The first member's lips pursed, giving her a wary look.

"A talent like Frankie comes once a generation. And yes, even with hybrids being born by the minute."

"I just think the reason we're in this mess in the first place is because we put all our eggs in one basket," she countered. "We should have had a backup."

"The reason we're in this is because some fucktwat on the American team decided to eliminate their teammate for unfound glory," the other woman member shouted. Her fist hit the table, shaking the carafe of water in the center.

Montgomery glanced over at Sharice. Her audacity to say what she did, fueling the woman's outburst, left him in awe. She obviously felt remorse. Saving her own skin took priority.

If the committee ever found out about her involvement.

Heads would roll.

"Has Frankie responsed to the organization's proposal?" the second man asked.

"A select panel of committee members will witness his time on the scheduled deadline. Whether Donovan shows up is the real question." Montgomery picked up his glass and took a drink. "I think he'll show."

Sharice looked surprised, like the others.

"His doctor would have to sign off on it," Sharice said, frowning. "I believe we've stated before that would require a new lack of responsibility on their part. Who in their right mind would sign off someone with a heart condition to train at an Olympic level?"

"His," Montgomery stated. He set down his glass. "If anything goes wrong, we'll have recourse to sue the shit out of him."

The other woman member let out a loud sigh.

Everyone sat contemplating the situation. Losing Frankie hit the franchise hard. There were still a few die hard haters but the threats and near assaults had ceased. Americans were frustrated at their status in the world. The swim team was the country's golden goose, guaranteed gold medals.

Not anymore.

Currently, the United States looked like a cluster of petty, sore losers.

Team player

Frankie remained still beneath the water, his eyes focused on its movement. He could see the lane separators buoying around him and down the length of the pool. The water stung his eyes initially before he donned his goggles. With his hands planted flat against the wall, cool tile on his back, he looked like a merman clinging to the side of a rocky hill. His hair waved around atop his head, splaying straight up.

For a long time he had thought about what it would be like to get back into his old routine. The water soothed him. The way it hugged every inch of his body in a vice grip so there was no other way out except to fight against it. A battle that Frankie dominated each time.

He pushed off while still under, gliding forward before coming up with his first stroke. Each one, he turned his head to the side, taking in air then copying the move on the other side. He reached the other side of the wall and emerged right in front of the small timer he had set in front of the lane. The tiny remote fob for it lay inside the left side of his body-suit. He had pushed it to stop the timer when he finished his last lap for a 1200 meter stint.

Movement on the left caught his eye. Coach Craig came around the corner from the main entrance of the pool. Seeing Frankie, he stopped in his tracks then walked over. Frankie checked his watch. He had lost track of time. The American swim team would come in not far behind for practice.

"What the hell are you doing here?" Coach Craig yelled. "You should know better than to be here. This is the team's time slot for the pool. And you aren't on it, so get out of there before I call security to report trespassing."

Frankie pulled himself out of the pool. Water ran down him in tiny rivers. Coach Craig glanced at his chest and looked away uncomfortably. As Frankie bent down to pick up the timer, he saw Coach Craig take a peek at the display. His eyes squinted, his expression struggling to combat his awe.

"I'm sorry," Frankie said. "I didn't set my watch. I'll be more cautious next time."

"You shouldn't be allowed in here in the first place," Coach Craig snapped.

Frankie grabbed his towel off the nearest bleacher seat and walked past him to the rinse station. Coach Craig didn't move, his head tilted down as if in thought. The team came in single file wearing their uniforms with the matching duffel bags on their shoulders. A few of the athletes gaped at him, not believing their eyes.

Fitzsimmons stopped walking as Frankie got closer.

"Good to see you, Frankie." He patted the side of Frankie's hip, whispering. "I was worried. Glad you're back in the water," .

Frankie looked over and saw genuine concern on his face. "Thanks."

Ravi and Blane kept their distance, not making any attempt to approach him. They simply nodded to him in acknowledgement. Frankie gave one in return. The awkward atmosphere made everyone tense. Coach Craig finally turned around.

"You need to leave."

Frankie glanced over at him then resumed walking to the locker room. His heartbeat raced, thumping hard inside his chest. The whole situation had frightened him. He never wanted to run into the coach or the team.

Coach Craig barked orders at the team, ordering them hustle to the locker room and get changed. While they trickled back to the pool wet from the rinse station, he paced the tile, deep in thought. The digits on Frankie's little timer burned in his mind. It beat the current world record by a whole three seconds.

Impossible! That heart reconstructed had parts of it regrown. How could it be fully functional?

Not only that, but stronger.

That Frankie had access inside the building, let alone the pool, meant the committee authorized it. He dreaded what they were up to. As much as he wanted his team to win gold, he couldn't justify having a drug addict representing the country. The committee's agenda be damned.

He took stock of the team. *They won't tolerate it either.* There were other rumors besides the drug use. Word spread that Frankie was promiscuous as well. For all he knew, Frankie could have been spreading STIs. He heard whispers that even teammates had taken the gamble and tapped that ass. Coach Craig shuddered. He always condemned fraternization. They apparently didn't listen.

"Alright! Get your shit together! Let's go. You all know your drills." He clapped his hands, the sound traveling in a ripple through the pool area. "I want to see better times from you today." His stern tone directed at Ravi, then Blane and Fitzsimmons."

God help us, they're the team's only hope.

Coach Craig sighed inwardly. And that meant another year of maybe a silver or bronze. The country's ranking had slid even further, making them twelve in the world. All because of Frankie and his fuck up!

He watched the team start their drills and frowned. The timer flashed in his head again. His gut instinct told him the committee knew about it and would have him compete in the upcoming games without having him attend trials. The only reason they would chance certain backlash for it sprung in his mind.

A guaranteed gold medal and a new world record.

You selfish pricks!

He saw his three hopefuls swim towards the wall, the overhead timer running. Slower than turtles.

Once again, Frankie sat in his cardiologist's office waiting for the man to show up. The exam table felt almost comfortable by the time he appeared. Wearing blue scrubs and a lab coat, the man looked ready for a shift in the emergency wing. He sat in the chair across from Frankie and adjusted the seat so they were eye to eye.

"What brings you in here this time?"

Frankie picked up the forms and handed them over. Dr. Holgate snatched them from his hand and looked over them, flipping the pages. He stared at Frankie, his eyes narrowing.

"Let me get this straight." He seethed, leaning forward. "The Aquatics division wants me to sanction your participation in a," he waved one hand in the air, "what?"

"It's a test heat."

"And you're too stupid to say no. Guess the drugs really did rot your brain." The doctor slid off in disgust. "You want to kill yourself to prove something, go right ahead. I'll have them ready in ten minutes or so. You can wait in the lobby."

Frankie followed him out of the exam room. They parted ways at the end of the hall. Dr Holgate turned right towards his office. The receptionist glanced up at Frankie, then quickly averted her gaze. He went to sit on the hard, fake leather sofa.

Less than ten minutes later, Dr. Holgate came out with the forms and handed them to Frankie.

"I hope I don't see you here again."

As he walked off, Frankie pushed the forms in the manila envelope they had come in. He gave the receptionist a friendly nod and left. Only four hours before the test. The elevator arrived and Frankie rode it down to the ground level. His ride sat close to the entrance, so he jogged to it and got in.

The silent trip felt ominous. Frankie knew his driver didn't like the idea. When they arrived at the Aquatic Olympic Center, Frankie grabbed his duffel bag and got out before the driver could protest. No one would talk him out of redeeming his record.

In the locker room, he slammed shut the cube he stored his belongings in and sat down on the bench, taking deep breaths. For the test he went with a pair of black speedos, not wanting to deal with the long leggings. The scars on his chest had reddened from anxiety.

Let them see what it all looks like. Frankie said to himself. Slapping his hands on his thighs, he stood and headed for the rinse station.

Three committee members and two judges sat at a six-foot-long table placed at the far end of the pool. Gerald sat in the second seat from the right. Coach Craig stood off in the shadows, both arms crossed in defiance. He struggled with containing his disbelief at seeing Frankie come out of the rinse station. Frankie donned his swim cap over wet hair while tucking the stray hairs into the sides.

"He actually showed up," the first judge said, stunned.

"Well, there's no turning back now," the committee member next to Gerald said.

An assistant came over with the forms and gave them to the committee member on the end. The member went through them, frowning with each turn.

"This doctor," he scoffed. "And I use that term loosely. He's signed it all." Gerald's hands clenched in anger. The member looked over and saw him. "We got a medical crew waiting in the wings, just in case."

Frankie went to the center lane and stepped onto the dive board. He shook out his arms and hands then got into position. The assistant stood on the tile floor in the middle of the pool area with a whistle held between his lips.

The judge pointed a remote fob at the timer. Once the whistle blew, he hit it, starting the clock. Frankie had launched off on the money, his long arms windmilled in the water, making his body seem to glide. He touched the wall and did a quarter turn to push off again.

As he began his approach on the last lap, Gerald leaned forward in awe. The others caught sight of it too. The first judge's eyes went wide.

"Is he slowing down?" He asked almost in horror.

The timer continued to run. Frankie touched the wall and the timer stopped at his previous Olympic record exact time.

Gerald became furious. "What was that?" he yelled.

Frankie went to pull himself out of the water and stopped.

The other committee member gripped the table as he too leaned forward.

"Did you just slow down to match your old speed?"

Frankie seemed confused by the angry faces before him.

"You said I had to swim my world record to get it back."

"That didn't mean you hold back your true speed," the member spat.

"How about we try this again." The second judge stared down at Frankie vehemently. "This time, without trying to deceive us into thinking you can only do this much."

Frankie stared at them in confusion. He met Gerald's eyes, then reluctantly swam back to the start point. They made him test for every form.

Especially the backstroke.

⤸

Two coworkers walked down the aisle laughing and joking, elbowing each other. They got close to Frankie's cubicle and slowed their pace, eyeing each other before snickering.

"Hey, loser." The first one called out. "How'd you get back on the team?"

"You don't represent us. Why didn't you join the junkie team instead?" The other said.

Frankie ignored them even though he could hear them over the music in his ear buds. The first one stepped closer.

"I'm talking to you, asshole." He leaned into the cubicle.

The other guy snorted.

"That's why you deserved to have your heart shredded."

Another coworker came around from the other side.

"Really? You should be ashamed of yourself for even saying something like that."

The two flinched, moving away from the cubicle, looking embarrassed and scared. The coworker nodded towards the elevators.

"If you're not going to apologize then why don't you go off somewhere?"

The second guy hung his head, averting his gaze.

"Sorry man. I didn't mean that."

The two slinked away, leaving the coworker standing

next to Frankie's cubicle. He rested an arm on the top of it. Frankie removed his earbuds.

"Don't worry about those bastards. They have no home training." He pointed to him with a pinky finger. "By the way, you don't have to worry about funds."

Frankie tilted his head in confusion. "Funds?"

"Yeah, for your trip to the Olympics. We did a collection box and got enough to cover the expenses with some money left over for spending."

Frankie looked up at him, surprised by the news. He didn't think anyone would contribute to getting him to the venue. His plan involved asking for a loan from Gerald, even though he repeatedly told him it would be a nonrepayable gift.

"That means a lot."

"Hey, a bunch of us think the whole thing sounded shady to begin with. Just go out there and get us some gold medals. We'll give you a sendoff the week before."

The coworker walked off and Frankie leaned on his desk. He heard about the conspiracies too but never followed up. Total strangers believed in him and not the drug rumors. It gave him a little more faith in humanity.

～

Frankie got home and laid down staring at the ceiling. Gerald had already left a week ago for the World games' preliminary set up in Australia. The night before, he had his fill of him. *That asshole! He fucked me all night.* Frankie had to take heart medication he hadn't needed for weeks because of that man. He exhaled, then sat up to stare out the window. Flowers were wilting from the heat. Shade cascaded across the ground with the setting sun.

On the floor of his closet, the doors wide open, lay his luggage with clothes and electronic accessories strewn atop it. He had switched out different outfits three times, still not sure what he should take. During competition days, his uniform sufficed. He figured he'd rest in his room on off days.

In three days, he'll be on a dreaded flight with his teammates, of whom the majority despised him. Fourteen hours of misery on a subsonic commercial plane awaited.

The sunlight died on his side of the room, casting the whole condo in a gloom. A few faint strands of it rolled through the kitchen window. The hum of the refrigerator overpowered the silence.

He almost missed Gerald's overly warm, muscled body. *Stop.* Frankie got up and stripped while heading to the bathroom. He needed a shower.

Coming out, his hair dripping wet flinging about as he dried it with a towel, he saw the notification light on his phone blinking. He draped the towel around his neck and checked to see who it was.

Speak of the devil.

Gerald's name and number stared back at him.

He debated if he should call him back. If he waited too long, he might get a second one in the middle of the night, disrupting much needed sleep. Standing naked at the end of the bed, Frankie hit the dial icon and listened for the call to connect.

"Why'd you wait so long, sweetheart?"

Frankie rolled his eyes. "I was in the shower." He didn't have the stomach to tell him he hadn't checked his phone since he left work. "Just got out."

A long pause followed. "Are you still naked?"

For Christ's sake.

Frankie closed his eyes. "I just got out, so yeah."

"Could you…"

"Absolutely not." Frankie shut down whatever thoughts Gerald had of getting a picture. "What were you calling for?"

"I had a bad day and wanted to hear your voice."

"I'll be there in a few days."

"You don't miss me."

It wasn't a question which irked Frankie.

"Don't do that. You know that's not true."

Frankie bent down to grab a shirt from the pile on the luggage, then a pair of pajama pants out of the bottom dresser. He moved the phone from one ear to the other as he dressed.

"I can't stand it."

He knew what that tone meant.

Frankie could only imagine how Gerald felt being in the same room with his ex-wife, pretending to still be together for the sake of her family's reputation. Even when he joins him, they couldn't be seen together. The logistics would have to be worked out.

"Don't kill her just yet," Frankie joked. Gerald went silent. "I mean it."

"I only want you, Frankie."

Frankie looked at the time on the phone.

"Go to bed. We'll talk when I get there."

For some reason it felt like they had reversed roles, with Frankie being the more adult person. Gerald seemed to have a hard time being apart. So needy.

"Alright." Gerald finally relented. "I love you."

Frankie sighed. "I love you too. Goodnight."

He padded into the kitchen and got a bottle of mineral water from the fridge. From there, he headed into the living room and plopped on the couch. He dug out the projector remote from where it had sunk between the cushions, then hit the power button.

The image on the screen made him seethe. That little Italian shit, the current world record holder who everyone said had a worse personality than him, walked through a crowd pushing and shoving spectators out of his way. He didn't spare women or children.

The caption on the bottom of the screen said, Italian world record holder, Paulo Boresccio, guarantees another gold medal, citing no one can come close to him.

He's in for a rude awakening.

Petty Games

Coach Craig walked up to the airline's gate agent inside the airport and pointed to the digital screen for departure flights.

"Excuse me. What's going on with our flight?"

The man at the counter looked up, following his finger.

"Oh. That flight is canceled due to a mechanical issue."

"Now look. We have to get to Australia by the end of the day. You want to be responsible for Team USA missing their flight to the Olympic games?" He said it loud enough for everyone in ear shot.

The man's counterpart, a woman at the next counter, gave Coach Craig a dirty look. She stepped over.

"Sir, we are in the process of getting a new flight. If you would be patient, the situation is being handled." She pursed her lips.

"This is a dire situation."

Coach Craig folded his arms in defiance.

"We understand that." She returned to her counter and nodded at her coworker. He too began working at his console. "I'll update you when there is news."

He went back to where the team clustered off to the side. After sitting for twenty minutes, he got up and paced the floor. All the members had not arrived. Frankie was probably enroute. He got a call from another stating he had a family emergency and would take the next flight out. His assistant coach gave an ETA of forty minutes.

"Sir," the woman gate agent called to him. He hurried over. "We have room to accommodate your party on an earlier flight. It leaves in an hour. Do you wish to take that one?"

Coach Craig rubbed the bottom of his lip as he turned

his upper body at the waist to look back at the team.

He turned to face her.

"That sounds fantastic."

"As long as all passengers on your roster are accounted for, we can transfer them over to the new flight manifest."

A young athlete in a Team USA uniform came running up to the third counter, ramming into it out of breath.

"I'm sorry but I think I missed my flight. I was supposed to be on the 8:17 one with the Diving team."

The female gate agent held out her hand for the young man's passport. She typed for a while then looked up at him.

"Yes, that flight has already gone. It taxied out an hour ago. Because you were listed under the Aquatics Department account, I would need to call for authorization to put you on another flight as a single."

Coach Craig stared at the agent in front of him.

"We are also under that account. We have two spaces open. Can't he take one?"

The gate agent looked over at her counterpart. She waited for her to check the data and nodded.

"Yes, we can do that. I'll add you to their flight roster."

The young diver's body slumped in relief. Coach Craig despised athletes who couldn't get anywhere on time. He let it slide this time, going over to pat the young man on the shoulder.

"Can't have you missing the most important game of your career."

"Thanks so much, Coach Craig. I can't believe my phone died and my taxi was stuck on the highway because of an accident."

Worse luck ever, Coach Craig silently pitied him.

The agent handling the situation, gestured for him. He stepped back over.

"I will need your roster for the transfer. Everyone's here, correct?"

"My assistant coach should be here any minute but yes. One second."

Coach Craig walked to the waiting area where he set his bag and rummaged through paperwork.

He stared at the updated list with Frankie's name on, frowning at the thought of handing it over. A light bulb went off in his mind and he shuffled further to find the roster from a month ago without it. He pulled that one out.

"Here you go," he said to her as he walked up to the counter. She took it from him and scanned the bar code at the bottom. The screen populated with each name. "I'll go get my team ready."

He stood in the center of the cluster and clapped his hands together hard.

"Alright, boys and girls, let's move. Get any bags you need checked and head to the counter. We lucked out on an earlier flight, and it leaves in less than an hour."

The team perked up, moving to get themselves and their belongings together. Fitzsimmons gave an angry side glance. Coach Craig motioned with his hand for the man to get going.

What would the committee do? Fine me?

He smirked, his mouth down-turned.

A liaison escorted them to the gate entrance, and they went through TSA. Once cleared, the entire team hustled towards the gate. Boarding had already started. The gate agent there smiled.

"You got time still, please line up. Have your passes ready."

They handed over the flimsy strips of paper with barcodes on them to the agent, then waited for the beep before passing. In single file, they walked down the ramp. Coach Craig had to go last. A small commotion came from the main aisle of the terminal.

He turned to see his assistant coach running between patrons, muttering, "Excuse me," as he went.

The assistant coach, Zach, came up to him huffing. He leaned against the counter to catch his breath.

"Man, I can't believe I made it."

"Can't believe we're going to get there with time to spare."

"Everyone is on board?" The assistant stood, taking one more deep breath.

"You and me are the last ones."

"Awesome. Let's get this show on the road."

They went through and got to their seats on the plane.

Coach Craig prayed with all his might that Frankie wouldn't show up early and they hold the plane. He gave an old roster, sure. But the canceled flight would still have his name on it.

He didn't relax until the plane taxied down the runway and took off in the air.

The driver pulled up to the curb of the unloading area at the airport. He popped the trunk, got out and took Frankie's bags out. Frankie exited the sedan wearing his Team USA uniform and stared up at the airline sign. He turned around and grabbed his bags from the driver.

The two men slapped their hands together into fists then hugged, patting each other on the back.

"Go show 'em you ain't dead yet," the driver said, slowly disengaging.

"Really?" Frankie half grinned.

"Bad choice of words," the driver shrugged.

"No worries. See you on the flipside."

Frankie made his way through the giant turnstile, seeing the reflection of the driver slamming the trunk shut followed by a mad dash behind the wheel as a security guard came to tell him to move. Inside the terminal, he went up to the gate agent. He looked around and didn't see any of the team around, assuming they must have already gone through TSA and waiting at the gate. He was an hour and a half early for the flight and saw the cancel status on the overhead digital board.

"Hi." Frankie greeted the young woman behind the counter. "My name is Francis Donovan. I'm checking in for my flight to Sydney, Australia. It should be under the American Aquatics Team. But I see it's canceled. Can you tell me what the new one is?"

She took in his uniform and went pale. Her fingers typed on the keyboard under the monitor.

"Can I see your passport, please?"

He took it out of his pocket and handed it to her. She frowned, picking up the phone next to her then turned away so he couldn't hear the conversation. When she turned back, hanging up the phone, she gave him a forced smile.

"Can you wait just a moment?" she asked nervously.

Frankie could tell something was up.

A supervisor came out the door behind her and walked over. She turned and motioned for the male agent on the next line and he came over. Another, upon hearing the conversation, joined in. Frankie could have easily adjusted his hearing to know what they were saying. He let them sort it out instead.

"Oh my god!" The first agent whispered, covering her mouth. "It's my fault. I didn't check all the passengers flagged with the team account."

"That's true," the supervisor said. "Then again, he gave you an outdated roster. Your saving grace, if any is that you scanned it for verification."

"I should have noticed too," the male agent said. "There were two spots open, and we only filled one."

"What do we do? There isn't another fight until the red eye tonight?" The second agent asked.

"That flight is full, he'd have to waitlist." The first agent said. "Even if he gets on, there's no way he would make it for open ceremonies rehearsal."

The supervisor took a deep breath and returned to the counter.

"Mr. Donovan, I am so sorry. There was a situation when your original flight was canceled. We found an earlier one for the team. Your coach apparently gave us the wrong roster. Of course, we should have checked."

Frankie jerked his head right then left, blinking in confusion. The wrong roster? No. Coach Craig did that on purpose. It was definitely the gate agents' fault for letting it slide. A man in line at the counter on the side of him stared at them in awe.

"You stranded one of our Olympic athletes?" He asked too loud. People in the airport seemed to stop and looked over at the airline counter. "He's going to miss the ceremonies."

Gasps erupted from people nearby. The supervisor's lips went thin as she addressed the man. "Sir, we are handling the situation. Please refrain from causing any unnecessary disruptions."

The man averted his stare. "Hmph!"

"We'll have to waitlist you on the red eye. That way you

can at least be at the gate." The supervisor nodded to the counter agent still holding his passport. She finally handed it back. "I'll make a call to the committee to see about an authorization to get you on."

"I have money. I could pay for my own flight if that's an option," Frankie suggested.

"I'm sorry, because of your status, we have to go through the Olympic committee. Please bear with us for now."

"Sure." Frankie tried not to show his relief. He didn't want to use the money his fans and coworkers had raised for his expenses. A portion of it had already been used for the flight deposit. "Thank you."

They gave him a temporary boarding pass and showed him to the express TSA line. He went through and found an empty row of seats at the gate. News of the snafu had spread. He could hear the whispers. Using his duffel bag as a pillow, he stretched out on the row and closed his eyes. He needed to stay calm.

His heart threatened to come out of his chest.

⌇

Assistant coach Zach sipped on an alcoholic beverage while looking out the window. He laid his head back and let out a sigh. They were halfway into the flight, ready to cross the borders where phone signals could be restored. Last minute instructions from the committee would be relayed.

As the assistant coach, he took care of the small stuff so Coach Craig could focus on the team.

His phone started to ping with the first notifications. Then it kept on pinging. Coach Zach flipped open his phone and saw a slew of messages scrolling his screen.

What the hell?

All of them were from the committee. The tagline on every one: Francis Donovan.

It felt like a boulder hitting the pit of his stomach. Since he hadn't heard Frankie's voice, he assumed the athlete was asleep, conserving his energy.

He opened the first message. As he scrolled the rest, his fury deepened.

-You better explain this bullshit.-

-How did this actually happen? I need details on this.-

-Have you lost your goddamn mind?-

-Donovan better be on the next flight out!-

-If Donovan misses the opening ceremonies, I will have you crucified for this.-

Coach Zach undid his seat buckle and shot up from his seat. He turned around and found Coach Craig kneeling in his seat talking to the athlete in the seat behind him.

"Where's Frankie?" Coach Zach yelled. All the team members stared up at him, startled. Some averted his eyes. "Answer me."

"I think he's in the back asleep," a team member replied.

Coach Craig frowned, turning his head to the assistant.

"What are you going on about?" He asked angrily.

The assistant walked over to stndd mere inches from him.

"Frankie," he seethed, "is not on this plane. You know that." He pointed to the team members who wouldn't look at him. "And so do they."

"Back off, assistant," Coach Craig removed his knees from the seat and stood before him.

The two men faced off, sharing one breath. Turning the atmosphere on the plane tense. Regular passengers watched in fascination. A few with new smartphones started recording.

"What have you done?" He held up his phone with the messages still on screen. "Explain it. Tell me the justification for leaving one of our athletes stranded in the airport with no way of getting to the games."

"Oh my god!" A woman gasped, covering her mouth.

"What is he talking about?" Another team member asked, looking around.

"You said everyone was accounted for." The assistant didn't back down.

"Sirs, please." The flight attendant came down the aisle and placed a hand on their shoulders. "I need you to return to your seats."

"You call them back," the assistant said, heading back to his seat. "I won't clean up your mess this time."

Fitzsimmons met his gaze as he walked past. The look

on his face told the assistant all he needed to know. Coach Craig had done this out of spite, jeopardizing a gold medal for their country.

He was in for a world of hurt.

Throughout the day, Frankie used the restroom and went to the newsstand store for water and snacks. He could hear passengers talking amongst themselves about his situation. The gate agents seemed nervous.

Three hours before the red eye, those passengers flowed into the gate area. An announcement followed.

"Good evening. For those of you on 1321 to Sydney, we have an Olympic athlete who needs to get to Australia. If any passenger is willing to give their seat, please come up and we will get you on the morning flight with accommodations and bonus miles."

No one would give up a red eye. Frankie settled back down in his spot. Neither security nor the gate agents came over to ask him to move. A man went up to the counter, leaning sideways on its edge.

"Which athlete is it?" He asked. The agent, not wanting to cause a scene pointed towards Frankie. The man scrutinized him for a bit then his eyes narrowed. "Nah, I'm good."

He went back to his group and engaged in a whispered conversation. They glanced over at him with horror and disdain. Even the waitlist passengers frowned over at him. Frankie closed his eyes. They weren't getting on either.

Morning came and again the waitlist for the next flight filled up. Another announcement on Frankie's behalf still had no takers. The same waitlisters sat frustrated and exhausted, having bad mouthed Frankie to everyone yet in the same boat.

By the afternoon, every airline gate agent knew about the situation and started to panic. He would not be going to the rehearsal ceremonies or the main event.

A passenger, upon hearing his old competition name from others and the announcement, came towards him.

"You show up late for your flight and now everyone has to accommodate you?" He snorted in disgust. "You shouldn't even be on the team. Maybe next time you'll put the crack pipe down and get here when you're supposed to."

Frankie didn't open his eyes. "Get away from me." He said in a calm, soft tone fueled with anger. His eyes opened to glare at the man.

The man's face contorted.

"How 'bout you move so other people can sit?"

He reached down to smack Frankie's legs off the seats. Other passengers let out cries of shock.

A security guard came over and blocked his swing.

"Sir, I'm gone need you to get back to your seat and not harass other passengers. Assault of a person in the terminal is a criminal offense."

"He's not a passenger," the man replied tersely. "He's taking up seats…"

"Sir," the security guard said impatiently. "Take your seat or I will have you removed."

The man's face flushed with rage. His balled-up fists lay on the sides of his thighs. With reluctance, he went back to where the rest of his party stared at him in shame. The gate agents' angry looks followed him.

Frankie sat up and took a sip of water from the bottle at his feet. He wondered how the committee would take it. Gerald would be enraged.

Sharice sat in on the video conference with the other committee members to hear Coach Craig's reason for the flight incident via phone. The plane had landed four hours ago. The man refused to come to the office complex three blocks from the dormitories.

Probably the smartest thing he's done.

She couldn't imagine him holding his own against the committee. Gerald sat eerily silent. His demeanor oozed fury. Even her father appeared beyond livid. She almost pitied the coach. Almost.

"So?" The first committee member spat. "What do you have to say for yourself, Bergenheim?"

The Coach's voice sounded far away as he answered.

"I must have given them the wrong roster," he replied.

Was he in a tunnel?

"The roster has nothing to do with it," a female member chimed in. "You should have had the previous flight manifest transferred over. Why didn't you do that?"

There was silence on the other end. Before he could respond, Gerald leaned forward.

"Where is Frankie?" Gerald's tone frightened the room.

"I think he's on the red eye. It was the next flight out," Coach Craig said.

"That flight was full and Frankie not on its manifest."

"What?" Coach Craig sounded confused.

Sharice shook her head in astonishment. He fucked up. His pettiness and hatred towards Frankie would now cost him his job as an Olympic coach.

"As is the morning flight." Gerald restrained himself well. "So, I ask again. Where is Frankie?"

The long pause finally broke.

"You reinstate him against mine and the team's wishes and expect us to just accept that?" He yelled.

"Exactly," Montgomery stated, cutting off his flow.

"I…" Coach Craig sputtered. "And what then? He goes on a drug binge and screws it all up again? Make us all look like asses in the eyes of the world?"

"Your job, Bergenheim," Montgomery said tersely, "is to get the team to the games and push them to win. It seems you can't even do that properly."

"You know what," Coach Craig said in a vicious tone. "I ain't got time for this. You want him on the team, then he's your responsibility. Not mine."

The line went dead. A page boy knocked on the door frame. "Excuse me." He leaned his head in at an angle around it. "I have the information you requested."

Montgomery waved him in. The boy handed him a folded piece of paper. Sharice took out an American twenty-dollar bill and gave it to him. The boy graciously bowed and left the room. Her father opened the paper.

"It seems Frankie is still at the airport. The airlines are desperately trying to find a flight for him." He folded the paper back up and tossed it on the table.

"Do we have any jets nearby that can get him?" The chair

woman asked.

"It would take another twelve hours to do so. He still wouldn't get here until tomorrow. After the ceremonies."

With the meeting adjourned, Sharice walked off to the nearest empty office space and dialed the number of an old acquaintance she knew was coming soon. She walked back to the door and peeked down the hall to check her distance from Gerald.

Seeing him far enough away, she ducked into the room, bringing her phone to her ear right as they answered.

"What's up?" The man asked. "You haven't called me in over a year."

"I need a favor."

The man laughed loudly for a moment, then went silent. "You're serious."

"Please. I wouldn't ask if it wasn't an emergency."

"It depends what it is."

"One of our athletes got stranded at the airport. Could you find him and bring him with you? If you don't have room on your plane, I understand."

"One of our athletes," the man began, "got stranded here? At the airport?"

"The coach thought it would be a great prank."

"Then he should be fired." He paused. "Who is it?"

"Francis Donovan." She cringed as she said his name.

"Frankie Mel Donova?" The man cried out. "You people are worse than I thought. How did you get him to agree to come back in his condition?"

"It was his decision," she yelled, in defense.

"Right. Sure. I'll get Frankie for you."

"Thank…" the line cut.

Sharice let her hand drop, resting at her thigh.

Vindication

Frankie felt someone looming above him. He opened one eye and saw a boy of eight or nine smiling big. His dark curly hair touched the top of his ears in a wild mop. A gap in the front off to the side indicated a missing tooth. Next to him, a tall man came into view. The white polo shirt and black slacks screamed corporate dick.

"Hey there. I heard about your situation."

"It seems to have spread," Frankie deadpanned.

"Well, I have a private jet and was heading to the games. The opening ceremonies are always full of chaos, so I won't be there in time for that."

Frankie slowly sat up, his sides hurting from lying on the uncomfortable chairs.

"As long as I get there, it doesn't matter."

"Cool. Can I get your stuff for you?"

Frankie slung his duffel bag over his head and across his chest. The man took hold of his roller bag and walked off. As Frankie followed, the little boy practically attached to his hips, the crowd cheered. Applause resounded and the gate agents yelled out congratulations and a safe trip.

They walked for a good thirty minutes until they arrived at a private runway. The attendant took Frankie's bags and hauled them off to the undercarriage. A walk on scale weighed him and he followed the man and his son onto the plane.

Frankie had to duck as he entered the cabin. Inside the furnishings were plush. Veneer, hard wood accents and tables made it look like a swanky cigar room. There were eight seats, two by two on each side, that swiveled.

The attendant came up behind them.

"We're ready for take off once you get secured in your seats, sir."

"Thank you." The man steered his son to the window seat of the second row on the right. Frankie took the first-row seat near the aisle. The man sat across from him. "I'm Robert, by the way. The shrimp is my son, Robin. Having your own plane has its advantages."

"I'm very grateful. Thank you." Frankie buckled in.

With the cabin door sealed, the attendant sat in his seat by the door. Frankie felt the plane shimmy as the engine started.

Australia, here I come.

Once the plane reached altitude, Robert and his son unbuckled and went to sit at the small round table behind the seating area. The boy stared intensely at Frankie, then moved to the sofa bench across from the table.

Robert chuckled. He rubbed the kid's head, messing up his hair.

"Dad! Stop!"

"I apologize for him. He's a big fan of yours and kind of awe-struck right now."

"Really?" Frankie focused on the kid. "How old are you?"

"Eleven," he replied proudly, puffing his chest out to sit straighter. "I'm going to try out for my school's swim team next year."

"Is that so?" Frankie looked over at the man. "I'm not really role model material."

The kid's face changed to irritation. His mouth went thin as he exhaled through his nose.

"I never believed any of that stuff they said about you." His little hands balled into fists. "Besides." He met Frankie's eyes. "Even if it were true, you're still one of the best athletes in the world."

Frankie's eyes went wide. His heart sped up like a freight train engine. Those words humbled him. He knew he had superfans but never addressed why. Or how they truly felt about him.

"Yeah, we didn't fall into the mass hysteria," Robert said. "Everyone went marching around with pitchforks ready to end you. It was too convenient for my tastes."

"You didn't do any of it, did you?" Robin asked.

Frankie smiled. "No."

"I knew it!" He turned to his father. "See, dad? All they had to do was ask."

Frankie fought back tears.

That's right.

No one ever bothered to ask him if the rumors were true. Going outside was not an option the first six months after the incident. He heard paparazzi outside his hospital room trying to get nurses to collude with them in getting some pictures or an interview.

Vultures. Every last one of them.

Robert seemed to also feel the tension in the cabin. His son got the hint as well and reached down into the cabinet under the table.

"Let's play a card game."

Frankie tilted his head. "What are we playing?"

The kid grinned, his eyes twinkling with amusement.

"Go Fish."

His father glanced up, shaking his head. Frankie snorted, leaning forward to stop the laugh threatening to erupt. He let out a short, "Hah!" Then joined them at the table. His tall frame made him look gigantic amongst the two.

They played a few rounds, talking about swimming, training regimens, the state of the planet, and other random topics. Nothing personal.

At the halfway point, Frankie got extremely tired and went back to his seat, which reclined into a bed. His legs stuck out a bit, so he curled up. Within minutes, he fell fast asleep.

A hand shook his shoulder. Frankie forced his eyes open and turned his head towards whoever it was. The kid's smile beamed at him.

"We're getting ready to descend. You gotta sit right."

Frankie nodded and slowly rose. His body felt stiff. He faltered, light-headed as he rose halfway, using one hand to stop him from falling back down.

The kid placed a hand on the small of his back to help.

"Thanks, kid."

"It's Robin," he pouted.

"Sorry." Frankie replied weakly.

Robert came over and grabbed hold of Frankie's hand, pulling him upright while the kid brought his seat back up.

"I know we made an unspoken pact to not talk about our personal stuff. But I have to say this." He leaned against the headrest of Frankie's seat. "You have no business competing in these games. You should have told the committee to go to hell."

Robin stood back and nodded. "When dad said we had to take you to the games, I was super happy. Then I thought about it and really worried for you." One corner of his mouth went up. "I don't want to see you get hurt again."

Frankie placed a hand on his head.

"Thanks. I'll be alright. Slow and easy, right?"

"Not too slow." Robin stared at him dubiously. "Can you really swim at top speed like before?"

"I can swim faster," Frankie said mockingly.

"Okay," the man steered him away. "Let's get in our seats."

The smooth landing made Frankie wish he had a personal jet. The commercial airlines always had pilots who thought dropping onto the runway was the right way to do it. At the FBO on the other side, away from the commercial flights, the plane settled on the tarmac. The attendant opened the door to let the stairs fold down.

The man, his son, and Frankie exited the plane. A warm breeze brought the scent of greenery, fuel, and heat. Despite the setting sun, the temperature remained sweltering. The runway crew loaded their luggage into a sedan waiting a hundred yards from them. They followed suit, along with the attendant. The driver standing outside closed the doors behind them and got back in.

The beautiful scenery of lush trees and rivers lined each side along the main road. In the distance, the newly built Olympic complex loomed above. Bright lights strobed across the sky. The sound of music carried all the way to them.

Opening ceremonies were in progress.

The driver followed the signs for the back entrance and waited in a queue with other important attendees arriving late. When they finally came to the dock area where people were escorted to their seats in the arena, the attendant got out to retrieve Frankie's luggage. The man and the kid got out too.

As Frankie pulled the strap of his duffel bag over his head to lay it across his body, the kid came around from behind the car. He held a dark brown stuffed bear with a tan muzzle wearing a red checkered ribbon around its neck.

"This is for you." The kid held it out to him. "I hope it makes you feel better whenever you need to hug something."

Frankie took the bear, placing it under his arm, and squeezed it.

"You're a great kid. Thanks. I'll do that."

"I hope you win a lot of medals." The kid cried out as he got back into the car.

His father reached out a hand and Frankie clasped it tight.

"Don't push it. If it don't feel right, walk away. You owe them nothing."

"What if I owe it to myself?" Frankie asked softly.

"Same rule applies." He walked backwards to the car. "Good luck."

Right as they drove off, a games official came up to him. The portly man huffed as he walked, beads of sweat forming as he came out of the air conditioning beyond the entrance. His reflective vest glowed.

"You Donovan?" He asked, out of breath.

"Yes." Frankie turned to face him.

"Your country is already near the seating section. We can't sneak you into the procession."

"I figured as much."

"We're going to have security escort you to the dormitories." The man shook his head. "Shame you're missing the main event."

"I'm not."

"Come again?" The man asked, confused.

"The main event is when I get in the water."

Frankie tapped the keycard on the door panel of his dorm room and pushed his roller bag in first. He walked to the last bed on the right near the window and fell onto it, dropping his duffel bag on the floor. The stiffness in his body from the long flight lingered. He gripped the stuffed bear in his left arm.

Colored lights flashed outside the window. The opening ceremonies were in full swing. He didn't want to turn on the television to watch it. The thought depressed him. A buzz from his jacket startled him and he tried to answer it quickly to stop the vibration. Gerald's name graced the screen.

"You okay?" Gerald sounded angry.

"Yeah. Just tired."

"That son of a bitch is going to pay for this."

"It's fine." Frankie didn't want to start a war with Coach Craig. "He knows what he did."

Gerald paused for a moment.

"Need me to come check on you?"

Frankie snorted. "Like you could sneak out of there and not get flack from the committee."

"I'm not in my seat now, am I?"

"I want to sleep. That's all." Frankie could barely keep his eyes open. "Maybe tomorrow."

"Okay. I'll come see you in the afternoon. Your debrief should be done by then."

"Sure," Frankie yawned.

"Sweet dreams, Frankie." Gerald hung up.

Knowing he would get hot during the night, Frankie struggled to get his jacket off. He tossed it on the floor as well and laid back sideways on the bed. Right before he closed his eyes, he caught a glimpse of the bags on the beds on the other side of the room.

Damn you Coach Craig. You did that on purpose too.

A door slam woke Frankie from a dead sleep. He sat upright and turned his head towards it. There was no one else in the room, but he saw the unmade beds. Looking over at the digital clock, he saw the time and cursed inwardly. The debrief would start in twenty minutes.

Those bastards didn't even bother to wake me!

Forgoing washing up, he grabbed his uniform jacket off the floor, shoved his phone in the pocket and left the room. He checked the other pocket to make sure his ID card was still there. An elevator opened as he approached. Four people were inside. He got on and tried to ignore the shocked stares.

At the conference level, he followed the signs to the USA meeting room. The debrief hadn't started yet. His teammates all turned around when he entered. Some sneered, while others looked at him with disinterest.

Only Fitzsimmons nodded at him.

Coach Craig stood at the front of the room talking with the assistant coach, who looked ready to tear his throat out. What happened there? They both turned towards Frankie for a second, then resumed their heated conversation. When they were done, the assistant coach sat in a chair off to the side.

"Alright people!" Coach Craig yelled. "For those of you who this is your first rodeo, you got one job. Win medals and make your country proud." He glanced over at Frankie. "Conduct yourself accordingly."

A few nervous laughs erupted. The Coach Zach's malicious stare burned into Coach Craig. One team member raised a hand.

"What is it?" Coach Craig snapped.

"Uh, just wanted to address the elephant in the room. Why is Frankie Mel Donova here?"

The tension thickened. Coach Zach leaned forward.

"Can you match his swim time?" He asked angrily. The member averted his eyes. "No? How many medals do you have?" The team member shifted uncomfortably, along with others. "Answer!"

"None."

"There's no need to be nasty…" Coach Craig began.

"You shut up!"

"Excuse me?" Coach Craig stepped towards him then thought against it as the team gasped in unison. "I could fire your ass right now."

"I dare you." The way the Coach Zach hissed made it clear Coach Craig had overstepped his authority.

He turned back to the team. "Unless you all are clones of Frankie, you already know why he's here. Don't ask stupid questions."

A deafening silence lingered.

After what seemed like an eternity, Coach Craig cleared his throat and began the debrief. When it was over, everyone filed out of the room. Coach Zach came up to Frankie and handed him his packet. Frankie pulled out his lanyard and put it on.

"I'm glad to see you, Frankie." Coach Zach said. "But I want to tell you, don't push it. I don't care what those committee fucks say. These medals are not worth your life. Got it?"

"Loud and clear. Don't worry. I got this." Frankie could see how his low energy tone made the assistant coach wince with concern. "Trust me, please."

He walked out with Coach Zach following. At the end of the hall, Coach Craig stood talking on the phone, giving Frankie the look of death. The team dispersed, heading to any of the various welcome meet ups. Frankie went up to his room.

Gerald stood waiting outside his door as he stepped out of the elevator. The austere navy suit with a white shirt sat splayed open and the top three buttons undone complemented his frame. His hair lay slicked back, the ends curving slightly upwards at the shoulders. He had gotten a haircut.

Why is he so sexy?

Frankie frowned, disappointed in himself for not reigning in his thoughts.

"You look exhausted, sweetheart," Gerald embraced him as he got in range. Frankie sank into his arms, feeling safe. So warm. "Come on." He took the keycard from Frankie's hand and tapped it. They entered the room and Gerald grimaced, seeing the names etched on the duffel bags sitting on the left two beds. "I should request a single room for you."

"Once the meets start, none of us will be in here for long."

Frankie sat on the foot of the bed and took off his shoes and socks. Gerald helped him out of his jacket and sat in the middle of the bed, undoing his own.

He turned Frankie around to face him then sat cross-legged. Gerald rested his forehead on Frankie's.

"I want this over with," Frankie said softly. "I wanted to prove how strong I am." He pressed against Gerald. "I'm not." Frankie fought back tears.

"I know." Gerald placed a hand behind Frankie's head. "I didn't want you to do this."

"I'm afraid."

"You can always back out." Gerald lifted his head. "I can deal with the committee. You are more important than their shitty agenda."

Frankie felt weak. He slumped into Gerald, not able to catch himself. Gerald noticed and gently turned to lay him down on the bed. Frankie couldn't open his eyes, no matter how he struggled. His eyelids fluttered rapidly.

"Stop." Gerald caressed his face. "You need to sleep more. You're jet lagged and probably overexerted yourself mentally. That takes a lot out of you."

Frankie managed to tug his sleeve.

"Don't leave me," he whispered.

"I'm not going anywhere." Gerald eased next to him.

Frankie fell into a deep sleep full of nightmares and doubt.

Warm water cascaded over Frankie, soothing the tense muscles of his body. He relished it for a while. Then his eyes flew open. He tried to sit up and his body refused. Frankie found himself naked in the bathtub with Gerald sitting on the edge of the tub wearing a masked look of worry.

"What happened?" Frankie could hear his words slurred.

"Is he awake?" A man's voice called from the doorway. The owner of that voice came into view. His lab coat had the Olympic logo on the upper right side. "Good. I can't believe his cardiologist didn't change his meds."

"That's a different discussion to have later," Gerald said. He looked down at Frankie. "Let's get you dried off and back in bed."

"What time is it?" Frankie asked, still struggling to form the words.

"Late. Your roommates are probably not going to be back

soon from whatever party they attended."

"Whaat?" Frankie's eyes stung.

"Curfew. They have to be back by eleven tonight."

The Olympic physician set a bottle of pills on the sink.

"Make sure you take these once a day. With your history, I don't want to see you spiraling out. I'll have the officials work around the drug testing so you don't get disqualified for it."

"Thank you."

Gerald reached out to shake the doctor's hand.

When they both heard the room door close, Gerald lifted Frankie out of the tub, wrapping a nearby towel around him.

"Just say the word, Frankie. And we stop this."

The packed seating inside the Olympic pool arena showed the spectators; excitement to see new rivalries form and the spectacle that was the Italian world record holder. He would swim in the second round of qualifying meets. Today, Frankie would return in the first heat after two years of silence.

He adjusted the speedo tank top body suit, letting it snap against his wet skin from rinsing off. His swim cap clutched in one hand, he patted his stomach, then donned it, making sure he tucked all his hair inside. He made his way to his lane, passing athletes from other countries who did a double take, not sure if they knew who he was.

All the better. 400 Meter Freestyle. Piece of cake.

"Competitors, please proceed to your lanes."

Each athletes stepped onto the dive platforms and waited for the announcer to finish telling the audience who was in which lane.

"On your mark." Frankie eased down into position, touching the board right in front of his toes. "Set."

The buzzer sounded and they all took off. Frankie kept an easy pace, yet still came way ahead of the others. He figured might as well get it over with. On the second turn, he sailed nearly a whole lap ahead.

The commentators watched the meet progress in awe.

The woman tapped her tablet with the stylus while her counterpart yelled into his headset.

"Francis Donovan of the United States is blowing everyone out of the water. A full stretch ahead, he could set a new record!" He glanced over at his partner and saw her point the stylus at the swimmer's name.

"What's up?" He asked, muting his microphone.

"I know that form anywhere. I forgot all about this."

She used the write function to write out Francis Carmel Donovan on the screen. She crossed out the cis and made it Frankie. Then car, circling mel and capitalizing the M. Lastly, she removed the n in Donovan. The male commentator's eyes bulged.

"Are you serious?" He nearly cried out. "What the hell? Why would the committee not tell anyone they brought him back to compete?"

She gave him a sarcastic look with pursed lips. "You really have to ask that? He changed his name and made such a brand of himself that many forgot what it was before." She switched on her mic.

He raised his brow. "You aren't going to...you wouldn't."

"What an unprecedented comeback for the former gold medal record holder, Frankie Mel Donova. He is truly in better form than before."

Gasped erupted from the audience. Some leaned forward to scrutinize him more. On the last lap, with the record time poised to be blown, they all watched, stunned as Frankie seemed to slow down. His outreached hand touched the wall one and a half seconds behind the record.

Like a slap in the face.

An insult to the other swimmers who were giving their all. Frankie didn't care. He pulled himself out of the water amid the roar of cheers and insults. His swim cap came off with one swipe of his hand, letting his long dark hair flow past his shoulders.

A reporter came running up to him as he walked back to the rinse station. She blocked his way and shoved a microphone in his face. The light from the live feed camera glared.

"What's it like being back after so long? Are you planning

to regain your status? What's next for Frankie Mel Donova?"

Frankie gave a deadpan stare. "Frankie Mel Donova died in the water two years ago." He resumed walking, leaving the reporter with her mouth gaped open.

He could hear the reaction from the spectators. No one expected that response.

The commentators sat speechless in the press section. They turned to each other. No hand waving or over the top cries of victory. He barely acknowledged that he had won the heat, his place in the finals secure. Not one athlete could beat his time to overcome him.

Francis Donovan took these games seriously. He came to dominate.

Frankie didn't stay to watch the Italian swim his qualifying meet. No reason to. With over-the-top flair and an arrogance Frankie had never flaunted, the young athlete entered the back area accompanied by four escorts. He systematically insulted and shoved any reporters who came up to him out of the way.

One reporter asked him what he would do if he didn't win. The Italian asshole literally spat at him. All of it on live stream. Frankie sat in the far corner of the locker room out of sight, watching with contempt.

"Disgusting!" the male reporter said as Boresccio walked off. "At least Frankie Mel Donova had class and wasn't a total dick to us."

Boresccio stopped. He turned around, eyes blazing.

"Fuck that has been piece of shit. You all treated him like a pariah but I'm the enemy?" He flipped all the cameras the bird. "Eat shit!"

Time to go.

Frankie pulled on his jacket and went towards the exit. He needed some air. As he passed a small press reporter, he saw their eyes widen while looking at their phone. They raised their heads and caught sight of him. Frankie shook his head. The reporter's expression fell, but he nodded in agreement. Not this time. Frankie made a circular motion with one finger, signaling after the qualifying heats.

In the tunnel that led outside the arena, Frankie squatted

against the wall and hung his head. He rested his forearms on his knees and exhaled slowly. His insides pulsed and his heart thumped erratically.

Did I push too much?

Or. Frankie looked up. His body still needed to adjust to the new medication.

He felt fine the past few days. Better even. Of course, he wasn't going full throttle in the pool either until today. With his time, he wouldn't have to swim again until the finals. Rest would be top priority.

⌒

Dim light crept through the window of his quiet dorm room. No one had drawn the curtains shut. He lay on the far edge of his bed, his feet dangling off the bottom. One arm stretched out above his head, the other tucked under his chin. He stared at the cityscape coming to life as the sun set. The Olympic flame burned brightly, illuminating the town below.

The door clicked open, and his roommates sauntered in. They didn't look his way as they plopped onto their beds. Ravi pretended to rummage through his duffel bag on the floor while Blane scrolled on his phone.

"Why did you come back?" Ravi blurted without looking.

Frankie glanced over at him. He didn't move, returning his gaze to the view.

"The committee cleared me."

"You could have said no."

"Right?" Blane tore himself from whatever mesmerized him on his phone. "We were going to win without you."

"That's not why I…" Frankie brushed off the rest of his comment. He didn't feel like arguing.

"Since you're not going to let anyone else bring home medals, we'll have to prove them wrong."

Frankie frowned, not understanding his logic. Where did he even get that from? Blane went back to perusing his phone. He could feel Ravi staring at him still until he got up and went to the bathroom. Frankie sighed, closing his eyes.

⌒

The live stream views for the 400 Meter Freestyle finals jumped to record numbers. Everyone wanted to see the fight for dominance between Boresccio and Frankie. Cameras were everywhere inside the pool area to catch all angles. The volunteer workers already activated the 360 view.

On the other side of the pool near the last lane, Boresccio swung his arms, stretching them side to side. He wore a black full body long sleeve speedo with the Italian flag on the front. His black swim cap, adorned with his goggles, also had it on the back. He glared at Frankie as he stood at his own lane.

Frankie knew why. The same reason everyone in the arena fell silent as he entered. He wore his speedo leggings, showing the scars on his bare chest. Although faded over the years, one could still decipher the ugliness of what it used to be. He wanted them to remember what happened. And that he would not be denied.

A few athletes from other countries slapped him on the back, greeting him with, "Welcome back, Frankie." He nodded to them. The announcer blared at them to take their places. He stepped up onto his lane's platform. Lucky number seven.

Boresccio stood in front of lane ten. He donned his goggles, pointed two fingers at his eyes then turned them to Frankie. The crowd erupted at the obvious challenge. *Really?* Frankie didn't respond. He would break the world record once more and show that brat and the world how much he had been holding back all this time.

"On your mark."

Frankie grinned, then took a deep breath, returning a stoic expression. The horn blew and he dove in without a splash, sailing across the water like a fish. He came up half a lane ahead of everyone else. Out of the corner of his vision, he could see Boresccio catching up.

Right where I want him.

With each turn, Frankie gained more lead. He could see the Italian getting frustrated, his strokes too aggressive. Most swimmers didn't pay attention to the others, focusing on touching the wall at the end. Frankie had a vested interest in doing so. When Frankie felt he was at the right pace, he averted his eyes to the end.

The muffled cheers let him know he had done what he set out to do.

He touched the wall and came up to thunderous bouts of cheers, cries, and chants. The commentators were losing their minds on the live feed that echoed in the arena.

"Francis Donovan, aka Frankie Mel Donova, has broken the world record by two seconds! I can't believe it. What a machine!" The male commentator exploded.

"This is a total upset for the previous holder, Paulo Boresccio. Just, there was not even a competition. Donovan blew it out of the water!" The female commentator's voice conveyed her disbelief.

Frankie didn't smile. He climbed out and raised one hand high in the air, then let it drop. Two Russians and a swimmer from Great Britain came up hugging his shoulders, slapping him on the back again.

Boresccio screamed in a rage, drawing attention. His body bent back with his fists shaking in the air. He stood and shoved the nearest official out of the way when they advised him to calm down.

Frankie finally looked up at the board.

Oh?

In the Italian's desperate strokes to beat him, he lost his form and ended up in third place. The Australian swimmer took silver. Serves you right. Frankie suppressed his joy and headed for the rinse station. Reporters mobbed him before he could get there.

CHAPTER FOUR

Isolation

The swim team avoided Frankie like the plague.

Isolation appeared to be the name of the game when it came to Frankie. The team used every tactic in the book to steer clear of him when not competing in the same heat. Sometimes even then. He didn't mind the alone time. Their way of treating him another story.

He walked a few laps in the hallway of his floor to clear his mind before heading to the elevators. Three of his teammates came out of a room laughing, slapping each other on the back. They spotted Frankie and their banter abruptly stopped. One of them stared at him in disgust while the other two merely stood in silence.

"Come on," the first one said, hitting the guy next to him in the chest. "Let's take the stairs. Get some steps in."

"Right." The third guy answered.

They turned around and headed for the stairs in the opposite direction. Frankie waited for the door to slam shut before going up to the elevator panel and pushing the down button. His chest hurt. He took a few deep breaths during the ride. When the doors opened on the main floor, he felt a little better.

Athletes getting breakfast in before the start of the games packed the restaurant. Too many people. He kept walking and went to the take out order line. The server entered his order on the POS system. He paid with the card his coworkers loaded with the fundraiser money.

An empty bench along the outside of the restaurant called to him. He slid down onto it and waited for his number. Leaning back, he closed his eyes and let his head rest on the top of the bench.

"Too good to eat with us, huh Frankie?"

He opened his eyes to two teammates looming over him.

"I was allowed to do that?" Frankie stared them down.

They squirmed, not answering right away. The one who spoke finally said, "We don't want you eating with us either." He frowned.

"Then what's the issue? I'm sitting here by myself not bothering anyone. Yet you two come over and harass me for not sitting with a team who couldn't care less about me."

"Well, that's your fault now, isn't it?" The other team member retorted.

"Get away from me." Frankie's tone made them step back.

The two walked away, glancing back once and flinching to see his face hadn't changed. Frankie heard his number over the din of voices and got up.

In his room, he walked past Ravi and Blane talking, and sat on his bed. He removed the contents of his bag one at a time, spreading out each container. The first one he opened had the fried egg sandwich. Next was the bacon and toast, then a container of smaller ramakins filled with condiments.

Ravi and Blane's conversation got louder, attempting to annoy him. When he continued eating his breakfast in silence, they eventually got up and left the room. Good. The way they acted around him lately creeped him out. One night he woke to find them staring at him from across the bathroom.

Finishing his food, Frankie decided a light workout would do some good. Another gold medal needed to be won.

〜

The relay's popularity brought in enough spectators to fill every seat in the aquatic center. There were more news crews, journalists, and commentators than usual. Over the years, one team dominated the scene. And it was not the Americans. They won silver the last two times and a bronze before that. Sweden and Australia were the ones to beat.

Frankie competed at eighteen in the one where they won their first silver. Coach Craig advised him it wasn't a priority and no need to go all out.

So he didn't, and they paid the price each time. The team struggled in the games after his incident, squeaking ahead by a few nanoseconds ahead of Germany and a full two seconds behind Australia.

Both teams seemed to smirk at the American team in a unified rebuff of their talent to win. Frankie stood apart from the rest of his team. Not by choice. They simply kept their distance. The cameras flashed, catching the awkward scene.

"Swimmers, please proceed to your lanes."

Frankie stayed away, being the anchor. He had a feeling he would need to go all out in order to catch up on time. If Coach Craig hadn't pulled Fitzsimmons at the last minute for a different competition, they wouldn't have a problem.

"On your mark."

The first swimmers climbed onto the platforms and got into position. They flew off into the water at the sound of the horn. Frankie watched each lane, giving more attention to Germany and Australia. They were pulling ahead by the third turn. As the sixth relayers plunged in, it looked like a last call. The US team swam in desperation, trying to get out of fourth place.

The last swimmers came up to their anchors, touching the wall. Frankie dove in right as his teammate's fingers grazed it. When he turned his head while coming up for air, he peeked at the clock. Yep. Gotta' work at it this time. He adjusted his form and glided forward, passing the third and fourth place swimmers. On the last turn, he sailed past Australia and Germany, creating a full second gap. No reason to squeak by.

He touched the wall before everyone else and could hear the roars of cheering before he surfaced. On the side of his lane, his team were hugging each other, shouting in victory. Not one of them came to help Frankie out of the water. He pulled himself out and took off his cap.

Boos sounded. At first, Frankie thought they were for him. Then he saw the cameras aimed at the team. The other swimmers berating their conduct.

"You celebrate and leave out the guy who won it for you?" A swimmer yelled.

"Is that how the American team works?" Another said.

"You ride the coattails of the one who works the most?"

"How disgraceful," a commentator tsked. "Being mad at him is one thing. Ignoring him during a competition? That's beyond the pale."

The team looked around in confusion, then anger. Coach Craig stood dumbfounded near the rinse station. Frankie didn't blink. He walked past his team, not showing any emotion. No arm raised for victory or blown kisses from him. Even the news crews stepped away, noticing the mood.

"Good job, Frankie!" A French swimmer called out.

"You did great!" Another country's swimmer said.

The German and Australian team caught up tosurround him, patting him on the back and shouting congratulations.

"Should have known when we saw you as the anchor," the Australian captain laughed.

"They bring you back for this reason," the German captain added. "We hoped you were out of shape."

Frankie grinned. He stifled a snort. For the first time in a long while, he felt vindicated.

They parted ways to have a talk with their coaches. Coach Craig blocked Frankie from going past him and waited for the rest of the team to gather behind him.

"What the fuck is going on in your heads?" He seethed under his breath. "We look like a bunch of entitled assholes with no sense of sportsmanship for our own goddamn team!" He looked around hoping no one heard his raised voice. "Get to the showers!"

Coach Craig crossed his arms and stared Frankie down. The two men didn't waver. When neither spoke, Frankie moved away, turning towards the rinse station.

"Good job, Frankie. We got our first gold in decades."

Frankie didn't reply. He waited for the rest of his team to rinse off then went, doing so alone. More cameras flashed. It was a shit show.

As the head of the committee, Montgomery had no patience for Coach Craig's excuses. He stared at the video screen, rubbing his fingers together to keep himself from wanting to reach through and strangle the man.

Every media outlet ran the story, with footage, about how the American Men's Swim Team acted following the relay where they won gold. He wanted everyone in sync for optics at the medal ceremony held later that night.

"I don't know what kind of ship you're running, but until your time is up, you better get those boys in gear. They are nothing without Donovan."

Coach Craig's brow scrunched up as he averted his eyes from the screen. Then he turned back heated.

"You bring him back without our consent, knowing how much he disgraced us, and you want us to all just wrap our arms around him and sing kumbaya?" He yelled.

"Exactly." The head of the committee replied bluntly. Coach Craig sputtered, not sure of what to say next. "You have one job. Do it."

Montgomery disconnected the line and the screen went dead. He rose from his chair and paced the small office in his hotel suite. Vitriol towards Frankie had reached an all-time high and only subsided less than a year ago. There were still haters in the midst. The committee had waited too long to curb its course.

Still looming over their heads were the culprits responsible for the attempt on Frankie's life. So far there seemed to be no movement. No chatter on the forums. Which made him anxious. He knew a plot was in the works, seeing Frankie back in full swing after such a devastating injury.

We must do our due diligence this time.

⤚

The beer garden and pub, a few blocks from the dorms, neared full capacity. Loud voices mixed with music assaulted anyone coming in. A round of beers covered every table, accompanied by nachos, pretzels, and hot wings. Wearing their uniforms, the athletes didn't care about who saw them.

At one table sat two Germans, two Australians, one Englishman, and a Swede. One of the Germans caught sight of Frankie entering the pub and waved him over.

"Frankie! Come! Drink with us!"

Frankie waded between tables to get to them.

The Swede patted on the empty chair next to him. He sat down and a stein of beer immediately slid in front of him. He stared at it for a moment, not sure if he should with his medication. Not wanting to be rude, he picked it up and took a sip.

"How you holding up, Frankie?" The British athlete asked, leaning forward so he could see him.

"Best I can," Frankie replied, taking another sip.

"Can't believe your team did that at the relay," the Australian said. "Knocked me right out."

"Those assholes were never good guys." The German nodded at Frankie. "You know that too."

Frankie lowered his eyes. True. They didn't want him on the swim team from day one. Being the golden goose made it much worse.

"Here's what you do," the other German said. "You move to Germany, get your citizenship, and apply for our team."

The Swede almost spit out his beer. "Say what! No, no. He needs less stress, not more."

They all laughed at that. Frankie started to feel more relaxed. He always had a good time around other countries' athletes. They understood.

Frankie woke up feeling heavy. Like slush flowed through his veins. His movements were sluggish as he struggled out of bed, moving the stuffed bear to the side. For the second day in a row, he couldn't get functioning right until hours after. It happened suddenly and he didn't know why. His medication worked fine as far as he could tell. Something else must be aggravating his system.

Of course, he probably pushed himself too hard.

He had won gold at every event with ease, only to sleep hard at night. Making his way to the bathroom seemed to take forever.

Am I moving in slow motion?

He stumbled into the shower, still wearing his pajama pants, and turned the water on, rotating the dial towards cold. The shock woke him up.

Banging on the room door startled Frankie as he finished getting dressed, tying his shoes.

"Hey! The bus is leaving early due to traffic!" The voice on the other side called out.

"Thanks!"

Frankie grabbed his duffel bag and headed out the door. In the hall were athletes waiting for the elevator or heading for the stairs. He didn't have the energy just yet for the stairs. The doors opened on the first floor, and he followed the rest of the team to the giant coach bus with the US Swim Team plaque on the front passenger window.

He sat in the second row behind the driver and leaned against the window. No one sat next to him. Coach Craig gave him a dirty look as he climbed up, the assistant coach behind him.

Today he had the 200M Butterfly. Not his best event. He hadn't competed in it since his second Olympics and won silver that time. To medal in it now would be a miracle. Coach Zach leaned over into his seat, making Frankie jump as he turned to look at him.

"You don't look well, Frankie."

"I'm good. Just slept bad." Frankie tried to force a smile. No go.

"I need you to tell me if you can't do this," Coach Zach whispered. "I won't jeopardize your health for this."

"I know. Thank you."

Frankie waited for him to back out of the seat and return to his before resting his head back on the window. The bus pulled off and Frankie closed his eyes.

Cheers from the crowd reached Frankie under the water in sporadic levels. They seemed to cut out every other second. A cloudiness occupied his mind, causing him to lose focus on his form. Touching the wall at the end of the final lap became his main goal. Nothing else mattered. He needed to get out of the water fast. His body wouldn't listen.

His time a few nanoseconds from the leader would earn him a silver. Frankie desperately reached out towards the wall as he got closer and relief came over him when his fingers brushed the smooth tile. He popped his head up and the deafening sound of victory and cheering hit him hard.

A tightness in his chest made him breathe in short bursts. Gotta get out! He pushed his swim cap off and placed both hands on the edge of the pool to pull himself up. Almost past his waist, weakness attacked his limbs, causing him to slip back into the water.

He heard cries erupt from all around him. Hands grabbed hold of him and pulled him out of the water. Someone laid him on his side as he tried to catch his breath. His heart thumped so hard he thought it would come out of his chest.

"Where are the medics?" A man cried out in a panic.

Another swimmer knelt beside him. "Frankie! Can you hear me? Are you alright?" He leaned closer.

Frankie's eyes fluttered. His impaired vision saw blurs of color with misshaped faces. An all-white blur with no face loomed over him.

"Let's put him under for now."

Thank god!

Frankie wanted nothing more at that moment than to sleep. He didn't' even feel the needle.

"What happened?" Gerald demanded.

The doctor on call at the medical center gave him an exasperated glance, then returned his focus to Frankie lying sedated in a private room.

"Looks like exhaustion. His nutrient levels are low, which means he probably hasn't been eating properly." The doctor turned his head towards him. "Who is his coach? Aren't they supposed to monitor their athletes' diets?"

"That's another issue I will deal with it later. Is he done?" Gerald asked tentatively.

"It would take more than this to stop an Olympic athlete. He just needs some rest." The doctor stood straight. "And a balanced meal."

"Thank you." Gerald rubbed his forehead.

"In my professional opinion, he shouldn't be in these games in the first place."

"Couldn't agree with you more."

"And yet, you let the committee go forward with it."

Gerald glared at him, his hand falling clenched at his side. "You think I didn't try?" He yelled.

"Not hard enough." The doctor walked past him. "If you had to hide him to stop it, you should have done that. By any means necessary."

Stunned by the doctor's remedy, Gerald didn't' move for a long time. The man was right. He knew the committee would have hunted Frankie down to the ends of the Earth. With a heavy sigh, he sat in the chair next to the bed. His eyelids got heavy, and he dozed off.

The sound of the television woke Gerald with a start. He raised his head, which had fallen on the bed by Frankie's arm, and looked over towards it. Olympic newscasters were reporting on the incident at the pool again to give viewers an update. The organizers postponed the medal ceremony, rescheduling it for tonight.

"Guess I better look like I'm alive, huh?" Frankie's voice sounded gruff.

"Here." Gerald filled a plastic cup with water from the carafe on his bedside table. "Your throat is probably dry as the desert."

Frankie took the cup and gulped its content in one shot.

"It feels like my tongue tried to fuse to the back of my mouth." He held out the cup and Gerald filled it again. He drank it slower this time.

"You going to the ceremony depends on what the doctor says." Gerald's tone tensed. "Which brings me to the problem at hand. When was the last time you slept or had real food?"

Frankie glanced at him with disinterest, then averted his eyes. He took another swig of water before answering.

"I got three hours the day of the event. Had a hard-boiled egg and some toast. I wasn't hungry but ate it anyway."

"Frankie," Gerald said angrily, then let his shoulders slump in defeat. "You have to do better."

The empty cup rolled from Frankie's hand as it dropped onto the bed.

His shallow breathing alerted Gerald that he had fallen back to sleep. He hadn't been awake even ten minutes.

A bad sign.

Attendance at the medal ceremony reached max capacity. The overhead lights blinded the athletes as they made their way to the podiums. Pushed in a wheelchair across the grass, Frankie gave a few waves to the spectators. In a white track suit with red and blue stripes along the sleeves and pants legs, he resembled the all-American boy. A messy ponytail kept his hair away from his face.

After looking up at the first place winner, for the first time, he didn't mind not receiving a gold. Getting onto the lower podium would be a pain in itself.

A ramp covered the usual stairs on the side. The medic rolled him up the steep incline, then locked the wheels when he faced out towards the field. Once the podiums were occupied, the announcer started the ceremony.

Frankie barely paid attention, forcing himself to stay alert when the man giving the medals got close to him. He bent down as far as he could so the man could slip the silver medallion over his head. When he rose, the medal fell against his chest.

The three winners lifted the medals in the air with pride, then became solemn as the gold medal winner's national anthem played.

Despite not being the focus, the cameras panned to Frankie more than once. The ticker at the bottom of the broadcasting screen ran the words, 'Francis Donovan squeaks out a silver after medical emergency during competition'.

They forgot to say film at eleven, Frankie scoffed.

Fighting did not sit well with Frankie especially after a competition. The doctors released him for events the day before. Today he finished the 50 meter with gold and again his body seemed to have too much weight. This time, he clawed himself out of the pool and left the aquatic center before anyone noticed his condition.

Back to his dorm room, he opted for a nap before food.

Both denied as he walked in on Ravi and Blane arguing about…him.

"This is bullshit!" Blane waved a hand back, almost smacking Frankie in the chest as he came in. "We almost had a chance. Then this fucker miraculously returns?"

"He's not some super being," Ravi retorted. "You saw that last event. He's not in top form. We got this."

Frankie walked to his bed and plopped down. They turned to stare at him, finally acknowledging his presence.

"Why'd you come back, Frankie?" Blane stepped towards him. "Huh? Why couldn't you stay down?"

"Why are you even still alive?" Ravi asked angrily.

Blane's expression went blank, and he glanced back at him in horror. Frankie tilted his head at Ravi.

"I'm tired. I don't want to…"

"Some of us want to be the top dog too, Frankie!" Blane shouted.

"None of this means anything to you," Ravi stated. "You only became a swimmer out of obligation. Then you just wanted fame."

Frankie grabbed the stuffed bear off his bed and stood.

"What are you doing?" Blane asked, cautiously.

Frankie got a few feet from him. "Move. Please."

"Where do you think you're going?" Ravi came from between his and Blane's beds. "We're not done yet." Blane didn't move, blocking his way. "Hey!" He smacked Blane in the arm.

Frankie pushed past them and left the room. *I'm tired.* He took the elevator to the first floor. Paparazzi flooded the walkways. Fuck! A restaurant employee grabbed him by the arm and pulled him into the kitchen.

"You can get out through our delivery dock." The man steered him to the back. "I saw your swimming. You look like you're having a hard time. These vultures won't leave you alone if they see you."

They opened the dock doors and held them for Frankie.

"Thank you so much." Frankie bowed his head to him.

"No worries. Get some air. Recharge. Win more medals."

Frankie walked down the empty alleyway and rounded the corner onto the main street. He squeezed the bear tight against his side. The setting sun painted a pinkish orange glow down the sidewalks, making the cobblestone road darker in contrast.

Tourists outnumbering the natives, talked loudly while their poor attempts to navigate the crowds were met with not so gentle outbursts. Not a soul approached Frankie. He liked being swallowed up by the masses to the point of invisibility.

He found himself in front of the pub. His shoulders slumped in relief as he peeked through the window and found it a third full. He walked in, taking the two top nestled beside the hostess stand near the kitchen. With his back against the wall, he moved the other seat close to place the bear on it.

The owner finished drying a stem glass, tossed the towel over one shoulder, and came towards him, depositing the glass on the counter to join the rest. Each one shined like crystal. A burly man at six feet four inches and weighed about two eighty, easy, the owner had the heart of a mama bear. Nurturing and ferocious if necessary.

"Frankie!" The owner opened his arms in greeting. "What brings you down so early?"

"Too much going on at the dorms."

"Ah, yes. Reporters and such. It gets worse the last week or so before the games end."

"I know." Frankie scratched the side of his head, his movement slow.

The owner noticed. "You look tired, my friend."

Frankie smiled. "I haven't eaten much today. Guess I'm all out of gas."

"That won't do at all." The owner's face scrunched in disappointment. Frankie hung his head, knowing how the man felt about athletes not eating. He voiced it quite plainly the last time. "I'll bring you some Hungarian soup and bread. You finish that, I bring you nice fish with steamed vegetables."

"I'm sorry," Frankie said softly. "I didn't mean to impose on you. Or make you worried."

"Don't mind that. You eat."

The owner slapped the towel on a small flip counter attached to the side of the bar. It wrapped around neatly, hanging in a perfect fold. He entered the kitchen and Frankie heard yelling. A few minutes later, the man came out with a bowl the size of his hand filled with thick, creamy soup. He set it down in front of Frankie, followed by a giant spoon and a fancy red napkin.

"There you go."

More patrons arrived, grabbing the owner's attention. Frankie thanked them silently as they headed for the bar. The last thing he wanted was a lecture from the man. He took his time eating the soup, savoring each mouthful. When he finished almost forty minutes later, the owner kept his word. Not long after, a beautiful plate of broiled fish with perfect portions of vegetables and risotto arrived.

By then, the pub had filled up with more tourists than athletes. Again, Frankie felt relieved. He ate in peace, hidden away from prying eyes.

Frankie nursed a stein of ale up to closing time. The owner gave him a wary look as the last few customers drained theirs, then went over to the bar to pay. As the last one left, the owner locked the door and Frankie shot down the two fingers of ale in the bottom of his glass.

"Not wanting to go back, huh?" The owner hovered.

"Is it that obvious?" Frankie tilted the stein back and forth, noticing its heavy weight even empty. "I just need a minute to get my bearings and I'll get out of your way."

"You know what? I have a better idea." The owner took the stein and set it in a bin on a roller cart. "I got a small room with a cot back here." He pointed to an area past the kitchen. "It's got a latex mattress so it's pretty comfy."

Frankie's gaze bore into him. "Are you sure? I don't want you to get in trouble if they come looking for me." Then he lowered his stare. No one would look for him. If anything, they would be overjoyed by his absence.

"We both know that's not happening." The owner motioned for him to follow. "Come on. Looks like you aren't going to last much longer."

Frankie kept close behind him, the bear under his arm

staring at him sideways. The two men went up four shallow stairs in the back. The room was indeed tiny, a rectangular space about five feet wide and ten feet deep. A cot sat on the right side with an LED lantern at the end.

A neatly placed blanket and pillow sat atop it.

"Sometimes, on busy nights, it isn't worth it to go all the way home only to come back a few hours later." The owner stepped back down onto the second step. "I'll get you up when I do so you can make it back to the dorms."

"Thank you. I'm forever in your debt."

"Get some sleep, Frankie."

Once he heard the owner and the closing staff cleaning up, Frankie unfolded the blanket and laid down, resting his head on the soft pillow. Better than the ones in the dorm! He pulled the blanket over him, clutching the bear closer to him, and fell asleep.

Dreams eluded him.

Tragedy Redux

Frankie felt off kilter. He couldn't put his finger on it but his whole body seemed to pulsate.

A soft tapping on Frankie's shoulder made him open his eyes. He looked up at the owner, a troubled expression on that meaty face.

"I tried to wake you off and on for twenty minutes. You okay to make it back?"

Frankie forced his sluggish body to sit up. His vision hadn't cleared yet so he sat staring at nothing for a moment. He nodded, although not sure himself.

"I'm calling you a ride. You can't walk straight."

Frankie nodded again. That was probably for the best. The owner left and came back ten minutes later. He handed him a take out bag with four strips of bacon and a grilled toast with a cooked egg in its center.

"I'm sure you've had one of these before. They call it eggs in a basket in England. It ain't much but should hold you for a bit."

This time, Frankie stood, having to duck as he went down the stairs. He pushed the bag in his left pocket, his right arm occupied with the bear.

"Oh." He looked back at the unmade cot. "I forgot to…"

"Don't worry about that. Get going. Your ride is here." The owner patted him on the back as he passed him. "Take care of yourself. Maybe come back for a victory drink later."

"Will do. Thanks again." Frankie gave him a half smile then went out to his ride.

The last eight days of the games meant the media swarmed the dorms in full force. Frankie instructed his driver to let him out around the side doors. He used a prepaid card for the fare adding a tip even though the country didn't do that. The kitchen staff barely acknowledged him as he walked through.

He peeked out the door towards the main walkway before stepping out, hurrying to the elevators. A reporter spotted him right as the doors closed. He saw his excitement turn to disappointment on their face.

Inside his dorm room silence greeted him. Blane and Ravi must have already gone for breakfast with the rest of the team. His duffel bag had been removed from the window seat and placed under his bed. The zipper closed only halfway. What was the point of that? Just close it all the way.

He took the toast and bacon out of his pocket and ate it while sitting on the bed looking out at the Olympic flame. He now resented its existence.

"Crap." Frankie set his food down and reached into his duffel bag, rummaging for his medication. He had to take it with food. The last two times he forgot, he ended up ill. That perplexed the doctor. He said it shouldn't do that.

"Well, it does," he said testily.

He found the bottle and almost took one before realizing he had to wait until after his drug test. I'll take it before the competition. He plopped the pill back in the bottle and sealed it. Taking up his toast, he resumed eating.

The one-hundred-meter backstroke. A short, down, and dirty event. Frankie rarely did that one. He found it non-taxing after a major heat. The games were winding down. He took his medication in front of the officials after they declared his drug test clear. Coach Craig watched with a disgusted look on his face the entire time.

Frankie got undressed, his speedos worn underneath, and went to the rinse station. His sluggishness lingered, getting worse. He shook it off, forcing his mind to engage on the task at hand. Donning his swim cap, he headed to his lane and slipped down into the water.

Instead of a comforting coolness, his body heated up as if steam would rise. It subsided after a few seconds, the water warm to touch. His vision blurred.

I'm okay. He commanded himself.

The announcer's voice became almost inaudible. But he knew the routine, so didn't need their cues. The only sound required was the sound of the starting horn.

The horn blared, signaling the swimmers to take off. Frankie pushed off with everything he had yet fell behind three others. He struggled to keep his form, every stroke like lifting bricks. A shot of pain went through his whole body. He remembered that feeling.

No!

Tears filled his goggles as darkness flowed around him.

Screams erupted from the stands while lifeguards and medics rushed to the pool. Two lifeguards jumped in to retrieve Frankie before he sank to the bottom. An official turned to the newscasters and made a cutting motion across his neck to stop the live feed.

The medics were prepared with a shot of regenerative gel, a defibrillator, and heart electrodes. They had learned from before. As the lifeguards dragged Frankie's lifeless body onto the tile, the medics went to work. The one holding the scanner stared at the image with disbelief, then rage.

"That's impossible!" He yelled. The other medics looked over and their expressions mirrored his. "What the hell is going on?"

Frankie's heart damage appeared worse than before. Volunteers rushed over carrying a tent to hide the recovery procedure. Reporters got a few shots before it blocked their view. A transport unit came through and stopped outside the tent.

"Put him down right now. We can't do anything here." The first medic ordered.

His counterpart pulled an injection gun from the kit and inserted a cartridge of blue liquid. He set it against Frankie's neck and hit the plunger. The monitor showed his vital signs blip once, then go flat.

"Okay, we got him in suspended stasis. Let's move."

They gently rolled him over to place the stretcher under him and brought him back, strapping him in.

With two on each side, the medics lifted then carried him to the transport unit.

Not long after the unit sped out and the tent moved back near the rinse station, the arena became a wall of sound. Voices mingled with cries overtook the announcers on the PA system. Coach Craig stood rooted to his spot by the bleachers where the rest of the team sat.

"What just happened?" One member yelled. "How could this happen twice?"

Coach Craig stared at the tiled floor, confused. He looked up and caught sight of two committee members calmly walking down the side stairs to exit the aquatic center. They glanced over at him, then averted their gaze. Coach Craig's eyes widened. In an instant, he realized what a fool he had been.

He had done Frankie wrong on every level.

A bolt like a jackhammer hit Gerald as he argued with Sharice and her father in their suite's living room. The glass of bourbon he held fell to the floor with him dropping after. Crouched on one knee, he clutched at his heart, the pain unbearable.

"Frankie," he cried out weakly, not having the energy to muster much more. Sharice and her father stared in horror as he began screaming. He forced himself to stand. "Frankie!" He croaked from a sore throat. His legs shook with every step as he trudged in a daze towards the door.

"Gerald, wait!" Sharice went to stop him. He slapped her hand away and turned to her. The hatred in his eyes made her flinch. "Please. You're in no condition to go anywhere by yourself."

Her father's phone rang along with Gerald and Sharice's. On the widescreen television, the news flashed across the bottom, then the live feed switched to commercials. Sharice's father listened intently to the person on the other end, then snapped his phone shut.

"Richards!"

"Yes sir?" The personal assistant came into the room, stopping cold when he noticed Gerald's state.

"Get the car ready."

"Yes sir." The man hurried out of the room.

Two other men entered.

Sharice's father pointed to Gerald. "Stop him."

Gerald turned his attention from Sharice, ready to fight his way through the two goons nearly twice his size. He didn't get the chance. Right as he took one step towards the door, the one on his right took him out with a punch to the stomach.

Having, the air knocked out of him forcibly bent him over as his vision blurred. For good measure, the goon brought an elbow down into the middle of his back.

He went flat onto the floor and consciousness fled.

Chaos flooded the medical center as the technicians rolled Frankie through its doors. A team of cardiologists were on hand and heart surgeons rushed to the operating room, already scrubbed in awaiting him. From the time they received the reports, they coordinated on a plan.

Committee members signed paperwork in the administrator's office. They couldn't stop the media. Those vultures would not be denied, refusing to leave until they got an update on the situation. Many already questioning Frankie having a massive coronary from drugs two years ago.

It happening twice? All the conspiracy theories came flooding back.

Montgomery walked into the office with Gerald not far behind, rubbing his stomach to ease the pain. He had no choice but to order his bodyguards to take him down, seeing his former son-in-law on the verge of madness. His gaze fell on the media crews as he walked by earlier. The committee could not hide the truth this time.

"What are we looking at?" He asked the medical center's administrator.

"At least ten hours of surgery to get him stable. Then we can get him into a cryochamber and transport him back to the United States."

"A cryochamber?" A committee member cried out. "Will

that be enough to save his life?"

"I am leery of this too," the chairwoman said. "From the initial report, his heart is basically shredded. Like a shrapnel bomb exploded inside it."

"Nothing so dramatic, but yes, it is bad." The administrator sat down at his desk. "These authorizations," he gestured to the paperwork spread across the surface, "will allow us to regrow the organ while repairing it during cryostasis."

"How long will he be inside?" Montgomery asked.

"Minimum? Three months, maybe six."

A loud smack made them turn to see Gerald leaning against the door frame with one hand planted above his head. His face contorted in pain, he let out a small cry and slid to the floor.

"What is going on?" A committee member yelled.

The administrator met Montgomery's eyes.

"Oh dear god. He's Francis Donovan's soul mate." One hand ran down his face, swiping it across his mouth. "He needs to be sedated until Donovan comes out of surgery."

"I agree." Montgomery said.

The committee members stared in shock at Gerald then Montgomery. Chairwoman stepped towards him.

"You kept something that important from us?" She reared back. "Does your daughter know?"

"Of course, she does." He glanced back at the administrator. "When will the toxicology report go out?"

"Within the next four hours."

"Not much time." He turned to another committee member. "We need to bring Dr. Novak back and get him on board. The more we contain this with people already in the know, the better position we are in."

"I'll have him here in four hours whether he wants to or not," the man replied, leaving the room.

Two nurses came to the door and used an injection gun on Gerald. He slumped to the floor and the male nurse picked him up with ease, depositing him on the gurney behind him.

"What a travesty," the chairwoman sneered. "Again!"

⌒

The lead detective in charge of the incident faced the US Swim team and their coach inside the dormitory complex's conference room. Two of his officers blocked the door with two more on the other side to prevent anyone from entering. Coach Craig sat off to the left, his arms folded, and his head hung low. The team looked around at each other with apprehension.

"As our protocol states, you are all to remain in this facility until we have interviewed everyone. If any of you know where Blane and Ravi are, please come forward now." The detective searched their faces. No one moved or spoke. "Then we shall begin." He held up the team roster. "I will go in alphabetical order."

For almost two hours, the team members were called one by one and escorted to a separate room for questioning. They returned silent, not acknowledging each other. Tension grew. Coach Craig nervously fidgeted in his seat, knowing they didn't need him to give a statement.

Every time the detective came back, he stared at him with pity.

During their interview, a team member broke down in tears. The detective stopped his questioning and motioned for his partner to hand the young man some tissue.

"Why are you upset?" the detective asked after the team member stopped sniffling. He had gone through three tissues. "My understanding is that the team did not like Frankie."

"That's not true!" The young man slapped his hands on the table. "We just," his face scrunched up, baring his teeth, "were disappointed."

"And, you knew nothing about any conspiracy to kill him?"

"Absolutely not!" He started crying again, tears falling on his hands.

"Blane and Ravi?"

"All I remember is them saying since their events were done, they would go travel to other parts of the country until it was time to come back for our flight home."

"When was that again?"

The young man's eyes widened.

"Right after breakfast that day."

The detective nodded. Everyone told a consistent story. Which left Coach Craig as the only person who knew the most about the attempted homicide.

"That's all I need. Let's get you back to your team."

The detective gave his partner a head tilt as he escorted the team member out the door. He would take each interview and compile them in a digital file for further scrutiny. The two officers at the conference room doors held them open for him and his charge. Still red eyed from crying, the team member sat down in the chair he vacated earlier.

"That will be all for today. Please keep yourselves available for more questioning if needed."

The detective and his officers left, not without giving Coach Craig an angry glance.

Silence engulfed the room after the detective left. The mood fluctuated between sadness and rage. Ten minutes went by before a team member spoke. They turned to Coach Craig.

"You knew, didn't you?" The team member turned a furious stare towards him.

"What the fuck?" Another member cried out.

"Does this mean all this time; Frankie never did any of those things?" A third asked.

"It's true." A member from the back said. "I went into his room to flush that white stuff while he was out. When I opened the baggie, it smelled sweet, so I tasted it. Nothing but powdered sugar mixed with some ephedrine."

A team member close to the center glared at his teammates. "I never, not once, thought Frankie was a drug addict. His pride as an athlete wouldn't allow him to do that. You all should be ashamed of yourselves, the way you treated him."

Many hung their heads while others got angrier.

"He started it," a team member retorted. "Pretending to do drugs in front of people. How were we supposed to know the difference?" He yelled.

"Because he never popped a piss test," Fitzsimmons replied. "You, me, and everyone else knows you can't fake those. No matter what weird rumors about bribes that floated around."

"Answer my question," the first team member addressed Coach Craig.

They all stared at him. The assistant coach sat on the opposite side of the room, seething. Coach Craig didn't look up. His fingers dug into his biceps.

"You knew those assholes tried to kill him the first time and you and the committee just brushed it off? Like his life meant nothing?" The teary-eyed team member yelled.

"Oh, they cared," a team member said. "He got the best medical on the planet so he can come back and win more golds. Isn't that right, coach?"

"You let us believe all that. Even dogged him like everyone else," the second member said.

Coach Craig's head snapped up, his face bright pink.

"I didn't make you treat him like shit! You all did that on your own. Don't you dare blame me!"

"We do blame you!" Coach Zach shouted back. "Your job was to make sure our athletes were safe and in good health. You tossed all that in the garbage to do the committee's bidding. Frankie should have been a priority."

"You shamed Frankie for drugs but let two murderers stay on the team." Fitzsimmons' hard stare bore through Coach Craig. "That's some bullshit."

He stood, towering over everyone, and walked to the door, not looking back as he exited the room. The rest of the team followed suit, leaving Coach Craig and the assistant alone.

Coach Zach crossed over to stand before Coach Craig. He waited for the man to look at him.

"I always thought you were overly obsessed with training, pushing them to the edge. To let those two keep competing and hand Frankie over to those fucking committee wolves." He shook his head. "Where did your moral code go?"

The assistant coach left. Coach Craig sat in the silent empty room staring at the wall. He jumped from his seat, yelling, as he kicked his chair into the wall behind him, causing a loud thump.

His eyes burned with tears that squeezed out the corners. He grabbed a nearby chair and threw it across the room.

His yelling brought a few dorm employees to the door.

"Sir!" The woman in charge of the conference room cried. "Please, calm down! If you continue to damage company property, we will have no choice but to report it to the authorities."

Coach Craig stopped his rampage and turned to her. She stepped back. One of her coworkers moved in front of her as a shield. Coach Craig slowed his breathing, his chest heaved as his heart beat hard and fast. With clenched fists, he bowed to the employees.

"My apologies. I will leave."

They moved out of his way as he walked past them. His blurred vision didn't stop him from finding the elevators. He went to his room and sat on the bed, placing his head in his hands.

"Fuck!" He bent over until his forearms touched his thighs. "Goddamn it!"

Those committee assholes! He raised his head, letting the tears fall. "Frankie." His arms fell to the side, and he let his head fall back. They set me up. Which didn't absolve him of his actions after the fact. He should have dug deeper. "I'm sorry, kid. I truly am."

The team despised him. He had no clout with them or the organization as the committee hinted in their last meeting. A knock on the door startled him. Without looking through the peephole first, he opened the door.

A fist smashung him right in the face, sent him stumbling backwards to land on the bed. Coach Stan stood in the doorway, his expression oozing contempt. He stepped into the room, slamming the door shut, and went to tower over him.

"I knew none of it smelled right. Frankie was no drug addict! Not with his body in optimal condition. When I saw how much the committee dirtied their fingers to make a meal out of him, then flip their tone on a dime, that clued me in."

"I didn't know!" Coach Craig yelled, ready to stand up.

Coach Stan grabbed him by the throat, pulling him close so they shared the same breath.

"You should have," he hissed. He let go, shoving him back. "I'm partly to blame as well. I should have fought harder and told all of you to go to hell."

"They kept me out of the loop," Coach Craig said, rubbing his neck. "I never thought they could do this to the team. To Frankie. I didn't think…"

"Exactly. Neither of us did. And we should know better. The committee has always covered its own ass."

The two men stopped talking. Coach Craig slumped on the bed while Coach Stan stared out the window. There was nothing more to discuss.

The games were playing on the big screen in the Olympic Rehabilitation Center's lounge, where Dr. Novak had been forced to work two years ago. His heart sank as he watched Frankie go under. Anger fueled his rage as he jumped from his chair, flipping over tables, and throwing chairs while screaming.

Another doctor came into the room and tried to stop him. It took three more staff members to wrestle him to the floor. By that time, his rage turned to sorrow. He cried, his body limp against the doctor beneath him.

Within two hours of the incident, two men in suits barged into the lounge demanding he grab his things and come with them. The rest of the staff cleared the room, not wanting any part of whatever drama would commence.

You sons of bitches!

They had already gone into his assigned housing to collect his passport and a few clothes. When they shoved through the open car door waiting in front of the building, a small bag sat on the seat beside him. They drove above the speed limit to the airstrip and there he boarded a committee jet.

Dr. Novak entered the private wing of the medical center escorted by two committee strongmen twice his size. *I'm not going to run.* He caught sight of the members standing in a cluster near the nurses' station having a hushed conversation. Sharice's father turned to nod at him, then resumed talking.

The only reason I am here is for Frankie!

The committee could go to hell. Someone tried to kill him again, this time worse than the last.

He knew the toxicology report would show the same drug from before in his system.

Dr. Novak walked towards the committee members who turned to face him.

"This is your fault! I begged you to pull him out of the games. That you needed to find out who did this."

"Calm down, doctor." Montgomery replied sternly. "We couldn't possibly have known they would try again. I will be talking with the local authorities in an hour."

"It's too late," Dr. Novak spat. "They are long gone by now, I assure you."

"This country is bigger than you think. They can't fly out without alerting the organization. You need to focus on your job. We will handle the rest."

"Where's Gerald?"

"Sedated."

Of course. He couldn't imagine feeling the same pain as his soulmate in real time. What a mess. Leaving the shit show of the media and the police to the committee, he went to the surgical observatory to watch the last hours of Frankie's surgery.

At least twelve other doctors were in attendance, some taking notes on their tablets. The overhead cameras recorded the procedure.

Frankie's chest lay splayed open, the tangled mess that used to be his heart sat still in the nearest surgeon's hands. Each surgeon took turns working on it with their specialty. Bags of regenerative gel sat in rows inside a tray. Four already lay flat at the bottom, empty.

When the organ looked more or less normal, they inserted the electrodes and shocked a small amount of jules through it. The monitor beeped slowly, his heartbeat barely registered. They closed him up, leaving the nurse's assistants to clean up. Even with advanced medical technology, this operation proved to be an almost impossible feat.

Dr. Novak couldn't stop staring at the amount of blood everywhere. The transfusion machine had been going the whole time. How much did they use? A doctor walking past stopped next to him. He stared up at the man.

"Heard you sounded the alarm the first time."

"Yeah. And I got sent to the Siberia of Olympic medicine for it."

The doctor snorted, nodding in agreement. He slapped his hand down on Dr. Novak's shoulder.

"Now they have to answer to all this." He slid his hand off. "Damn! To take out another athlete. For what?"

"That's the question, isn't it?" Dr. Novak stood.

He followed everyone out of the observatory.

Time to get a summary from the surgeons at a private meeting in the conference room. They would get cleaned up first. He figured another hour before it started. In the meantime, he headed for the doctors' lounge, where he knew a widescreen television broadcasted the aftermath of the breaking news.

"What this report tells us, is that someone tried to kill Frankie Mel Donova the first time and that the organization did nothing," the American female news reporter cried out indignantly.

"They didn't do nothing," her counterpart sitting beside her said. "They covered it up, then brought him back from the brink of death to win more medals." He shuffled the papers in front of him. "He's nothing but a well-oiled machine for the U.S."

"Do they even care about our athletes?" Her lips pursed. "And what about the culprits? Have they been caught?"

Her partner raised a hand to the side of his face, listening to the voice coming through his earpiece. "We have a break on that. The country authorities are doing a press conference right now."

"We'll be switching to that live feed," the female reporter announced. "And return with our feedback afterwards."

The screen changed to a stage with a navy-blue curtain as a backdrop. Various sized microphones littered the dark wood podium. Standing front and center, the head of the country's military stood bracing himself on its edge, both hands gripping the sides.

Behind him were four soldiers, two Olympic games organizers and four US Olympic committee members.

Cameras constantly flashed, creating a strobe effect. The man shielded his eyes until an official motioned for the owners of the cameras to stop. He cleared his throat.

"Good morning," he checked his watch, verifying the time past midnight. "I appreciate you all coming at this hour. As you know, there was an attempted murder at these Olympic games."

"An hour after receiving the toxicology report and previous information, we sent out a bulletin to every border official to stop anyone from crossing until further notice. The media and other organizations were not informed in order to catch the suspects in a net."

He drummed his fingers against the podium. A few camera shutters clicked.

"I am greatly concerned that the committees had not briefed us of the situation beforehand. This could have been avoided with security protocols in place for Mr. Donovan's safety. Their delegate will now take over this press conference. I will answer questions at a later time when we have more details."

He stepped away and left the stage with an expression of ire and disgust. Behind him, his soldiers had similar looks. The head of the Olympic Games Committee came to the podium. Camera flashes resumed.

Scapegoat

Gerald struggled to sit up in the hospital bed. The bright overhead LED lights made him squint. Their harsh assault hurt his eyes. He found the bed's remote and pushed the icon to raise the head to his level. Comfortable sitting up, he reached over to the side table for the tv remote.

"Don't do it." The man's voice came from the doorway.

Gerald retracted his hand and waited for his vision to clear. Dr. Novak walked over to him and took his wrist to check his pulse.

"Believe me. This whole shit show is not for the faint of heart." He let go of Gerald's wrist. "You seem stable for now. That's good. You need to remain strong for Frankie's sake."

"How long was I out?" Gerald dislodged his dry tongue from the side of his mouth. He smacked his lips. Dr. Novak poured him a cup of water and handed it to him. He took small sips despite his urge to down it like a shot. "Please tell me they caught those two."

"It's been about a week. And no, they haven't."

Gerald gripped the plastic cup, denting its sides. He let it go and Dr. Novak refilled it.

His father-in-law and two other committee members came into his room. Dr. Novak frowned at their presence. He went to get up, and Montgomery raised a hand to stop him.

"Please stay seated." He yielded the conversation to the committee member behind him.

"These are tumultuous times," the committee member said. "The masses want answers. Someone to blame."

"We can't have the world lose faith in the organization or the committee's ability to function."

The other member chimed in.

Dr. Novak and Gerald glanced at each other, knowing the situation they were about to find themselves in. Gerald downed the rest of the water and set the cup on the table.

"There's no need to get up in arms," Montgomery said. "I can see it on your faces. We just need everything to die down for a moment. Take the focus off us."

"You will both be compensated and remain caregivers for Donovan." The first member flicked his nails, the clicking sound getting on Gerald's nerve. "Of course, you will abide by our instructions."

Gerald leaned forward. "The only way I would ever agree is if I am out. My committee seat stripped. I answer to no one. All ties severed."

The two members balked, the first clenching his hand. "You don't get to dictate the outcome."

Montgomery gestured for him to stop.

"That's only fair." He turned to Dr. Novak. "You can pick any facility you want to work in after taking care of Frankie. It will be under the radar for a while, but once the dust clears, the stack of recommendations should satisfy the medical association."

Dr. Novak's lips curled into a sneer.

"My only priority is Frankie. I wouldn't leave him no matter what your committee decided. So, I'll take your offer," he spat. "I had a feeling you would throw us under the bus to save your own asses."

"That language is uncalled for," the second member said.

"Fuck you, you bureaucrat!" Dr. Novak yelled.

The two members' heads reared back at his outburst. Montgomery didn't flinch. He eyed Gerald.

"Fine. We'll take the hit. It doesn't matter. The media will see it for what it really is." Gerald eased back on the bed. "I don't care anymore."

"Good. With that settled, we are scheduling a press conference a week from now. Your speech will be ready. Dr. Novak will stand beside you."

"In other words, I'm to keep my mouth shut." He snorted.

The committee members turned and exited the room.

Montgomery held back.

"I'm sorry for what you're going through. I had no idea the two of you were soul mates until after the first time. By then, it was too late. I wish you luck."

Montgomery left. Gerald covered his face with his hands. Tears seeped through his fingers. Dr. Novak placed a hand on his arm. They stayed that way for a long time. Neither spoke, knowing their lives were about to turn upside down.

⌒

Frankie's cardiologist fumed in his office chair and glared at the committee members sitting across from him. They had arrived unannounced. He heard the two men yelling at his nurse, demanding she set up a meeting. Berating her with harsh words to do her job and fetch him. As he made his way to the front desk, she appeared traumatized in the hallway, running into him.

She now remained standing by his side while they spewed their ire at him. He didn't get paid enough to endure the situation at hand. Her erect posture told him her emotional status wouldn't last long.

The sun had moved so only a few rays came through the large picture window behind him. Thin beams cast shadows on one side of the room. Metal marbles softly clicking against each other soothed his nerves.

"You signed off on this?" The first member slapped a stack of papers on his desk. "What the hell's wrong with you?"

Holgate glanced down to see the release to normal routine with his signature on the bottom that would be on every page requiring one. He frowned at it, realizing what they came for.

"No cardiologist worth his salt," the member said,

"Or their integrity, for that matter," the second member interjected.

"Would do this," the first member continued. "As a top tier certified Olympic doctor, you are held to a higher degree of scrutiny."

"He wanted to get back to training based on your suggestion." Holgate pointed a finger at them.

The second member's face scrunched in anger as he leaned

forward, inches from his.

"You didn't give a shit about Frankie's health. If anything, your actions appear to border on attempted manslaughter."

Holgate slammed his hands on his desk, his demeanor turned to fury. Through gritted teeth, he replied, "I have never sent a patient out hoping to kill them! How dare you come in here. In my office and accuse me of that!"

"Right. Because you never voiced that opinion to him, ever." The first member taunted him.

Holgate froze midrise from his chair, stunned silent. He lowered himself back down, balling his hands into fists. His nurse clutched the clipboard held against her bosom tighter. Shame and sorrow covered her face.

She looked away towards the wall.

"We should have your credentials pulled." The first man sat straight, tugging his jacket sleeves back down to his wrists. "We don't need doctors like you in the organization."

Holgate's anger flared.

"You son's of bitches set us all up with those lies. Making the whole world think Frankie was the worse thing breathing air. And now you want to cover your asses by throwing everyone who believed it under the bus." Holgate's gaze bore into them. "Fuck you. I dare you to try and strip my license."

"Why make this difficult?" The second member asked, tilting his head. "We all know you're a shitty doctor who only caters to patients you like. The rest be damned. Removing your Olympic authorization would put you right back into private practice."

"You would only lose less than one percent of your patients." The second member raised a hand palm up and shrugged. "No skin off your game."

They got me. Damn!

The doctor knew he had fucked up the moment he heard about the second incident. No way something so specific could happen twice. There were obviously spies in his office if word of his verbal abuse towards Frankie got out. They were right. His bedside manner when it came to athletes he deemed unworthy had gotten out of hand.

"You want to punish me? Go ahead. What happened to

Frankie is on your hands, not mine." The two men balked at him. "He would have never given me those papers to sign if you hadn't suggested it."

They rose, keeping their stares focused on him. The two dispatched organization suits had completed their task to intimidate.

"We will be in touch with the medical board. A decision should come within sixty days." The first member snorted before turning away. "I hope you rot."

As they exited the office, Holgate gave their backs a scowl. "The same to you."

Sniffling from his left made him turn to his nurse. Tears streamed down her face. She let go of the clipboard with one hand and tried to wipe most of her face, instead smearing it.

"I hated the way you treated him, even knowing what they said he'd done. He was just a kid, really." She went to the door. "I'm sorry. I can't."

"I know." Holgate fell against the back of his chair, letting his head rest over the top. "Take the rest of the day off. I'm closing the office for the day since the last patient is done."

She nodded without looking back and went down the hall. The doctor ran a finger across his bottom lip. He had no recourse if they went through with their threat.

Looking back on his interactions with Frankie, regret filled him. *I should have done better.* He became an accredited Olympic doctor because of his top rating in the cardiology field. *And now I'll lose it.* All from being arrogant, thinking himself above treating losers.

He leaned over his desk, setting his elbows on the surface, and placed his face in his hands.

"Frankie." He felt the tears threatening to fall burn his eyes. "I'm so sorry."

The podcast group watched the press conference, a mere fifty yards away, unfold before their eyes. More than a hundred press people crammed inside the hotel ballroom with camera flashes brightening the place. Armed guards covered every exit and blocked the media from getting no closer than one hundred feet from the stage.

News cameras set up in the corners avoided obstructing the view. They had brought minimal equipment, knowing the event wouldn't take long. Years of covering the Olympics gave them a clear insight into how the committee operated.

On stage, Gerald, his demeanor that of defeat, addressed the audience from the podium while Dr. Novak remained silent behind him on the right.

His expression barely contained his hostility.

"Here it comes, guys," the cameraman whispered. He raised his small handheld up to capture the footage. Using the zoom feature, he focused on Gerald and the doctor.

"It has become clear that after the first attempt on Francis Donovan's life, Dr. Alois Novak and I made an error in judgment when we decided to cover it up. Instead of funneling our resources for him, we prioritized the organization's status and reputation."

His deadpan delivery was not lost on anyone in the room.

The podcaster snorted, scrunching his face at the stage.

"Utter bullshit," the cameraman blurted.

"That's an understatement," a reporter nearby said.

"These two are nothing more than sacrificial lambs," a lady further away added. "Sent to the slaughter."

"The Committees are covering their asses," a reporter behind them said.

"What we did was egregious and knew there would be consequences if they came to light." Gerald lowered his gaze, looking down at the podium. "As of midnight this day, I have resigned my position on the US Olympics Committee."

Loud gasped and curses against the committee erupted.

"Dr. Novak has turned in his resignation as an accredited Olympic physician." Gerald raised his head. "We truly regret our actions and the pain it brought to Francis Donovan and the nation."

Gerald stepped away from the podium and left the stage with Dr. Novak amongst a slew of questions being hurled. Neither turned back to acknowledge them.

The podcast cameraman lowered his camera and checked his images, a scowl glued on his face. He glanced over at his team and shook his head in disgust.

"The committees are the only ones who need to be ashamed. No one is going to believe this shit."

"It's sloppy." The reporter behind them snapped. "No way do they think we're crucifying those two for this."

"This," the podcast reporter said, waving her hand, palm up, across the room, "is a distraction. Something else is up. I think there's more to it and they are protecting another person."

"Did they go for it?" The first committee member asked as he sat at the conference table with his counterparts inside the boardroom. "Where are the feeds? Are Gerald and the Doctor being dragged?"

"Not in the least." Montgomery gestured with a finger at the widescreen on the wall.

The news anchor's terse expression as she discussed the news conference jarred him. Multiple comments from other media groups displayed on the ticker tape at the bottom of the screen.

"What could only be described as a farce, the U.S. Olympic Committee trotted out Gerald Ivers and Dr. Alois Novak to take the blame for the Francis Donovan tragedy."

"This entire incident is a disgrace," her partner said. "You can't tell me they didn't know about the whole thing. The committee probably knew before those two."

Montgomery picked up the remote and hit the mute button, tossing it on the table afterwards. He sat back in his chair while straightening his jacket. His lips went thin as he glared at the carpet.

"We knew this would be the outcome," the chairwoman said. "I don't see why you all have your panties in a bunch." She scoffed. "Gerald finally got his freedom."

"He's not going anywhere!"

The third member slammed his fist down.

"He's too valuable to the organization. We'll let him take his little hiatus."

"And when we need him back, he will do as he's told," another added.

"That is correct," Montgomery said. "We will let him think he's untethered, for now."

The chairwoman shook her head at them.

"You won't learn, will you? That one will bite the hand that feeds. Keep pushing an abused dog and he'll eventually go rabid."

She rose from her seat, leaving them to fume at her remarks. Montgomery ran a hand down his face and let out a loud sigh. Her words pierced deep. The same went for Frankie. Who in their right mind would let go of a golden cow? Never mind two.

❧

Dana stared out the window seat window of her plane not taking in anything beyond it. Her mind and body felt numb. The committee paid for first class on the next flight out of her hometown following the news of the incident. Her husband tried for hours to console her as she watched it happen in real time. The phone rang four hours later. Her parents were unreachable, again.

"Ma'am?" The flight attendant placed a hand on her shoulder. "You need to exit the plane."

"Oh." She lifted her head and undid the seatbelt. "I'm sorry. Must not have been paying attention." The corners of her mouth twitched, trying to form a smile. She failed.

"It's okay. I understand." The flight attendant's face went stern. "Please know we are rooting for Frankie to recover. He's in all our thoughts and prayers."

Dana's eyes widened in shock.

"Thank you," she replied softly.

"I, for one, never believed any of it. I'm just sad that I was right."

The attendant moved out of her way so she could step out into the aisle. Dana leaned down and pulled her small travel bag from under the seat.

"I'm glad. Thanks again."

She walked out of the plane, down the rampway. At the end, inside the terminal, two committee members and two armed guards waited for her. She recognized Phillip Montgomery. The other man she gauged as a representative from the Olympic Global Organization. Bureaucrats! They had no interest in Frankie except as a commodity.

"Mrs. Everston," Montgomery greeted her, extending a hand. "It's a shame we meet again on such dire circumstances. She stared at his hand and refused to take it. He lowered it. "We have made accommodations for you at the hotel nearest the medical center."

The five of them moved through the terminal exit. They took the elevator to the parking garage's fourth level. A sleek black SUV backed out of its spot as they approached. The driver got out to open the doors. Dana hugged her bag close to her as she got in.

One guard sat in the passenger seat while the other sat with the OPO rep in the last row. Dana and Montgomery occupied the middle seats. The first half of the ride they remained silent, the tension in the air getting awkward with each moment.

"I want you to know," Montgomery broke the mood. He kept his focus on the passing scenery. Dana didn't turn to him either. "We took every feasible action to protect Frankie from harm. If we had known it would come to this." He abruptly stopped. Dana saw his fist clench tighter.

"Did you?" She whispered. "Cuz, to me, it seems like you prioritized getting him back in the water than ensuring his safety."

"I can see why you would think that." He raised a hand for his head to rest against the window. "It wasn't enough. We could have done better."

The vehicle turned onto the medical center's private road entrance. An armed guard escorted them to a parking spot close to the elevators. Dana exited the car, followed by Montgomery and the two men. They rode to the fourth floor.

The doors opened to a chaotic scene with reporters, law

enforcement, and hospital staff trying to do their jobs while hindering each other.

Enforcement officers became middlemen, thwarting the media from getting past the main nurses' station. Dana watched them clamber towards the hallway leading to the ECU, yelling at and pushing hospital workers to get by. Montgomery nodded at the officers and to her amazement, their tactic changed on a dime.

Security physically assaulted media people, pulling them away to the waiting room by the elevators. One reporter caught sight of Dana and tried to get to her. His opened mouth and outstretched hand disappeared as an officer grabbed hold and yanked him back.

Cameras flashed, temporarily blinding her. She raised her hand to block it.

Don't these assholes know where they are? Who uses flash in a hospital?

"Come, Mrs. Everston." Montgomery placed a hand on the center of her back and guided her past the blockade the nurses created against the media. The staff parted to allow access to the hallway. "I don't need to warn you how bad it may be when you see Frankie."

He stopped at the ECU wing's entrance so she could continue alone. Grateful to be away from him, Dana slowed her pace, remembering the last time she saw her brother in the ECU ward of another country. She could hear the soft beeps and hisses of machines as she got closer to the room.

Her heart made loud thumps, as if it were about to burst from her chest. She clutched the front of her blouse while squeezing her eyes shut.

When she opened them, the giant bed covered in wires and tubes seared into her soul. In the center of it all lay Frankie, in female form, her body nearly swallowed by them. The monitors above and to the right displayed slow pulsing lines, too slow for a steady beat.

She gasped, unable to stop tears from falling. Her hands covered her mouth. Frankie resembled a corpse. Much worse than the last time. Movement from the left of the room made her turn around and flinch.

In a chair set far away from the hospital bed, Gerald glared at her.

"Why are you here?" He asked, barely containing his hostility. "I told you before, I'll take care of Frankie. You don't need to do anything."

Dana angrily stepped further into the room, dropping her hands. She stood across from him with clenched fists.

"Is this how you took care of him, then?" she spat. "No matter who you think you are to Frankie, he is still my brother." She poked herself in the chest. "My flesh and blood! You don't get to say what happens to him. I do."

"Right," Gerald snorted. "Because now you're so concerned."

"How dare you!"

"Frankie needed someone to be on his side. To know who he was and not believe all that bullshit in the media. You, his family, couldn't even do that. None of you ever had faith in him."

Dana went at him in a flash, one hand raised to strike his face. He dodged it, bobbing his head to the side and knocked her hand away to the opposite side. She staggered back, holding her hand already turning red from the impact.

"Really?" Gerald's cold stare bore into her. "I'm not the one you should be hitting. I'm the only one who gives a damn."

For the first time, she got a good look at Gerald. His gaunt appearance and disheveled clothes were signs of how long he sat watching Frankie. The way his gaze never wavered when she entered the room. Everyone else he deemed insignificant.

There was no one else in his eyes or on his mind except Frankie. She stepped away from him, a realization creeping inside her.

"You're," she paused, not wanting to believe it. "You're Frankie's soul mate," she finally got out with a whisper. Her anger rose. "You should have protected him!"

The doctor and his nurse, carrying a tablet, entered the room.

"I need you both to refrain from yelling, please." The doctor stood at the edge of the bed next to Dana.

The nurse went about checking the monitors.

"Mrs. Everston, since Gerald is listed as first contact, he has already approved the medical documents and authorized transport to the United States once Frankie's condition stabilizes."

"I'm his next of kin! I should have been notified of any changes to his contact information."

The doctor glanced uncomfortabli, from her to Gerald.

"I'm sorry, it wasn't my call."

Dana unclenched her fist in defeat, her head dropping until her chin hovered her clavicle. She let the tears drip to the floor, not caring anymore.

"My team has recommended putting Frankie in a cryochamber. The facilities organization will be here by the end of day tomorrow to assess the procedure."

His words, though she heard every word, muffled in her ears. She didn't' move. The rest of his words were lost as she tuned him out. She understood better than anyone how much she had failed her brother on every level.

Making excuses for their parents' lack of love and empathy. Turning a blind eye to his suffering in the whirlwind of fame.

A wall of darkness blocked her view, followed by arms wrapping around her. Gerald's large frame engulfed her like a heavy blanket. Her face pressed into his wrinkled dress shirt, the scent of faded cologne and cigarettes invading her nose. Without saying a word, Gerald's gesture did the work. She cried, soaking his shirt. He didn't let go.

She felt the doctor and nurse silently leave the room. No one else needed to see her melt down into despair.

⸻

Only two Olympic Games reporters and their cameramen were allowed in Frankie's hospital room to broadcast the Olympic official awarding her the Gold medal from her previous event before the last. Montgomery stood against the wall by the door with Gerald, Dana, and the Olympic Organization representative, .

"On behalf of the Olympic Organization we present

this Gold medal for the 100 meter Freestyle in swimming to Francis Carmel Donovan." The official held up the golden disc secured to an inch wide red ribbon for the cameras. "May you have a speedy recovery and prosper in life."

He laid the medal atop Frankie's chest, arranging the ribbon so it appeared to be around her neck. Then stepped away to let the reporters raise their DSLR cameras to get still shots. After a minute, Montgomery nodded to the doctor and his nurse waiting in the doorway.

"Okay, I need everyone out except family." The doctor came into the room and moved out of the way so the visitors could leave. Everyone except Gerald and Dana vacated. He turned to Dana. "Would you take the medal?"

Dana stared at the gold glinting in the light. She moved towards it, then stopped. The doctor gave her a puzzling look. She caught Gerald's gaze, then went to remove the medal from Frankie. Walking back to him, she placed it in his hands.

"You keep it for him." Her hand closed around his in a fist. "I don't deserve to have it."

Gerald nodded. When she released his hand, he shoved the medal in his pants left pocket. From the side entrance of the room, footsteps grew louder until they reached the double doors. They were flung open to reveal an entourage of men in lab coats surrounding a floating machine shaped like a capsule.

"Greetings," the man leading the group said. "We are here to take Francis Donovan."

The man's cocky demeanor and joyful expression disturbed Gerald. Dana glanced over at Frankie's doctor for an explanation. The doctor frowned at the man's outburst. Without invitation, the group entered, taking up most of its space along with the machine.

The capsule tilted vertically and positioned itself next to the foot of the bed. Its shell split in two and the front half lowered to set on the floor. A vat of clear liquid with a hint of icy blue sloshed inside. The inside walls had multiple ports on all sides.

"You have to be careful with the tubes," the doctor started

to explain. "And make sure the monitor stays connected while you…" Four of the men converged on Frankie, pulling out the tubes, snatching off electrodes, and removing the IVs with brutality. The alarms went off. "What the hell are you doing?" He yelled as he and his nurse tried to stop them.

Two more men from the group pulled them away while Gerald and Dana watched in horror. Blood splattered on Frankie's gown from the IVs. The last monitor flatlined before being disconnected. The leader stood near the opened capsule.

"It doesn't matter if he's breathing or not," he declared. "The cryochamber will sustain him for now."

"That's no reason to be cruel!" The nurse snapped while struggling to get free of the man holding her back.

"It's not cruelty." The leader smiled. "I'm in a hurry."

The four men in lab coats lifted Frankie from the hospital bed and carried her to the capsule. They dumped her in the liquid. She sank slowly, the liquid denser than it appeared. Tiny tubes slithered out of the ports and entered her flesh. The top part of the capsule lit up, displaying a slew of monitor feeds.

"Connecting vital signs to database." The AI voice filled the room. "Initiating sleep sequence."

Thick red fluid went through the tubes and into Frankie. The display screen showed her vitals slow to a crawl, then rest at a steady wave right above death. With Frankie fully submerged in the basin, gel like tubes snaked into her nostrils and a mask of similar material covered her mouth.

"Ready for cryo. Closing the hatch."

The top part of the capsule lowered down over Frankie. The vat went dark, engulfing Frankie in darkness as the edges connected and sealed shut. No visible lines appeared along the capsule to indicate where it could open.

"Let's go." The leader gestured for his men to move. Rising two feet from the floor to hover, the capsule glided out behind the entourage. The leader glanced back at the doctor, then Gerald. "I will send the retrieve documents and the proof of possession by end of day."

CHAPTER FIVE

Justice and Retribution

Five miles from the border of Bookham, Australia, a barricade of four International Crime Investigation Bureau vehicles blocked the main road. Officers knelt, with guns drawn, behind their vehicle's open doors, while Detective Armondo stood in front carrying a bullhorn. His trench coat fluttered in the wind, his tie sideways brushing his shoulder. The wind swirling around the ground, pushing dirt and rocks whistled along with the hum of engines idling.

Across from the barricade sat an old beat-up sedan with two men in the front seats staring out at their situation. They had nowhere to run or hide. Off in the distance, another caravan of police cars formed a second blockade behind them. Detective Armondo raised the bullhorn and clicked the switch.

"Exit the vehicle slowly with your hands above your heads. Do not resist or we will be forced to use violent measures."

After incidents of hybrids with talents resisting arrest, authorities around the world implemented new protocols. Officers could no longer take a chance on being maimed or killed by a telekinetic or some other form of weapon. Even if the report categorized the criminal as a regular human.

Ravi sat in the driver's seat, glaring at the man. His dark eyes seemed to churn with fury at being caught. Blane, in contrast, looked bored, almost carefree.

Like he knew this would happen. No surprises.

Armondo smirked as he lowered the bullhorn. The other four police cars screeched to a halt, swerving sideways to make a line. He watched Ravi's hands tighten on the steering wheel.

Blane glanced over at him with disinterest before opening his door and stepping out, both hands up in the air. He knelt on the ground, then laid facedown.

He knows the drill.

Two officers came out from behind their car doors to place the thick, one inch wide plastic cuffs on him. They hauled him to his feet and shoved him into the back of their squad car. Ravi's hands slid from the wheel, and he sat back, contemplating his next move.

"Don't be stupid," Armondo said through the bullhorn. "Come out and stop this stalling."

Ravi angrily shoved the door open and stepped out. He stood straight, his head held high as his glare bore down on Armondo. With disrespect for time, he slowly raised his hands in the air, his gaze never wavering. And that is where he stopped.

Armondo nodded to two other officers, and they rushed Ravi to the ground. He struggled, managing to kick an officer in the groin. Two more came to subdue him. He didn't stand a chance. Pride. That's what Armondo figured. Ravi seemed to be the mastermind behind the whole incident.

Blane happened to be there for the ride.

With both suspects apprehended and secured in the back of the police cars, Armondo pulled his cell phone from his inside coat pocket and hit the 4 to quick dial headquarters.

"We got them."

The silence on the other end lingered longer than he liked.

"Are they harmed?" The man on the other end asked.

"No. Blane came quietly. Ravi decided to fight for some reason."

"Where?"

"Southwest, near the border of Bookham, way outside the Olympic sector. They were smart. Didn't move too far inland knowing about the restrictions."

"Australia has agreed to have them extradited to the states for trial. Get them prepped and ready for departure."

"Yes, sir."

The line cut, he placed the phone back in his pocket and glanced back at the two suspects in separate vehicles.

Ravi flailed around in the backseat, kicking the doors and windows while cursing. Blane appeared to have fallen asleep. The complete opposite of their dossiers.

Everyone described Blane as a hothead who spoke his mind and never sugar-coated anything. Straightforward, no nonsense. Ravi emitted a silent, aggressive personality. He acted on impulse, yet in a calculated way. No one had ever heard him yell even after winning a meet.

What am I seeing? Armondo couldn't make heads or tails of it. *Has he snapped?*

He went to his black SUV and slid into the driver's seat. His body sagged from exhaustion. For three months, they collected tips and data on their whereabouts and another two to pinpoint their current location. How they managed to evade authorities for so long irked him.

The squad would get much needed rest after delivering the suspects to the nearest ICIB check point. There were safe houses all over the planet with transports to take criminals where they needed to go.

The bureau had been created out of necessity. Too many crimes committed with culprits fleeing countries and not enough manpower to cover everywhere. Whether it was the correct decision remained to be seen.

◡

Overhead lights flickered to life, illuminating the stark white hospital room. Their shine bounced off the twelve-inch square tiles on the walls. The monitoring machines soft hum gave a cold ambience. The cryochamber in the center of the room hissed as cooling exhaust sprayed from beneath. It grew stronger, covering the floor with cloudy mist.

The towering eight-foot main console at the end changed from black to blue. The cryochamber lid cracked open to create a seam around its perimeter, then slid into a hidden compartment in the console. White wisps of air swirled around, obscuring the body within.

"Regeneration sequence now complete," the console's soothing, feminine voice announced. "Bringing patient out of cryosleep."

Tiny electrodes detached themselves from the pale, clammy flesh. A bright blue light zapped across the body, making it arch up a few inches off the slab.

Frankie opened her eyes and let out a pitiful cry. Dr. Novak rose from the chair he had placed far from the chamber. He walked over and caressed her forehead.

"I know. It hurts." He smiled down at her. "Welcome back to the living, sweetheart." Frankie screamed, her back rising off the slab as she tried to get out. "Shh. It's alright." He eased her down and hit an icon on the console.

"Administering sedative." The last electrode didn't detach, instead filling with yellow fluid that emptied into Frankie's left arm. "Heart rate is elevated. Organ remains stable."

Novak placed a hand on Frankie's breasts, feeling the thump of her heart. A thin white scar ran down her sternum. He watched her eyes slowly shut.

"Now you have a new heart, just as strong as you."

Gerald burst frantically into the private hospital room, his hard breath matched the wildness in his eyes. His gaze scanned the room and landed on Frankie sleeping peacefully. The bed elevated her head ten degrees, enough to let him see her face full on. He stumbled towards the bed, then fell to his knees, clutching the sheets as his head planted in them.

Novak came in, placing a hand on the top of his head. Tiny beeps from the monitors echoed, disrupting the silence.

"She's going to be okay. The worst part is over."

Gerald raised his head. Novak removed his hand and stepped to the side. Gerald caressed Frankie's forehead as he tried to focus on her face. His vision blurred from tears filling his eyes. He wiped his face with his other hand, then straightened his posture.

"What are the details?" He glanced up at him.

"I'm waiting for her sister to arrive. Whether you like it or not, she is next of kin."

"I know." Gerald's shoulders slumped.

"Don't wake her," Novak ordered. "We need to keep her down a little longer. It's a light sedative to make her sleep."

Gerald nodded, then moved away from the bed into the

nearby chair. His body sagged against the back as if made of gelatin. The doctor pursed his lips, watching his gaze go lifeless. Within seconds, Gerald fell asleep.

Too much excitement.

Novak scratched the side of his temple, wondered how to keep Gerald from going overboard. Frankie needed support, not coddling.

A new home.

Frankie scanned the foyer from her wheelchair while Gerald pushed her along to give her a lay of the land. Still not comfortable in her newly regenerated body, she shivered every so often from tingling sensations. *I can't shift anymore.*

The arrogant boy turned mega star had died. His legacy complete. Frankie didn't know how to mourn his previous life.

Gerald seemed sympathetic, but she knew he felt a small sense of joy. They didn't need to hide their relationship any longer. The burden of shifting all the time had been lifted. Yet, Frankie still felt an invisible weight pushing down on her. Freedom came too easily.

On the living room table, stacks of product endorsements stood out amongst mountains of flowers and stuffed animals occupying every inch of furniture. Gerald removed a giant plushy giraffe from the sofa so she could slide onto it.

Her body wouldn't cooperate half the time, infuriating her. Gerald would talk her down from the tirade of profanity she unleashed. She did that a lot lately.

"Did you go through all those?" Frankie asked, nodding towards the pile of endorsements.

"Yeah." He plopped down beside her. "There's even one from Sports Talent Magazine wanting to do a photo shoot for the cover."

"Huh?" Frankie's brow furrowed. "Like one of those trashy spreads?"

"Yep." Gerald laid his head back to rest on the top of the sofa. "Swimsuit and all."

Frankie took stock of her body's condition, glancing down at her mediocre sized bosom.

"The fans ain't gonna get much out of it."

Gerald rolled his head towards her.

"They'll get more than they should. If you do it, that is."

"Every promoter shunned me for years and now they want to…what?"

"Don't worry about them." Gerald lifted his head and eased onto her lap. Frankie ran her fingers through his hair. "I need you to get better first."

Frankie let out a sigh. This living arrangement would be temporary. She decided her next move two days before leaving the medical facility. The college dean visited the week earlier to discuss the work study she hadn't completed to participate in the Olympic games.

She had yet to talk with Gerald about it, knowing he would pout, get all melancholy on her. *So possessive! And needy!* Frankie let the strands of hair slither around her fingers as they slipped through. Gerald snuggled deeper in her lap, his legs curling like that of a child.

"I love you so much, Frankie," Gerald slurred, on the verge of sleep.

When he went still, his breathing even, Frankie leaned over and kissed the side of his head.

"I know," Frankie whispered. *I love you too.*

〜

Sports Talent Magazine's photography director snapped his fingers at his assistants between pacing with a frown and crossing his arms. The back half of the small studio sat in a pit of darkness while gel lights lit up the other half. Black umbrellas surrounded a raised circular platform where Frankie lay in its center wearing the US Women's Swim Team one piece suit.

One assistant fussed with arranging the loose tendrils from the slick backed do under her head. The other touched up the neutral make up. When they finished, they stepped away to give the director a full view.

While the photographer stood behind his camera set on a tripod, Frankie watched the director pace a few more times, glaring at her.

He finally went still, his expression changed to elation, clapping his hands together in glee.

"Perfect!" He shouted. He angrily waved the assistants out of the lighted area, then stood by the photographer. "I want full on wide shots. Some sexy angles and overheads." A ladder on the edge of the umbrella ensemble waited for just that.

Frankie stifled a grimace.

As a dominating male swimmer, she had no qualms about showing off that body. Now, she felt self-conscious, the top part of the faded scar from her heart surgery peeked out of the swimsuit. That's what they wanted to show. That she survived and had the receipts.

"Okay, Frankie, I need you to look over this way." The director motioned to her right. "Don't smile but give me lighthearted, a bit of redemption of some sort."

This is bullshit! Frankie yelled in her head. She tired of people telling her to be grateful. Redemption? Screw that! Nonetheless, she tried to appease the man, feeling sorry for the photographer in the same boat, not able to get clear of the man's clutches.

Frankie gave the photographer a look of sympathy. Their eyes met in agreement.

"That's it!" the director jumped for joy. "That's the look! More. Get more of those from the top too."

The photographer removed the camera from the tripod and climbed the ladder. He clicked a few rapid shots, then came back down. Frankie settled in for the long haul. The director's demands were just getting started.

Midday sunlight coming through the kitchen windows' sheer curtains gave the eating area a soft glow. Bright enough for them to see clearly yet dim enough to not hurt their still half sleep eyes. They had slept in and now sat disheveled at the table eating three egg omelets, thick cut maple bacon, and avocado toast.

Gerald's hair had gone wild. Raised sections stuck out from the sides and back. A few wisps clung around his ears.

Frankie's fared no better being matted in the back. They both wore baggy pajama pants with matching long-sleeved tops.

She snorted. Peak laziness.

Gerald stared at the magazine cover for quite a while, making Frankie nervous. The magazine had sent over the proof copy ahead of its publication in two weeks. Frankie splayed across at an angle like a pinup model with a side glance that said pity me. The blue swimsuit with red and white stripes on the side hugged every inch, enhancing her silhouette.

In big italic letters on the bottom left corner, Frankie Mel Donova is dead. Francis Donovan Shines Through, assaulted her eyes.

"Well, that's pretty tasteless," Gerald finally uttered.

"Yeah, I didn't approve that."

"Wanna sue that prick?" Gerald asked, already reaching for his phone.

Frankie stopped him halfway. "Don't. It doesn't matter. I got paid regardless." Gerald gave him a stare that made her flinch. "Stop that. You're only mad because everyone will see me half naked in female form for the first time." He's not wrong, but his obsession with her bordered on territorial.

"I don't like it. No."

Frankie tilted her head away from him.

"I'm not sexy, huh?"

Gerald's face flushed. Frankie tried to unsuccessfully stifle a giggle. Gerald turned to her.

"You know that's not what I mean," he snapped.

Feeling sorry for him, Frankie wrapped her arms around him. He swung around in his chair, so their noses touched. *God, he smells good.* Frankie closed her eyes and breathed in his scent. The slight hint of sweat mingled with faded day-old cologne.

"What are you thinking right now?" Gerald asked.

"Mmm...nothing much."

Gerald squeezed tighter. "I don't want you getting sucked into their schemes again. They always find some way to use you. This shit is to show they have remorse." He moved away less than an inch. "And they don't."

"I know that." Frankie pulled him back closer, brushing her lips against his. Her nostrils flared.

"Are you…smelling me?" Gerald's lips parted hers.

"Hmmm."

Gerald tilted his head and kissed her, sinking his tongue deep in her mouth. Frankie did the same when his retracted for a moment. When they disengaged, both seemed out of breath.

"Fuck, you drive me crazy, Frankie."

"That's part of the reason why we need some time away for a bit."

The mood went sour in an instant. Frankie slumped, not meaning to do that. Gerald rubbed her back.

"I'm sorry. I feel like it's the wrong decision, though I know it isn't." He rested his head in the crook of her neck. "You need time to get your life in order and so do I."

"Your kids hate me." Frankie blurted out. "We can't be okay if they hate me."

"I'll fix it. I promise."

Frankie ran her hand up his back.

"It's not like we'll never see each other. Just not living in the same space. I'll have two days off every ten days."

"I know. It sucks."

Frankie lifted his head from her shoulder and cupped his face. He didn't look at her so she kissed him again. Gerald pulled away, this time locking his stare.

"I'll miss you too much."

"You're such a big baby." Frankie grinned, then resumed kissing him.

Gerald finally relented, picking her up and carried her back to the bedroom. Breakfast would have to wait a bit.

High Tide

Media cameras and reporters pushed and shoved the police escorts, fighting for a better glimpse of the Olympic swimmers turned attempted murderers. A sea of armed guards swallowed Ravi and Blane as the entourage made its way into the courthouse.

Out of public outrage, the judge granted cameras to be present for the preliminary hearing. They wanted to hear the two state their case and give a plea. Despite getting a fair trial, the world already viewed them as guilty.

People crammed the courthouse hallways, leaving the group no choice but to force their way through. They finally arrived at the prisoners' entrance of the assigned courtroom and slowed down. No one else occupied that space, allowing them to spread out. Armed guards standing at the double doors opened them for the group to enter.

Inside the courtroom, media crews jockeyed for positions in the back and along the sides. Spectators filled every pew. Blane and Ravi's parents sat behind the defense table in the first row. They had angry expressions with hints of fear. The two prosecutors on the other side glanced over at them, pursing their lips in pity. Committee members occupying the first row across from them did the same.

Blane and Ravi's guards ushered them in. The handcuffs stayed on until both sat behind the table next to their lawyers. Ravi rubbed his wrists once they were set free. Blane shook his hands to bring back circulation. The guards at the jail had secured them too tight.

The bailiff stepped in front of the bench, hooking his fingers in the waist of his pants.

"All rise for the honorable Judge Rendenburg presiding for the international courts! This hearing is now in session!"

Judge Rendenburg entered from his chamber and walked up to his seat set high above the rest. His thinning grey hair lay slicked back, making his blue eyes stand out. A dark blue like an ocean storm, they bore into the masses. He would be in no mood for amusement.

"You may be seated." He arranged his robe sleeves to sit above his wrists and leaned over the tablet the bailiff set before him displaying the synopsis of the case. "What do we have here?"

The bailiff cleared his throat and replied.

"This is the case of attempted murder by the defendants Ravi S Abenashid and Blane Hardy of one Francis Carmel Donovan. Agents captured the two along Australia's Bookham borders after fleeing the scene."

Judge Rendenburg looked out at the lawyers.

"You may proceed."

The first prosecutor stood, shooting a nasty stare at the defense.

"Good morning, your honor. As much as we agree to let these hearings proceed in the United States, the country of this crime's origin would like a say in where they will be held for the length of their sentence."

The first defense lawyer jumped out of his seat.

"Your honor! The prosecution is giving out a verdict before the trial has even started. That shows prejudice. I would like him to be removed from these proceedings."

"That's uncalled for!" The prosecutor snapped. "I was merely stating what the country preferred if the outcome found them guilty."

"Then you need to choose your words carefully," Judge Rendenburg admonished him. He glanced over at the defense attorney. "Keep the drama down. I have no patience for it."

Both lawyers flinched at his iciness.

"The incident occurred on diplomatic Olympian soil," the first defense attorney said. "Therefore, the proceedings can continue in the United States."

"I know the rules of jurisdiction, counselor," the judge

replied, his eyes narrowing. He flipped through the hard copy again, then rested his forearms atop them. "How do your clients plea?"

"Not guilt..."

"Why is it just us here, huh?" Blane blurted out loudly.

"Counselor, control your..." The judge got out.

"I mean, we aren't the only ones at fault." Blane tsked and leaned back in his chair. "That Montgomery woman on the committee is the one who got that drug for us in the first place."

The courtroom went still. No one spoke. Blane looked proud of himself. Ravi snorted. Blane slapped the defense attorney in the abdomen. "Finish telling them, not guilty."

Their second lawyer buried his face in his hands in defeat. The first lawyer straightened his jacket and clearing his throat, said, "My clients plead not guilty, your honor."

Whispers of Sharice Montgomery's name grew louder. The prosecutors' expressions turned grim. Judge Rendenburg whacked his gavel on the block.

"Order! Everybody shut it!" When the din of noise died back down, he pinched the bridge of his nose. "The two of you will remain in custody and be held at the temporary prison until your court date. Proceedings are set for three months from now."

"Your honor!" The defense lawyer cried out. "Three months is too long."

"Yes, counselor. I am aware you'd think so. This will give them time to reflect on their actions that led them to this unfortunate outcome."

With the slam of his gavel, Judge Rendenburg stood. The bailiff stood before the bench.

"This session is now over. All rise!"

Everyone stood as the Judge made his way through the chamber doors. The moment it shut; the courtroom erupted. Officers came to take Blane and Ravi. They didn't fight or yell obscenities this time.

Media commentators and journalists yelled out questions to them and the lawyers.

"Is this a ploy to shift blame? Why do you hate Frankie

Mel Donova? Is the committee hiding the truth? Was this a plot by the committee to kill Frankie?"

It went on for a good two minutes before the court guards ushered them all out into the hall.

The prosecutors came over to the defense table as guards escorted the horde out.

"What the hell is going on?" The prosecutor demanded. "Why are they randomly throwing a respected member of the U.S. Olympic committee under the bus for their shit?"

"Respected, huh?" The second lawyer smirked. "She is the third party. The committee covered it up. We said we'd try to keep it under wraps."

The second prosecutor's eyes widened in disbelief.

"You were going to obstruct justice for some corrupt entity? You need to be removed!"

"Keep your panties on, junior," the second defense lawyer snapped. His words rankled the prosecutor. "That ship has sailed. We have no intention of helping the Montgomerys."

The defense lawyers left, nearly shoving the prosecutors out of their way. The first prosecutor sighed and turned to his counterpart.

"Get on the phone and request, no demand, a warrant for the Montgomery residence. And set up an interview with Sharice Montgomery. I want to hear what she has to say."

"On it."

The younger prosecutor hurried out of the courtroom.

"What the fuck?" The prosecutor said under his breath.

This was supposed to be a clean-cut trial. The committee. It didn't surprise him that they would be involved. Another monkey wrench to deal with. Out in the hall, the media lay in wait to bombard him with more questions. He could see the defense struggling to make it through without answering.

This is going to turn into a circus.

〜

The Montgomery estate buzzed with lawyers and legal consultants moving through the abode in a frenzy. Everyone went on damage control after Blane dropped the bombshell that Sharice had supplied the fatal drug.

Papers ruffling, cellphone conversations, and an old school fax machine blended to create an unbearable noise.

Sharice paced the lounge room adjacent to her father's office. The fury etched on his face as he watched the newsfeed frightened her. The district attorney announced they were sending officers to get her statement.

Depending on what she said, her freedom might be in jeopardy. Her lavender pantsuit suddenly felt constricting. She tried a breathing technique to calm down, shaking her hands to loosen the joints.

From the doorway, she could see her father talking with the family's head attorney. Both men stood mere inches apart, whispering with stern expressions. Neither glanced her way, knowing she stood there watching. The anxiety worsened. Sharice tugged her suit jacket tight across her to make it fit better then headed towards the family room downstairs.

Quiet greeted her as she entered the room. This area her father deemed off limits for their visitors. Gabe sat in one of the plush chairs with its back against the window. He looked sullen. Payton turned from perusing the built-in bookcase. Anger and disappointment exuded from him.

"Tell me it's not true." His voice came out terse and low. Sharice stopped in her tracks. "Tell us you weren't responsible for what happened to Frankie."

Tears streamed down Gabe's face; his head hung with his chin resting on his chest. She saw Payton's hands clench tight. Sharice stepped back, covering her mouth with one hand. *What could I possibly say?* This is what she feared the most yet had no answer to give them. She dropped her hand.

"I never wanted this to happen. You have to believe me."

"Is that why dad left?" He asked, his brow scrunching.

"Part of it, yes."

"So he knew what you did?"

Sharice nodded. Gabe looked over and glowered at her. The intensity made her shrink inwardly. Payton turned away from her. She could see his body shaking.

"Sharice." Her father's voice startled her, and she stumbled as she faced him. "Come with me."

He eyed his grandsons before escorting her to another

wing of the house where had set up the interview room. Along the way, she kept glancing back towards the family room.

"It's done," her father said. "You can't fix this."

"I never wanted them to hate me," Sharice squeaked as tears filled her eyes.

Her father stopped. Without looking at her, he said, "Don't you dare go in there crying like some victim. Straighten up and tell them what you need to."

His bluntness slapped Sharice out of her despair. She had almost forgotten. Montgomerys do not show weakness in a crisis. She straightened her posture, adjusted her jacket, and wiped the moisture from her eyes. The enemy lay on the other side of the door ahead. And she had to make them leave her family alone.

Her saving grace came in knowing that the evidence of where the drug came from had gone missing in Australia. She assumed her father had gathered everything for the sake of the family. She convinced her friend at the lab to go on a vacation, then take a new position at a high security medical center until the dust settled.

That may not be feasible anymore.

The doors opened and two officers stood on each side. A tall man in a grey suit stood in the center of the room. A dusting of white along the sides of his hairline gave him a distinguished look.

"Have a seat, Ms. Montgomery." The interviewer gestured to the seat opposite him at the table. "This is your home, so please be at ease." He looked up at her father. "My apologies, but we must question her alone."

"With three men in a closed room?" Her father stared the man down. "Absolutely not."

"It will only be me. My officers will be outside with you. I am certain Sharice can handle herself quite well in these situations. She is a former Olympic athlete, is she not?"

Sharice almost smiled at that. Her father, knowing the man spoke the truth, nodded, and left the room with the two officers. The door shut and the man's demeanor shifted to a hostile nature.

"Sit down."

He did so first, laying his hands flat on the table.

"We have a lot to talk about." Sharice slowly sat in the seat, glaring at him. He hit the recorder button and leaned back. "Now, let's hear how you managed to get an experimental drug and why you tried to kill an Olympian."

The closed session court had a camera crew set up in the back, taping the proceedings. Judge Rendenburg only granted one network approval. A small group of spectators, including committee members, sat in the court watching Ravi and Blane sit alongside their lawyers without a care in the world.

In the front row behind the prosecution table, Frankie and Gerald avoided eye contact with Ravi and Blane. Frankie appeared pale and sickly, while Gerald wore his malice outright.

"We are here to establish motive," the prosecutor said, standing. He brushed one hand down the front of his jacket. "The defendants' attempt to commit premeditated murder should justify at minimum ten years."

"That's a bit excessive considering the victim is in the courtroom. My clients' supposed hatred is conjecture at best." The defense lawyer shrugged. "We haven't even determined if it was attempted murder."

"Huh?" Blane yelled as he turned towards the prosecutor. The gavel came down. That didn't stop him. "I never wanted Frankie dead. I adore Frankie."

"Counselor, control your client!" The judge yelled.

The defense lawyer opened his mouth to speak, but Blane cut him off.

"I just didn't like what an ass he became over the years." Blane turned back around to face the judge.

"Since Mr. Blane has decided to volunteer his feelings," the prosecutor stepped around the table. "Then maybe he can tell us why he conspired with Mr. Abenashid."

Blane gave him a side glare. "I didn't."

Ravi's intense expression turned hateful as he eyed Blane. Something about it seemed to warn him, yet Blane remained oblivious, giving the prosecutor and his lawyer pause.

"Superboy here," Blane gestured to Ravi, "wanted some ass and wouldn't take no for an answer. Said he would drug Frankie if he had to. I knew he would do it regardless. Found out how toxic as shit Ravi was when Frankie puked all over the first time while he was getting strokes in. So I made sure he wore a rubber whenever he hit it. I figured, might as well get some too."

The courtroom went silent.

Judge Rendenburg stared at Blane in disbelief along with his lawyers and the prosecution. Every spectator and news crewmember sat stunned. Frankie gripped the rail of the divider before her, fighting back tears. She glanced over at Blane. He blew her a kiss. Gerald wrapped his arms around her shoulders and held her tight. She visibly shook.

"So you see. I liked Frankie. Just not as much as he did," Blane pointed to Ravi. "Frankie wasn't exactly that great a lay." He tilted his head to see Frankie around the prosecutor. "Sorry babe."

Ravi's expression became void of emotion and he sat back in his seat as if nothing strange had transpired. The lawyer next to him covered his face with one hand and whispered, "Lord, have mercy."

The Prosecutor blinked rapidly, tilting his head to one side, then brought it upright.

"You do realize you just confessed to the rape of a non-responsive person?"

"What? Nah. We didn't do nothing violent like that. Frankie never knew. Plus, we weren't the only ones hitting that." Blane smirked. "Everyone wanted a taste of Frankie."

"Your honor, I would like to request a recess to consult with my clients," the defense lawyer croaked.

"Granted. I think we all need a minute to gather ourselves." He banged the gavel as he said, "we resume in one hour." He pointed the gavel at him. "Get your people in line, counselor."

Within seconds, the attending media rushed out of the courtroom to give their reports and commentary. The hall outside became a wall of sound.

Once the judge disappeared through the chamber doors,

the defense lawyer whirled around towards his clients.

"What the actual fuck?" He yelled. His partner dropped his hand from his face and let out a deep sigh. "We are trying to keep you from swinging and you spout that shit!"

"What? He's trying to say I hated Frankie and wanted him dead. I was just letting him know no way."

"Good god." The defense lawyer plopped down in his chair, taking a breather before gathering his things. "Let's go. We need to have a come to Jesus moment kind of talk."

⌒

Cat calls and whistles echoed throughout the cell block as Blane and Ravi were paraded down the narrow corridor. The wrist and ankle restraints had just enough slack to prevent them from falling over. Instead of walking, their feet shuffled, the drag along the grates causing a chuff sound.

One guard ahead twirled his billy club, occasionally hitting the bars of a few cells to intimidate their occupants. Two more guards followed the new inmates, pushing them forward when their minimal strides made them slow down.

Blane and Ravi's heights warranted the guards' tension. Both were well over six feet, the norm for swimmers, which meant they towered over their escorts. If their ankles weren't shackled, they could have overtaken them with a few footsteps.

"Alright!" The lead guard stopped before an empty cell. "Here's your new home, princess." He turned and winked at Blane. "Get comfy here during the trial." The bars slid open like an automatic cage. "In you go."

One of the rear guards pushed Ravi out of the way and shoved Blane into the cell. He stumbled forward, catching himself before he could fall. The guard roughly grabbed one arm at the elbow and spun him back around to release the restraints. Blane smirked, rubbing his wrists when the guard left the cell.

"Oh, you think this is fun and games?" The lead guard scoffed. "Let's see if you still think so a week from now." He looked Blane up and down, then snorted.

The cell door slammed shut, leaving Blane inside the tiny

three by five concrete hole. A bunk bed sat against the right side of the wall and a metal toilet jetted out across from the cell door, suspended less than a foot from the floor. Blane sighed as he plopped down on the bed.

"Guess I'll wait for the welcoming service."

He knew the drill. A few inmates would be let loose to teach him a lesson during free time while his cell remained magically open. Despite the warden ordering him and Ravi to be kept away from Gen Pop. No matter how hardened a criminal they send, Blane would lead them on before giving them the business.

What worried him the most came from knowing Ravi since childhood. He or both of them would end up in solitary confinement before the week ended. He almost felt sorry for whoever came after Ravi.

That crazy fucker ain't having it!

Blane sat cross-legged in the middle of the bed and leaned against the wall. He let his breathing slow while his arms hung loose, his palms laid up. Being in jail meant nothing to him. His situation would be temporary, unlike Ravi's. Blane always went with the flow, doing whatever he wanted as long as it didn't hurt anyone. This time, he messed up. Not getting clear of Ravi's insanity.

"Can't believe I'm part of this shit show," he breathed out, closing his eyes.

After the hearing next week, he would sit down with the lawyers his parents were sending and lay it all out for them. Until then, he had to survive. He remembered a few inmates leering at him earlier. He opened his eyes and looked out at the spiral of cell blocks surrounding an open center three levels below.

"Gotta steer clear of those homos and jail bitches coming for me."

For an entire week, he tracked four guys who watched his every move. They leaned close to each other whispering while keeping their eyes on him. Doing fist bumps afterwards.

Bring it, you sickos.

He didn't have to wait long.

On the tenth night in jail, Blane lay on the bottom bunk in his cell when he saw his gate door slide open.

Wonder how much those shit heads gave the guard?

The four men crammed into the tiny cell, blocking the entrance. The biggest one stood before Blane, making sure he had nowhere to run.

"I heard you like ass fucking chicks. Maybe it's time to give you the same business."

"You bet not," Blane said, sitting up. "I'll make you regret that decision."

The big one nodded to the others. One stayed at the entrance while the other two grabbed hold of Blane, flipping him over to pin him face down on the cot. The big guy pulled his sweatpants off and position himself behind Blane.

"Oh, you gone scream when I get in there." He pushed his sweats down below his ass cheeks to let his erection loose. "Hold him down tight," he ordered the two.

Blane struggled to get loose even as he felt the big guy's dick tearing open his anus. *Yeah it hurts like a son of a bitch.* He had a plan. The moment he felt it go all the way in, he clamped his sphincter muscle down hard, putting the man's dick in a vice grip. All the while, he thrashed about.

"Stop moving around!" He could hear pain in the big guy's voice. "Hold him down," he snapped at the two convicts.

"We're trying," the one on the right said, gritting his teeth. "He's strong as hell."

Olympic athlete. Duh. Blane silently chided.

Blane bared the pain and tossed his body side to side, causing a strain on the big guy's johnson and not allowing it to be pulled out.

"I said stop!" He went to hit Blane and ended up striking the guy on the left.

A wet snapping sound followed by the big guy howling in agony made the other two loosen their grip enough for Blane to twist his body more. The man started screaming as he tried to get his dick out. In a panic, the two let him go and moved towards the entrance. Three guards came running and yanked the three out.

Blane relaxed his muscles, releasing the big guy's dick. The broken member slid limp onto the cot.

"Told ya you'd regret it," Blane smirked.

One guard came and hauled him out, still yowling like a wounded animal. Blane turned onto his back and saw the blood splotches that came from his ass being violated. Another guard yelled into his radio, calling the medical ward.

I just have a hurt asshole. No big deal.

He'd been in worse pain than that.

Blane could see other inmates gathered around to get a glimpse of the show backing away as the riot squad arrived to shut the block down. Everyone got ushered into their cells and locked in.

The infirmary reminded Blane of the makeshift medical wing in his hometown after a natural disaster hit when he was a kid. Only the basic care administered until transporting the patient to the main center. He would stay there since his injury didn't warrant more attention.

On the bed to his left, a prisoner lay rigid, his fists and teeth clenched tight as he tried to endure the pain from what looked like a nasty knife wound and a broken leg. Blane squinted to get better focus and saw the abdomen wound seemed wider and more jagged for a knife.

An attendant, followed by four men in white scrubs, escorted a floating gurney. They stopped at the prisoner's bed. While two of the men slid the prisoner off the bed onto the floating one, the attendant turned to Blane.

"Your sicko buddy is an animal. He went too far."

"Right. Cuz, we're supposed to let anyone do what they want to us without a fight."

"Maybe you should have thought of that before you tried to commit murder," the attendant snapped. "What kind of person uses their fingers to stab someone? Breaking limbs. He almost killed those men!"

"So what?" Blane looked further down the row for Ravi. "I don't see him in here."

"He's in solitary confinement." The attendant grabbed the data from the bed's display on the foot of it, transferring it to his tablet. "That's where you're going when they release you from here."

After strapping the prisoner down on the gurney, the entourage headed for the exit.

"For our own safety?" Blane snorted.

The attendant stopped halfway out the door.

"For ours."

Blane waited until they were gone to sit up. His lower extremities throbbed with invisible daggers piercing them in rapid succession. The doctor hadn't given him a pain killer in two hours since the last dose wore off.

Bastards!

He took a few deep breaths and waited for the pain to subside a bit before laying back down. He had an appointment with his family lawyer tomorrow.

Time to get the hell out of here.

Two guards escorted Blane down the dreary grey hallway towards the visitor room third on the right. One pulled his keycard on a zip cord and tapped the outside door panel. A loud buzz erupted, then a click signaling it unlocked. They shoved him inside and slammed it shut.

Sitting at the metal table were two men. His lawyer and the lead investigator, Armondo wore nice suits. Blane pursed his lips, the left corner of his mouth raised. They resembled drug dealers. And probably just as crooked, knowing the dirt on his family's hands. For all he knew, Armondo could be on the take.

Why else would he be there?

"Come." The lawyer motioned for him towards the chair opposite them. "I heard what happened to you. You were supposed to be in isolation until our meeting. The guard is being suspended without pay."

"But not fired, cuz he didn't really do anything to me directly, right?"

"Yes. Unfortunately." The lawyer let out a sigh. "Blane, I need you to tell me what the hell happened."

"I would like to know as well." Armondo rested an elbow on the edge of the table.

"Look, like I said," Blane leaned back in the chair until the front legs rose from the floor. "I had no beef with Frankie aside from his behavior. I had no idea Ravi was trying to kill him. That's not what I signed up for."

"You didn't turn him in." Armondo said.

"Nope. When we heard he lived through that, I gave Ravi the riot act. He said it was an accident."

"And you believed him?"

"I had no reason not to." Blane rocked forward, the chair legs hitting the concrete floor with a bang. "Until now. Knowing he lied to me."

"But you still didn't turn him in. Why did you run with him?" The lawyer asked.

"At that point, I knew there was no getting out of it. I was an accomplice for all of that and what's her face wasn't going to go down without taking us with her."

"I'm sorry, but again," Armondo raised both arms up, his hands splayed open. "You ran with him and didn't try to get away."

"Are you for real?" Blane stared the two men down. "No way was I poking that crazy motherfucker! I stayed to keep him on the level. To have him turn on me and kill me was the last thing I wanted."

"So you're be willing to testify against him?" Armondo asked.

"Nah. Do I look stupid?" Blane rested his handcuffed wrists on the table. "I'll give you my deposition and I split. No courtroom drama for me. I've had enough."

Armondo frowned, crossing his arms as he sat back. His lawyer seemed to contemplate the deal. Blane could tell the two men were on his side. The problem lay with how Ravi would react.

"You're going to have to explain this to the public. They won't like the fact that you just went along out of some presumed fear."

"As opposed to what?" Blane snorted. "I don't care. Whatever. Just get me out of here so I can disappear."

His lawyer nodded.

Looking over at the detective, he gestured at the door.

"Shall we?"

Armondo rose from his chair. "The judge ain't gonna like this one bit."

"No one will." His lawyer stared him down. "I need you to keep it low. We're having you transferred to solitary until we get you out."

"Yeah, don't go apeshit like your man, Ravi. He put four prisoners in ICU." The detective frowned.

Dang, I missed it!

The whole thing must have went down while he was in the infirmary. He heard snippets about it afterwards during recovery. The outcome didn't surprise him. He slumped back in his chair, his legs spread apart, with one leg straight out to the side. His handcuffed wrists rested at his crotch.

Gotta wait a little longer. That's all.

Exclusive interview! Sat in bold letters at the bottom of the television screen with the details in smaller case below it. Blane spills reason why he didn't run or turn Ravi in when he had the chance. The ratings went through the roof as people all around the world streamed the program.

Blane sat on a neutral-colored loveseat in a staged studio. The camera lighting appeared too bright. The background was a CGI of a living room mantel. Across from him, barely in range of the cameras' sight, sat the interviewers.

A well-known pair of entertainment journalists who kept abreast of the story.

Only ten minutes into the interview and the pair stared in disbelief at Blane.

"So, let me get this straight," the first interviewer said. "You simply went along with Ravi to save your own ass?"

"Absolutely. If he went so far as to try and kill Frankie, there was no hope for me if I crossed him."

"You didn't think the authorities would help you?" The second interviewer asked.

"Is that a real question?" Blane snapped.

A short silence filled the room before the first interviewer came back.

"What about the upcoming trial? Don't you want to see justice for Frankie, who you say you love?"

"I love Frankie to death." Blane's hooded expression surprised the two. "But I'm not dying for her. Self-preservation takes center stage on this one."

"Then what are you going to do?"

"Get as far away from that monster, so when he gets out, he'll have a hard time finding me."

The second interviewer snorted.

"You think he'll get out in a couple of years and just, what? Go on some kind of manhunt?"

Blane's voice took on a serious tone.

"Ravi holds a grudge." He stared the two down. The camera zoomed in for everyone to see the seriousness in his eyes. "Until he's satisfied."

The two interviewers leaned back, terrified by his words, and demeanor.

Taking Interest

The dark ocean water swayed like gelatin, nudging Frankie's body, causing her to almost veer off course. Bubbles flowed from her breathing mask as she exhaled. Her dive suit fit tight, eliminating her curves. The blue-black material worked as camouflage so far down.

A giant stingray swam directly below her. She reached out and let her hand glide across as it sped off.

Silence. Glorious yet frightening. Frankie peered up where clearer waters waited. Sunlight shimmered across the bright blue so far away. Topside were people, pollution, and laws. She brought herself into a standing position and waded for a while observing a school of fish. The stingray would probably turn around detecting a meal.

A tiny beep alerted her time was up. The small pouch attached to her gear bumped against her thigh. She had collected the required samples before taking in the ocean view on her own. With an inward sigh, she made her way back to the surface. The sludgy water warmed, becoming more fluid. Sunlight invaded her eyes through the goggles.

Frankie burst from the water, buoying next to a ladder secured to the side of the rig she called home the past three weeks. She removed her mouthpiece and took hold of the lower rung to pull herself along. At the top, she turned around and flopped her butt on the ledge. The wetsuit made a splat, farty sound as it slid across the smooth deck.

"Well, excuse you," Cameron, one of the other divers, joked as he padded towards her.

She looked over at the young man coming towards her. Tall, slender, and muscular, his suit defined every part.

His slightly tanned face had smooth features. The tussled dark hair, still damp, framed his head like a bird's nest above his ears. A pretty boy.

"That's getting old," Frankie sighed.

"Really?" He gave a devilish grin. "Still funny though." He leaned on the rail and stared down at her. "Need some help?"

Frankie glanced up with a frown. Her body had yet to fully recover. Diving, though therapeutic, took a toll on her. Hence, why she sat not removing her gear. *I hate this!*

"No. I'll be out of these in a moment."

His body engulfed hers as he leaned over, whispering in her ear. "Nah. We got a meeting in an hour. Boss man wants a report."

She could feel the hotness of his breath as he spoke. Too close. As always. His lips barely touched the tip of her ears. He sat back to kneel behind her and unzipped the suit. She felt the cool breeze hit her back. Unclipping the sample pouch, he set it against the wall. Frankie slowly yanked at the sleeves, freeing her arms.

She sat slumped over in her plain navy-blue two-piece bikini that contrasted with her paler skin. Her whole being felt lethargic.

Cameron dragged her the rest of the way onto the deck, took off the foot fins, and pulled the suit at the ankles to release her legs. Like wet sausages, they thumped down. She wiggled her toes.

"Can you stand?" Before she could answer, he had her by the underarms, sliding her to her feet.

"Cameron," she tried a forceful tone and failed. "Let go."

"You sure about that?"

Frankie's limbs felt made of jello. It took everything she had to stay standing and Cameron knew it.

"Fine." Frankie gave in. Cameron bent down to retrieve the sample pouch, then handed it to her. "I can't leave my gear like this."

"I'll circle back and get it. Come on. You need to take a shower and get dressed."

Cameron led her to the lower level where the sleeping quarters lay. They entered the long bay.

Each door had a number on it. Frankie used the railing to alleviate Cameron's burden. They stopped at number eleven. Frankie took out her keycard from inside her bikini top and tapped the panel on the side of the door.

"I got it from here, Thanks."

"Glad to be of service, Frankie." Cameron let her go, not without grazing his hand down her hip and across the top of her ass. "See you at the meeting," he said cheerfully, walking away.

Frankie went inside and shut the door, hearing the locking mechanism engage. She slid to the floor and let her chin rest above her chest. If Gerald had witnessed that… she let her mind trail off. Nothing good would come of thinking that.

All twenty members of the diving crew crammed into a tiny space with rows of metal folding chairs arranged in a curve split in the center. The boss used an empty desk that sat in front of the far wall as a seat, one leg dangling off the edge, with the other foot planted on the floor.

She wasn't paying attention to what the boss had been saying. At one point, she certainly dozed off for a few minutes. Cameron offered his shoulder to rest her head. I shouldn't encourage him. The meeting ended up short, which Frankie thanked the gods for.

"So, good work everyone." The boss's voice cut through Frankie's napping, forcing her to sit upright. "As a reward for being ahead of schedule, take the next couple of days off. Enjoy the coast. A skiv will be ready at O' Eight thirty. You get to sleep in." Murmurs of approval circulated. Not being up at the crack ass of dawn always made them happy. "On that note. Dismissed!"

Everyone got up and headed out the room. Frankie eased to her feet. Cameron side eyed her.

"Want me to walk you back?" he asked.

Frankie jolted at the thought. He didn't seem to notice.

"No, I'm good. Going to take a walk along the mid deck for some fresh air before mealtime."

"Alright. Let me know if you need anything." He left first, glancing back once to make sure she still stood straight.

Exhaling to regain her composure, Frankie walked out into the main hall and turned towards the open entryway that led out onto the deck. She strolled along the perimeter of the giant ocean rig to take in the midday sun setting. At one of the corners, she stopped and pulled out her phone, hitting the auto dial key for Gerald. He answered after the first ring.

"Hey, beautiful."

Frankie cringed at the greeting.

"Hey. I just wanted to let you know I have a couple of days off starting tomorrow. The boss is rewarding us for getting the work done ahead of schedule."

A long silence followed. Frankie already knew what dirty thoughts swirled in his head.

"What time are you coming ashore?"

"Skiv is taking us out at eight thirty. I should be there around ten."

"I'll meet you at the crabcake restaurant."

"Okay. See you then."

"You sound tired." She heard the worry in Gerald's tone.

"Yeah, I'm going to lie down after this."

"Take care of yourself, baby."

Ugh! Frankie rolled her eyes. "I am. See you tomorrow." She hung up before he could spew some other sappy term of endearment.

"I love you, I do," Frankie said. "Just…"

Everything seemed so complicated.

⌒

The ferry crew threw the ropes to their counterparts on the docks, who secured the vessel as its passengers debarked. A steady stream of barge workers, finally waking up for the clear day, headed towards the tiny town along the coast. Light conversation mixed with laughter emitted from them. Seagulls circling above cried out their high-pitched squawks that pierced the eardrums. A few workers winced.

"It's too damn early for that." A worker plugged one ear with a finger and jostled it.

"It's almost lunchtime," the coworker next to him laughed.

"Yeah, well, we just got up a couple of hours ago."

Frankie held back a chuckle. The man was right. She felt groggy having slept in later than usual. It happened every time they got a day off. Not enough time to adjust. Cameron walked beside her, his confident stride matching hers. The way he smiled sent red flags in her mind.

He expected something.

With two months left of work study, Frankie wanted to finish it out drama free. Cameron made it hard to imagine, spreading rumors about their non relationship. He constantly invited himself to join Frankie on land stays, despite having met Gerald. As if he could complete on the same level.

They approached the local diner, and she could see Gerald through the window. He sat patiently on the long bench at a table with two chairs on the other side. Not checking his phone or looking around the room. Her skin prickled at a weird sensation coming off Cameron.

The two men's eyes met.

And there it was. What normally appeared to be subtle accompaniment turned into a smirky challenge. Frankie went stiff, seeing the way Cameron stared down at Gerald.

Oh no! Frankie glanced at him in awe.

"Huh, didn't know you were going to be here too, man," Cameron lied loudly. He turned to Frankie. "You should have told me, babe. I'd have come prepared."

The babe reference made Frankie's head snap upright. Gerald tilted his head in puzzlement.

"Why wouldn't I be?" Gerald crossed one leg over the other and leaned back. *God, you sexy…* Frankie felt her breath get caught in her throat. "I'm always with Frankie when I have the time and she's not working."

Cameron pulled one of the chairs out for her. She hesitated, her plan to slide beside Gerald on the bench dashed. She glanced at Gerald again and he gave her a tight-lipped smile. Go with it. Frankie sat down. Cameron joined her in the other seat.

"Well, I take good care of her in your steed." Cameron grinned as he toyed with the laminated menu on the edge of the table. "Right, Frankie?"

Gerald's sense of calm frightened Frankie.

Not one emotion graced his face. A blank canvass. He's fuming inside. *Because he knows I would never.* Frankie took a deep breath and tried not to react.

"I need you to stop trying to provoke him." Frankie turned her head to Cameron. "I'm not sure what your goal is but please, don't."

"What do you mean? I'm just stating a fact, is all."

"That may be true, but it's coming off the wrong way."

"Huh? We like each other's company." He grinned, "What's wrong with that?"

"I said don't," Frankie clenched her fists on the table.

Cameron's eyes narrowed. His entire demeanor turned volatile. Yet his even tone came in contrast.

"I thought we had a mutual understanding." He pointed two fingers, waving them between him and Frankie. Then his hand dropped flat on the table, smacking against the menu. "Or were you just being a tease this whole time? Leading my dick on for fun?"

Frankie sprang from her seat. Cameron followed to stop her from moing away, grabbing her wrist.

"Let go of..."

"Is that it? You think you're special because you used to be some hotshot Olympian?"

He went to pull her closer. His grip released as his body went sailing across the room, crashing into the empty booth on the other side. He quickly regained his footing and stood, moving towards Frankie, then stopped.

Gerald blocked his path to Frankie, his deadpan eyes piercing Cameron's soul. This is bad. Frankie slid an arm around Gerald's waist and pressed her face against the crook of his neck.

"I put up with you coming along with her because I knew you weren't a threat." Gerald's delivery sent shivers through Frankie. "That ends now."

"Ha!" Cameron sidestepped towards the entrance, his eyes never leaving Gerald's position. "You two deserve each other. A broken freak rebuilt on the country's dime and a has been too old to compete anymore."

The diner went silent. People stopped eating.

The staff paused.

Cameron realized he had overdone it. The treatment of Frankie from the first attempt on her life brought shame to the entire country. A subject no one made light of. Frankie kept a death grip on Gerald as she felt him try to get loose. So strong! It took everything she had to hold on. The head waitress walked down the center of the diner to stand before Cameron.

"I'm gonna need you to vacate the premises." Her southern twang held back anger. "And I don't need to tell you why, either."

"Sure." Cameron backed out, still not severing his gaze with Gerald until he turned down the sidewalk.

The patrons and staff resumed their activities, their conversation now steered to the current event. Some of Frankie's coworkers sitting at their tables awaiting food tried to hide their embarrassment. The boss would hear about the altercation.

Damn it!

Frankie felt Gerald's body relax, so she released her hold. Her arms hung lifeless as her tingles ran up and down them, her fingers going numb. Gerald seemed to sense her plight.

"Are you alright?" He spun around and cupped her face in his hands. "Come on. Sit next to me."

They moved as one onto the bench seat. Gerald guided her head to his shoulder to rest on.

"I wasn't going to kill him," he reassured her. "But he was going to be hurt in the worse way."

Frankie tensed. Rage consumed her. The sensation of a boulder pressing on her chest made her breathing hitch.

"That fucking prick," she muttered, fighting back tears.

"I know. Shh." Gerald rubbed her arm. "Don't cry over something like this. I got you."

The head waitress came over to their table. Frankie sat straight, wiping the tears away.

"Your foods coming up in about ten minutes." She pointed to Gerald. "Your man already ordered before you got here. How about some pie in the meantime?"

"That sounds," Frankie sniffed. "That sounds great."

"That's the spirit. Keep ya chin up. It's on the house."

She walked off. Suddenly Frankie's funk lifted. She chuckled, then let out a full laugh.

"Ahh, shit." Frankie turned to Gerald. He smiled.

"There's the Frankie I know."

They both laughed together, stopping when the plate with a giant slice of Dutch apple pie and two forks came. Dessert before the main course would always be a good call.

⌒

"What do you want to do with them now?" The chairwoman asked the rest of the committee seated at the long table in the conference room. "Our golden goose is out of the games and his soulmate refuses to work with us for the greater good of the country."

"We need to give them some space for a while, is all." The secretary of events replied. "Let them see us as a nonthreatening entity."

"Are we?" Montgomery asked, raising his brow. "I can be persuasive if necessary."

The chairwoman raised a hand, palm up, signaling him to stop. In the aftermath of his daughter's scandal, the committee voted, at his suggestion, to demote him and appoint a new leader. She didn't like being the one scrutinized for every failure.

"That's part of the problem. You goaded your daughter into snatching Frankie off the dive team. The catalyst that brought the committee and the Olympic world to its knees."

Montgomery scoffed, tugging down on the lapels of his suit jacket to straighten it. His associate across from him nodded.

"These brats need stern direction. One of them called me a talentless bureaucrat fucker when I tried to guide him through a press junket."

A member snickered as another snorted midway, sipping his drink. A spray of coffee flew from his almost pursed lips.

"It's not amusing!" He slapped the table, making the water carafe shake. The coffee press still had weight and got merely jostled. "That creepy bastard."

"Oh come on!" A member laughed. "They're still young. Let them vent. We are their natural enemy." He wiped droplets of coffee off the table with a napkin. "Until the competition starts."

"We have to bring them back into the fold somehow. Trainers? Consultants?"

"Get Gerald back on this board," the chairwoman demanded, staring directly at Montgomery. "That's our first priority. Even with all that's happened, he is still trusted among his peers."

"As for Frankie," a member at the end of the table spoke, "I think consultant first, then move her up the ladder to trainer without it being blatant."

"She has already proven herself good at coaching with those two fuckheads despite losing them as well in this mess," the coffee drinker said.

"Three Olympic swimmers down in flames in one blow." The chairwoman clenched one hand into a fist. "We're the laughing stock of the planet."

"Let's not go that far." Montgomery relaxed in his chair. "This is a minor setback. We still hold the world record and the most medals for swimming. And diving, I may add."

"If we find Blane, we could get him back as well." The member at the end said.

"True." The coffee drinker took another sip and set his cup down. "One of our goals is to have a next generation to mold. Let's wait until after Frankie and Gerald push out a couple of offspring. Same for other swimmers opting to sit the next games out."

"A shame about Ravi. With a bit more coaching, he would have risen to the next level." The member at the end reached for the water carafe to refill his glass. "Such a waste."

"No love lost for me." The coffee drinker said. "We don't need some psycho who lashes out in the extreme out of envy."

"Then it's settled." The chairwoman swiveled her chair around and grabbed a crystal decanter of whiskey from the rolling tray behind her. "We have a plan." She set the whiskey on the table after pouring two fingers' worth in her water glass.

The whiskey made its round to every member, the coffee drinker pouring some into the last remnants in his cup. When it came back to the center of the table, they rose their drinks.

"To our next successful agenda." The chairwoman said with a hint of sarcasm.

Montgomery watched the newsfeed playing on the eighty-inch flatscreen in the den. He stood legs slightly apart with one hand in his pants pocket while the other held the remote. The same clip ran on every channel. Big, bold letters at the top of the feed read;

CONVICTED EX OLYMPIAN ESCAPES DURING SENTENCING!

The news anchor leaned closer to the cameras. Her eyes widened to the point they almost seemed to bulge out. The fear on her face made the corner of Montgomery's mouth twitch. How comical. As if she would be in danger somehow.

"Be very aware, law enforcement has deemed him extremely dangerous. He may have acquired a weapon along the way, despite taking down multiple officers with his bare hands."

That didn't surprise Montgomery. Nearly half of the Olympians were hybrid or had alien DNA. Some of their hidden talents lay dormant naturally or via drug regimen. Elite humans with more power than the average human.

Which is why Olympians are categorized as dangerous. Why they are not allowed to roam the masses without a leash. Because their emotions are unstable.

Montgomery turned off the feed and tossed the remote on the nearby side table. He shoved his other hand in his pocket and stared at the carpet for a moment. A presence from behind made him look up and turn around. His daughter stood in the doorway, her face terror stricken.

Her cell phone, clutched against her bosom rang, startling her. She fumbled to hit the call icon.

"Hello?" She gasped.

"You saw the news. I need you to ask your father for more security. That nutjob will come after you. Promise me you'll take every precaution." Gerald's voice boomed out of the tiny speakers. "Are you listening?"

"I…yes. I got it." Her voice shook.

"Sharice!"

"I said, I got it!" She yelled back, ending the call.

"Don't worry about this," Montgomery said. "He would be an idiot to show up here."

"I don't live here anymore." Sharice glared at him. "You threw me out, remember?"

"You will stay here until he is caught."

"Absolutely not!" She stepped back from him. "I've been on my own all this time. I can take care of myself. You want to send guards to my apartment building, that's on you."

"Then why are you here?"

"To get some things for the boys." Her face contorted. "I'll be out of your house in a minute."

She stormed off before he could say anything else. Montgomery sighed, dropping his head towards his chest. Their relationship became strained after the investigation. The only reason he forced her to their condo on the other side of town was for her safety. Too many paparazzi vultures swarmed the house. At least they would have to work a little harder to get access to her.

This meant something else. No matter what, he would protect his daughter even if she didn't want it.

∽

Stupid!

Sharice scrambled backwards on the floor, looking for a path to the door before Ravi could get to her. He had come busting through the bedroom balcony, shattering the glass. Shards flew everywhere. It woke her from a tortured sleep, and she knew immediately Ravi had either got the drop on the guards her father would have sent, or he found a way around them.

Now, in her home wearing a only a nightgown, she stared down a crazed former athlete. The look in his eyes permeated the dark. Glass crunched under his combat boots with his advance towards her.

"This is because of you," Ravi said calmly, brandishing a hunting knife.

Where the hell did he get that?

Her blood ran cold. The serrated edge gleamed in the glow coming from the streetlights.

"All you had to do was get rid of the tracks and keep your mouth shut."

"Fuck you! I never wanted to kill Frankie. You're sick in the head."

She flipped over to make a dash for the door. He caught her by the ankle, pulling her away.

Oh hell no!

The moment he got her around to face him, she head butted him. His head snapped back for a second, then he punched her square in the face, catching her off-guard. But not enough to stop her from returning one back. As a former athlete herself, she wasn't going to let him off unscathed.

The two fought like animals, exchanging blows, crashing into furniture. She got a few cuts, trying to dodge each swing of the knife. He moved with precision, like he wanted to dissect her. The noise eventually gained attention. Sharice could hear people in the hallway.

The running of feet.

Huh?

She heard the apartment door burst open with a crackling split, followed by a whine as it swung on its hinges. Within seconds, four men in suits came into the room. Sharice watched in horror as Ravi subdued them in quick succession before heading back out the way he came.

Sharice lay propped on her elbows, breathing hard. Her nightgown covered in her own blood from the four deep gashes on her body. The one on the side of her face right above at the brow line seeped blood into her eye.

Her hands shook as she wiped it away. Tears mixed in as her lips quivered.

I won't cry! I won't!

She held it in for a few seconds more before bawling her eyes out.

Gerald stormed into Montgomery house, making a bee-line to the common room where he knew his sons would be comforting their mother. Montgomery didn't stop him or tell his servants to do so. He walked into the room and saw both boys red eyed, their tears dried up.

Sharice looked like she fought for her life and barely won.

The bandages on her arm and face filled him with fury. She may be an awful wife, but he never wished her dead. He cautiously moved towards them. The boys clung desperately to their mother, as if letting go would mean losing her. Gerald wrapped his arms around all three.

"Why?" He whispered. "Why didn't you let your father help this time?"

"I know," Sharice sniffed. "I thought." She wiped her nose and pulled out of the hug. "I thought I could take him."

Gerald let go and sat up to stare at her. Ravi and her were equal in height and build because she kept up her training regimen to stay fit over the years. That may be. He knew Ravi packed more muscle and weight.

Still, she could hold her own.

"The whole point was to not engage him at all."

He ran his hand atop his sons' heads.

"You were scared, huh?" They nodded. "You have to take care of your mother, okay? Don't let her out of your sight. She's sneaky, you know."

They cracked a smile, leaning into her. She winced without letting them see and took a deep breath.

"They're doing a full manhunt." Sharice got comfortable on the settee. "I don't think they'll find him."

"Well, if he tries to come after you again, he'll be in for a rude awakening."

"Yeah." Sharice grinned. "My father's not messing around this time."

He glanced over at her father standing in the door frame. Pure malice oozed from him.

"Cops are idiots," Ravi said while straddling Frankie on her living room floor by the kitchen.

One hand squeezed her neck, holding her down while the

other held the hunting knife, his new favorite toy. He had cut open her nightshirt, the only thing she wore, to expose her body. The knife grazed across her breasts, creating thin red cuts.

"I couldn't kill that committee bitch because her father sent a bunch of assholes to protect her." He tapped the knife below her breasts. "Everyone is so fixated on her that they forgot about protecting you, Frankie. They assume I wouldn't try a third time." He leaned down, his lips almost touching hers. "Third time's a charm. Isn't that how the saying goes?"

Frankie kept her breathing even, showing no fear. They had fought for what seemed like eternity. The only reason Ravi got the upper hand came from her slipping on a piece of plastic that broke off during the struggle.

"What'll it be, Frankie? Should I gut you like a pig and sever your neck? I'll enjoy watching you writhe in pain while I do it."

Frankie tilted her head, locking eyes with him. He saw the defiance in her. His lips pulled back to expose gritted teeth. Drool dripped onto her neck, sliding down one side to the floor. Right as he raised the knife to plunge it in, she bucked upward, lifting him with her. He slid forward enough for her to bring her thigh into his crotch. The impact sent him flying over her head, and she rolled out of the way into the living room.

Her ankle, already swollen, had turned blue and purple. She couldn't run. She had no intention to either. Ravi regained himself and pivoted to one knee. He came at her. Frankie smirked. She let him tackle her but not bring her down. He struggled to get her back to the floor while trying to get a good angle to stab her. Frankie wasn't having it.

A few feet from the window, Frankie slumped to the floor, surprising Ravi enough for her to use all her strength to lift him. Her ankle screamed from the weight. With one inhuman toss, she sent Ravi through the window. Glass went out with him as he landed in the backyard.

The neighbors on both sides stopped to witness the incident. And that made them aware that Frankie had been in trouble. The wife on the right screamed.

Ravi, bloody from cuts, got to his feet. He glared at Frankie with a hatred she had never seen, then took off through the back gate. The man on the left house talked to a 911 operator on his phone.

Frankie took a deep breath and flopped on her back to the floor. Gerald would be back any moment after checking on Sharice and their sons. Ravi better run far. Frankie snorted.

If Gerald gets a hold of you, it's all over.

CHAPTER SIX

Resurface

The dull LED lamps cast the small bedroom in a grimy blue with hints of grey. No outside light came in. A metal plate attached with bolts covered the window. Only the sound of the occupants breathing could be heard.

The smell of antiseptics and dirty diapers lingered.

Two infants slept fitfully in a makeshift basinet next to the double sized bed. A thin blanket shielded them from the cool air of the ceiling vent that blew every few hours. An I.V. stand held a half empty pouch of what seemed like clear liquid until the light hit it at a certain angle to reveal the tint of green. The tube snaked across the side of the bed where the needle sat embedded in the forearm of its patient.

Her swollen belly slightly moved as the life inside squirmed. The imprint of tiny hands moved beneath its surface. The woman gasped with a hard intake of air. She kept her eyes closed to alleviate the sting from the light reaching her eyelids. The pain medication in the drip would last maybe three hours.

Her legs periodically broken to prevent escape were not healing fast enough. This would be the fourth time.

She counted her days in captivity. Almost two years.

In that span, her body went through numerous experiments, surgeries, and beatings. None of which stopped during her pregnancies. Including now. Her captor took great pleasure in all of it. He would gleefully reminisce about his work study at some clandestine clinic while carving her up.

She surmised their intake consisted of runaways and the homeless youth.

His experiments were straight out of a horror film.

He studied DNA manipulation on Bi-Genetic hybrids with dormant or nonexistent shifting capabilities. The clinic's main goal to permanently change a person's sex came out of misguided agendas from anti-hybrid groups and irresponsible doctors refusing to listen to science.

After six months of torturing his prey, he succeeded.

He raped out of cruelty, not dominance or frustration. The resulting pregnancies were merely another experiment to see if he could achieve it. He often threatened to kill the infants if she didn't find a way to comfort them.

Keep them quiet.

How could she when they and herself were beyond mal-nourished, damaged and constantly sick? She did her best. And, escape to where? She had no clue what kind of place he had taken her.

A beep sounded. The liquid stopped flowing.

Blane opened her eyes.

Footsteps sounded outside the heavy door. The clanking of a bolt, then a high-pitched buzz, made her tense. Easing the door open halfway, her captor stepped into the room.

Ravi tossed a small plastic bag on the table near the door. He glanced over at her, scrutinizing the I.V. pouch's levels.

"How many times do I have to tell you? Taking more won't make it go away. That pain killer caps out after a certain dose."

She didn't respond. He came up next to her, leaning down so that his face hovered less than an inch from hers.

"Look at me," he commanded. Blane turned her head to the side and locked eyes with him. "Answer me when I'm talking to you."

"I'm sorry," she whispered.

"No you're not." Ravi gave her a malicious grin. "You know what?" He stood. "I'm bored. Maybe I should finally just get rid of all of you." He moved to the basinet and picked up the youngest baby. Both infants screamed. "Shut up!"

Blane struggled to roll onto her side, one arm reaching out for her babies. Ravi palmed the child like a football.

"Please," her voice a raspy shriek. "Don't."

"Make them shut the fuck up!"

"Please, give them to me. I'll try. I promise." Tears blurred her vision. She could barely make out his features. "Ravi."

He raised the baby in the air and drew back his arm, ready to throw it against the window's metal cover. Blane moved with lightning speed, knocking over the basinet, and tackling Ravi to the floor. She ignored her pain as she landed on her side, catching her baby. The pain exploded through her whole body. She felt wetness gush out of her. Looking down, she saw the darkness of blood in the blue light.

The other infant had fallen out of the basinet. Ravi pushed himself off the side panel of his medical locker where he landed and got to his knees. He punched her in the small of her back. She howled, then clenched her teeth.

No. No more.

He doesn't get the satisfaction of hearing my pain.

The other infant waddled over and bit Ravi in the fleshy part of his arm. Ravi backhanded him, sending him almost back into the overturned basinet. He resumed attacking Blane, seeing her helpless as the head of the baby inside appeared, coming out on their own.

Blane screamed, not able to move.

Ravi loomed over her, leering. "I'll stomp the shit out of it the moment it's out," he seethed.

Despite the excruciating pain, Blane whirled towards him. To his surprise, she delivered an uppercut right under his jaw. Ravi went backwards, stumbling further before landing on the floor where his head hit the edge of the table.

While he tried to get back up, disoriented from the blow, Blane braced herself against the locker and pushed out her child. She quickly dug her fingers in his mouth and nose to remove the membrane that obstructed his breathing. In one pull, she got it out and her newborn son screamed. The umbilical cord detached, no longer needed.

Hybrids gave birth differently.

Bloody, and out of her mind, Blane went towards Ravi. He held the side of his head while lunging for her. She took advantage of his position and rammed him. He got another punch off into the side of her face. Her body rocked back, then straightened as she straddled him.

"I'll fucking kill you!" Ravi got one hand around her neck as he reached for a metal rod that had fallen off the table onto the floor. "No one will ever find your body or those things you gave birth to. I may have not been able to kill that committee bitch but I got to take my revenge on you for snitching on me."

He swung the rod, hitting her in the shoulder when she tried to dodge it. A lock box on the table caught her eye. She leaned forward, knowing he would take a shot. The metal rod hit her in the chest. Because of the angle, it didn't do as much damage than if he were sitting up.

Blane got hold of the lockbox. *So heavy.* Which worked in her favor as she let it drop onto his forearms. He cried out in pain; the rod leaving his grip.

"You fucking cunt!" He rose his head to butt hers,

Her shaky hands lifted the lockbox again, and she brought it down with as much force as she could muster. She saw his head bounce from the impact. His eyes rolled up in their sockets, but he still seethed, saliva oozing from the corners of his mouth.

Blane lifted it again. And again. And again.

Silence made Blane stop mid downward swing. She looked at Ravi's still body and dropped the lock box behind her. A chance! She didn't know how long he would be out. She grabbed the basinet blanket off the floor and wrapped her newborn inside.

Using the sheets, she swaddled them to her with the newborn in front, the next youngest on her back, and the oldest on the side of her hip. The pain killer would start wearing off soon. The only sounds from the older two were sniffles while the newborn remained eerily silent. Feeling his heartbeat meant he was okay.

A key lay on the floor. By its shape, she recognized it as belonging to a vehicle. How else would he have gotten around to get supplies? Blane snatched it up, her body protesting with every movement.

Outside the door, she found herself in a dark hallway. She used her hands to feel along the walls until she saw light to her right. She turned and made her way to it.

An old wooden door with windows so dingy the light barely cut through sat at the end of that hallway.

She hesitated before it.

What am I doing? No time!

Blane opened the door and stepped into early evening sunlight. Desert. Nothing stretched for miles. She made out a road off in the distance. She looked around and found the vehicle off a ways on the side of what she now saw was an old abandoned house in the middle of nowhere.

An old model sedan that any joe shmoe would drive sat parked nose out. Blane unwrapped the babies and set them in the front passenger seat. She knew that was wrong, but had no time. The oldest slid to the floor, giving more room for his younger siblings.

"Good boy."

Blane pushed the key in the ignition and turned. The engine roared to life, making her wince. *Shit!* He could come running out at any moment. She whipped the car around and gunned it to the road. From there she sped onward until she ran into a town. She looked for a hospital sign and followed it.

Right before dusk, she screeched to a halt in front of the emergency entrance. The staff on duty lounging outside looked over at her. She stepped out of the car.

The two nurses by the door gasped as the paramedics loading up their gear dropped it all and rushed towards her.

"Please. I need help. My ba…" The world tilted and darkness closed in.

Two orderlies, a nurse, and a doctor, wheeled Blane down the corridor in a maddening rush. They burst through the swinging doors of an empty room and began triage followed by a full examination while another nurse came in to start an I.V. drip.

"My god, she's a mess," the first nurse exclaimed. "It's a miracle she's even alive."

"I say she gave birth maybe a few hours before she got here. Hell, less." The orderly used the fabric scissor to cut off the bloody nightgown. He almost dropped them as he cried out, seeing the scars of surgical cuts on her abdomen, chest, and limbs. "God almighty!" He took a deep breath, composed himself, and continued.

"What kind of monster would do this?" The first nurse finished attaching the tube for the drip. "I got this." She stuck Blane's arm with a pen sized blood taker and let it fill up. "We can get a DNA hit with this."

She left the room, and the doctor leaned over Blane.

"She's a strong one. Look at that bone structure. Tall too."

"I bet she's a former athlete." The orderly turned around to grab a gown from the nearby drawer.

The doctor held a hand signaling for him to wait. "We gotta fix this first. She may have stopped bleeding, but there's a lot of damage."

"Come on, doc. She can't just lay here naked."

Another nurse came into the room.

"I'm gonna have to agree on that. She's been through enough. At least give her some dignity, even if we're going to operate." He placed a hand on her bare feet. "This is all messed up."

"What about the babies?" A second orderly asked as he helped his associate get the gown over Blane.

"The newborn is headed to the NICU. We sent the other two for a full checkup."

"Alright." The doctor grabbed a mask and surgical gloves from the drawer on his side. "Let's fix her up."

The lab technician stared at their screen, shocked at the blood results. He turned to the doctor's assistant. Both didn't speak for a long time.

"Is this right? It can't be." The technician tapped the screen to zoom in on the DNA markers.

"This person is designated as a male hybrid with dormant shifting abilities that would never manifest." The assistant looked closer and frowned.

"Yeah. But this isn't a forced shift. Someone did a full on sex change by tapping into it."

"It's barbaric. The procedure itself would take weeks, months to complete since it has yet to be perfected."

"And very much illegal, unethical, and experimental."

The technician's harsh tone matched his anger. "Only a handful of clinics are doing such things on the down low and get shut when found."

"And then to impregnate her to seal the deal." The assistant shook her head. "Monsters."

"Well, the cops are tracing her steps. They should find out where she was being tortured."

The second part of the sequence finished, and an alert flashed across the screen.

Data pertaining to identification is now rerouted to law enforcement. Please contact authorities for any information.

"What the hell?"

The technician slapped his hands on his desk.

"Looks like our Jane Doe is someone important." She patted the technician on the shoulder. "Don't fret. I'm sure they are coming to talk to us and her soon."

⌒

Detective Armondo saw the hospital data come in on his laptop. It started the moment he logged in with an urgent message icon attached. He sipped his coffee mug and waited for it to finish. When it did, his eyes went wide as he turned and spit out coffee onto the floor. He sat straight in his chair, getting comfortable, then read the entire report.

Blane Hardy. The urgent attachment held a message from his superior to head out to the crime scene. The list of injuries, the assessment of bodily harm, and babies.

Dear god! Babies!

And yet, she lived. The detective leaned back in the chair, his eyes never leaving the screen.

A notification tag caught his eye. Whenever an Olympic athlete got into anything dire, the Olympic committee got notified. Of course. He set his mug on the desk and grabbed his coat. No need to wait. Two officers met him at the modified tactical Humvee for law enforcement.

He got in the front passenger seat.

"The quicker the better," he said to the driver. "The faster we can get the local team off this case, I'll feel at ease."

The officer in the back seat brought out a fourteen inch

tablet and tapped the screen to wake it up. Files for the case flooded the entire space.

"It's gruesome. Not gonna lie." He looked over at them. "May need to gird our loins on this one."

"I'll determine that when I see it."

The Humvee sped off onto the main road and headed to the next state over where Blane met evil.

Montgomery paced the living room of his estate with one hand on his hip and the other rubbing the bottom of his lip. The disturbing news of Blane's resurface nauseated him. *This is not how it should be!* The committee's plan to bring Blane back into the fold crumbled.

There was no doubt in his mind who administered such travesties on her. Ravi would be written off. His career and life as a swimmer ended at that moment. A ping alerted him to a communication. The committee probably wanted an emergency meeting.

◠

Blane's eyes flew open as she tried to sit up. Her arms got tangled in tubes running from her body to multiple IVs. She took in the hospital gown and the heavy blanket covering her feet to keep them warm. Not hospital issue. Again, she struggled to sit up.

"Whoa, whoa!" A nurse cried out as he entered the room. "You gotta stay down."

"My babies," Blane got out before coughing. Her throat felt like she had swallowed sandpaper.

"They're being taken care of."

Detective Armondo came in and stood at the foot of the bed. Blane lurched forward, ignoring the pain firing through her body.

"Ravi. Did you find him? You have to catch him before he gets too far." She gasped at the pain flaring. "I gotta get out of here. We're not safe. He can get in anywhere."

"Blane," Detective Armondo said calmly. "It's alright."

She stared at him while the nurse eased her back onto the bed.

"You got him? Did he say anything?" She could hear the desperation in her voice.

"He's dead, Blane."

"Huh?"

"You killed him."

Blane felt her body go cold. A sense of bewilderment and fear gripped her.

"What?" She shook her head. "No, I…I," she couldn't think of any more words.

"You bludgeoned his head with a lockbox. His face looked like ground meat. Cracked the back and front of his skull from that and the impact on the floor."

"That's a bit uncalled for," the nurse chided the detective.

Blane covered her face with her hands and let out an anguished yell. Tears flowed, seeping out past her hands. Anger, relief, and shame sent her into a state of despair. She could hear the monitors going haywire. The nurse scrambled to get a sedative injected into the drip.

"You did good, Blane." Detective Armondo gripped the bar of the bed frame. "No one on the planet would fault you for this."

The sedative kicked in hard. Blane didn't have time to finish her thoughts. She fell into a deep, dreamless sleep.

⌣

Every news media outlet across the globe ran the story of Ravi's demise. They replayed the scandal for days, bringing back memories of how it all began. Again, the committee came under scrutiny as the ones to blame. They should have booted him out after the first attempt on Frankie's life. Blane would get reprimanded with a suspension and back in rotation.

Hailed as a coward for running away after his release, the public now saw the situation in Blane's eyes. They understood his fears from two years ago. Ravi was more than an attempted murderer. He was a monster. One that knew how to administer the worse harm on another human.

Blane sat up at an angle in the hospital bed, watching the split screens on the television mounted close to the ceiling tilted downward. She saw footage of her former self. A tall, muscular man with an entire swimming career ahead of him. For some reason it didn't make her sad.

That body no longer served her. She continued flipping through the feed with indifference.

The doctor poked his head through the half-opened door. "Can I come in?"

He glanced up at the screen. His brow furrowed.

"Sure." Blane shrugged. "This is your domain, not mine."

The doctor went to the side of the bed and pulled a mini scanner from his lab coat pocket. He ran it over Blane's head, chest, and wrist.

"Your vitals are looking a lot better. How do you feel?"

"Like I got the shit kicked out of me," Blane replied nonchalantly. There were seconds of silence. She looked over to see the doctor recovering his composure after shock. "What was I supposed to say?"

"No. That's perfectly accurate." The doctor sighed. "We are waiting on authorization to move you to a different wing before release. The media is starting to get aggressive, finding ways to sneak in here during off hours while you're asleep."

"They never pass up a good story." The doctor hesitated to speak. "What? Oh, are those child services people coming around again?"

"Unfortunately, yes. They're actually outside."

At that moment, loud arguing erupted from the hallway. Multiple voices heated in anger battled each other with harsh tones and profanity.

The doctor's lips thinned. He swung open the door.

"Need I remind all of you this is a hospital?" Four adults glared at him in defiance. "If you can't conduct yourselves like civilized people, I'm going to ask you to leave."

The two committee members took a step away from the two child services reps. Blane could tell what they beefed about. Her babies were up for grabs. The four came into the room. More than allowed. She saw them as a wall of enemies.

"Miss Hardy, your recovery is our main focus. That being said, you are in no condition to care for two infants and a newborn. We're only removing them temporarily from your care."

"That's a hell no." Blane tossed the remote onto the bed at her lap. "Who do you think kept them alive all this time from that animal?"

"We get that…" The woman tried to counter.

"No, you don't," Blane spat.

"We are prepared to house them, mother included, in a secure facility for rehabilitating athletes." The committee member interjected. "There will be a childcare wing on site."

"Why? I'm not part of the swim team anymore. Why are you staking claim to me and mine?"

"Whether you're competing or not, you are still part of the Olympian community," the second member said. "Your wellbeing is our priority."

That statement gob smacked Blane. She always knew the committee had an agenda.

"We will get an injunction, if necessary," the other child welfare rep threatened. "Blane was up on criminal charges. Attempted murder at that, and now she's actually killed someone. We need to evaluate her mental state and the best environment for those children."

His obvious disdain for Blane sparked the argument anew.

"How dare you bring that into this!" The first committee member roared. His face's dark skin took on a reddish tint as his eyes bulge with rage.

Exactly. That fucker. Blane chewed on her bottom lip.

"I'm stating the facts!"

More yelling and accusations flew, both sides not acknowledging her presence. Already determining she would be a nonfactor in the discussion. It went on for another minute or two. Then the male rep took it up a notch.

"That," he pointed to Blane, "has no business raising anything," he yelled back.

"We will file for suitable guardians and take custody of those children as we see fit!" The female rep added.

Blane narrowed her eyes, ready to tell that woman where to shove it, when two people she never expected burst in.

Angry, and out of breath, Frankie Donovan yelled, "You're doing no such thing. Theyre coming with us. We're taking them in."

"You want a fight, bring it on," Gerald goaded them. He locked eyes with Blane. "You okay with that?"

Blane felt tears welling up. *This again!* She was tired of crying. It didn't fix anything. Frankie came over and grabbed her face, averting her gaze at her.

"I need you to be okay. You deserve to be okay."

The two stared into each other's eyes for what seemed like an eternity, the rest of the occupants silently watching them. Blane tried to stop the pain in her chest. She burst into tears, leaning into Frankie's breasts like a small child.

"We're done here." Gerald stood at the foot of the bed, blocking the four's view.

The child welfare reps backed out; their faces contorted in fury. Both committee members' expressions shifted to something shady. The doctor ushered them into the hall for a stern talk.

〜

Plushy. Almost too comfy.

Blane's body sank into the papasan, letting it mold around her. It sat near the far wall of the living room, giving her a full view of the room and the bay windows looking out the front yard. She lay curled up in a cream-colored, short-sleeved t-shirt and light grey lounge pants. Her thick wavy hair hung loose down her back, its weight straining her neck. She refused to cut it. The babies liked playing in it.

All three slept in the playpen in the center. The thing looked out of place among the neutral toned furniture and glass side tables. Greys, whites, and tans filled the entire front of the house. That aesthetic comes from Gerald's bougie ass. Blane smirked, shoving her hands between her thighs to warm them.

The front door opened.

Blane glanced over to see Frankie barely getting inside before the oldest infant sped past her, making the sharp turn around the divider headed staright for Blane.

Aww shit! She didn't try to block the little boy. Just braced herself for impact. He dove right into her chest, his face planted in her breasts. He raised his head and grinned.

"Yeah. Get off." The little boy didn't listen. Instead, he smacked his tiny hands on her cheeks and squished them. "Seriously." Blane's voice came out muffled.

"Pretty," he giggled.

"Jacob, stop that!" Frankie lifted the boy off.

His face scrunched up and tears sprung.

"Fine." Blane sat up from her comfy position long enough to take him back. He snuggled against her as she laid down. "Such a brat."

"Because you cave and let him have his way," Frankie said. She checked on Blane's babies. "How long have they been asleep?"

"I don't know. A few hours maybe."

"You can't let them sleep all day." Frankie wiggled their toes, then poked their cheeks.

"Don't. They wake up, they'll be all greedy and I don't feel like feeding all of them yet."

"First of all, they should be on different eating schedules for now. What are you doing?"

Blane stared at her. Frankie plopped onto the sofa next to the papasan.

"I can't help if I don't know what you're thinking. Talk to me, Blane."

"What's there to say? I can't go back to being a guy. Don't want to anyway. My kids are my world. This is how it is now." She tussled Jacob's dark hair. "What's the point of regretting stuff that happened before?"

Blane averted her gaze from Frankie.

Yeah, no point.

Because she relived it all in her nightmares.

The Last Lap

Not one media person got a glimpse of Blane during the investigation or after. The committee shut them all out to give her the time she needed. Wild speculations regarding her mental state circulated, how she looked, and if the law would bring the hammer down for Ravi's death.

There wasn't a jury on the planet who would convict her. Prosecutors found themselves on the bad side of the public whenever they hinted at bringing charges. Add to that the Olympic committee throwing their weight and money behind her, the act went moot in less than two months.

Ravi's family did interviews for two major networks then went silent. His parents came across as cold. Both spoke calmly about their son, painting him as a young man on the path to do great things. That pressure from the athletic community caused his troubles.

All excuses.

The U.S. Olympic committee convened at their headquarters in a conference room large enough to accommodate the full body. Twenty members in attendance showed various expressions of disdain and frustration. The ones in charge of the Aquatics Division looked even more so. Yet another travesty to handle on their end. Gymnastics and Ice Skating had a ton of scandals but nothing like what they faced.

Montgomery spoke first. He wanted to get it over with.

"We must regain the public and our athletes' trust. I fear the only way to do that is to start over. Our top competitors are no longer viable."

"They're not even thirty yet!" A member snapped. "You can get another four years out of them and a couple of more."

"Morale is," the aquatics chairwoman said, "lacking. And I'm being optimistic."

"If that's the case," the gymnastics chairman said, leaning forward, "then you might as well put your team on hiatus and implement the breeding program as planned."

"You limp along with the team you got, hope for a comeback and start training their children for the next generation." The head of Track and Field lit a cigar and pulled one of those venting ash trays out of her purse sitting on the floor beside her chair. She took a couple of hard puffs and set the cigar along the ashtray's rim. "Do it in rotation. You can't have half your team out on child leave."

"We've already started with Frankie. The facility will be contacting us about the most compatible team member for Blane." Montgomery pointed to the cigar. The Track and Field chair reached down, pulling another from her purse, and tossed it to him. He caught it in one hand. "Hopefully she's not too far gone not to accept a soulmate."

"I don't understand," another member frowned. "Blane has three offspring from Ravi. He wasn't exactly top tier but still an Olympic level athlete."

"According to the DNA testing, Ravi wasn't compatible. Actually quite toxic." The aquatics chair replied. "His DNA percentage is less than ten. Those infants are purely Blane's."

"Which I see no issue with," the gymnastics' chair said. "A top five Olympian is good enough for me."

"With Blane permanently female, maybe we can persuade her to switch over if her body can get into competition shape." One member suggested. "We couldn't get Frankie back in that capacity. This is another chance at doubling our stats."

"That ship has probably sailed." The Track chair said, taking another puff. "Our best option is getting her into the trainers' program. Our main agenda is to combine top DNA to produce super athletes." Smoke swirled downward into the ashtray. "Plus, a soul mate is another ball game."

The room went silent for a moment. They contemplated the needs of their agenda going forward. Still in the early stages, it required a fresh approach.

"Regarding Frankie," the chair of the committee finally

spoke. "And Gerald. You need to coax them back into the fold as consultants or coaches. Their expertise is essential to raising new talent."

Montgomery finished clipping the tip of his cigar and lit it with his engraved pocket lighter. He took a few puffs, then leaned back in his chair, staring at the ceiling as he blew smoke. He lowered his gaze to stare at them.

"I'm working on it. The first step is to revitalize their passion for the games."

"And how on earth would you do that?" The Track and Field chair scoffed.

"Oh," Montgomery caught the ashtray she slid towards him and tapped his cigar against the rim. "I have a plan in motion."

⌒

A group of athletes loitering near a sundae shop at the training dome's outdoor food court stopped talking as their gaze tracked the newcomer. Their eyes bulged while their mouths dropped open.

"Holy shit! Is that Blane?" The first blurted.

"Damn! If I'd have known this was how he looked as a chick, I'd have hit that in a heartbeat."

The second licked his lips, shaking his head.

"Yeah, that's hot as fuck."

The third scanned Blane's body like a creep.

I can hear you, you fucks.

Blane walked towards the donut shop next to the sundae stand. She would normally blend in with the other athletes. Her notoriety made that impossible now. Frankie had kicked her out of the house for the day, saying she needed to get some fresh air and get back in touch with society.

She waited in line, conscious of her soft body despite working out three times a week. According to the doctors, getting her muscles back would take more time. Her six-foot three frame felt heavy.

The giant boobs ain't helping either.

Blane glanced down at them. Double Fs.

Ironic.

Her already sculpted ass became bulbous. The mounds equaled her bosom.

Similar whispers of talk like the three guys swirled around her. She found it comical considering she wore her usual plain short-sleeved t-shirt and grey sweatpants. Her hair lay loose and wild, with a few tangles from the baby yanking on it. Those guys would have never known what she could look like, since her shifting abilities remained locked and dormant. If Ravi hadn't…

Blane placed a hand over her mouth as nausea hit her. She took a few deep breaths, then removed it.

"Hey," a male athlete came up to her. "Let me get that for you," he nodded at the donut shop's menu.

"And what?" Blane shot back. "I owe you a date and you brag about how you almost got in my drawers?"

"Really, Blane?" the guy sneered at her. "You always got something vulgar to say."

"Oh, you thought because I'm a chick with kids, my personality was supposed to change?" Blane snorted. "Fuck off. I'm still me."

"Well, that's a turnoff," the first by the sundae shop sighed.

"Speak for yourself," the third said. "I'm all in."

"Huh." The guy in line sneered. "Maybe you'll get a taste of having your ass blown out like you did all those chicks you hooked up with over the years."

Blane turned to her side and stared at him.

"What are you getting on about? Those bitches let me ass fuck 'em. If they didn't want it, they should have said so before that."

"See, I was trying to be nice and buy your order. Yeah, you're right. You still got a nasty mouth. You should be grateful anyone wants that," he looked her up and down, "after being used up and shredded."

All hush fell on the courtyard. The guy stepped back from her while looking around at the other patrons. Glares bore into him.

Blane stood stunned, not sure how to process his words.

Her eyes narrowed and her lips pulled back, baring her teeth. Before she could respond, an arm swung in front of her, blocking the guy's view.

"You're out of line."

Fitzsimmons stepped in front of Blane.

"How can you even say some shit like that?" the second sundae guy asked.

"I'm sorry," the guy mumbled. "I know that was wrong. I fucked up." He raised his gaze to meet Blane's. "I didn't mean that."

"Whatever." Blane clenched her fists at her sides, fighting back the hurt that threatened tears. "I couldn't care less what you people think of me."

The guy walked away, glancing back once with sorrow. Fitzsimmons turned around to face her.

"I know that hurt. You're not okay." He nodded at the donut counter where the cashier waited for her to order. "I got this."

Blane nodded back. The donuts were more for the babies than her. None of them should be eating so much sugar.

"Thanks, Fitz." She opened her hands and rubbed them on the sides of her thighs.

"You are super stunning. Can't blame the guy, really."

"Then he needs to figure out how to talk to chicks cuz that ain't it."

Fitzsimmons snorted, bending slightly forward as he covered his mouth. He gave her a side glance.

"Uh, you can't talk. All those women were not impressed with your lack of charm. They wanted to hook up with the fifth ranked Olympian on the planet."

"Fuck you, Fitz. I had plenty of game."

"Sure."

They walked up to the counter. Blane ordered a dozen assorted donuts. More than she needed.

⁓

Facility three housed the abandoned hybrid children and those with talents. There, the scientists did experiments on them while raising them in a secluded environment. It touted the latest in medical technology. They were the first place to go if you wanted to know more about Bi-Genetics biology, their DNA, compatibility runs, and anything else related to hybrids.

Zoned as their own countries with full autonomy, each facility had rules for contact with the outside world. Facility three despised government channels. Organizations with sketchy agendas fascinated them.

The facility representative sat at the conference table among the US Aquatics Olympic Committee members. He slowly sipped hot tea from a fancy China cup with a matching saucer. His dark brown hair reminded one of milk chocolate flowing in a fountain. It hung in slight waves an inch past his shoulders. Long lashes accentuated the bright hazel pools of his eyes.

His calm demeanor and purposeful movements made the committee nervous. The austere black suit and tie with a white shirt didn't help. A bodyguard in similar attire stood near the closed door. Also unmoving, not cracking a smile. The representative set down his tea.

"I see you wasted no time implementing our suggestions." The smooth tenor of his voice oozed disdain. "You sicced Erik Fitzsimmons on Blane within a month. I take it you've moved forward on the others."

Montgomery tsked, his body tensing with ire.

His colleague on his right held his arm back. He relaxed, taking a deep breath, and replied,

"Isn't that what you recommended? The sooner we get them to produce offspring, the less down they need. Your people said that."

"Hmm. True."

"Why are you here? We have no business with your facility at this point."

"Oh?" The representative raised his brow and made eye contact with Montgomery. "Every child must go through intake and registered for monitoring in case any develop talents."

The committee simultaneously took sharp inward breaths. Intake at the facility subjected infants to extraction of brain fluid, body scans, and blood draws. They used shock treatment to activate pressure point cylinders. Montgomery remembered the news story that aired not long after aliens revealed themselves on Earth.

"We never made any such deal!" The chairwoman cried.

The representative looked over at her deadpan.

"There is always a deal with hybrid humans. Especially those in the higher tier, like the Olympics."

"What if some of the offpring don't show any Bi-Genetic traits? You'd have caused trauma to an infant for no reason." Montgomery knew his point fell on deaf ears.

Picking his tea up, the representative took another sip, his eyes narrowed above the cup's rim.

"You want to use our services at no charge? You should know better."

"Damn monsters!" Another member threw out.

The air in the room suddenly went dense and an invisible weight crashed down on the members, pinning them where they sat. The member who utter monster lay with the side of his face on the table, his teeth gritted in pain. Montgomery, plastered into his chair, his back and neck arched painfully, saw the amber glow in the representative's eyes.

Right as the pain became almost too much to bear, the weight lifted, his eyes reverting to normal.

"Careful." He said, continuing to sip his tea. "I'm quite sensitive to name calling."

Montgomery lifted his head off the back of his chair. This solidified why Bi-Genetics with talent frightened him.

❧

Gerald stared Montgomery down with contempt. The man rarely came to visit and only when he required a favor for his daughter or from Frankie. He stood in the kitchen across from him on the other side of the island while Gerald poured himself a cup of coffee. Montgomery didn't ask for any and Gerald didn't offer.

"Frankie's not here. I'll let her know you stopped by."

Gerald's gaze never left the man as he leaned on the counter sipping his coffee.

Montgomery took his hands from his pants pockets and turned to him, letting out a sigh.

"I'm here to talk with you, Gerald."

Alarm bells went off in his head. "I'm not coming back on the board." He set his mug hard on the surface.

"I'm not asking you to." Montgomery tilted his head. "Are you going to let me tell you what it is or are you going to stand there continuing to speculate?"

A tad embarrassed, Gerald stood straight, relenting to the situation. Montgomery saw his cooperation and placed his hands flat on the counter.

"There's an all-star Olympics game coming up in four months. A chance for the old guard to show the new kids how it's done."

"You're joking." Gerald glared at him when he didn't answer. "What does that have to do with me?"

"We want you to participate. As you know, a husband-and-wife team, old enough to be grandparents, won the gold in your event last round. Surely, you're capable of giving them a run for their money."

"What's the catch?" Gerald wasn't buying it.

"No catch," Montgomery lied. "The country needs the world to see we are still in the running. That even our veterans are good enough if necessary."

"So the committee wants to strut us around like peacocks to show our false might?" Gerald snorted and took a swig of coffee. "Cut the shit, Phil. No one is going to swallow that garbage."

"Nevertheless, we have put in our application and were accepted." Montgomery scanned Gerald's body. "I'm sure it won't take long for you to get back in the flow." He turned around, waving a hand in the air. "I'll see my way out. Don't forget to log into the system to register."

Gerald waited until Montgomery drove off before he slammed down his mug, sloshing coffee across the counter.

"Son of a bitch!"

They got me. They got me good.

"Fuck," he sighed slowly. "I should have seen this coming. So stupid."

He had let his guard down since the committee kept away for the past two years. Three years would be asking too much. Gerald grabbed a few paper towels from the roll over the sink and wiped up the spilled coffee. He wouldn't refill his mug. Caffeine would only fuel his anger.

Cool water cascaded from the kitchen sink faucet onto the large colander filled with fresh fruit. Flecks of dirt and greenery seeped out of the holes, then down the drain. Frankie stood drumming on the edge of the sink as she watched. She didn't turn around as she spoke.

"Do you think you'll be ready by then?" Referring to the all-star games after he told her.

"What?" Gerald grabbed a bag of portioned iced cubes from the freezer part of the refrigerator. "Why wouldn't I be? I got four months."

"Well, I mean," Frankie's nose wrinkled, making her mouth twist upwards to the side, "you are kinda old." Frankie shut off the water and shook the colander, tossing the fruit around.

"Frankie," Gerald warned her, gritting his teeth. He set the ice next to the container of protein powder by the blender. "Don't."

"You mad?" Frankie tilted her head over her shoulder. "Seriously? Tell me again why you're still not competing?"

Gerald paused. His injury had long healed. He didn't really have a valid reason other than fear. He braced himself on the island and his breath hitched.

The 2016 incident replayed in his head. The snap of his right leg and left arm as they hit the hard packed snow. His head ramming into the barricade before everything went black. The sound of the helicopter life flighting him out to the nearest medical facility in Sochi.

Arms wrapped around him from behind, startling him out of his reverie. Frankie laid her head against his back. He realized his breathing had become anguished.

Damn it!

"I'm sorry. I didn't mean to bring that up."

"It's fine." Gerald placed one hand on top of hers at his waist. "That was in the past. I'm over it."

"Liar."

Gerald managed a tiny smile. "Yeah."

"Alright." Frankie let go. "I'll help you."

"Huh?" Gerald turned around. "Do what exactly?"

"First of all." Frankie gave him a side glance. "You need to get back in Olympic shape. Not just athletic."

"That won't be a problem."

"Umm…when was the last time you skied for five miles straight under a time limit?"

He opened his mouth to reply, then shut it. He had nothing. She was correct. The most he had done involved some leisure skiing during vacations. Nothing at any serious level. He glanced at his abdomen. Still harboring a six pack, it needed tightening up.

"Fine." Gerald ran a hand across his midsection, now feeling unhappy about its state.

"Those old farts went up against competitors half their age. Hell, more than that. And they won gold, beating all of them. What's your excuse again?"

"Okay, first. They are not 'old farts'," Gerald rose to make air quotation marks with two fingers. "They're seasoned Olympians." Frankie snorted while scooping powder over ice in the blender. "Stop laughing. Second, I could come in right behind them if I wanted."

"Why not win?" Frankie tossed a handful of various fruit into the mix. She pushed the top for the blender down. "I won't help you if you're not going to win."

She hit the button. The grinding of ice and chunks of fruit being pulverized drowned out all other sounds in the house. Gerald looked over and saw Frankie staring at him with her finger on the button.

I get it.

The fierce look in her eyes made his soul shrink inside. He forgot how competitive Frankie could be. Gerald had a feeling his wife would be worse than his old trainer.

Upstream

Hordes of spectators lined the pathways of the Biathlon event. The route opened for practice runs before the games started the next day. Lots of athletes reconnected with jovial laughs and harsh rubbings of criticism. A thin layer of clouds blocked the sun's intensity, its paleness still bright enough to hurt everyone's eyes. Less wind meant a good shooting day.

Less calculations.

A group of younger athletes surrounded the current gold medalists on the slope atop the finish line. They fired off questions mixed with congratulations and hints of envy. The two let out hardy laughs.

Redford Banks' full beard glistened from melting snow, his bushy brows raised high as his eyes widened. His wife, Janie, stood beside him, her head thrown back. The blonde pigtails peppered with grey hung down the front of her jacket.

Digging his poles into the snow, Gerald averted his gaze. They were indeed older than him by almost ten years. The man's barreled chest and barely there beer gut added insult to his mood.

His suit felt tighter than normal despite his body being in the best shape it's ever been. Frankie drove him like a slave.

"Ivers!" The man's voice boomed, carrying down the slope to assault his ears. Gerald winced, not wanting to engage. He had no choice. "Is that really you?"

Gerald looked up and saw the two within a few yards of him. Time to play nice.

The big guy whacked him on the back, pushing Gerald's upper body to bend over as he planted his weight so he wouldn't fall. He let out another hardy laugh.

"Look at you! Still got that strong core. Take more than that to knock you down."

"Is that what you were trying to do?" Gerald stood straight. "Nice seeing you, Red."

"Well, it would have been funny, for sure."

"Come to show up the newbies?" His wife asked.

"You're both here. No need in me joining in on the fun."

"Oh come on!" She gave a sheepish grin. "You gotta give us a run for our money," she chided.

"Wait, you're getting paid for this?"

"Sponsors and all," Red grinned. Then his expression turned serious. "Those committee fuckers got you on a leash, don't they?"

"Look," Janie placed a hand on his shoulder. "Doesn't matter. You do this because you want to. Not for their sake."

"Show those assholes you still got clout." The big guy smiled wide. "If you beat one of us, I'll buy the first round."

Gerald caught sight of Frankie in the crowd close to the barricade. "If?" He smirked. "I may have been out of the games for a while. That doesn't mean I can't bring it."

The two followed his gaze.

"Is that really Frankie?" Janie asked, dropping her hand.

"Oh!" Red laughed. "You gotta impress your woman. I get it."

Gerald tilted his head back, inhaling the arctic air. He breathed in through his nose and let out a huge puff of air. His chilled breath drifted upward. He glanced over at the two. Beating them would be a miracle. As much as he believed in himself, reality stared him in the face.

A group of four younger competitors walked towards the three of them. Gerald recognized one as the seventh-place winner. Top ten looked great on a portfolio. Medal wins got you fame and power. Red and Janie turned away.

"That's all you, son," the big guy called out while walking off. "Encourage them well."

Gerald sputtered a protest to not be left alone. The four stopped a few feet from him.

"Mr. Ivers!" The seventh place athlete said with excitement. "I can't believe I get to meet you."

"I'm just a guy."

Gerald awkwardly fidgeted with his poles.

"Nah," the one next to the kid said. "We studied you growing up. You're iconic."

"Yeah, none of us would have known how to hone our skills if it weren't for you," the third gushed.

"Totally, spot on." The fourth added.

"I really appreciate that."

The group talked with him for a few more minutes, then left to get to the start point. Gerald waved after them.

"Have a good run!"

"Yes sir!" They yelled back.

He took another deep breath and made his way to do the same. The first run would get the kinks out. Only two were needed for good muscle memory. Practicing in the mountains at home didn't hit the same as the actual track.

Everything ached. Gerald regulated his breathing. He kept his eyes closed while lying on the firm hotel bed that now felt extremely comfortable. The top part of the thermal body suit bunched around his waist exposed his bare chest that rose and fell in slow succession.

He could feel his heartbeat thumping against his hand. The darkness helped ease the throbbing in his eyes.

The mattress on each side of him sunk down, and a presence loomed above him. He felt Frankie's thighs straddle atop his waist while her hands slid up to the top of his pecs. Her lips lingered above his. Her breath smelled of sweet fruit.

How am I supposed to resist that? He lifted his head, so their lips met and kissed her deeply. She inhaled, forcing their mouths to seal.

When they disengaged, Gerald, finally able to take a breath, forced his eyes open. Frankie looked concerned.

"What is it?" He whispered.

She pushed around his sides and right below his hips. He winced, sucking air through his teeth.

"I'll get some heat pads and oil so I can massage that out."

She moved to get off. Gerald stopped her, grabbing her waist. "Not yet. Just a little longer."

He closed his eyes again, feeling Frankie's weight pressed on his body.

"So needy." Frankie eased off him.

Her tone carried her exasperation.

"I always need you." He tried to clear the pins and needles tingling where she had pushed.

"Well, I need you in top shape for the first run tomorrow. I'll never let you live it down if you don't get in the top five right off the bat."

Gerald looked over at her tinkering around in the medical kit supplied by the committee. Slave driver didn't correctly identify her training aesthetic.

God, I love you.

He shut his eyes once more, seeing her walk back to him with an arm full of supplies. Frankie was going to make him feel better.

The number of spectators and camera crews surprised Gerald. All-star events didn't get much press and tickets were limited. Mostly rich people or those with influence grabbed them for networking. Attendance appeared triple in size. Regular folks outnumbered the privileged.

That's why all the committees stressed participation!

Gerald shook his head, sending flecks of snow flying back into the air. He would tuck his hair inside his suit's hoodie when he got to the start point. The overhead holo-screens showed each stop section and a feed of the crowd at the finish line. He caught sight of Frankie immediately, despite the cluster surrounding her. Her expression told him she expected him soon.

Alright. First runs always made him nervous. No matter how much he gauged the competition, there would always be someone with more ambition, more conviction, than him. At the same time, his confidence stemmed from others under-estimating him.

In his younger years, the masses saw him as the pretty boy. His older self, they deemed him the hot guy. Apparently, you weren't supposed to be good looking in his sport.

He wore a long brown trench coat usually for ranchers.

Its fabric blocked wind better than the new windbreakers' thin material. Most of the young competitors sported bright colored body suits with sponsor logos.

Must be nice. Those days are over for him.

"All participants. Please proceed to the starting line."

The female voice boomed through the speakers.

Gerald adjusted the rifle's strap across his shoulder and headed off. A short burst of panic came and went, making him a tad nauseous. He took a few deep breaths to calm himself.

Show 'em what you got!

The run went smoothly. Like he had fallen into the zone, oblivious to the other competitors. He moved with clarity, not missing any targets while gaining speed towards the end. His mind didn't register the cheering of the crowds until he crossed the finish line. Startled, he glanced up and saw his time and ranking.

Third. Right behind the reigning gold medalists and a newcomer. I'm in the top five. Frankie jumped up and down in a frenzy, a huge grin on her face. The elation flying off her seemed contagious as others around her followed suit.

Red came over and slapped him on the shoulder.

"Well, hot damn! I'm gonna have to take this more seriously if you gone run it like that!"

Gerald pursed his lips and stared at him. He pushed the hoodie off, letting his dark mane loose to let the wind do what it pleased. Strands of hair whipped into his face like a spider's web.

'You should be that regardless. These All-Star games are not for slacking off."

"Whoa!" Red raised his hands in protest. "No need to get all insulting."

"I…" Gerald swiped the hair from his face. "Sorry. That's not what I intended."

Red laughed, throwing his head back.

"Ivers, you're always so intense. Loosen up, son." He whacked him again. Gerald couldn't hide wincing. "See you at the final round."

The moment Red left, Frankie nearly mowed Gerald

down with a head on attack, hugging him at the waist to stop his fall. Her lips smashed into his. The holoscreen displayed their kiss for the world to see. Not caring, their mouths open for a deeper connection.

He could hear the whispers from the crowd.

"Is that Frankie Mel Donova?"

The committee stressed keeping their relationship a secret until the right timing.

Hmph! There goes that.

Gerald thought this may be their doing. Why now? They ended the kiss with him staring into her eyes. Frankie seemed to have the same thought. She let out a long sigh and pulled him closer, laying her head in the crook of his neck.

"Now you need to hold it or break it." Her hands came over his back, resting below his shoulders. "You know what I want, though."

"Yeah." Gerald smirked. "You want me to win."

They stood for a few seconds amid the swirling speculations, then moved out of the way for the next athlete coming down the last stretch. Fourth place would come almost two minutes behind the leaders. Gerald checked the times again. Way faster than normal. The rest of the pack would need a miracle to keep up.

And, that's how we like it.

His competitive streak fired on all cylinders. Tomorrow he would give the big guy and the newbie a real run.

"Damn Ivers! You were right on my ass the whole time." Red wrapped his arm around Gerald's neck, putting him in a choke hold. "That poor kid got discouraged halfway and slowed down."

Cheers roared, drowning out the AI voice nnouncing the winners. Gerald could see Frankie forcing her way through the masses to get to him. Janie came up and dragged Red's head down for a kiss with Gerald still in his grip.

Gerald glimpsed the young man who came in third. Not the one from yesterday. He whooped and hollered, jumping onto the back of another man. Probably his coach. The third winner from the day before crossed the finish line in eighth place. His dejected expression coincided with his demeanor. He stamped his poles into the packed snow and cursed.

The kid reminded Gerald of his first Olympics when he, too felt angry and disappointed in himself. He and the big guy were so far ahead, faster than yesterday, he must have panicked trying to keep up. Which was his first mistake. He should have calmed himself and went at his own pace.

"He's young. He'll get over it," Gerald said as he wiggled his way out of the choke hold. Frankie ran up and stopped a few inches from him. She met his gaze. Neither said anything for a few seconds. "I didn't win. I'm sorry."

"Huh?" Frankie's face scrunched. Gerald stared at her, confused. "You got silver after not competing for over a friggin decade." She reached out and pulled him to her. Her mouth covered his as her tongue invaded. When she let go, she smiled. "I'll take it."

"You know what?" Red yelled over his shoulder, his wife snug against his chest. "I'm gone buy you a round anyway."

"Here they come. I'm surprised they didn't make their way through before we got down." Gerald nodded to their left. Red let out a heavy sigh. "Our bane of being the best."

The horde of reporters and media outlet correspondents rushed as fast as they could in the snow towards them. One set went straight for Red while another swarmed Gerald. A middle-aged man in a too tight snowsuit shoved a mini mic in Gerald's face.

"Gerald Ivers! Congratulations on winning silver. How does it feel to medal after over a decade?"

"Uh, I'm still an Olympian." Gerald would take that from his wife, not this asshat.

"My apologies. I wasn't trying to be insulting."
Bullshit.

An anchorwoman pushed her way in.

"How did you prepare for this run? Truth be told, our colleague here isn't wrong. It's been a while."

"My wife helped me get in competition shape and with my training."

"Your wife?" The reporter's gaze fell on Gerald and she noticed Frankie attached to his side, her arm around him.

"This is your wife?"

"Yes."

An eerie hush fell over the event area.

"Isn't that…" she was about to ask.

"Frankie Mel Donova helped you train?"

A reporter from behind yelled out.

Something about the way he blurted it out made Gerald tense. An ominous feeling crept in. Within seconds, the press changed gears. They bombarded Frankie with questions.

"How long did it take you to learn the sport?"

"Was it hard to keep Gerald motivated?"

"When did you decide to help him?"

"Are you going back to swimming?"

Frankie leaned forward. The cameras caught her face. The holoscreen displayed the feed and everyone got to see her larger than life-sized.

"First of all, the person you're supposed to interview is the medalist." Her harsh tone left no bones about how she felt. "Secondly, I retired after my fucking heart imploded in my chest. So no, I'm not going back to swimming. What the hell is wrong with you people?"

The hush deepened. A loud, raucous laugh broke the mood. Red pointed to Frankie.

"She may not call herself Mel Donova anymore, but that is pure, unfiltered Frankie."

Little by little laughs erupted. Frankie frowned.

"So you're the new power couple of the Olympics," the first reporter said.

"Oh, hell no," Frankie rolled her eyes.

The interviews went the normal route after that. Each media person snaked around the athletes to get a shot at the top ten. Because even though they didn't win, they were the top tier of the Olympics. The only athletes allowed to compete in an All-star event were medal holders.

～

Waitstaff hustled along the narrow pathways between tables in the packed restaurant full of more athletes than regulars. Loud conversation and laughter filled the room. Beer flowed from the bar taps nonstop.

Celebrations all around.

At the big top in the far corner, the patrons kept their excitement subdued.

Red chugged half his stein of lager and slammed it down like the Nordic he was. He wiped his upper lip with two pinched fingers.

"So, you two been on the down low for years, huh?"

Frankie halted eating a French fry. Gerald sniffed, tilting his head to one side before straightening it again. He scratched his temple.

"Something like that." Gerald didn't enjoy talking about it.

"After hearing what Sharice had done, I felt bad for you," his wife said. "How did you put up with all that for so long?"

"You don't just leave the Montgomery family without a valid reason."

"Pfft!" Red picked his stein up. "The Montgomerys are not all mighty. Fuck em." He drained the rest of his beer, letting out a loud gasp of refreshment.

"Maybe not, but they sure have the power of one," Frankie replied as she shoved the fry in her mouth.

"But seriously." Janie leaned towards Frankie. "You trained this arrogant bastard back in shape enough to win silver in an all-star game? That's some next level shit."

"She was more of a slave driver than a trainer." Gerald picked up a shot of tequila from the center and tossed it back. "About killed me."

"Stop saying that." Frankie gave him a side glance. "Makes you sound like a pussy."

Everyone at the table and the surrounding two either gasped or half spit out their beers while drinking. Gerald looked sideways at the ceiling, not wanting to engage.

"Frankie," was all he got out.

Red burst out laughing. Others followed, lightening the awkward mood.

"You never had a filter," the big guy roared. "Classic!"

"Just saying," Frankie mumbled. She finished chewing another fry. "He always kept in shape. I only made him kick it up a notch."

"Well, you did great. Maybe I can get you to give me a hand before the next games," Janie suggested.

"How you gonna try stealing my wife to train you right in front of me?" Gerald gave her an admonished stare. "Shouldn't you two be retiring?"

"What for?" Red raised his brow. "We win gold after ten years on the circuit and you think we should quit? Nah."

"That's it," Gerald pointed at him. "Ten years. You got in the top ten but never medaled. Either the competition declined, or you were struck by fate."

"Exactly!" Red motioned for the female server coming his way. Her short skirt grazed a man's shoulder, lifting it a few inches, and he looked over to sneak a peek. "Hey!" The big guy yelled. The man flinched in his seat. "Keep your eyes to yourself." He turned to his wife. "Fucking trash."

The server smiled, blushing with embarrassment. No one paid attention to the man glowering at Red. If he went after him, he would be on his own. Going against the big guy would be a stupid move on his part.

Four committee members sat in a booth four tables away around the supporting wall. An audio detector placed in the center of the table aimed towards Gerald picked up the conversation, recording it. They leisurely ate their meal, sipping on beer steins covered in thin ice sheets melting away.

"I say we got them right on the money."

The first member brought his burger to his mouth and pointed his pinky at Gerald's table. He took a bite and spoke while chewing.

"They won't have a choice being added to the list."

"Frankie on basic training with Gerald mentoring. Sounds like a good plan." The second member picked up his beer. "Here's to getting our top athletes back."

The other three raised their drinks as well, and they all took big gulps.

"Now all we have to do is keep Hardy and Fitzsimmons

together and on board." The third member held his stein near his chest. "Then the cycle will be complete."

Gerald spotted the committee members out of the corner of his eye as he down his beer.

Holy shit!

He watched Frankie's eyes widen when she also found them. She sneered, ready to get up. Gerald placed a hand on her thigh and pressed hard. She turned to him. He shook his head. Red followed their gaze. He didn't look surprised.

"Did you really think the two of you would get out of their clutches?"

Gerald angrily turned to him. "You knew what they were after this whole time?"

Red gave him a stern stare. "And you didn't?"

Gerald felt the sting of his words. He hit the nail on the head. Deep down, he recognized the gears at work. As a former committee member, he should have seen it coming. Getting him to participate in the All-Star games became the catalyst. What they didn't bet on was Frankie training him.

They both fell right into the trap.

Tranquil Waters

An official meeting with Frankie and Gerald in front of the committee took place at their local Olympics center. Each level of the fifteen-story building housed a training area, the aquatics in the lowest and one below. The offices occupied the top three. Its white stone and silver siding gleamed in the late morning sun. Not much heat came down. Only enough to slowly melt more of the dirty snow along the sidewalks.

Gerald and Frankie entered the building, displaying their badges to the guard. They rode the elevator to the fourteenth floor and did the same for the receptionist. Wearing a black tailored suit Gerald resembled his former self as a committee member while he adjusted the black and white marbled necktie.

"They're waiting for you in conference room five." The receptionist pointed to her left. "Straight down the hall to your right."

"I remember, thank you." Gerald glanced over at Frankie.

The white pencil line dress slimmed her curves. She wore her hair in an austere bun with a few strands left out on each side. Like a corporate dick's wife. As beautiful as he said she obviously was, she could tell he didn't approve.

I don't either!

They had to look professional. She made no promises to act as such.

Gerald held the conference door open for her and she felt the mood of the room. Smugness. Yeah, they knew. A member stood and motioned towards two empty seats at the center right of the table. Right between two of the members from the all-star games.

"Frankie, Gerald. It's good to see the two of you healthy." The chairwoman greeted them. "I'm glad you accepted our invitation."

"Invitation? More like a summons," Frankie blurted. She immediately regretted her words. "My apologies." Gerald pulled out the chair for Frankie to sit. "Thank you."

"Such feminine grace," a member smirked. "Never thought I'd see the day."

Frankie tensed, forcing herself not to respond. *Fuck you!* She yelled in her head. Gerald placed a hand on the small of her back as he sat beside her.

"That was uncalled for," the chairwoman snapped. She turned her attention to Frankie. "You're both here to hear a proposal. There is no pressure to accept if you feel it won't benefit you."

"Is that right?" Gerald's jaw had already gone tight.

"Gerald, your engagement with the younger athletes sparked a lot of interest. All they could talk about is how they would implement the wisdom you gave, wishing they had more time with you."

Gerald looked away towards the door. Frankie wasn't sure if the chairwoman lied or not. She knew that happened at the games. The feedback seemed iffy.

Montgomery spoke next. "We are not expecting you to take a seat on the committee. What we need is for you to take part in the mentorship program. If you feel the need to coach in conjunction with your role, that is also acceptable." His gaze bore into Gerald as the two men locked eyes.

"Keep that machismo bullshit out of this!" The chairwoman sighed before addressing Frankie. "Your training methods were impeccable. You don't need me to tell you what we want. I hope you consider the trainer position."

"And who am I supposedly training?" Frankie looked around the room at the other department heads. "I have no desire to work with the swim team."

"Oh no!" The head of gymnastics waved a hand. "Core training specific to the division you'd work with on a rotation."

Frankie frowned. She expected a full-on fighting match. The proposals sounded reasonable.

Nothing sketchy about it. Her malice deflated. Glancing at Gerald, she saw his hostile demeanor change as well.

"What about the pay?" That would tell Frankie what it really came down to.

"You will be handsomely compensated." The chairwoman slid a brochure card across the table. "These are the salary tiers for the various positions in the organization."

They leaned over to scrutinize the list. Frankie found the core training role. She masked her surprise, not wanting to show her hand. Gerald made a low hiss as he raised his head.

"Daycare is included, and all expenses accrued for doing your job will be covered." Montgomery gave them a crooked grin. "Is that not satisfactory?"

Yep. They got us real good.

Frankie's shoulders slumped in defeat.

"Sounds about awful to me," Blane deadpanned while bouncing the baby on her stomach. "Cracking the whip on some snot-nosed narcissist who'll buck your authority at every turn. No thanks."

Frankie shook her head. She picked up the toys scattered along the floor.

"Honestly, it doesn't sound all that bad. If I can handle Gerald, those up and comers will be a cake walk."

Blane turned her head towards her. "And they provide daycare? I wouldn't mind either."

"Be careful." Gerald walked into the kitchen, setting down a bag of groceries. "They probably have you on their radar. You're the fifth ranked Olympian in the aquatics world. I wouldn't put it past them."

"Oh, they already did. All I need is to finish my degree and accept the swim trainer position."

"How do they ask you to take it on and not ask the reigning record holder?" Frankie scoffed.

Blane glanced over at her. "Because, unlike you, I have always been a swimmer."

Frankie's brow furrowed. Those were the facts. And she had declined to do it anyway.

"Plus, it'll keep me busy besides being home all day."

She laid the baby on her stomach. "Anything to avoid those vultures, Ravi's parents."

"What?" Frankie stopped picking up the toys and fell onto the sofa. "Why?"

"They feel that since Ravi's jizz helped create my babies, they should have a say in their spiritual upbringing to secure his legacy."

"That's bullshit." Frankie tilted her head back. "Didn't they get the DNA measurements from the facility?"

"Yeah. His contribution is at twenty percent and dropping. His shit was toxic, so he had to strip most of it for the pregnancies to take hold."

The way Blane explained it so nonchalantly made Frankie ill. As for Ravi's parents, they had some nerve.

"What are you going to do? Do you want to use our lawyer?" Gerald called out.

"Naw. The committee is handling it for me. They got way better lawyers than our own."

How convenient. Frankie glanced over at Gerald. The committee moved fast.

The doorbell rang, startling them in the gloomy silence. Gerald walked around the counter and went to answer it. He opened the door to Fitz standing with his back at the doorway.

He turned around and smiled.

"What's up?"

"That's what I'm asking," Gerald replied, perplexed.

"I'm here to pick up Blane and the kids. Get them out of the house today."

Gerald moved so Fitz could enter. He raised his brow at Blane. "Is this a thing now?"

Fitz lifted the baby off Blane and turned him around to cuddle.

"What?" Blane sat up. "What's wrong with Fitz?"

"That's not what I'm implying," Gerald addressed Fitz. "What exactly are your intentions?"

"Are you her father now?" Fitz snorted. "Maybe we're soul mates. Did you ever consider that?"

"Not even remotely." Gerald gave him a dubious stare.

Frankie's head snapped forward.

Is that it? Those fuckers.

She finally understood what agenda the committee indulged in. The first generation of super athletes bred from the current top tier. Their blatant plan left a bad taste in her mouth.

⌒

After spending two hours strolling in the nearby park with Fitz lightening the load, Blane still felt exhausted. Hauling three infants took a lot out of her, even though Fitz carried the little one. The sun shined bright in the partly cloudy sky. Birds chirped happily, flying from tree to tree.

Friggin birds. Chirping.

Blane's lips pressed together as she exhaled hard through her nose. Something about their cheery disposition always bothered her. The smell of fresh cut grass and shrubbery made her eyes water. The pungent aroma stung her nose.

Guess I got allergies now.

So much yelling. From the children frolicking through the park and parents calling out to them to stay within sight. Which kids don't listen to at all. She watched other parents wrangling their smaller children in strollers, carriages, and on Velcro tethers. One woman had five kids. Her struggle to keep them together made Blane thankful for her three.

"It's because they're probably a year or more apart," Fitz broke her observation.

"Huh?" Blane wiped the corner of her eye with the bottom of her palm. "How so?"

"The baby will stay put, even the one-year-old. But the three and up, they will want to take off for the hills every chance they get."

"Ha!" Blane understood that. She remembered how her older brothers would go 'exploring' despite their mother yelling at them to "get back here" while she carried their three year old sister with Blane in tow at her side. "Almost forgot Mom went through that."

Her mom.

They hadn't spoken in months. Neither of her parents ever

283

encouraged her during her entire Olympic career. Dumping her into swimming was their way of getting Blane out of their hair. As a boy, Blane kept himself in constant trouble. That didn't mean being ignored didn't hurt.

Fitz wrapped his free arm around her, pulling her close. Blane instinctively rested her head on his shoulder.

Nope. Not gonna cry.

"It's not your fault." Fitz squeezed her. "Your family has to deal with their own guilt. They don't get to push that on you."

"Yeah. Would have been nice to have one that gave a shit about me." Blane stopped pushing the stroller. She stood still, fighting back the pain wanting to resurface. "All I ever wanted was for them to at least see me. They didn't even have to love me."

She gripped the stroller's handle. No matter how hard she fought, the tears dripped down onto the blanket covering the two infants. Seeing her cry, their faces scrunched up.

"No, no." Blane reached in and wiggled them by the chest. "Momma's alright." They sniffled. "I promise, I'm okay." She wiped her eyes and straightened her posture.

"You're tired." Fitz adjusted the baby in the swaddle wrap. "Come on. We're close to my place. Can you make it to the car or do you want to wait and I'll come back with it?"

"I'm tired, not dead," Blane snapped. "Let's go."

Fitz got all of them in their car seats then threw collapse the stroller, throwing it in the back of his SUV. Blane dozed off the moment the vehicle went in motion. In the short twenty minute ride, she dreamed of swimming in the lake by her childhood home. No one else around to disturb the quiet time between them and nature.

The jolt of the vehicle stopping woke her up. She found herself slumped against the door, her face pressed on the glass. Lifting her head left a smear of skin oil and drool. She struggled upright, fumbling with the door handle until the door opened.

"Here." Fitz tossed the house keys. "Get inside. I got this."

Blane glanced back at him, undoing the car seats. She left the front door open and stood in the doorway. Fitz came up and handed the baby to her.

Fast asleep, his cherub face seemed angelic.

"You little hellion. So glad you're asleep." He did pretty good with Fitz holding him.

That's not fair.

With her children settled in the guest room remodeled into a nursery for them, Blane headed into Fitz's bedroom. Flopped backwards at an angle on the bed, she let her feet dangle off the sides while one arm draped across her face.

"You gotta get in right." Fitz chuckled as he scooted her legs straight onto it.

"Sorry," Blane mumbled.

She didn't see or hear anything else after that. This time she dreamed of her early years in competition. The water felt different than the lake. It pushed and pulled, fighting her with every stroke. And yet, Blane's determination to conquer it made her come out victorious.

Those were the days. Her dream faded to black, putting her in a deep dreamless slumber.

Blane bolted upright from a dead sleep, her breathing coming fast. Her eyes slowly adjusted to the dim lighting of the room. A small lamp on the side table gave a dull glow, casting more shadows than light. Beside her, Fitz slept with one hand on his bare chest. The other lay right above his pelvis.

She reached over and traced the definition of his abs.

I used to have those.

Hard packed muscles full of power and strength. Her fingers moved along lazily until they reached his other hand. Blane halted for a second, then ran her finger along his pelvis' equator.

"If you keep doing that," Fitz whispered huskily, "I won't let you go."

Blane glanced back at him. "You say that as if you want me." Blane slid her hand off him.

Fitz rose next to her. "Because I do."

"Ha!" Blane smirked. "No one ever wants me. Not like that, anyway."

"You're wrong."

Fitz turned her face towards his, sealing her mouth with his. Blane didn't resist. She accepted his kiss, breathing in his scent as his tongue invaded her lips to find hers. He gently laid her back down, sliding his body atop her.

The plain grey shirt got removed in one pull over her head. Blane felt the weight of her breasts released. Fitz tugged her sweats off along with her underwear.

He kissed her more. Blane cupped his face to keep him there. Fitz's hands roamed her breasts and the sides of her ass. When they both came up for air. Fitz stared into her eyes.

"Why are you letting me do this? Aren't you a little afraid?"

Blane looked off for a moment, then resumed her focus on him.

"Because I know you won't hurt me like he did."

Fitz's breath seemed to hitch. He didn't move for what felt like minutes, then pulled her legs around his waist.

"I would never hurt you like that. Stay with me."

His lips sealed hers again, and she felt him enter her. It didn't hurt. Tears slid down the sides of her face. She could tell he told the truth. He really wanted her. Someone finally wanted her.

～

Blane set down the tote with the last of her belongings, revealing her barely showing stomach. By the end of the day, she would be completely moved in with Fitz. She looked around the living room to make sure she hadn't left a toy lying around.

"I can't believe you're with Fitz, let alone pregnant." Gerald came into the room carrying a storage cube of bed linens. "You could have waited."

"Tell that to the one shot wonder," Blane pointed to the front door where Fitz walked through.

"Huh?" Fitz stood next to Gerald. "What did I miss.?"

"I knew he had knocked me up. It felt like being sprayed with a garden hose on blast when he came."

"Ew!" Frankie halted at the end of the hallway. "What the hell?"

"That's..." Fitz shook his head. He picked up the tote.

"Don't tell people that, babe."

Blane shrugged, folding her arms. Gerald's eyes stayed wide in shock. He caught Fitz's stare. They both had to deal with partners with no social etiquette. The struggle was real. Frankie let out a sigh and hauled the swinging basinet she had to the door.

"Well, at least you'll have a home. I worried about you."

"Couldn't wait to get rid of me, huh?" Blane grinned.

"No. We weren't going to let you leave if you didn't have somewhere stable to go." Gerald pushed the door wider, so the basinet went through easily. "I'm just not a fan of your choice."

Fitz jogged back from his car.

"Really? I ask again. Who are you, her dad?"

"He is old," Blane said.

Gerald's chin tilted upward, his expression indignant.

"Don't." Frankie came back. "He's sensitive about that."

"I. am. Not. Old." Gerald smiled while saying it like a ventriloquist.

"I know." Frankie gave him a deep drive by kiss as she walked to the kitchen.

"Remember what I said." Gerald's face went stern. "The committee has something up their sleeve."

"They always do." Fitz patted him on the shoulder. "Don't worry. We're not stupid."

"That's not the reason. I don't trust them. Frankie and I are already caught in their net."

A loud clank from the kitchen made them all turn. Frankie stared at the frying pan spinning on the floor. She looked up.

"That's a sign. I'm not cooking."

Blane snorted. With all the babies at the center to keep them out of the way during the move, they had adult free time.

"Cool. Let's go eat at that steakhouse by the square."

"I could eat." Fitz walked out to the driveway. "Who's driving?"

After dinner, they all went to pickup their children. Fitz and Blane hauled her three infants into the house, then got them into their cribs. Blane plopped onto the bed, sitting upright as her head tilted towards the ceiling. She let out a heavy sigh.

"This was a long day," Fitz said, taking off his shirt and tossing it on the chair by the door. "The little monsters are worn out."

"I feel like karma has come to bite me in the ass."

"Really? How so?"

"I'm pretty sure I was a little shit growing up."

"As opposed to?" Fitz's brow raised.

"You know what?" Blane grabbed a pillow and smacked him with it.

Fitz knelt beside her on the bed, looming above her.

"Are you seriously thinking about taking that training position?"

"Sure, why not?"

"Then what was all that about Frankie teaching you swimming techniques before?"

Blane smirked at him. "Uhh, I'm always looking to up my game. I thought maybe he knew something we didn't." She lay on the bed. "I figured I'd have to find a way to make it work for me, not just copy him like Ravi tried to do."

"Huh, that makes sense." Fitz eased down beside her. "So you didn't get much out of it."

"Frankie is an anomaly. She's some sort of sea creature."

Fitz snorted, not holding back his burst of laughter.

"A sea creature? Seriously?" He wrapped his arms around Blane, pulling her close to spoon.

"Yeah. But the fact remains, she never wanted to be a swimmer. And still doesn't."

∽

Blane sat with her body tense in defense mode across from Ravi's mother in the Abenashid family kitchen. She watched the woman tickling the baby, making googly sounds. An ache in her chest grew tighter. The last time she visited over three years ago, everything seemed okay.

On every hiatus, Blane would accompany Ravi to his parents' home for at least a week being fed traditional Indian meals. They stayed close, even sleeping together in Ravi's bed. Not once did Ravi touch him in an inappropriate manner. They would lie there talking about swimming, life, and the awful food at the training facility.

The house looked the same. Everything inside, the way she remembered. She glanced at the mandala patterned cushions on the wooden chairs they sat in at the kitchen table. Giggles and laughter from the living room behind them let her know Ravi's father kept the other two children occupied.

Without looking up, Mrs. Abenashid spoke.

"We're not the enemy, Blane." She stopped playing with the baby for a second. "We get it that his genes are not prominent. It doesn't matter to us if it's only twenty percent. These children are the only parts left of him we have."

Blane fought to keep her composure. She understood perfectly. Her hands balled into fists. Mrs. Abenshid leaned forward, placing her clasped hands on the table.

"The two of you were stuck together like glue. The way he looked at you with such adoration when you weren't paying attention. I worried about what that meant as you both got older. I always thought you were such a pretty youg man." She tilted her head to one side. "Then you'd open your mouth."

Blane frowned at that. Everyone said the same thing. What did that have to do with her looks?"

"Even Ravi knew better than to use that language around us in the house." She paused. "I don't know what happened to make him hurt you the way he did."

Her voice faded as Blane's mind slipped back to her time in captivity.

She saw Ravi looming over her, his breath warm against her face while he held a needle in one hand.

"You were my ride or die."

Anger and disappointment etched his face.

"I had so many plans for us."

His eyes narrowed.

"You got off the ride."

Blane shook her head to clear away the memory, both hands covered her face to stifle the small cry that escaped her lips. Mrs. Abenashid raised the baby to her bosom as he started to cry, seeing his mother in distress. She patted him on the back to soothe him.

Her voice returned in full volume.

"Please know that you have always been treated like family here. Even more so now," she addressed Blane. "Let's finish our cake." She gestured to the untouched plate in front of Blane. "Dessert always makes you feel better."

Blane lowered her hands, revealing her tear-stained face. They were indeed that close, going everywhere together. The one tragedy that filled her with sorrow in all of it.

She had lost her best friend.

Anxiety gripped Sharice the moment she pulled into Gerald and Frankie's driveway. The boys sat in the back, neither wanting to sit in the front with her. That happened sometimes when they got into arguments, and they threw her sins in her face.

I deserve that.

Doesn't make it hurt less.Gerald tried to reason with them. Told them they didn't have to like her, but they had to respect her. She thanked him for that.

The front door opened. Frankie came out carrying the youngest child. Sharice saw the boys in the rearview mirror hesitate to get out. The same rule applied to Frankie, and they still had mixed feelings after all this time. Frankie set the little boy down and he sprinted towards the car, slapping both hands on the back passenger door.

"Hey, get back here." Frankie stepped onto the driveway. "You'll get hurt if they open that door."

His cheeks puffed from pouting, and he moved back right as the younger son popped the latch. The door barely missed his head.

"That's dangerous." Gabe chastised the boy. "Don't go running up on cars like that."

The little boy stared up at him with doe eyes, then raised

his arms. The other door slammed shut. Reluctant at first, Gabe took a step back. When he decided to approach, Payton stole his moment by swooping the boy up and carried him past Frankie into the house.

"What the heck?" He yelled. "I was going to carry him!" He dashed into the house after them.

Neither said hello, good morning, nothing.

Sharice got out of the car and walked towards Frankie. The two women didn't speak at first.

"Sorry about that," Sharice finally spoke. "They're in a mood today."

"Oh, that pre-teen angst thing? Yeah, I know."

"Frankie, I…" Sharice struggled with her words.

Frankie raised a hand to stop her, shaking her head.

"It's still too early for that. We will never be friends as long as we have this weirdness between us."

"I don't know what to do. How can I fix it?" Sharice held back tears, not wanting to show weakness.

"You don't," Frankie said bluntly. "None of this can be fixed. All I ask is that you respect me as well and treat my children right."

Sharice's shoulders hunched forward. Her quivering lips pressed thin, moistened with tears that ran down her face. She sputtered, sending flecks of tears and saliva into the air. Frankie sighed, stepped closer, and embraced her. All Sharice could do was lean against her, crying like a wounded child.

"Oh, shit," Gerald breathed as he came out the house.

She gently pushed herself off Frankie, wiping her face with the palms of her hands.

"Hey." She greeted Gerald.

Frankie inspected her shirt.

"She got snot and what not on me." Sharice saw the dirty look. "She's worse than a baby."

Sharice's expression fell into embarrassment. She opened her mouth, ready to protest, then saw Frankie wink before going inside.

"Thanks for dropping them off. We could have swung by to get them since we're leaving for the center in an hour."

"No, it's fine. I have a meeting with my father."

She frowned. "I don't like how they did that to you and Frankie. They should have asked."

"But that's no fun. They like clandestine agendas."

"I'm still bitter." Sharice crossed her arms, embedding her hands under her armpits.

"I know. You should figure that shit out. Nothing stopped you from competing in the non-medal all-star games. Your injury is healed enough."

"I just, it just." Sharice shook her head. "It hurts knowing that's all I could ever do."

"Maybe if you ask nicely, Frankie can get you on the books for strength training sessions."

She chewed on her bottom lip, glancing away to stare at an ant crawling along the stone.

Such a hard worker, aren't you? She asked it silently.

Getting lessons from Frankie sounded more like punishment. Despite that, she gave it real thought.

"Possibly." She mumbled, letting her arms drop. "I better get going. He likes punctuality."

"I don't envy you." Gerald stood in the doorway. "Drive safe. We'll bring them back Sunday night."

Sharice nodded as she walked backwards, then turned to get back in her car. She hit the ignition button right as the door slammed shut. She winced, not meaning to do that. Gerald waited until she drove off to go inside. The door closed. It made her think of it as a euphemism to her life over the past couple of years.

Yet, another was opening. Frankie's hug felt safe, secure. It surprised her. All that jealousy and hatred towards her? Completely unwarranted. She understood that not long after the first incident.

Today, she would tell her father to leave her family alone. That included Frankie. She needed to solidify her independence, even if it meant being disinherited. Which she knew her father would never do. He would indulge her for a few years. That's all she could ask for. A short reprieve from his and the committee's schemes.

Activities for every age were in progress for family day inside the Olympic training center. Mini obstacle courses and bouncing houses took up half the front section near the entrance. Licensed childcare workers navigated the little ones to age appropriate events.

Turn out ended up double than expected.

Family day also included bring your child to work. Gerald's sons followed him to the indoor shooting range while Frankie headed to the gymnasium for a training session. Ten kids aged nine to thirteen were lined up in front of the targets, taking calculated shots. He unzipped his track suit jacket and clapped his hands.

"All warmed up?" They leaned their mock rifles against the distance stands and gathered around him. "I'll be looking at your form and accuracy today. It's been four weeks, so I want to see a good amount of improvement."

Dejected looks spread amongst them. Payton and Gabe stood near the back wall, out of the way to watch. The first four were terrible in their eyes. Four weeks? They should be better than that. The two gave each other knowing stares.

Their grandfather taught them how to shoot when they were five and seven. He took them skiing all the time without their parents. Granddad told them they couldn't be bad at it when their father was a gold medal Olympian.

No pressure. Right!

Frankie arrived when the seventh kid stepped up to aim. His cocky demeanor didn't live up to his demonstration. He did way better than the previous ones, getting four out of six. Frankie rolled her eyes at his proud grin.

"Is that the best you can do?" Gerald burst his moment. "This is what you're proud of? Am I wasting my time here with you?"

The oldest and tallest of the kids, the guy turned on Gerald. "Maybe you're not as good a coach as you think. My dad pays you a lot of money to train me because you're some has been from his day."

The rest of the kids backed away, seeing Gerald's face flush with anger.

"Maybe if you listened and followed directions better…"

"I'm better than any of these plebes!"

Before Gerald could reply, Payton stepped towards them.

"I can shoot better than that and I don't have a coach. You're just making excuses for your crappy shots."

"Oh yeah?" The kid tossed his mock rifle. "Prove it."

"Son," Gerald reached for the rifle.

"I got this, dad," evading his father's attempt to take the rifle and stepped up the stand.

He raised the rifle, his stance perfect, and took a few even breaths. With each squeeze of the trigger, he hit all six targets a few seconds behind the record.

The older kid tsked, not happy about being showed up. He snatched his rifle from Payton's hand.

"This is bullshit."

"Watch your language." Gerald pointed for him to join the others who already went.

"You got nerve after the way you talk to us," he snapped.

"I'm an adult, you're not." Gerald turned to Payton. "Not bad. Your form could use some work."

"Then teach us," Gabe said. Gerald's head whipped around with a stunned expression. "We can win gold medals, too. It's in our blood, right?"

"Yeah, we just have to try out for the Olympic team next year." Payton stood next to his brother.

"That's…" Gerald tried to keep calm. "I don't…"

"You can't let that guy represent you," Gabe thumbed at the oldest kid.

"He's got a point." Frankie glanced over at Gerald. "Would you rather have some random coach teach your kids the ropes or you get them to the promised land yourself?"

Fuck! Gerald rubbed his forehead. This isn't what he wanted. *Wait.*

"How are you this good at it in the first place?" He watched the two of them stare at him as if he were an idiot. Of course. Even Frankie rose an eyebrow. "Never mind."

Frankie leaned closer to him. "I'll bet you money they are on the tryout roster as alternates until there's official paperwork."

"Wouldn't put it past the old man." He turned to his sons.

"Fine. I will get you enrolled."

"Cool." Gabe laughed. "We can show that guy how it's supposed to go." He tilted his head towards the oldest kid again.

On the other side of the range, a committee assistant volunteering as a gofer resetting the targets picked up the last shredded piece and stepped out of sight. He pulled his phone from his track suit pants pocket and dialed his boss. The line picked up on the third ring.

"I have confirmation. Our plan is now in full effect," he whispered into the receiver.

"Good. The next generation will bring us back on track to reclaim our glory."

The line went dead, and the committee assistant snapped the phone shut. Resuming his volunteer work, he smiled.

"God bless the USA."

~END~

ACKNOWLEDGEMENTS

Thank you for taking a chance on this first spin off from my Curve of Humanity series. I hope you are enjoying it as much as I did writing it. This book series is a lesson of hope in the face of futility. My belief is that one day humanity will take a good look in the mirror and do better.

A huge thanks to NaNoWriMo (National Novel Writing Month) for giving me an annual kick in the butt. Without them I would not have known what I am truly capable of achieving.

To my peeps at:

NIWA (Northwest Independent Writers Association),

PNWA (Pacific Northwest Writers Association)

20Booksto50K.

You all keep me humble, reminding me to be fearless and keep going when it all seems too daunting. I appreciate you so much.

BOOKS BY MAQUEL A. JACOB

CURVE OF HUMANITY

ORIGINS

SHADOWMEN OBJECTIVE

PURGE SEQUENCE

CRIPPLED EARTH

AFTERMATH

THE CORE TRILOGY

CORE OF CONFLICTION

SEEDS OF CONVICTION

BONDS OF CONTRITION

WRATH OF ACQUISITION

ACTS OF TRANSGRESSION

WELCOME DESPAIR

A COLLECTION OF SHORTS

THE BLOOD SAGA

BLOOD DOCTRINE

BLOOD DOMINION

BOOD DESENSION

ABOUT THE AUTHOR

Hi there. I'm Maquel A. Jacob. My passion for the written word emerged from the age of seven, reading everything I could get my grubby little hands. Including encyclopedias and thesauruses. At twelve, I got hooked on my first encounter with a Stephen King novel. Each one inspired me to write my own brand of fiction. Combining multiple genres to keep things interesting.

I am a HUGE Anime fan, love a great bottle of wine and rock out to heavy metal music. The Pacific Northwest is where I currently reside, spinning imaginary worlds in my head and day-dreaming.

For cool limited-edition Swag, updates, FREE short stories, Newsletters

...and more, become a Patron!

https://www.patreon.com/maquelajacob

Visit the Website

Visit:www.majacobauthor.com

Buy direct at maquelajacob.com

Like on Facebook

Follow on Tumblr and Twitter @MaquelAJ1

Join the conversation on Discord

Check out the Publisher MAJart Works on Instagram

Also find me on Goodreads